# The Red Ring
## Maggie Stuart • Book Two

### Jen Frankel

## Also By Jen Frankel

✪

### The Blood & Magic Series featuring Maggie Stuart

Book One: The Last Rite
Book Two: The Red Ring

### Coming soon

Book Three: Heaven & Hell

# The Red Ring

©2013 by Jen Frankel & Wildcard Pictures
a Xeno Productions publication
Global CS Edition
Contact: Wildcard Pictures
         info@wildcardpictures.com
www.wildcardpictures.com / www.jenfrankel.com

ISBN: 978-1492863687

All illustrations ©2013 by Jen Frankel
Cover illustration includes "Mada Premavesi" by Gustav Klimt (1912)

To all the coffee shops I've loved before. . .

# 0

## Look Back In Anger

✪

*Once upon a time, I found myself in a Klimt painting. There I was, or a fair imaginative proxy, with Char, and Arabella his terrifying daughter, and a little boy who achingly reminded me of Peter, the child who was more than a child.*

*Not that long ago, in fact. And turning the page from Klimt's gold-columned "Love," the painting that evoked my past, I found one that seemed to evoke my present.*

*She'll always be Klimt's "Girl" to me, although officially she's* Mada Premavesi, 1912. *God, how I loved her! She's got straight, chestnut hair of the exact shade I'd always thought of on myself as mouse brown, and the same dark eyes as I inherited from my father.*

*I smiled when I saw her—no, I grinned. Big and completely, grinned like a lunatic in the library. I pulled out the notebook I carry in my pocket, a little one in fake black leather with gold tooling I picked up at a Goodwill for a buck, nearly empty and better than new. The first page I left blank in it, because on it I could see the barely visible impressions of whatever had been written on the page or pages overlaid above them, the ones that had been yanked out to resell it as a nearly-new item. Someday, I meant to run a pencil lightly over them to find out what had been written there by the stranger who'd donated it—but then again, maybe not. The mystery was tantalizing and thrilling. Who knew what the reality would bring?*

*I noted down Mada Premavesi's name, smiling all the while, then went back to her image in the book. First thing I'd do when I got home would be find her again on the Internet and print out a copy for myself on the color laser.*

*She was so comfortable, so radiant, in a dress that seemed way too young for her but somehow just right. It reminded me of a brown dress I loved when I was a few years younger, a thing from my past kept in the back of my closet as a kind of tribute to a younger self. This was a girl poised on the brink of mysteries herself, and confident she'd meet them head on. I loved it. I loved her. She spoke to me of my potential and my struggles. I could imagine myself inhabiting her as Klimt stood at a distance with his brushes and easel, trying to capture her proud, free essence. This was me: joyful, magical, right.*

*I have to remember Mada-in-me when I get too hard on myself, when I feel the weight of my past and the uncertainty of the future. Joy is too beautiful an emotion to put aside, no matter how dark some days are. Now—if only I can get through adolescence without forgetting that.*

✪

Sometimes, I still dream of flying.

I'm high over the subdivision, Westbrook laid out like a railway model, winding stripes of gray between vacuum-formed plastic trees. The breeze has a bite to it, cool on my face and legs, and I fancy I can feel wisps of low-hanging clouds pulled through my fingers as I glide.

I can see the old public school, Westbrook Elementary with its tarred roof and surrounding green yard. I can almost see flames flickering in the sky above it. I can almost feel the rush of warm air I imagine might greet me as I approach, the sense of foreboding, the fear that starts my heart beating faster.

But that's just wishful thinking.

✪

Three years ago, I had been in a battle. I fought an evil magician with the fates of a good many people in his hands. For the sake of those people, I made a sacrifice. I gave up a gift that made me powerful enough to have anything on earth I wanted.

Three years, and I hadn't stopped either thinking about it, or agonizing over the decision I had made. I still had the scar from one of my more violent confrontations with the Burnt Man (one of which I actually had very little memory, ironically), and I still had the ring which had once belonged to Arabella, the Burnt Man's daughter. Hunt had pulled it off her dead finger and given it to me, his idea of spoils to the victor, I guess.

The scar I carried in a long white streak from my left shoulder to the elbow. The ring, with its huge ruby, sat in the bank at the mall, wrapped in red velvet, my token. It hummed when I picked it up with the echo of a power now lost to me. I would never sell the ring, even though it was painful to have it in my possession. It was all I had left of an adventure that had affected so many people in Westbrook, and of which only two of us here had any memory.

I had time over those three years to think a lot about what had happened. I wished—no, I guess I don't wish none of it had happened. Everyone wants to be a little different, don't they? A little special? Even if no one else knew what I had found myself capable of down there in the catacombs, I did. It was a source of pride, I thought, knowing that I could fight when I had to, and to consider the consequences of my actions before I did. But I still wasn't sure if all that was going to be a benefit to me in the future. In a way, at almost sixteen, I was already living in the past like someone whose great acts are done and gone, a memory. How could the rest of my life approach what I'd experienced by thirteen?

Since Char, I'd been nothing. No hint of my being special, or unique, or valued. Nothing ever happened to Maggie Stuart. Nothing. And so, Arabella's ring was in a safe-deposit box, rented jointly in my mother's name and mine, ostensibly for a bunch of near-worthless Italian and Greek coins I'd found in a drawer.

And now, I dream of flying and while I dream, I squeeze my eyes tighter, hoping to return to a place I'd desperately tried to escape at the time. It's perverse, isn't it?

✪

Hitting fifteen the previous October, still, was a bit of a benchmark for me. It was, for one thing, the year I knew for sure I would never be any taller than I already was. I hadn't grown an inch through all of fourteen, and I was finally willing to accept that five feet, two inches was it.

The great outer world was starting to impose more and more on my little reality. I spent more time going into the big city. There was hardly any excuse not to. Westbrook is only ten minutes by GO-train to the end of the subway line, and nothing goes on here in the 'burbs. I was watching more television this year as well, reading less, caring less about school, and looking for ways to fill my time.

In the past, there was never a problem. When I was thirteen, I didn't have much in the way of friends, but my imagination was better company in those days. I think that after Char disrupted my life, everything I could imagine sort of paled in comparison. Now, heading into grade eleven, I had a brain stuffed full of useless facts I'd gathered through my non-interactive reading years and an apathetic outlook. Nothing interested me.

After—the 'incident,' I'll call it—I went on medication for severe depression and for a hard-to-shake lung infection. I got very sick, and lost a lot of weight. Maybe that's what stopped me growing at five foot two. Worse, I was utterly unable to be honest with the doctors about what was making me so crazy.

Eventually, they weaned me off the medication, which was kind of like turning my head inside out with a toasting fork. No one told me you could get addicted to penicillin. Found out that gem through Google. I hallucinated a lot, and went through attacks of paranoia. I was fun to deal with at school, as you can imagine. None of this was very good for my standing with my peers.

It didn't help that none of them remembered I'd saved their lives. All of them, Scott, Aaron, Jason. My little friend Peter had found a family, I guessed, and disappeared. Hunt and I had talked about that, when I was promising to try to forget everything myself as well.

We had been sitting on the bluff overlooking Char's ruined domain, his subterranean palace flooded, his lineage extinguished. The sun had set and the sky was black. In the distance, Toronto glowed like a forest fire on the horizon. Moonlight was all we had to see by, silver and sad. Tamblyn, Hunt's brother, was passed out at our feet. Loss of blood will do that.

And Hunt gave me some instructions. For the good of all those involved, he promised. Neither Peter nor his new parents would have any idea what he'd been through in those deep, subterranean caverns, and I was under oath not to try and find him. I would have liked to talk to Jason about all of it, about how strange and unnatural I still felt, but I'd promised not to. The promise was binding because I agreed with Hunt. There was no need, even if Jason or the others had flashes of memory, to put them through the trauma they'd experienced for a second time. They should be able, because I couldn't, to forget. No need for all of us to be psychotic.

It was hard for me to revisit that decision, because in so many ways, it made less and less sense as time went by. What *had* happened to Peter? Orphaned doubly by the loss of Char and his family, and then by the destruction of the only world I thought he might have ever known... what had happened to him? Maybe it was a blessing that he wouldn't remember anything, but then again, he'd seemed to have grown very close to Scott during our ordeal. Maybe they'd both have been happier to have their memories—and each other.

Since the incident, I couldn't seem to fit with anything around me. It had been bad enough before. I mean, angst goes hand in glove with teenage years. That's what I've read, and it seems borne out by experience. There has to be someone who gets ignored and kicked around at school. Otherwise, where do all the underdog stories come from?

I couldn't get my mind around anything I was supposed to. School—who cared? Boys and sex—no urge in that direction at all. Partly because, well, screwed up as I was, who would have me? Friends—who would want me? And how could I make them understand what made me tick when I was forbidden to talk about it? I stayed aloof in all situations. I tried to have as little effect on the world as a water-strider did on a lake. If I could have disappeared completely into a carpet or a forest, I would have done it.

In the summer, I had two problems. I had to stay away from the house as much as possible—I'll explain that later. And I needed money for school supplies. So, what do you do during the summer, when you're underweight, insecure from a couple of years of paranoid delusions, and still (need I say it?) a geek? What everyone does, when they need money and have no qualifications: they go to work in the fast food business.

I worked at the local McD's for the whole summer, and that's where life started impinging on my sensibilities. Against my own better judgment, I developed this sort of crush on a guy my own age who was almost always working the same shifts. I'll call it a crush, but I don't think that's exactly the right term. I couldn't have cared less about kissing him or anything. I just thought he was interesting and I wanted to talk to him. I thought I might be able to relate to him, without Char's presence looming as it always did when I tried to say anything to Jason, or Aaron.

But this guy, he was openly contemptuous of me, and I just got more and more pathetic and awkward around him. I spent most of my time at work trying to avoid him, so I wouldn't do anything to add to his poor impression of me. The rest of my time I spent trying to find some way to stop thinking about him, and to stop being so rough on myself over my own unruly feelings.

Then something happened to put the shoe on the other foot, I guess. More crappy karma. My boss, a guy more than twenty years older than me, invited me into his office in the middle of my shift and told me point-blank that he wanted to sleep with me, and in no fancier language than that. I told him that, although I would be sixteen in a few months, I had no interest in having sexual relations with him or anyone else. He told me he didn't believe me, and actually informed me that the latest statistics were that one hundred percent (or so near as to make no difference) of all teenage girls have sex before their sixteenth birthdays, and it is in fact not healthy to abstain any longer. I was disgusted, as you can imagine.

The next steps were very simple. I put in a request for transfer the same day, and it was granted thankfully fast. I only had one shift scheduled before my transfer to the other store, and on that day I played sick. I started working at a new McD's, further away from my house, but I didn't tell my mother that the change had happened at my request. My first introduction to sex hadn't been hand-holding in a movie theater, or a shy kiss on the porch after a date. Me, who'd never had a date. I'd been propositioned—unethically not to mention illegally—by an older and, yes, reasonably disgusting man . I knew it shouldn't be a big deal, but it made me feel filthy and I hated it. Somehow, I thought it had to be my fault, that I was tainted from my experiences and a normal adolescence was forever beyond me. It was like having the first drug you were offered be crack cocaine, instead of pot or booze.

And I had no one to talk to about it. To return to what I said earlier about wanting to be out of the house as much as possible: my relationship with my mother is terrible, has been since the events of three years ago. It has been hard to trust her. The magic, or whatever, that I used to erase all memory of the Burnt Man from the minds of those who knew about him has had another effect on my mother.

She's the other person I meant when I said two of us had some memory of what happened back then. Apparently, I couldn't erase everything for her like I did for everyone else; I guess couldn't purge her mind completely of things like that her house was almost burned down, or that I had been kidnapped. She worried almost constantly about where I was and what I was doing, about the memories that wouldn't connect, and especially about Nick, my father.

He'd left town as soon as the incident was over, because it was easier for me to erase the entire trip to Canada from his mind than it would have been to pick and choose. Without Damon's manipulation, he was not aware of any great urge to track down his Canadian offspring, and, as far as he was concerned, the re-awakening of his feelings for my mother had never happened.

The over-protectiveness was really hard to take, especially since I had literally nothing to hide. I think she still remembered, at some level, the stress of losing me, even for that brief period of time. Either that, or she was harkening back to an even earlier time when I was just a baby and my dad made off with me during their split. Yeah, even with the recent traumas excepted, my past was pretty screwed up.

So. In much the same fashion as always, I was tip-toeing around my house, keeping everything to myself. If Jan didn't notice me, she wouldn't ask awkward questions. The closeness that had developed briefly between my mother and myself during the incident had disappeared after.

I settled in for a long, painful adolescence. I read a lot of books, the same as before, drew some pictures that I never liked too much while hoping for a miraculous rediscovery of the talent I'd shown so briefly while with Char, and surfed the Internet in an abstract way that avoided social media. You really wanna have a Facebook page when no one wants to be your friend? No thanks.

I had no interest in getting close to anyone, especially after that summer at McD's. I felt, irrationally but immovably, that the reason my manager had come on to me was because I had dared to have a crush on the other guy, a punishment for giving in to feelings. If I was cheerful sometimes, it felt like a lie. I was lonely, and the question of what I was lonely for sometimes made me nervous. I tried to be stoic, but sometimes I just wanted to curl up in someone's arms and be held. I couldn't help remembering the feel of the Burnt Man's mind, pressing against my own, and his whispers as he indicated his realm and the empty throne by his side, "This could all be yours. . ."

Given the choice again, I don't know what I'd do.

1

Wishful Beginnings

✪

The first person I saw the very first day of grade eleven, or at least the first person I noticed, was Scott Saunders. I don't know why I should have been so surprised to see him unchanged by the summer but he was—same curly dark blond hair and long body, a gait that bordered on the lumbering—eminently recognizable. I followed him from the parking lot into the main building, to the boards where our names would be posted alongside our home room numbers.

I said "Hi," as I checked my classroom number, and he indicated he'd heard with a little nod. He seemed particularly smug and I felt snubbed. It wasn't like he was one of the big heart-throb football players or anything. In their way, the group he belonged to was just as outcast from the popular crowd as I am. There's nothing like getting dissed by someone way, way down the social ladder to really make you feel truly unworthy.

There wasn't anything to do in the half-hour before class, so I sat down with my back to the wall, and took out a book to read. I'd made a brown paper cover for it, one of the works of Aleister Crowley—I figured it was better to have everyone think I was reading dirty books than something weird and occult. Some things are deviant yet acceptable. Others make people nervous, and I seemed to do that easily enough without pressing the issue.

Our school is called John Diefenbaker, after the former Prime Minister, but that gets shortened more often to "Dief", or to just "J.D.", like the whiskey. Almost everyone who used to go to Westbrook Elementary ended up at Dief, so I've been seeing the same faces nearly all my life. It's funny how that could be true, yet I can say I don't have a real friend in the lot. Jason and I were friends once, pretty good ones, and I got along well with Aaron Scribner too, but that was in the part of the past neither of them remembers. But then, maybe what I had with them was intensity, because we were all in danger and helping each other out. We didn't have history, and I think that might be more important in the long run. I couldn't imagine how I'd get to know either of them again.

I turned a couple of pages without reading a word. Scott was still standing by the board, meandering back and forth. The hall was crowded, mostly confused grade nines from the conversation. I was kicked and tripped over, and stepped on numerous times, but Scott stayed and so did I. I was curious to know who he was waiting for. Spying was the only way I had of keeping in touch, pitiful though it sounds.

The first bell rang, and the school song started, giving me about five minutes to walk the one short corridor to my home room, which was actually my second period class, just to make matters more confusing for newbies. This was for the benefit of anyone with a first period spare. My actual first period class was drafting, the only thing I was really looking forward to this year. Home room, period two, was Grade Twelve history, which I was dreading. I stood, and was about to go to class when…

…when Scott's companions arrived. Old home week at the Psych-Me-Out ranch. I hadn't seen Jason Lawson since before the summer. He was tanned and nervous. He had always been very tall, even in grade eight, but now he was filling out a bit and looked very athletic. I don't know why I was surprised that Jason and Scott were still hanging around together.

The other two were girls, Rae Kennie and Suzanne something. Rae was a star volleyball player, popular and pretty. Suzanne had arrived from another school the year before and had rocketed up the high school pecking order to princess status almost instantly. I knew very little about either of them, except that it annoyed me to see Scott and Jason with them. Somehow over the summer they'd moved up on the social ladder. Probably about the same time I was being hit on by a horrible older man with tobacco and sweat hanging around him.

I was too far away to hear their exchange, but whatever was said got Scott as agitated as Jason. Suzanne opened her gym-bag and handed

Scott an old, large book. He slipped it into his own bag, and the four of them disappeared toward their new classrooms. I felt a tingle that was far too much like the feeling of my powers that were gone forever, and I was almost in tears when I reached my home room. Seeing them was like looking in a window at a party someone forgot to invite you to. I walked a little faster.

✪

My classroom was full of grade twelve students, and not a single one that I knew. I slid into the only seat left in the room just as *O Canada* began over the P.A. The teacher motioned for us to stand, and I did, with a crash the volume of a 747 at liftoff. The contents of my bag scattered up and down the aisle, and one of my paintbrushes just kept on rolling, up towards the front of the room.

I hardly noticed the kindly grade twelve girl who helped me collect my things and shovel my books back into the knapsack. All I knew was that the whole class was laughing—at me.

I zipped the case just as the national anthem finished and slid back into my desk, color rising in my cheeks.

This being the first day of school, we'd have an auditorium in the morning, then run through an entire day's schedule in fifteen minute long periods after lunch. There was a pep rally on the football field planned for the latter part of the afternoon. We would be out an hour early, which was more a tease than anything else. Another year in school. *Don't think about it, Maggie,* I told myself, and concentrated instead on filling out all the first-day-of-school paperwork.

When we had been given our timetables, the grades nine to eleven assembly was announced. I was the only grade eleven in the classroom, so I had to stand, explain, and excuse myself. I was in the hall before I realized I had forgotten my knapsack inside, and had to return for it. Seriously, I could hardly look any stupider than I already did. On a first-impression scale of one to ten, I rated about minus fifteen.

I thought I'd finally got the hang of Dief this year. It wasn't easy. There were three wings, each constructed in a completely different era of the school's history. You'd guess each successive architect hadn't bothered to even look at what had come before when planning the expansions.

The oldest, the middle section, was a blocky, rectangular edifice on three levels which included the library, the cafeteria, and the office. The tech floor at the bottom was like a dungeon, half-sunk so that the windows were level with the grass outside.

That I could handle. Below there was an even deeper and much creepier level, where there were few classes but a lot of doors, and although a lot of other students used the sub-basement for quickie shortcuts between classes, I had never made it past the top of the stairs. Being underground doesn't suit me.

The other two wings were constructed about five years apart. Each had two stories, but neither building lined up in any way with the old school. The more modern annex had low ceilings and narrow halls and *almost* made sense, but the other was built like a labyrinth with twisting passages and odd-shaped rooms.

There were staircases to nowhere, and blind corridors turning unexpectedly into walls, and steps leading up just to go back down without even the excuse of a room or intersecting hallway. I hated the whole place passionately, and it gave me the creeps. People got lost all the time, although never permanently—at least as far as I knew. The layout of the school had given me enormous problems for the first couple of months of grade nine. But this year, I thought I had old Dief pretty much in hand. Maybe I was just cocky because my home room class was close to the main entrance and easy to find.

The only sort-of nice part of the school was the gymnasium, big and modern, with skylights and a gallery—but damned if Maggie Stuart was going to be caught dead in there. I was not in the least bit athletically inclined. The compulsory phys. ed. class in grade nine had been almost enough to kill me.

The auditorium nearby was another detrimental feature as far as being a place for functions was concerned, although I had a special relationship with it personally that I'll get to later. The stage in the auditorium had always confused me. It was convex, like someone had started with a nice, rectangular stage and cut a scoop out of the middle of it, for the orchestra we'd never have, I guess. It was a completely useless shape for any kind of play to be performed on it, because center stage was so far back from the audience. Maybe that's why Dief had never in twenty years put on a school show.

Now, the auditorium was full of students, not my favorite way to see it at all. Grudging every moment, I sat as far back as I could and stuck my knapsack under my seat. It was too dark to read, so I dozed instead. Mr. Philps, a.k.a. the Mouse, called for attention, twice, and the auditorium began.

The assembly lasted forty-five minutes and did nothing to instill me with the school spirit it was supposed to, and we were returned 'to the work of period one,' which for me meant sitting by myself in an empty classroom for the duration of the top grade's assembly.

Finally, the grade twelves returned, and we were released for lunch. I was the first one out the door. I would have given almost anything for a look at that book Scott and Jason had been passing around.

## 2

## Shapes of Things

✪

The kindly grade twelve who had helped me pick up my stuff caught up to me half way down the hall. She was plump and wore glasses, and was black, which made her one of a very select club at white-bread Dief. Somehow, on the periphery of the most cosmopolitan city on Earth, Dief had managed to draw its entire population from second- and third-generation WASPs. You couldn't even get good sushi out here.

The grade twelve had some pimples and a wide, symmetrical nose which was set off strangely by her small eyes. It was a kind face, but probably not one to launch ships or inspire sonnets. Who cared? Neither I nor the vast majority of humanity would either. Not having seen her before this year, I guessed she was new to the school. I found it hard not to stare at her, and then hard to pretend even to myself that I hadn't been staring.

"I'm Irene," she offered, and pushed her glasses up, maybe as an alternative to the standard adult handshake or to bridge the awkwardness I'd caused by my obvious rudeness.

"Maggie," I said, not wanting to sound too abrupt, although prepared to escape as quickly as possible. I started to walk, and she tagged right along.

She scrambled in her purse as we went down the hall, and pulled out a paintbrush. "I found this under my desk," she said.

I took the brush. "Thanks," I said, and stuck it through the neck of my hoodie under the strap of my bra.

I hoped that would be the end of it, but she just kept standing there. It would probably be rude to walk away, but I really didn't want to get into a conversation with her. "Are you an artist?" she asked finally.

"No," I said. "I just paint for fun. Look, I've got to go. Thanks again."

"Bye, Maggie," she said. "See you tomorrow." She didn't move, so I turned and continued down the hall as fast as I could. It was like talking to a little kid on the phone who doesn't know when to say good-bye.

Maybe having no friends did have less to do with everyone else, and more to do with how I didn't even try. How dare I, alone and aloof, how dare I judge anyone? I had already rated this Irene as a loser and an outcast, and that was pots and kettles in cacophony. *Maggie Stuart,* I told myself critically, *you are a class-A bitch and a hypocrite to boot.*

I considered going back to her, and maybe having a chat over lunch, but that's not really what I wanted. I wanted to be alone, which was kind of the crux of my whole situation. I figured no one could understand me, so my own company was all I wanted. Crud, it wasn't fair. I couldn't get past thirteen. I wanted to forget—but I didn't want to forget. The one thing that made me special—*Maggie's Amazing Disappearing Supernatural Power!*—was what was going to drive me crazy. I would probably turn out like my mother, trapped in a past no one else even knew about.

One good thing about Dief was that for a person like me who wanted to stay away from everyone there was always a secret nook to hide out in. My favorites were the drama club costume room, which no one ever went to, and the auditorium, as I promised before to mention. The costume room was in the attic and had a tiny semi-circular window about a foot from the floor, looking out over the football field. You could curl up on the floor with a book and have all the light you needed. It made me feel like Bastian in *The Neverending Story*, which was half the appeal.

The auditorium, by virtue of its proximity to nothing but the gymnasium's spectators gallery, was deserted except for school events. It was private, big and airy, and, most importantly, always unlocked. The costume room key always took me a couple of weeks to get ahold of, so it was the auditorium for now.

After sneaking in the door of the auditorium on the side closest to the gymnasium gallery, I ate my lunch quickly on the edge of the stage. I was feeling agitated. I wasn't sure why, except I knew I didn't want to spend another year in high school. Was I learning anything important? Debatable. Did I want to go to university after high school? Only if it would get me out of the glorified subdivision of Westbrook. There had to be some other way to do that. I had no idea what I was doing in school, except wasting time. Until what? A good question to which I had no answers.

I thought my brief encounter with Irene had disturbed me more than I cared to admit. I hardly talked at all anymore. I didn't say anything to my mother unless I had to, and didn't speak up in class unless I was called on, and believe me, I did everything I could to avoid notice. Being with Irene reminded me that conversation is a skill you need to keep doing to stay in practice. How long would it be before my brain seized up and I became mute?

That thought was funny enough to make me smile. *Maggie Mute.* My own company wasn't bad, I guessed. I could think of people I'd less like to spend time with.

I filled my water dish at the fountain outside the auditorium door and returned to the stage. Feeling a bit more relaxed, I laid out my paints and the small pad of watercolor paper. There was no doubt that someone in the office must know I came here every lunch hour, because I'd been doing it fairly regularly for two years now, but I had never yet been disturbed or questioned.

I started to sketch in pencil, with no idea at all of what I wanted to draw. First, I drew an oval, trying to get the impression I was looking at a circle from the side. The lines came without conscious intent, as if the pencil was pulling my hand along.

*Compulsive behavior, Maggie,* I told myself. Was this the feeling I'd had in Char's dream-world, when I had done portrait sketches for money? My hand had been so sure of itself. So many things I had refused to think about for so long, like the portraits. Why today?

The old woman who'd handed me the drawing supplies, whispering, *That's quite a talent you have there*—or something to that effect. I remembered her lined face, the ironic tilt to her mouth. Not like my own real grandma, dead now and almost forgotten, but like someone's grandma. The grandma I wished I still had.

That shop, in my fantastical version of Kensington Market, full of the coolest eclectic clothes and knickknacks and wild jewelry. I'd avoided any mention of Kensington when Jan and I made the rare shopping trip into the city. I was afraid of seeing for real what I'd previously only encountered in a dream.

So many memories, flooding in now, and the most urgent ones caught under the heading of "Semi-Fantastical." My real life was so basic and unremarkable nothing really stood out. When I found myself unexpectedly remembering anything, it was that time when I was thirteen, which of course I couldn't share, didn't share, with another person in the world. My only defense against total depression was to deliberately not think about what I'd lost.

School. What was I doing here? I though about all the authors I'd read of who'd dropped out of school after many fewer years than I'd already suffered through. I had no interest at all in being here. What kind of thoughts go on in the head of someone who quits school? My father had quit mid-way through college to take up painting. It was hardly likely I would ever get to talk to him about that. Nick was gone from my life like he'd never come to Canada.

My mind wandered, as my hand continued to work. Suddenly, I was thinking of Char himself, my *Burnt Man*, and the final ritual. I tried so hard to keep him out of my thoughts. He was gone from my dreams, but I guess I hadn't banished him completely. It was the memory of him that brought me back to the auditorium from wherever I had wandered, and I saw for the first time what I had drawn.

*Score one for the subconscious*, I thought. The oval had turned into a pentagram, and I had drawn a tiny bowl in the center of it. From the bowl, long, twisted streams of vapor rose and twined. Instead of finishing that original oval completely, I had drawn a gap in the circle enclosing the central pentacle.

I sat and stared at the drawing for a couple of minutes, then found myself unscrewing lids and squeezing paint onto my palette, and mixing colors.

Then I found I was thinking about Damon. This was the rawest place. My arms curved, and I tried to remember what it had been like to hold him there, dying. He had shaken so much. His skin has seemed less human then. I knew he wasn't *precisely* human, of course I knew that. But he'd never seemed so different as he did in that moment. His skin was icy, but it ran with sweat. Had I never noticed before how cool he was to the touch? The Burnt Man had always seemed that way to me. I could brush my fingers against my throat any time and remember exactly how cold his hand had been when he had gripped my neck at the beginning of that fateful last rite.

Damon had seemed less frightening, maybe because of the night I had spent in his apartment in the Dreamworld. The whiteness of that place came back to me, the curtains, the carpet, everything so pristine. And he'd carried me up the stairs into his loft, tucked the blankets around me, and left me with a breeze-cool kiss on my cheek. That was how people were supposed to behave toward each other. If I'd been fifteen nearly sixteen, and not a thirteen-year old in a twenty-five year old body, I would have fallen in love with him after that, maybe. If we'd had a few more days in the Dreamworld with that kind of pristine and subtle affection between us, I would have kissed him back.

Damon, and the Catacombs. Char. Hunt. Arabella. Sweet little Peter. All lost to me. Everyone who wasn't dead was gone and far away, or completely ignorant of what they meant to me. I think it wasn't so much I couldn't care about people but that the ones I loved didn't know me at all. That was the root of the loneliness. I wanted Jason, and Aaron, and Peter, and even Scott. I didn't want substitutes. I wanted Damon back, under different circumstances. I wanted my power.

I had wandered again. I had been so far from the auditorium it felt like a journey to come back to it. Twenty minutes of steady work had passed during my reverie, and the sketch was painted. I held it up, keeping the plane of the paper almost horizontal so the still-wet pigment wouldn't run. The watercolors had been a Christmas present from my mother, quite a surprise, since Nick, my father, had loved watercolors, and generally, all mention of him around my mother was completely taboo.

Who can say where paintings come from? I had looked into a couple of abysses already, I think. Maybe the darkness there had crept into me. Whenever I thought about Char, I felt myself growing hopelessly melodramatic, and here was the painting to prove it. The white candles I remember intending to paint were tinged with red and had blue-black smoke rising from and almost obscuring them. There was fire in the bowl at the center of the pentagram. I could imagine the mask-like faces of the Burnt Man's retainers collected in the background of the painting, and Jason Lawson, his face twisted with torment, screaming at me as he tried to wake my mind from inactivity.

Something broke all of a sudden, and I turned the still-wet painting upside down on the stage, collected my used brushes, palette, and water dishes, and left the auditorium very quickly.

The light inside had been dim, and in the hallway the fluorescents hurt my eyes. They welled up—but no. I was crying, and it had something to do with the brightness, but not much. *Maggie the Melancholy, Princess of Pain.* I had to do something to get myself out of the bad, sad, mad mindset. I had to laugh and relax and be easy with myself and with the world. I had to stop feeling like the only thing of value that had ever happened to me had almost also killed me, and had cost several people their lives. *Lighten up!* I ordered myself. I felt ridiculous.

It wasn't until I stood by the water fountain washing my brushes and drying them on my hoodie that I realized how fast I was breathing, almost hyperventilating. *And me without a paper bag,* I told myself, and the hysterical laughter welled up inside. It was also then that I became aware of the noise from beyond the door across the hall, from the auditorium.

3

## The Pretty Things Are Going To Hell

✪

I stood in the hallway listening. I could hear the buzz of the fluorescent lights above me, almost drowning out the other sounds—muffled muttering, guttural, hoarse sounds which couldn't possibly be English.

There was a rush of oddly hot air past my face and down the back of my hoodie. I sneezed and spilled dirty water from the water dish down my leg. It ran down into my shoe to where my foot felt cramped and sweaty. Zoned again. I had no idea how long I had been standing there.

The harsh, barely audible words thumped around in my head, and I crossed the hallway and opened the door to the upper level of the gymnasium.

The gym had a spectators' gallery running along one side, and it was into this that I entered. From where I stood, ten rows of benches, stretching the length of the gym, led down a steeply graded set of concrete stairs to the low railing prefacing the eight-foot drop to the level. The lights were off, and most of the illumination came from the four large skylights which dropped squares of muted sunlight on the gym floor below.

Only, the flickers playing on the glass basketball backstops weren't sunlight, but candlelight. And in the middle of the gym, there was a white circle marked out in chalk. A five-pointed star was drawn inside, and candles stood at the places where the star touched the circle. Other symbols—squiggles, arcs, odd-shaped letters—marked the circle within and without. Crouching by four of the candles, right away I recognized Scott, Rae, and Suzanne from the morning—and Jason.

Jason Lawson, my ridiculous public school crush who in Char's domain became something more than a just vain love-interest. He'd ignored me after the incident like the others, only occasionally hitting me up for homework help as he'd done before everything began. I missed him most of all because of the time I'd spent with him between our kidnapping and the final battle, and because he at one time had known more about me than anyone. I think I'd been close to him—I'm not much of a judge of things like that—and he didn't remember any of it.

Jason's and Scott's presence should have made the final member of the group almost inevitable, but somehow I was surprised anyhow. The fifth stood facing me, and it was he who recited in deep monotone the harsh, complex words in some foreign tongue. The huge, old tome that I had seen pass between Suzanne and Scott that morning was held in both his arms mid-chest level. Aaron Scribner's blond hair was parted on the left and hung limply to his ears. The light reflected off his glasses. I could imagine the blue of his eyes burning in the flickering candlelight. I had seen him in class over the years in much the same attitude, eyes blazing as he made his point. He seemed to be very intense all the time. In the circle, Rae was obviously very much under his spell, swaying slightly with every word.

I stood mesmerized myself as Aaron motioned to Scott, who picked up a matchbook from the floor beside him, lit a match, and tossed it into the center of the pentagram. It blazed up in a miniature blue-white fireball, and didn't burn out. I heard a sharp intake of drawn breath, from one or from all of them, I couldn't tell. The candle flames darkened to blue-black.

Dampness prickled in the small of my back under the heavy cotton of my hoodie, the first realization I had of the actual peril of my situation. I wasn't in control of myself, I knew as I tried to pull my eyes away from the glint of fire on Aaron's glasses. My breathing came fast and hard. I wiped moisture from my upper lip and temples and pushed away wisps of hair that had become glued to my forehead, but I couldn't look away.

Suddenly, something snapped. I squeezed my eyes shut and dropped my head to my chest. A sobby croak escaped straight from my throat, but it felt like I'd dropped the sound into a bubble and nothing of it went into the air to disturb the rite below.

My head jerked up. I saw again what I had attached no importance to before—a scuffed-out section of the circle. Someone had accidentally rubbed out a small arc, but it would be enough. That circle wouldn't hold anything. This much I knew, from what Mr. Hunt had told me in the Burnt Man's catacombs. If they actually succeeded in summoning something, they and everyone at this school, including me, would be at its mercy.

In a haze of heat and sweat *(why was it so hot here?)* I half ran, half slid down the ten concrete steps screaming "Stop, stop! Stop it!"

Below, Aaron, oblivious to me, raised his chin, his eyes burning their blue fire, and said some two or three words with great finality.

"Stop!" I screamed again.

Suzanne looked up at me with glazed eyes. Her lips curled as if she wanted to say something. Her brown hair, pulled into a thick braid at the back of her head, glowed in the blue light. Black smoke now rose from the candles.

"Close the circle!" I cried, hoarse now. Had I really lost my voice that quickly? Suzanne stared at me stupidly. The others hadn't noticed me at all. Red-yellow twists rose from the match in the center of the pentagram. It was smoldering now, fiery red but showing no sign of dying completely.

"It is done," said Aaron, his face still upturned.

With some little cautionary voice in the back of my mind telling me not to be so stupid and to get away as fast as I could, I threaded my legs between the bars of the gallery railing, hung in space for an instant, and dropped.

I landed badly, heavily, twisting one ankle under me. I was dimly aware of the pain, and of Aaron raising his hands to the ceiling, fingers spread, head still flung back. *You self-important, self-destructive prick*, I thought. The other four stared up at him.

I lay where I had fallen.

I took two deep breaths, with my shoulders collapsing forward, and got up. In the haze of the heat and sweat and pain, I stepped purposefully on my hurt ankle, to establish the extent of the damage. *Piece of cake*, I told myself with as much bravado as I could manage. I walked on, smoothly and quickly as possible toward Aaron along the perimeter of the circle.

It was about then that the smoke, rising in an intermingling of red, black and blue, coalesced into a formless smoky mass. The match died.

I stepped past Rae, using one cold shoulder to support me as I passed. Rae was beside Scott, and between Scott and Aaron was the hole. A thick piece of white sidewalk chalk lay by the matchbook Scott had dropped, by Aaron's left foot.

The shape above the pentagram shimmered and spun. It found the hole. I could almost taste its hunger. I felt a shiver in my mind and touched the place, empty now, where my power had sat. The form pulsated, and before I could imagine acting, it slid through the air and out the hole.

And the world exploded.

Aaron went down silently, thin red streaks across his forearms and cheeks. I felt myself thrown back from Rae, gashes that appeared across the backs of my hands stinging with salt from my sweat. I could just make out the shape of the thing darting around the circle of ex-observers who were now taking a very active part in the ceremony. Jason fell backwards, arms crossed tightly over his face to protect his eyes. The thing ripped in passing at his bare legs. Suzanne crouched low, her knees pulled under her. The back of her Polo shirt was torn in strips criss-crossing her back. Rae screamed and screamed to no avail as the thing cut her arms and bare shoulders and grazed the side of her face. Scott swung his arms madly at it, which seemed to anger it. It flew at his back, knocking him forward into the circle, unconscious or dead for all I knew.

Or cared, to tell the truth.

Pain burst out in my shoulders, my scalp, my bare legs. I clamped my hand over the sting on my cheek and felt warm blood gush out between my fingers. I was amazed that something so silent could deal out so much damage. My right temple bled as well.

I bit my tongue to focus the pain like Mr. Hunt had taught me in one of his lessons in the catacombs, but this only served to remind me of my throbbing ankle which collapsed under me, sending me down on my stomach hard.

*Focus. Deep breaths. No time for self-pity.*

Amazing myself, the pain receded to a dull, background ache as I inhaled slowly. Maybe it was the tickle in my brain that called out, siren-like: *I couldn't help feeling this was something to do with me.*

On my belly, I crawled toward Aaron. I tried to get over Scott, and lay for a moment across his legs, my hand on his back, feeling his blood soak into my hoodie.

I pushed myself over him in an intense exertion. The thing clawed my back. I screamed, but again all the sound seemed to fall dead, as if it hadn't gone past my own throat.

My brain and body were tiring, but I saw what I had to do. First, get Scott out of the circle so I could re-close it. I reached past the protective edge of the circle, took a fistful of Scott's hair, and pulled. He responded with a yelp of pain, but hauled himself out of the way. I grabbed the chalk and redrew the portion of the pentagram that Scott had erased with his body, and all but an inch of the original hole.

Then, I realized why the demon was still in the room, why it hadn't left the room, and why it attacked us. It had to be the reason for the match Scott had thrown into the center of the circle. Heat. And blood. Blood was the first lesson in magic. Heat might have been the second. No, never let anyone get the better of you was the second. *First, trust yourself,* said Hunt, *and secondly, no one.*

Aaron had dropped to his knees, and his fist was now tightly closed around the matchbook. Blood thumping in my head, I reached out and tried to wrench Aaron's hand open. Rae screamed again, losing momentum. Quiet sobbing rose from the other three as the thing continued to scrape and rip at them. Aaron's fingers were like marble, cold and smooth. I shivered at the feel of him, memories of Damon stabbing me again. But this was Aaron, not Damon, and this was now, not three years ago. I pulled his hair, which had worked so well with Scott. He looked at me then, wild fear in his eyes.

I grabbed his wrist and twisted. "Let go of the bloody matches, Aaron," I shouted, maybe unnecessarily loudly, but I was having trouble hearing with the sound of my pulse pounding in my ears. Bloody matches was apt, and I found myself laughing out loud. *I must sound like a lunatic,* I thought. Suddenly, the thing tore across Aaron's back. I twisted harder, and with the double onslaught, he relaxed and the matchbook dropped from his fingers into my hand.

I wiped blood off one hand and fumbled to strike a match. It flared up finally and I threw it into the center of the pentagram. The thing seemed to gain some dimension suddenly—I saw a hint of smokiness pause in mid air, before darting at the flame, suddenly the greatest source of heat in the room. I closed the circle, trapping it within the pentagram.

"Demon, begone," I said wearily. I could hardly hear myself over the noise of my own heartbeat.

The thing glowed red, then vanished with the fading of the match. There was a little puff of black smoke, then nothing.

The glass backboards and Aaron's glasses reflected the yellow flickering light of the five candles. There was a fleck of red in one corner of the left lens.

"Every ritual of a certain size needs blood," I said to no one in particular. "Lesson number one."

# 4

## Don't Look Down

✪

I stood carefully and threw the matchbook away from me. It was shiny red, covered in my blood, and Aaron's. It skittered over the tile, coming to rest by Scott's hand. He was lying in a fetal position, shoulders hunched against the pain, I would guess. His back was bleeding from a dozen wet gashes.

I clamped my jaw shut and raised my chin. I straightened my back as well as I could without pulling the hoodie off the places the blood had begun to dry, gluing it to the slashes. I took a couple of steps and grimaced. With each step, I could feel a squishy warmth in my shoes, soaking into the leather interiors. It was either more blood, or dirty paint wash. There were streaks of blood on the floor around Aaron.

I walked past Aaron, past Jason, across half the basketball court. The stiffness was settling into my ankle, and I wasn't sure how much longer I'd be able to walk on it. I pushed against the heavy gym door with my good hand, the bleeding one braced under my elbow. Now the immediate danger was over, I was furious more than anything else, and not really thinking clearly. I pushed the door open and balanced on the ball of my right foot as I looked back.

Two of the candles fell over and went out. Rae was rubbing at part of the circle with her hand. The old book must have been somewhere, but I couldn't see it. It should have been my first priority, but as I said, I wasn't thinking too clearly. All I really wanted to do was wash my hands of the whole thing. If there was a mess to straighten out, I didn't want to have to help explain. As far as I was concerned, I was never there.

I stepped into the hall and let the door close behind me. Then I ran.

Away from the gym, through two sets of double doors, up the stairs.

To hell with the ankle. Every step was agony, and it felt *great*. The second floor women's washroom in this wing was always deserted, and it would be a good place to clean up. *To hell with the ankle.* I wanted to throw up.

I ran, trying not to limp, and felt a tightness starting across the bridge of my nose, which meant I was about to cry.

I reached the top landing of the staircase and pushed open the door with my shoulder. If I could put off crying until I was inside the washroom, I could call it a good day. I didn't want to have to explain why my hoodie was ripped to shreds and covered with blood either, but I mostly just didn't want to cry in front of anyone.

Suddenly, three people came around the corner: a boy and a girl holding hands, and another girl carrying her binder, probably on her way to the library. The girl with the books gasped, and I was tempted to laugh.

I headed off their silence. "There's been an accident," I croaked, "that way," and inevitably, as soon as I spoke, started to cry. I realized, too, that my instincts for self-preservation were as unerring as always. I had pointed in the wrong direction.

All three went rushing down the hall in the direction I'd indicated. *Really worried about me*, I thought. I hoped they turned the wrong corner and ran into a brick wall. I went into the girls' washroom, giving up on walking normally and favoring my hurt ankle.

I stood in front of the large mirror to assess the damage. The washroom, as I had expected, was deserted. I had the sensation I was standing outside myself, looking at the girl with screwed-up eyes and tears running down her cheeks.

The ankle was swelling, but not badly enough to necessitate taking my shoe off, thank god. I'd ice it as soon as I got home. If I could get home without causing a scene.

My clothes were a horror show. Not all the gashes had gone all the way through the fabric, but enough had that between the blood and the tears, I was barely decent. All I could really do was wash them out the best I could and hope I'd stopped bleeding by the time they were dry enough to put back on.

I took a deep breath and started to pull the hoodie off my back.

Pain is not a big deal, if you have something else to think about. I was so busy assessing the rips in my shirt to decide if it was decent to walk home in, I was mostly able to ignore how hurt I must be. Really, it was no worse than a bad case of pins and needles.

And when I'd soaked some paper towels in the sink and started rubbing blood off my cuts, I was surprised at how minor my injuries really were. Just a fine criss-crossing of red lines, no great gashes or rips. The skin was barely broken, but my hoodie was torn in several places and had absorbed a surprising amount of blood. The back of my bra was scratched through, too. I hadn't noticed—which proved how useful the stupid thing was to me.

My shorts were in much better shape, only one small tear and since the hoodie had nearly covered them, the blood situation was negligible as well.

I could still feel that pins and needles sensation on my back as I soaked the hoodie in the bathroom sink, rubbing soap through the red patches of blood. The white of the hoodie turned gradually pink. Not my favorite color, but at least it was more or less uniform.

Then I set the shirt out under the hand-dryer and left it running while I went to the toilet. It had stopped by the time I was finished, but the fabric was still wet. I ran the dryer three more times until the hoodie was only slightly clammy and put it back on, not really caring at this point if I got a cold; that was the least of my concerns. In fact, if I got sick, all the better. Then I would have an excuse stay at home for a few weeks, if not forever...

On that note, I decided there was no way I could back to class for the afternoon. My clothes were excuse enough.

*How could they?*

If they only knew what they'd been through before! If they could remember the death and chaos that had accompanied the Burnt Man's plans for the four of us—Jason, Scott, me, and Aaron. Blood, and magic. I'd learned, in his realm, that the two are intrinsically connected. You want big magic, you need blood. Although, I supposed, in what they'd just done, the blood was an effect of the magic, not its genesis. Char didn't seem to have problems with blood on either side of the magic equation, cause or effect. I suppose he'd become indifferent to the use of violence after all the centuries he'd lived. Had he considered its use as pedestrian and morally acceptable as taking money out of the bank? Every ritual of a certain size, after all, needs blood.

I ran a hand through my hair. It felt greasy, and I could feel hard bits of dried blood matting strands together. Where I peeled it out, my scalp stung. *How could they?*

Then I remembered I'd left my painting stuff in the auditorium.

The painting.

I had forgotten. The candles. The blue-black flame. That hole in the circle.

A giggle jumped into my throat. I watched my face in the mirror, fascinated, as the edges of my mouth curled. I could almost see the fit of giggles climb out of my stomach and finally burst out.

I limped out of the washroom laughing so hard there were tears in my eyes. This had always been one of the ways my mind dealt with stress or fear. Too bad an inappropriate sense of humor wasn't on the list of things that make you cool.

Outside the auditorium doors, I picked up my water dish and paintbrushes. I washed them off as well as I could in the fountain and wiped the excess water on my hoodie. Little streaks of brown from the wet pigment stained the pink cotton even further, which just made me laugh even harder. I slid down the wall and lay there, with my head on my shoulder, until I regained some sort of composure.

I wiped my eyes finally, trying to keep my face straight. Then I went carefully to the auditorium doors and opened them.

Coldness hit me. I swallowed and blinked several times. Someone had turned the auditorium lights out, and the only illumination came from the hallway. All the laughter drained out of me, and suddenly I was scared.

My nose itched, and I rubbed at it. My other hand, the one with the thin red stripes running across it, had clenched into a fist. I could feel my injured ankle shaking. I took a ginger step toward the stage.

*Thup.* The slap of my shoe reverberated through the room. *Thup.* Again, slowly. I took two quick, uneven steps which got me as far as the edge of the stage, where two watery-green eyes stared back at me.

I hadn't painted those. I picked up the picture. A pair of slanted almond eyes floated, disembodied, above my pentagram circle. The eyes were in my style, the colors diluted just the way I diluted my paints, indistinguishable from my own work. They were also, indisputably, frightening. I would hesitate to say evil, because my style was perfectly replicated and hardly skillful enough to express so individual a concept, but it was unnerving.

The wounds in my back throbbed suddenly. Hand shaking, I turned the picture face down on the stage.

I put my brushes and dish back into my knapsack and zipped it up. As an afterthought, I reached out to put the picture in my bag with the paints, but my fingers stopped a couple of inches from the painting, and I wondered if I could bring myself to touch it again. I told myself calmly, rationalizing, that since my arm was already fully extended, I would have to lean forward to reach the picture, and would probably throw off my balance by having too much weight on my bad foot.

My hand retreated.

"Maggie."

I jumped, as if just to prove just how tense I was.

"Maggie," the voice repeated, impatient now.

I turned to see Aaron standing in the doorway.

"You okay?" he asked, moving slowly toward me.

I shrugged.

"Did I scare you?"

"Uh, yeah," I agreed. The fury I had felt earlier welled up again.

"I came to apologize," he said, pushing a piece of pale hair out of his eyes. I saw the splatter of blood in the corner of his glasses, his ripped shirt and the rustiness of dried blood on his jeans. His hair glowed yellow-white in the faint light from the hallway.

He continued. "We should have double-checked the circle. It was my fault. I moved the book over the chalk just before we began the ceremony. I must have rubbed it out. If it wasn't for you, we might all be dead now."

I wanted to explode. For all you'd guess from the tone of his voice, he might have lost some homework I lent him to copy. The tightness came back into the bridge of my nose. "What the hell—" I began. I stopped, and looked away from him. "How much more irresponsible could you be? Did you just—*assume* it wouldn't work? Figured your *brilliance* was enough to cope if it did?"

"You know—" he said, shrugging, and I looked back, very angry now. He was so smug—didn't he have any sense of responsibility? I thought of the blood on the gym floor, the mistake that might have cost one or all of them their lives. Shouldn't he be indebted to me? But no, ego prevented gratitude, obviously.

"Where's the book?" I asked, the only avenue of questioning I really cared about. A book of spells, something like that, anyhow. Probably a simplistic way of looking at it. But I was already convinced, I realized, that the knowledge contained in the book was meant for me. Why else had I become involved? Too much coincidence otherwise: seeing the morning hand-off, being in the right place to interrupt the ritual.

He shrugged. "I don't know. It was gone after the thing in the circle vanished. I thought—it—might have taken the book along with it."

I couldn't deny the possibility, although it seemed ridiculous to me. Still, I had no idea how that kind of thing worked. Our combined ignorance was rather stunning. "No one saw where it went?" I whispered a "dammit" under my breath that I didn't think he heard.

Now, when he replied, he sounded pissed off. "I wasn't really thinking about it," he said. "There were hurt people. Sorry for being so irresponsible."

"*GOD*dammit," I spat, the stronger obscenity louder than the mild one had been. Infuriated, I balled my fists, shifting to one hip.

Then I saw how bloodshot Aaron's eyes were. I made contact with them, beyond the splotch of blood on his lens. The redness wasn't in the whites, it was in the irises, but the color leaked out around the edges of them as if painted. Painted. Like the almond eyes in the picture, pigment on wet paper, leaking outwards. I felt the blood drain from my face, and the tightness moved to my throat.

"Demon," I said.

His mouth twisted into a grimace and he laughed.

"You're a more sophisticated thing than what was in the circle," I guessed. "Just saying *you are dismissed* isn't enough to get rid of you, is it?"

He snarled, which I took as amusement, but I saw the semblance of Aaron waver.

"You're losing control of that form, aren't you?" I said. "Maybe you're not as strong as all that." By reflex, I reached into my bag, keeping one eye on him all the time. Arabella's ring. But of course it wasn't there. I had carried my prize religiously for so long, thinking I had to be prepared all the time for the return of something like the Burnt Man. I had given that up a year ago, whether hope or fear I didn't dare decide.

It was time to bluff, or to lose. "Do you know who I am, demon?" I hissed, making a fist inside my bag. "Go tell whoever sent you to try something better next time." Then, with a sneer, "You are dismissed," I said.

His grimace faded, and the face twisted and seemed to collapse in on itself. His clothes took on the same texture as his skin, and his whole body shriveled and wrinkled. Then he dissolved, completely, silently, in a thin stream of smoke. "Go to hell, bastard," I whispered, terror now fully formed, heart beating a billion miles an hour. I carried weight somewhere, it appeared. Not at school, but with things called by magic.

And it was gone.

The picture lay on the stage, face up.

5

Strangers When We Meet

✪

I turned the picture back over to hide those nasty eyes. The best thing to do would be to rip it up, burn it, flush the ashes down the toilet. What else had escaped the circle besides the two I'd already seen? *Maggie Stuart, Demon Slayer,* I thought. It was ridiculous to imagine.

On the other hand... On the other hand, I was qualified as anyone I knew. Who better than Maggie Stuart, almost-Queen of the Night to sort out an occult bumble?

*No, don't even think it.* As far as I was concerned, I would act when necessary, but I wasn't going out of my way to correct Aaron's or whomever's lack of judgement.

I left the building quietly through the labyrinth of the tech dungeon. I guessed that the scene in the gym would be big news around the school by now. It was best to completely disassociate myself with it.

✪

By the time I got home, I was almost convinced the whole thing had been a dream. I spent the time before Jan—I mean Mom—got home reading some more Crowley, sitting in the big armchair by the window, with the key to the safe-deposit box containing Arabella's ring in my pocket.

I helped cook and clean up after supper, and watched T.V. until eleven thirty in the basement rec room. Mom came down for the news. We talked a little, no more than usual. And of course, managed to say really nothing at all.

I went to bed, feeling restless as usual. *Maggie Stuart, Opposite Girl.*

How could I justify to myself that, regardless of the danger they'd put themselves in and that I had run head-on into, today had been the best day of the past three years?

✪

In the morning, I found a silver chain that Jan never wore, and strung the key around my neck. After school, I planned to retrieve the ring. It would be a comfort, and protection, and would keep me strong through whatever the fallout of the previous day's events would be.

It wasn't necessary. I went to school, and it was as if nothing had happened. I didn't see Scott or Jason or any of the others, excepting a brief glimpse of Rae on her way to the volleyball practice after school. I didn't ask anyone if they'd heard about what had gone on in the gym the previous day. And, since very few people spoke to me at school anyway, no information was proffered.

Over the next few days, I got in the habit of saying hello to Irene every morning, so I'd have the control to head off any other interaction. The key stayed on the chain, a warning and not a ward. And I got back to the business of being depressed.

✪

Two weeks passed quickly, during which I began to believe that the fading ache in my ankle was nothing more than hysteria sympathetic to a hallucination. Even the torn hoodie at the bottom of my closet (the useless bra I'd just trashed) didn't seem like enough proof, especially since all the blood had washed out pretty well. It was like the 'incident' all over again.

Then, I found I had to believe again.

I woke up with my eyes full of sunlight. I had been thrashing around in sleep, I knew from the sheet wrapped around my legs. My dreams were often very vivid, full of images that haunted me for the rest of the day. This morning, I hadn't been able to recall anything specific. But I just couldn't shake the feeling that something important had been communicated to me while I slept.

The walk to school put me in a lethargic, dreamy mood, as if I hadn't quite woken up. We were in the middle of a heat wave. I guess you'd call it Indian Summer; we were nearing the end of September. It was already over twenty degrees, and only eight-fifteen.

I had a long drink at a water fountain inside the school. It was too early for most students to have arrived, and I planned to spend half an hour in the library before first period, after hitting the washroom.

I chose the girl's washroom on the second floor near the auditorium, because it was on the way to the library. I hadn't been there since the first day of school. I stood for a moment in front of the mirror, trying to summon to my mind the events of three weeks before. All traces of blood, of wet cotton smell, all had been scoured away long before. I felt like I was visiting the scene of some distant childhood memory, trying to capture a picture in my mind's eye of something that probably never existed to begin with.

I went into a stall, pulled up my skirt and down my panties. I started to sit, but slowly, because something had caught my eye.

My dreaminess intensified. Looking up, underwear around my thighs, I could see my reflection in the mirror above the sink, which was impossible. Had the mirror been moved? Somehow, I realized, my perceptions had altered and I was seeing—

What? Myself, in ugly brown print skirt and thin hoodie slightly off one shoulder. I never wore anything with less than elbow-length sleeves, no matter what the temperature, and I never uncovered anything of the other shoulder. Another movement captured my attention.

I could see, in the mirror, the next stall, and the man sitting curled on the adjacent toilet.

Blond, almost white hair. Small frame, but solid. Roundish Dutch face. A miniature Rutger Hauer, with a foolish, sensuous smile. The person in the world I could least expect to have anything to do with my business, Mr. John Thurl, my drafting teacher.

I gawked, watching myself and him in the mirror. He rolled his head slowly, cocked it to one side and looked back at me side-long through sleepy eyes. A half-smile raised one corner of his mouth.

He was sitting on the toilet seat, one knee pulled against his chest, one arm behind his head. It was—vulgar, especially since Mr. Thurl was so quiet and gentle. . . He spoke.

"Maaaaagie. . ." A long, low whisper.

"Shit," I whispered back, almost a hiss.

"Come, little Maggie," said Mr. Thurl. "I want to hold you in my arms. I want you, Maggie. Maaaaagie. . ." The sound trailed on to nothingness, a voiceless ampersand.

I said nothing, hoped he would vanish. Then. . . there. A footfall, in the washroom? A step ringing hollowly on tile in some acoustically deep room. I reached, to unlatch the stall door, and when I looked up again, my vision had returned to normal.

*Scream*. In my stomach, it sat and crawled—but I swallowed the bile taste rising in my throat and left the washroom stall. The door of the adjacent stall was hanging open. Naturally, there was no one inside. No one had entered the washroom since I had. Shaking, I must have washed my face a dozen times, in anticipation of tears that didn't come.

✪

When I arrived in class about twenty minutes early, the real Mr. Thurl took me aside. He looked as usual, calm and gentle. It wasn't easy to forget the look on the face of whatever I had seen in the bathroom. There was still something loose in the world, and it had chosen to visit me. I felt an ice-cube crawl on my neck as he touched my shoulder.

"There's someone waiting to see you, in my office," he said, and I went.

This was my second year in Mr. Thurl's class, and my affection for him played a bigger part in choosing drafting again than any particular love for the subject.

Mr. Thurl was just a good person, a very good teacher, intelligent and interested. He knew a lot about my home life, which is more than I can say for the guidance counselors at Dief. I was one of those kids who, in their professional opinions, had nothing to complain about and should stop being difficult. Mr. Thurl accepted that there were things I didn't want to talk about, but heard me out if had a particularly emotional outburst that needed venting.

Still, he couldn't have known who he was sending me into his office to greet.

My first thought was, *this must be a mistake*. The room, in semi-darkness, lit solely by thick glass-block windows three-quarters of the way up the wall, seemed empty.

Then I saw the dark head belonging to someone who sat in Thurl's great rolling office chair, his back to me.

My recognition, even with so little to go on, was immediate. A pit opened up in my stomach, huge and yawning like the emptiness of space. "Mr. Hunt," I said, and I wondered if his presence should make me happy. I felt a little guilt, a little anger, a little more fear. He was supposed to be long gone from Westbrook. It was a bad sign. If the cops knew he was here—but then, he'd been right under their noses for years without them catching on. No reason for them to suspect.

And I'd done my bit to make him safe. No one remembered the *incident*, so no one knew *the Hunter* had ever been Ontario. From what he'd said that last night on the bluff, everyone, including his own brother, thought he had died years before.

He stood and came to face me. His hair had grayed a bit at the temples, but he was otherwise unchanged. Maybe his life had given him as much abuse as one man can carry on his features long before I ever met him.

He was not overly tall, but he came close enough that I had to roll my eyes up to look him in the face.

Mr. Hunt was compact and dark, everything about him seeming full of gravity. He had been my science teacher for two years back at Westbrook Elementary, and my favorite teacher overall. He was often sarcastic, caustic, cynical, and, as I had discovered, dangerous. He had been included in the forgetting I had put on everyone who had been touched by the Burnt Man, but he had promised that someday he would remember, so that I wouldn't have to bear my memories alone.

He reached out and took my hand. I let him, resisting the urge to pull away. I could imagine for a moment his taking my hand more firmly and pulling me toward him. Revulsion? No, not the right word. Just plain fear, maybe.

"Maggie," he said, smiling, massaging my tendons almost painfully. His voice never went above a breathy whisper. "You've changed so much, and so little."

"I take that as a compliment, or not," I replied.

"Still like that, Mags?" His smile was sadder as he released my fingers. I started to feel that we were entering into another elaborate game, where one false word on my part would not only lose me whatever the prize was, but meant I would be excluded from all knowledge of what the game had been.

Mr. Hunt circled me slowly. I could feel his eyes on me, even when he moved out of my line of sight. I remembered Char and his games, when I had bluffed my way blindly through everything, somehow managing to find the right answers, and even score unexpected victories—and I mean unexpected to both of us. I had always wondered if my success hadn't given Hunt—the Hunter—an inflated impression of my intelligence. Or maybe my subconscious was doing the work, and I was just taking credit due.

Behind me, I heard him shut the door of Thurl's office. There was something different here from the last time I had seen him, something more—exciting? My neck tingled. It had been three years.

"You can't even guess why I'm here, can you?" said Mr. Hunt, his voice dropping even lower. Almost three years. He stayed behind me, speaking low into one of my ears. I, unsure of his intentions, did not turn.

"Oh, very good, Maggie," he said softly, with a hint of amusement in his voice. "Stay still, and let me enjoy the composition I've created. Such a pretty picture."

There was a tone, a quality in his voice that I don't think was there before, a smoothness where before there was edge. The fear was back, but I didn't feel like laughing. I wanted to turn to check his irises. Would the darkness in the office make more sense?

My stomach constricted as one of his hands slid over my scarred shoulder. "Maggie," he said, and was silent. I felt his fingers brush my neck, and then they were gone, and he was gone, the door opening and closing behind me. I didn't turn until I was sure he had left.

At first, when I had just given up the power and its absence made me lonely and half crazy with longing, I had thought about Char constantly, considering over and over any other option I had had at the moment I became again a normal teenage girl. I remained convinced that I had made the only decision possible. The place the power had sat in my body was still raw, like the abscess left by a pulled tooth. Close. I imagined running my tongue over my lost power.

After a few months, the sense of loss had dulled to a painful ache. I found myself flexing my fist, searching for the power that was no longer there. Postpartum blues. No, more like miscarriage. What would I have been doing now if I'd kept it? In the unlikely event that I was still alive, of course. Well, this was one baby I would survive.

I stood, until Mr. Thurl came back, wondering if it had been temptation, if Hunt had made some kind of offer that I had rejected by not comprehending it. So much like the games I had played with the Burnt Man. I felt slow and stupid. *Poor Maggie*, I told myself. *Senile before sixteen.*

"Maggie?" Mr. Thurl, kind Mr. Thurl who'd held my hand for an hour when I was coming off my medication at school, hallucinating and paranoid. "You okay?"

"Yeah," I said. "There's a man I haven't seen for a long time."

He didn't press, gentle man. Unfortunately, I really *did* want to talk to someone, but since I had no idea how to start, I kept quiet. He misinterpreted my silence for reticence. "Why don't you go home?" he said. My answer to everything, and often his. "I'll get someone to take notes for you." He must have thought I was going to cry.

"Thank you," I said and left the school, wondering where I would go.

6

Join The Gang

✪

I walked aimlessly along the school drive running behind the football feld bleachers, my eyes swimming, oblivious to my surroundings.

Suddenly, there was a shout from nearby. "Mags," called Jason Lawson.

I stopped, wondering where he'd come from, and let him catch up. "Hey, Jason," I replied, without much relish. I looked at him expectantly.

"I'm sorry, Maggie," he said. "I didn't mean to do anything, for things to go the way they did." His usual good humor seemed strained.

"What makes you think you have to apologize to me?" I asked, scanning his eyes for any sign of redness. There was none.

I spoke quietly, head turning away, not even sure after I'd said it if he'd heard, knowing that I probably had no chance of saying what I wanted to say. The anger I had felt before had faded, and all I felt now, weeks after, was annoyance at being forced to remember about my lost power. Hunt's visit had confused me and I was hitting a kind of sensory overload.

Turning back, I said, "I think that you should tell me what you want, Jason, and then you should go away and leave me alone while I decide if I'm going to do it."

"Why do you think we want you to do something?"

I resisted the urge to tell him that really, the only time he ever spoke to me was when he wanted something. Any interaction I'd had with him in the past few years had been about homework, and how I could help him with it, and that was all. I was also tempted to point out his use of the word 'we'. But I waited, and said only, "Hunt came to me today."

"Hunt." Jason's voice was flat. He obviously still had no remembrance of the time before, and there was no reason for him to think immediately of our grade eight science teacher.

I dropped it. "I think you should tell me everything." I started to walk again, and he followed me to the donut shop on the main road close to the school across from the bus stop. We got coffees and sat. The shop was almost empty of students. Hardly anyone skipped before second period. I could hardly imagine Jason Lawson skipping at all. Well, well, well, and all for little ol' me.

"We found the book in Aaron's dad's study," Jason began. "Aaron swears it was never there before."

"Who's 'we'?" I interrupted.

"Me, Aaron, and Scott. The girls came in on it later." He frowned. "The thing I don't understand is how our cuts healed up so fast. I was bleeding so much at first, but five minutes later, almost nothing. By the next day, there were just little lines." He looked at me for confirmation.

I withheld it, feeling righteously bitchy. "What I want to know is why no one seemed to know all. . . what happened."

"After you left," said Jason, "when the candles started blowing out, we all came back to normal really quickly. Rae and I cleaned up pretty well, and the others got out."

"Did anyone ask Aaron's father about the book?"

"Didn't have to. Mr. Scribner keeps a list of all his books on file. We checked the next day. Nothing even close."

I laughed and drank down the last dregs of my coffee. "Phantom books, appearing on shelves in the dead of might. Keep your libraries under lock and key."

Jason looked down into his coffee. *Inappropriate humor strikes again.* I wished I knew how to put him more at ease. Nothing appropriate would come to me.

Instead, perversely, I smirked and leaned back. "So, Mr. Lawson, just what makes you think I can help?"

"You can't," he said. "Not like this."

And he drained his coffee and stood.

I hadn't been prepared for that. "Hey," I said, keeping my seat, "Do you want help or not? I'm sorry," I added, to apologize for whatever offense he'd taken.

He sat, and the corners of his mouth twisted like he might cry. "This was my idea. Aaron probably wouldn't want me to talk to you. I think he was more scared by all of—*that* than he wants us to think. And Rae and Suzanne—they don't want anything to do with it, because they say none of it's their fault. Suzanne, more than Rae. Scott—"

"I don't think Scott likes me," I supplied, hoping it wasn't true.

"It's not that so much," said Jason. "I just don't think he figures we should trust you."

"And you do?" I asked.

He looked down. "Look, Mags, I don't know what to think. I don't understand anything about what's going on, and you seem to. I don't really know anything about you. I just want to stop it before anything really bad happens."

"What has happened already?" I said quietly, hoping he would lower his voice too. Especially with Hunt back, I was starting to get an acute feeling of paranoia.

"Death," he said, and stopped. "It sounds stupid."

"Tell me," I said. "I'll try not to pass judgment."

He took a deep breath, then offered to buy me another coffee. I decided it would be a good idea, and stared out the window at the parking lot until he returned.

"Death," I prompted, adding sugar and cream to my coffee. Black seemed like a bad idea today.

"Squirrels mostly," he said, cradling his coffee like a good luck charm. "They all look fine, except they're dead." He paused. "I mean, no tire marks, no blood. They could have all died of old age."

"Why do you think there's something wrong?"

"Because it's not random, it's personal," he said. "Around my house, around Aaron's, all of us, even the girls. Everything that comes within thirty feet of our houses that's alive and not human dies. It's like a curse."

"Cats and dogs?"

He nodded. "A couple of cats. I'm glad we all have backyard fences. And no pets."

"How long has this been going on?"

"Since that day," he said. "Long enough to realize it's really happening. I—I've been cleaning up dead squirrels and birds and—" He stopped, and looked into his coffee.

I took a quick sip of the coffee, succeeding in burning my tongue.

Had it really been three years since I had exchanged much more than a hello or *"sure I can help you with math"* with him? I was tempted to mention a couple of things he'd told me before, little secrets. And one big one. I mean, they weren't all that incriminating, but maybe it would be a good idea to set the seal once and for all on my "oddness." If they were going to treat me like an idiot savant—*here's Maggie to cure our ills!*—well, damn them, they may as well be scared of me. But then again, maybe not.

Jason looked at me, but refused to hold my gaze. I felt bad instantly so I leaned back and ran my hands through the ends of my long hair.

"Okay," I said. "From what I understand, what you did was summon something. I don't really know what. I mean, demons, whatever. There are a lot of forces in the world, magic ones, but not many people have appreciable contact with them." I looked at him, meaningfully. Maybe something leading would trip his memory. If he remembered on his own, I wouldn't be breaking any promises. "Some people have latent power, but I don't think many really use it, or know about it. Sometimes you can tell who's got it if you know what to look for, and how to look. Power emanates a bit, unless you're really good at controlling it. It's likely to make people around you nervous—"

I broke off. He was staring at me. *Stupid*, filling his head with useless information, just to show how knowledgeable I was. *Braggy Maggie.* I could have yet another cool nickname if I wanted.

"I'm sorry," I said. "I'm not helping."

"Is that really—do you really believe all this crap?" said Jason. His coffee was forgotten. Maybe I was doing okay after all. *Don't sweat the next seminar, Mags, you'll knock 'em dead.*

"I've just been doing a lot of reading." It was an explanation, not a good one, but attractive at least. It explained my hold on the facts, if not my interest in them. "Trying to distinguish between the kind of stuff that might actually be real, and the stuff people just hope exists. I think that basically, if something has a name in English, chances are it's a human, non-magical invention."

"What? You mean like fairies?" He was interested. I remembered now the Jason of grade eight. He read all sorts of horror books then, and he and Scott watched slasher flicks apparently almost constantly. I wondered if he still did.

"Not so much," I said, "I mean more like vampires and werewolves. I think the real things are a lot more amorphous and hard to put in neat little packages of 'eat garlic' and 'watch out at full moon.' Look, this is one of those conversations that could go on for hours getting more and more pointless, and all I'll feel is foolish, because I don't have any proof for anything. I don't really believe in most of it."

"But what happened back there was real." His voice had dropped to a whisper, and he leaned forward across the table.

"Yeah, I know," I said, "And something you summoned is still around. I'm thinking we'd better get it before it makes life miserable for any more squirrels." *Maybe more than one thing,* I almost said. I'd dismissed two, and I'd seen another this morning. No telling how many were out there—but there was no need to scare him.

I met his eyes finally, and he held my gaze firmly this time. My heart was beating fast, and again I felt on the verge of something big. At least this time, I would be taking the initiative. I had learned last time that I don't really like being kidnapped and used in someone else's game. This time, it would be different.

Of course, this time, I didn't have my power.

I smiled, and it must have gone through both our heads at the same time what I'd said about squirrels. Not that there's anything really all that funny about dying squirrels, but he was scared, and so was I, and we needed to get rid of some of that tension. So, greatly endangering our coffee, we both burst out laughing. It was a good long time before we could stop.

When we did, I was overcome, almost instantly, with a great sadness. This was what I had lost, what I had been missing in those years since time went blank. More than the power. In my lucid moments, I still knew this.

He grinned, and the smile seemed friendly and open, nothing condescending or patronizing like I had feared. "Thanks, Mags," he said. "You know, not many girls would even be interested, much less want to help." Then he spoiled it. "You and Rae—"

My eyes burned then, and I thought that if I didn't leave then I would cry. Emotion: unfair that we can't control it like we can decide whether or not to eat, or sleep, or run. "I am like no one you've ever known. Don't forget that, not ever."

That effectively ended the discussion. He went back to class; I had decided to continue home. Skipping first period could always look like oversleeping. Missing second as well started to look bad. I'd rather just be 'sick.' The administration at Westbrook High seemed to care more about appearance that the actual facts of a particular offense. I wasn't worried. Mr. Thurl would cover for me.

And I had some thinking to do.

And because I was afraid to get started, even though there was really nothing in the world that was more pressing for me to do, I walked. I love my neighborhood in some way I don't really understand, maybe because it's so much easier to feel at home if people don't come into the equation. The mature trees, the sidewalks, the way the sunlight falls through the leaves in patchworks of light and dark, the smells, the dandelions blown into soft dust in the air. I found myself smiling, so I guess I was okay after all, not so scared, or so lonely. I don't know what made me decide not to take the straight route home, but that's what I did. And I went up the hill on Fleance, and found myself in front of Scott Saunders's house.

I had been there once, maybe. I had a vague memory of delivering some homework there, in grade five or six, when Scott was out again with a broken something or other. The house was a low two-story, garage to the left, and a chain-link fence to the right, separating the front lot from the backyard. Scott's family had been here, like so many others in our subdivision, since its beginning, twenty years ago. The trees on the lawn were well-established, and the bushes were trimmed and in bloom. Through the flowers, through the diamonds of wire, I could see something, a flash of white.

A face. Eyes. I froze. The eyes stared, haunted and—wrong, somehow. Wrong. I narrowed my own eyes at them and they stared, fixed. They were nearly washed of color, almost pink as they caught the light reflecting off leaves, through leaves. My gut heaved; this was powerful. I was off guard totally. What was watching me? Another demon? And if so, why was it so familiar?

Then I had it. "Peter—" I called softly.

There was movement in the eyes now, they darted past me, then drifted back to my face.

The eyes were the color of faded blood, but not because of any magical inhabitation, just because Peter was albino, with no pigment at all in his irises. His hair was corn-silky and his skin as pale as snow.

I was back, instantly, in a subterranean cavern where soft,

mysterious light threw snakes of reflection from the pool to the walls, watching Peter's white-haired head bob through the waves of his own passage. I could remember Damon's hand on my temple, the other hand squeezing cool water onto my forehead—his shirt, his shirt soaked and —

All my memories from this part of my imprisonment in the Dark Man's fortress were sketchy. I was sick and partly delirious. My arm was infected and burning. Scott took care of me, and I played with Peter...

Peter. "Peter—do you remember me?" I stepped onto the grass and moved slowly under the canopy of the trees. "Peter."

The eye fixed me firmly again. Did he? Did I finally have an ally in this mess of a life? "Peter. Maggie, you remember me don't you? Down in the underground?"

Then he was gone, shrieking, into the depths of the backyard. I heard a screen door slam, and I ran, only registering absently the dead squirrel on the front lawn.

## 7

### In The Heat Of The Morning

✪

That night I avoided my mother completely by locking myself in my room upstairs with loud complaints of a headache, away from the click of laptop keys as she worked on a report. She'd used the same excuse countless times before to get out of conversation with me. We were two islands competing for isolation.

In my bedroom, I sat on the bed staring at the painting of the pentagram and the alien eyes until the light from outside faded and I was blinded with tears from over-strain. Then I flipped on the lamp on the bedside table and tried to come to terms with what had happened this horrible day.

Peter. He was here, in Westbrook, and at Scott Saunders's house. At Scott's. Hunt had told me he'd be adopted, but why had he ended up at Scott's? That had to be a mistake. Peter should have no connection with any of us. No one was supposed to remember anything about what had happened underground in the catacombs. No one, that is, except me. No one. I was the only one, and I had accepted that. No, I hadn't accepted it, but to have a false hope now would be worse than no hope at all.

Damn damn damn! A few years ago, I would have been pushing books off the shelves and tearing the bedclothes up. That was back in the days when I wanted my mother to hear me, and to come and comfort me. Now, I knew that avenue wasn't open. It wasn't that she was a bad person. Somehow, she just didn't have comfort in her, or maybe just no empathy for me. It was impossible to bridge the gap between us. Same problem as with everyone else. *Maggie Stuart has been through the fire, through an alchemical change, and she can't relate or be related to.*

Self-pity had definitely been one of my strong suits these last few years. Irony was there too, and I hoped it would counteract the worst of my sour moods. I felt way too young to be so angry.

I turned my attention back to the picture. The eyes were still there, and I found myself believing I had somehow painted them in, subconsciously trying to unnerve myself. That would be a good one. My own hands working against me. It would be nice to go downstairs to curl up on the sofa with a video, and shut the door on my room and all its unanswerable questions, but my mother was down there too and running that gamut was not worth the numbness the escape would offer. I was stuck until she went to bed, and that would be another hour and more.

The eyes. I hadn't painted them, and I was less and less able to fool myself as the sky outside my window became black. It would be a good night to go out walking—except that I knew the first place I would want to go was back to Fleance and to the Saunders house, and what would that do but cause me more impotent anguish?

I couldn't deny the memory of the picture flipping itself over either, or the fake Thurl's greedy eyes, or the little speck of blood on the demon Aaron's glasses. Or Hunt. How did he fit in? Did he?

First thing in the morning, I would go to the bank. I could do that and still get to school on time. I needed Arabella's ring, even if I couldn't use it. If my mere association with Char was powerful, an icon like the ring was invaluable. Then, I would find Jason, and we'd talk. Tonight, I would sleep on it, and try to come up with a plan for him. I didn't really expect to do much myself. I mean, it was their problem, their fault, and they should have to extricate themselves from the consequences of their actions. Even thinking it, I was lying to myself.

This was the only contact I'd had with the occult world since the 'incident,' the only time I'd been able to put any of Hunt's teachings to use in three years. I was damned if I was going to walk away. Hunt had explained he himself had no real magic substance about him. Everything he could do he needed props for—chalk, knife, candles—like the ritual Aaron had presided over, and some kind of magical writing to provide a map. I could do something like that too, in time. I didn't need my actual powers, if I could learn his way. This was my ticket back to what I had lost.

That decided, I stared at the picture for a while more. Yes, I had to conclude. The eyes, those watery, wicked eyes, were female. The longer I looked, the more sure I was. Who? Arabella? She was dead, and I wouldn't be happy at all to discover otherwise. She had nearly killed me —gleefully. I had her death, what I was sure was her death, on my conscience. But rather her death than her vengeance. If somehow she had survived our fight, she couldn't have survived the explosion which wrecked the Burnt Man's palace. No matter how ashamed it made me feel, I was glad.

One thing was for certain. There was at least one more escapee from the gymnasium to deal with, and it could by now be anywhere. I had no idea how far things like that could travel, if they could, if they were bound to those who had summoned them. Nothing, really.

My research over the years had really just been in the form of altering my already in-place reading habits. Where before I'd read just about any kind of novel, I had become pretty much addicted to books, fiction or non-, with an occult theme. But I'd never done more than dabble. I was going to have to be serious now, and that was good.

It was obvious. How could I have ever doubted that magic would come back into my life one way or another? When I came to believe it wouldn't come back on its own, I should have made something happen. I was unsuited to everything normal people talked about. My future had been set the moment Char set foot into my dreams, power or no.

Scott Saunders could object to my involvement all he wanted, because it would make no difference. I wasn't going to back down, or out. I was in. Jason had asked me, and I was not letting myself get left behind. I would be so damn useful that even the odious brainac Mr. Scribner would have no objections. I felt a little pompous already that it had been something found in his father's study which had begun all the trouble. At least I would never have done something as stupid as reciting something in a foreign language out of a book I knew nothing about, with all the tools of the trade laid out in front of me and with my friends as ritual participants. That was stupid, irresponsible.

Chalk and blood. Candles. It wouldn't be the same. Magic had always been a clean rush for me before, a slight tension in my stomach. A tingle in my extremities to let me know it was there. Doing things mechanically would be awkward, probably not nearly as satisfying. And who would teach me?

I lay awake for hours after that, even after I'd put the lights out and eventually pulled the blinds to give me complete darkness. Where there should have been fear or at least some gentle trepidation, I now felt excitement. I could hardly wait for morning to come, because then I would start building the life I should have, not the one I'd gained by default when Char's fortress fell and Maggie, chosen consort of a King, became again the stupid, scared, normal kid she'd been before.

✪

Crossing the parking lot of the strip mall to the bank, the sun up and the heat already brutal, I could hardly remember what I'd gone to sleep feeling so intensely. The lost exhilaration was much like my vanished power, something I remembered the effects of but couldn't recapture.

The alarm had been the first assault on the deep sleep I'd fallen into, and my mother's voice was the second. I rushed things to get out of the house early after waking at the usual time, because I hadn't dared to set the alarm for any earlier than I normally did. No, that might have led to questions, and those were to be avoided at all costs.

"Hi," I said to the lady at the information counter inside the bank. There was a long line for the tellers, working folk trying to get money stuff done before nine. I was hoping I could circumvent that channel. "I'd like to look at my safety deposit box."

"Certainly," she said. "Can I have your box number please?"

I gave it, and she handed me the book to sign in. This was one thing I had insisted on when my mother rented the box, that I would have full use of it and be able to get into it whenever I wanted. The bank preferred a minor to have a co-signing adult, but waived objections.

I admit, I never really thought the day would come when I wanted into the vault for this particular item. In the small room provided for customers to examine their valuables, I looked a long time before touching the ring. This was the sinister little bit of jewellery which had put Damon beyond my, or even his father's, saving. Without a bit of luck, I would have been dead too because of it. In a very real way, I wished I never had to see it again, much less carry it with me. It was a relic of a past I couldn't get back to.

It had a past of its own, of course. Before Aria, it had been owned by her mother, Char's wife. She was dead, as her daughter was dead. And Char had chosen me to be his new consort. I guess in a way the ring did belong legitimately to me as it belonged to no one else I knew of. Char's family was gone. I was, strange as it sounded, his only heir. Maybe. And maybe I was being far too generous about my connection to all the power the Dark Man represented. None of it was destined to be mine now, not without learning the ropes a different way than before, not without the same kind of struggle Hunt seemed to be involved in. And all his years and knowledge hadn't gotten him very far. When I knew him in the catacombs, he was acting as Char's lieutenant, a kind of glorified gopher. Char let him have the run of the place, but he also didn't let him have any real power. Hunt had a huge effect on the whole outcome, but Char couldn't have known what would happen from what he allowed.

I put the ring with its deep red stone on the chain around my neck, slipping it inside my clothing. The band was gold and my chain was silver, so I guess they didn't really match. It was a small consideration. More important was that Aria's ring, her mother's ring, *my* ring, was with me. I had an actual card to play, if it ever came to that.

✪

On the lookout for Jason at school, I had a problem I hadn't anticipated. His science class had been scheduled for a field trip and he was going to be out of the picture all day. He was taking biology, which I had opted out from, ending up in that history class instead. I had no interest at all in it, although I found myself wishing I had just to relieve the frustration of this day. My comfort was that there were no apparitions, no unexpected visitors, and no demands.

And then. . . well, things just kind of slipped by the wayside. I didn't see Jason at all the next day, so I didn't get a chance to talk to him that day either. But the third day, when I caught a distant glimpse of him from the seat I'd taken at the back of the cafeteria at lunch time, I found all my aspirations seemed to have faded away to beige wallpaper again.

Instead of going to talk to him I let myself be entertained by the cafeteria supervisor having a Jerry Springer-sized hissy fit on a couple of the workers over one of the lunch ladies not showing up for work and leaving them short-handed. I usually wouldn't have let myself enjoy those kind of fireworks, but I was having a mean-spirited moment. I chalked it up to wanting to avoid too much self-examination. I didn't think I'd like what I'd find. No stamina, no staying power. Just a whole lot of not much.

✪

Jason caught up with me as I was leaving for the day on Friday. Back behind him, hanging out around the wall of the school, I saw Aaron and Scott. They, obviously, didn't want to get too close.

"Letting you get your hands dirty?" I asked as Jason nearer.

He shrugged in a dismissive fashion. "I, uh, well, I just wondered if you'd had any thoughts on our. . . on the matter."

"You know I'm on the job," I said coldly. Then, I shook my head to clear it and my bad attitude. "No, look. I'm working on it, but I'm going to have to sit down with you guys, all you guys, very soon. I don't have much to go on." He looked at me, then glanced away. "What?" I asked. "Has something changed?"

Jason used his head to indicate the others. "Scott."

Scott Saunders. Didn't like me back in public school where I'm pretty sure he was the one who'd saddled me with the mercifully short-lived nickname "Froggie," and nothing, it seemed, had changed.

But no. "His little brother saw something. I don't know what it was, 'cause he was just screaming and scared. Scott can't get anything more out of him than the color red, whatever that means."

"When?" I said. I grasped one of my wrists with the opposite hand to hold them both steady.

"Monday," Jason said, confirming it. "In the morning sometime."

I sighed. "I thought as much." What a bitch I was. *Use something you did yourself to claim magic intuition, that's a good girl, Mags.* "Something outside in the yard—"

That's as far as I got before Jason's wild stare stopped me. "You—" he said.

But this was my chance, so I pressed on. "Can I see this kid? How old is he?"

"Soren? Ten, I think." He turned and shouted over his shoulder. "How old's Soren?"

Soren. Not Peter. Could I have been—No, of course I was right about who the child in the backyard had been. It was Peter, only now he had a different name, and a new family.

I heard Scott shout back, and he started jogging toward us. I had missed his reply, but Jason nodded to tell me he'd been right the first time.

Scott was quiet when he reached us. I felt very small and out of my depth. The look in his eyes was not friendly, not to mention that cumulatively Jason and Scott were more than two feet taller than me. I got the impression that Scott was fuming and it wouldn't take much to make him explode all over me. What had I ever done to him? In response, I began to take a more aggressive stance.

Jason, I could tell, had noticed the instant animosity, but pretended not to. "Well?" he said, to Scott. "What about letting Maggie talk to Soren?"

Scott laughed, brittle and angry. "Not on your life. I'm not having him scared any more."

"Well, maybe you can tell me what he saw," I countered.

"Sure," he said, but it was all sarcasm. He wasn't going to let me *near* Peter, or whatever they were calling him.

"Okay, Mags," said Jason, trying to take the focus and break the tension between me and Scott. "You just let us know when you want to get us together. We'll be there."

✪

I stayed away from school three days running the next week, wrote my own sick notes, and smiled sweetly when my mother asked me questions. Jan was really trying lately. Too bad it was mostly lost on me.

Hunt didn't show, and I wondered why. No, more than that. I was hoping he'd show, because I wanted something to put me back on track. I was the worst of procrastinators. Watching television, playing video games when Jan wasn't on the computer, and sitting in my bedroom with a book were not the actions of a devoted seeker of the unknown.

✪

Eventually, a day came when I bumped—literally—into Aaron

Scribner in the hall. There was a press of people around us. He didn't even look at me; I don't think he had noticed it was me he'd run into. I was torn between going after him, getting him to jump-start my enthusiasm for the problem, and slipping quietly away. Telling myself that what had happened in all likelihood was that the thing had already resolved itself, I did the latter.

Besides, he was insufferable, and always had been. He was the only person I knew whom I considered my intellectual equal—except that he usually placed higher than me in class testing. It pissed me off. My own particular conceit had long been than no one really intelligent would bother performing like a trained seal for the sake of a teacher's whim. That way, I could pretend I was still somewhat smarter, at least in the big picture.

But the events of the day were by no means over. After classes were over, when I had packed up what I needed for the night and was closing my locker, I heard my name. There's something pacifying about knowing no one at school wants to talk to you. You go around in a kind of bubble with your own thoughts for company. If someone breaks the silence around you, there's a weird time-lag where you have to remember how to interact with the world again.

"Hi," I replied, frowning. Rae Kennie was the last person in the world I would have expected to talk to me.

"I'm Rae," she said, as if everyone in the school didn't know. "I wondered if you wanted to get a juice or something with me."

I held my eyebrows level with effort. They were sending in the girls. Hadn't Jason passed on the message that I was willing to cooperate? But then, maybe that's not how it had seemed to him. And actually, until just now, it wasn't how it had seemed to me either.

"That's an odd proposition," I said, turning my back on her to snap my padlock closed.

"Oh, I don't know," she said, smiling, a hint of a laugh in her voice. "We've been in a couple of the same classes, and we've never really talked."

She was suggesting, I guess, that that was odder. I shrugged and let her lead. Things were getting more interesting all the time.

I walked the road from the school to the donut shop beside her in silence. She called hellos to nearly everyone who passed us, and between greetings kept up a pretty constant chatter about the last few week's events. I was grateful only that I wasn't expected to join in. She even had the decency not to ask me about my summer after a partial catalogue of hers—she hadn't been working except for two weeks at a children's day camp which sounded actually enjoyable. I prepared a reply in case she asked, and I'm glad she didn't. *I was working at McDonald's and my boss came on to me. You have that happen at day camp?*

"So, Maggie," she began when we were in the donut shop and settled, her with an orange juice and me with a coffee. Today, I was going for black. Being in this place, at the same table in fact, was reminding me over and over of my conversation with— "Jason said he talked to you about this mess we're in. I wanted to add my voice to the plea. Can you help us?"

"I don't know," I replied, looking out the window.

She accepted this and nodded. "I hope you'll consider it. I know there's nothing in it for you. There wasn't the first day either, but you came to our rescue anyhow."

Appealing to my sense of self-sacrifice was not a good place for her to start. It really got up my nose, in fact. She was wrong about one thing, anyway. I had already decided what was in it for me. For better or for worse, I was tied to this project—provided I could get off my butt. I just wasn't sure I wanted to help *them*. "What do you think happened? Maybe that's a good place to start."

She pursed her lips for a moment, considering. "Well, first thing, you know the thing that Jason told you about. . ."

*Dead squirrels.* I nodded.

"It's not like it was at the beginning. Not nearly so many. I think whatever was doing it is moving on or not getting the results it wanted. . ."

*Or just evaporating in the fullness of time*, I thought. "Go on," I said.

"Jason and Scott found the book at Aaron's, sometime near the end of the summer. I gather that Aaron recognized the language. He had some kind of guide for pronunciation, so he was the obvious person to be the leader. Suzanne and I were over at Jason's one day, and they told us about it. They needed five for the ritual." She shrugged, but it was less dismissive than self-castigating. "I don't know why I went along with it."

"Curiosity," I said, sucking my cheek in. *Let her get away with that. I know why people do things like that. They want to be special.*

"Yes," she agreed. "Mostly that, I'm sure. Mostly I thought Aaron was a bit crazy about all of it. I probably wanted to see him proved wrong."

"There are more things in heaven and earth. . ." I said.

She looked at me, friendly, and there was some kind of fondness in her expression as she laughed. "You can say that again. There are lots more things. My philosophy has taken a beating over the last few weeks." Then, more soberly, she went on. "I saw what you did that day. You seemed to know exactly what was going on. Is that true?"

Faced with such a direct question, I couldn't get it together to dissemble. "No." I smiled coldly, unwilling to like her. "I know a little bit, but I don't know what's going to happen. The basics I know, even though it's been a—I've never had the chance to try them out." Close. I'd come near to admitting to the past.

Rae's eyes focused with uncomfortable intensity on mine. She seemed to have forgotten all about her juice; it sat lonely and untouched between us. I took large sips of coffee to cover my growing discomfort. Then, she looked away and smiled herself. She said, "I don't know if this is going to come out of the blue, and I'd understand if you said no, but I just wondered. I go riding some weekends, at Merrymount stables north of town. I'm going in Saturday morning this week. Would you like to come?"

I kept my face blank, although she couldn't have surprised me more by sticking a fork in my hand. "Riding? Like, horses?"

She shrugged again in that self-deprecating fashion. She seemed to know that her confidence was somewhat threatening, and was doing what she could to make me feel comfortable. "I have a couple of horses there; my family owns them." The half-smile crossed her face again, apologies now for being wealthy, I supposed. "It would be absolutely free, no obligation to me or to the guys. But it would mean a lot to me."

No one had ever said anything remotely similar to me. I felt, quite despite myself, flattered. I shrugged, something not even resembling her easy gesture. This casual dismissive thing was a powerful tool, but I would have to work hard to master it. For Rae, it must be a natural. Now, a suitable response. I didn't want to sound too rude, or too eager. "That would be great," I said, my tone as perplexed as I felt. Surprised, I realized I really meant it. Me, on horseback.

Rae's face lit up, as if I'd done something which pleased her immensely but for which she'd only had a small, vain hope. "Great," she said, echoing me. "I'll pick you up at your house at eleven thirty—how does that sound? Oh—if you bring a bathing suit, we can swim afterwards."

"I'll be waiting for you at the end of the court," I corrected. It was more than just wanting to have some input into Rae's efficient plan-making. I didn't want to have any explaining to do on the home front.

"Excellent," she said. She stood, one smooth motion, sweeping the orange juice bottle off the table and into her bag. "I guess I'll save that for later." She smiled at me again, her eyes frank and friendly. I almost expected her to extend a hand for me to shake. "Thanks, Maggie. I'll see you Saturday."

I got out some kind of parting words, and she was gone. Not feeling like walking with her, I sat until she disappeared from view. Strangeness.

Home was the last place I wanted to be, the more I thought about it. Finally, knowing I would soon have to leave or buy a second coffee, I made a decision. It was time to start living up to my potential. I was ripe for a confrontation, and I needed some expert help. If Hunt was going to be hanging around, I would bring the one man who had some knowledge of him into the equation.

## 8

## Shadow Man

✪

John Tamblyn worked at the main police station in downtown Toronto. At least, that's where he had been when I'd last heard anything about him three years ago. Tamblyn was also, much to his obvious chagrin, Hunt's brother. It was a relationship that had, I gathered, caused him little but discomfort. Even now, I could picture the vast number of opened and re-opened wounds on Tamblyn's arms and chest, where Hunt had helped himself over the years to his brother's blood. A few of them I had made myself.

Hunt was an amateur magician. By that, I mean he was a practitioner of the non-intrinsic methods of magic. Chalk, candle, incantation. But blood is blood, and where there's magic, blood follows. Small magics require a trickle. The big ones, a flood.

Of course, I was in the same boat with Detective John Tamblyn as I was with Jason and Aaron. The score of the game was Maggie 3, Memory 0, as it were. The trick was to find some way to convince him to help me with Hunt.

And why should I need help with Hunt when I had won his loyalty in my confrontation with Char?

Because no one, not even the Burnt Man, really had Hunt's loyalty.

I needed every piece of information possible to get the slightest use out of my contact with him, and that was no lie. Tamblyn, if I could win him, would be my biggest ally. Hunt, if I could use him effectively, might be my only hope against whatever had come out of that circle.

On the way to the station, I thought over my options. Perhaps the smartest thing would be to start my research in a more standard place, like the public library. That was on my list, naturally, although my memory-scourge had no doubt wiped the Westbrook 'incident' right out of the books. Even so, there'd be something to aid me there, even if I had no idea what it would be.

But Tamblyn was a touchier thing, so I decided to try him first. I had Arabella's ring now; how could I fail? If this was a success, I might just have a chance. Where was Hunt? I had expected him back. Whether he wanted to play more games with me, or if something was going on which involved me, either way I really thought he'd have contacted me before now. What was the game this time?

I liked the police headquarters in Toronto on College near Yonge, a cool, glass and stone building with a facade like some architect's dream of childhood building blocks. There was a bustle of traffic through the place and I was, as a small girl, quite able to slip in without being challenged, making my way through the security gate in a cluster of kids around my age and several adult civilians who apparently comprised a youth group on a tour, bookended by uniformed officers.

I was nervous. It's funny, you can be perfectly at home in a big city, acting like nothing can scare you, and then a single step into a police station and you're furtive, and you figure everything you do is probably punishable to the full extent of the law.

In any case, it wasn't difficult to find out where Tamblyn's office in Homicide would be located, and then to ride the elevators up to the proper part of the building.

I slipped the tour group easily, ducking into a washroom, and headed up. The elevator doors opened on a clean hallway with the odor of efficiency and coffee. Directly in front of me was a desk at which was seated a young woman, probably mid-thirties, behind a stack of papers and in a casually-worn uniform. Her dark hair was curled neatly under her ears. The nameplate in front of her read, "Corporal Szaba, Carla." *Corporal Carla.* Nice alliteration. *Some day,* I guessed, *she'll be the equally fun Sergeant Szaba.*

"Hi," I said. Always speak before you're spoken to if you think you're doing something which puts you in the wrong. "I was looking for Detective Tamblyn."

"Friend?" she asked, sizing me up in an amiable manner. Her mouth had twisted with innocent amusement, as if she expected me to answer in the negative, and then laugh along with her at the absurdity of the suggestion.

"Actually, a friend of the family's." That was pretty much the truth.

"He's here," she said, satisfied, "but I'm not sure if he's holding audiences today. It's quite rare we have the honor of his presence, in fact. You caught him on a special day, but you probably knew that."

I shrugged, to let her fill in the blanks however she wanted.

"I'll buzz him," she said, full of good humor. "Who should I say?"

Her finger stabbed a button on the telephone, and she lifted the receiver to her ear. Tamblyn answered quickly.

"Maggie," I said, in response to her raised eyebrow.

She relayed the name, and then replaced the receiver. "He'll be down in a minute." One of her hands swept a curl back behind her ear, and then indicated a chair beside her desk. "You may as well sit. Quick he isn't."

But I hardly had time to rest the seat of my shorts against the seat of the chair before an office door down the hall rattled shut, and a thin, well-remembered figure came stalking toward Corporal Szaba and me.

The corporal nodded in his direction. "Brace yourself," was her advice.

I slipped the chain out of the neck of my shirt and grasped the ring for luck.

"Let's see. . ." said Szaba's voice, curious, and I gave her a glimpse of it before tucking it away again. Her eyebrow raised, and I imagined, as I went to meet Tamblyn, that I saw her look with an intensity of scrutiny quite out of proportion to the sight of a ring on a chain. That, of course, would be my own sense of the dramatic working overtime.

"Well?" demanded John Tamblyn, hands on thin hips. He was wearing most of a suit: jacket and nearly-matching pants. I found the lack of trench coat a bit disorienting, as if he somehow owed me a duty to look like some hard-boiled detective from a Chandler novel.

"I'm Maggie Stuart," I said. Rehearsals on the subway seemed to have done nothing after all to prepare me for the actual moment. "I wondered, could I talk to you for a moment in private?"

He grunted assent after a moment's thought, and I was left to chase after him all the way down the hall back to his office. *Good girl*, I told myself. None of what's at stake is on the table, and I managed to not even mention how important this was. *Let him think it's about a school project until we're behind closed doors.*

Tamblyn's office was the last in the row; not surprising if he was really as well-liked as I had gathered from the Corporal—in other words, not at all. Most of the glass-doored offices offered views inside, many were ajar, but Tamblyn's was shuttered and locked, even though he'd only come a few dozen meters away from it. Paranoid, anti-social, or dealing with very sensitive stuff.

"What is this all about?" he asked, roughly, as soon as the door was closed behind us. "I don't have any idea who the hell you are."

"No." I glanced around for a chair, but besides the one he had occupied behind the wide, cluttered desk, there was no sign. Not a place meant for the comfort of guests. Tamblyn had a small window, also shuttered, but the desk lamp made up for it. Although it was tilted ever so slightly in the direction of whatever visitor was forced to stand across from him. *Ready-made interrogation room.* "It's about Hunt."

If he was surprised, he gave no sign. "Hunt," he repeated, putting his fingers together to make little steeples. His tone was dead as if what I'd said had no meaning for him.

"Yes," I said. "He's been to see me. I've had dealings with him in the past, and I know about his relationship with you."

"Thank you," said Tamblyn abruptly. He rose and came around the desk. "Constable Szaba will walk you out. Good day," and he moved to open the door for me.

"Wait!" I cried. "I need your help. I—" And there it was. I wanted to tell him. The first real test of my little vow, and I was ready to break it. "I—know—" But I couldn't. The vow had been made for a reason. And the greatest reason for keeping it was so that my sacrifice shouldn't have been in vain. If I gave up my powers, and the world remembered Char anyway, what had I gained?

"Good day," Tamblyn repeated firmly.

I stood my ground. "Listen," I said. "I have some important things to say, and I'd like a minute, just a minute, of your time. Please. It would mean everything to me."

He stopped, and looked at me, blinking, a beatific smile on his face. His expression clearly said, *"You are not fooling me one little bit."* This was not going well at all.

"Hunt," I said. "I know about your relationship."

"You've said that," he said, rolling his eyes up and shut. "Hunt."

"You know who he is," I insisted. "I had dealings with him, and with—with Char. I know about your scars. Shall I show you?" The nearest arm tempted me. I could undo the cuff and roll up the sleeve. He'd been hacked to hell in Hunt's quest for arcane knowledge. But of course, I didn't have the balls to reach out. I indicated what I was thinking, a finger pointing, and Tamblyn pulled the limb out of reach.

"Okay," I said, changing my tactic. "Just answer me one question. Do you have a brother?"

Nothing from him.

"And there's—" I stopped. I had to stop short of showing off Arabella's ring, didn't I? Maybe not. "See this?" I pulled it out, the silver of the chain and the gold of the band glinting. The red stone gleamed with what seemed like more than reflected light.

He wasn't impressed.

"It belonged to Arabella, Char's daughter. Hunt took it from her, and he gave it to me." That was true, even if it didn't fill in all the circumstances. I pressed it toward him, expecting him to want to at least make an examination.

But Tamblyn acted as if I hadn't even offered it to him. "Ten," he said, and began to count backwards, hand on the doorknob.

Desperate, I grasped for anything I could remember to give myself a lever. What could I say to convince a man who thought he'd never met me, and more, who must remain convinced he never met me?

The long fingers of Tamblyn's free hand drummed out an impatient beat on his pant leg.

His hand. A picture came to mind. *The ritual—Hunt shimmies down the rope and falls the last few feet. His hands are bloody.*

*Later, as we sit on the bluff waiting for the sun to set, Tamblyn asks a question about—*

"Where's your ring?" I said, pointing at the fourth finger of his right hand. "A signet, wasn't it? Some kind of—"

The hand I'd indicated came down hard on the desk, and he rose. "This is a cute little game," said Tamblyn, face dark and nothing about his manner suggesting I should take his words literally. "I'm not interested in whatever you're selling, whoever trained you, whoever sent you. And I'm just starting to get mad."

And that was absolutely it for my interview.

Tamblyn wasn't rough, exactly, but he was firm, and the grip on my arm let me know he wasn't joking. He was pissed, and whatever I'd hoped, I was finished with this avenue of inquiry. If I was able to set foot in the building again, I would be very surprised.

I was aware, about halfway back to the elevator, that we were being followed down the hall. A glance over my shoulder and Tamblyn's elbow confirmed this. It was the corporal from her desk, who had obviously been away from her post and at the end of the hall where there was nothing but Tamblyn's office. Her eyes were narrowed now; she seemed intent on something. I could only assume it was something other than me she was interested in. Had she been listening in, *spying* on Tamblyn?

But when we got into the elevator, Szaba stopped, lips tight and dark eyes questioning. I had no answer for what she wanted, or which one of us, Tamblyn or me, she had been trailing.

The detective escorted me all the way out of the building, silent and fuming. Then, his hand still on my arm, he told me in no uncertain terms what he would do if I ever came back, and took my full name and social insurance number for good measure. I didn't even think to refuse. Then, he said, "Kid, for your own good, don't mess with this stuff," and that was that.

He watched me walk down most of the block and nearly out of sight of the building before he went back inside. I knew, because I couldn't stop myself from checking over my shoulder, again and again, like a total moron. *No trust, that guy.* I had had my first total failure.

It was strange seeing him in the foul kind of mood I'd put him in. In the only other contact I'd had with him, Hunt had had the upper hand and Tamblyn was the sweeter, meeker, younger brother. Actually, I only guessed that Tamblyn was younger. Or sweeter for that matter. Hunt's age was hard for me to place. I could almost swear he hadn't aged a day since the last time I'd seen him, while the detective seemed very worn down.

But Tamblyn wasn't going to help me. Also, I didn't feel very well disposed to the police in general after him, and wondered if that was going to be a problem in the days to come. I had a little, not wholly unattractive fantasy of all of Toronto embroiled in the outcome of these events. *Power-mad Maggie,* I told myself. The truth was, Tamblyn had shaken me. My hands were vibrating as I dropped my token in the collection box and headed home. I didn't feel like doing anything else today.

9

## All The Young Dudes

✪

*Tonight, I dream vividly. It seems to start as soon as my head hits the pillow. I see the book, like it had appeared to me in that fleeting glimpse. Big, heavy, substantial. The color of it shimmers in my memory—had it been as green as I thought? Were there hints of blue in the thick, creased cover?*

*Phantom arms reach, grasp, pass through me to take the book. My arms flailing, fingers outstretched, muscles in my shoulders straining. Why couldn't I touch the book? I watch frustrated and helpless as one after another of the other hands take charge of the old tome. It's keep-away, and I'm the perpetual monkey.*

✪

I woke with my alarm, blinded with tears. It was partly the anguished memory of the dream: a portent of being jilted by my future plans? The rest of the reason came from the past. Dreams were what had started my relationship with Char, and vivid dreams reminded me of him. It was startling that I thought of him fondly, as I lay in bed dreading the alarm going off again in a minute or two. Even Char I missed. Any one of the Dark Man's family or minions around would be better than school, teenagers, and mothers. What had I ever done to deserve this?

I did a quick drawing of what I remembered of the book from the dream in my sketch pad as the coffee brewed. Jan was gone; she usually was before I got out of bed. Unless there was something specific to talk to her about, I avoided her in the mornings. It was torture interacting before I got some coffee into me. She didn't like me drinking coffee, of course, but I had her believing I only did it if we ate in a restaurant. I always washed the coffeepot out before I went to school. Such subterfuge.

I wanted to feel excited over the prospect of riding with Rae on the weekend, but the part of me that used to be capable of that emotion inside me felt dead. I always seemed to be like that these days, knowing what I should feel but unable to reach the emotion. *Maggie's a tight-wound spring, and she feels it more necessary to be controlled than to have a good time,* one of the therapists had written during my post-Char depression. I wished I could let go sometimes, but around who?

School was becoming a problem. I was falling behind already. It generally didn't matter if I wasn't taking notes, because I could catch enough in class to pass tests and dash through assignments in the minimum possible time. But it was starting to look bad for me this year. I had gotten seats to the back and side in all my classes, and hadn't really paid attention yet. From the relative shelter of taller people in front, today I was studying a list I was compiling in my black notebook.

It was important to know who was who and where they could be reached. I had home phone numbers and addresses for the five ritual participants—I'd have to get cell numbers from them personally—and the name of that corporal who had seemed curious about me. Carla Szaba. No Szabas listed in the online 411 but lots of Szabos. Wonder what that meant.

What would happen if I asked her about Hunt? What would it take to punch holes through the spell of forgetting I had woven around Toronto and Westbrook? Strange, that my biggest obstacle for three years was something I had done to myself.

Tamblyn I had no address for, because he wasn't listed either, just the number of the police station. Imagining a worst-case scenario, I scribbled on the bottom of the page the three digits to be used in utter panic—*911*.

✪

I paid no attention in class for the rest of the day, because I was finishing my list of players and another of questions that needed answering. This second list I meant to tackle that day in the city at the main branch of the public library.

I knew where Jason's last class of the day was, and high-tailed it there as soon as I got out of mine. It was time to start facing this thing straight on. If it didn't get me access to Peter, at least I could subtly goad Jason into telling me more about him.

Unfortunately, Jason was with Scott, which instantly increased the chances that this encounter would go south. I figured I better make it as short and concise as possible. I tagged along as we moved outside with the rest of the departing student body.

Behind the two guys, I saw Aaron Scribner approaching. I could only term his walk a saunter. For the guy who had started all of this, he had a lot of nerve. No embarrassment, no concern. Just strut.

It took me a moment to remember I hadn't actually spoken to him since the confusion in the gym, or even seen him beyond that one collision in the halls and then that awkward moment when Scott and I had faced each other down about Peter. Had I been assigning to him the slick conceit of whatever had come to me in the auditorium? Scott, seeing my attention wander away from him, threw up his hands in disgust and turned to leave.

"Hang on!" Jason told him, and nodded to Aaron who now joined us. Aaron nodded back, and gave Scott a little tilt of his head as if giving him permission to go on. Maybe he *was* as smug as the thing that had aped him.

This was just a little too much for me. "Okay." I took a good long look at my watch. "Tomorrow, the three of you meet me at the coffee shop after school, and bring every scrap of knowledge you have about this mess. I have things to do today." Turning, I left them, not looking back until I was safely at the bus stop across the road. They followed more slowly, deep in discussion, heads bowed together. For a moment, I thought Jason was going to run after me, but the bus swept in between us and the chance was lost.

I drifted asleep on the bus and came close to missing the transfer to the GO-train. Saturday couldn't come too soon to suit me, I thought. Rae's company, and her sense, would be a balm after all this tangled mess of ego and bravado. Not that Rae was likely to be perfect or anything, but the three guys were a little too strung to be much use.

I switched to the subway at Kipling, and rode into Toronto the

Good.

The cars of the subway rattled along. I'd gotten a front seat where I could watch the progress of the train. I loved it up here. Even if it meant walking the length of the platform twice more than necessary, I usually bothered. There was one place in particular I liked to watch out for, between Royal York and Old Mill. It was cool, a place where you could almost swear there was an extra track running alongside the main one, and a spot where it looked like the extra one took a dive down into another, deeper level of subway, one which was never used.

Today, even though I was in my favorite seat at the front of the train, I hardly paid any attention to the trip. I was thinking about Jason and Aaron and Scott, and Peter, and trying to turn my mind onto the questions I had to answer before I met with the guys tomorrow.

After yesterday's disastrous attempt to enlist Tamblyn's help, I couldn't really afford to lose any other allies. We'd need, I was sure, Jason's courage and Aaron's smarts and Scott's straight-ahead tenacity and—

And what? I was still thinking like it was three years ago and we were locked underground in Char's fortress. This had nothing to do with that, except that the players were mostly the same. Correction— the players were the same people, but they'd changed over three years like, well, like I had. I'd no idea how things would go, if we'd even be able to work together much less be a help to each other.

What had I accomplished so far? I'd lost a potential resource by being under-prepared and much less than cunning, and I'd frightened a ten-year old boy out of his wits. Excellent record, really wonderful. If I didn't make any progress at the library, I'd have pretty much, well, nothing to show for the month and a bit since the botched ritual.

Any more successes like that and they'd have to build a new, non-matching wing for me at old Dief.

✪

It was a losing proposition, obviously; I knew it from the moment I set foot inside.

Around me, the core of the Toronto Reference Library rose stories high and the multicolored flow of people all around barely distracted my eyes from the obscene volume of information stored here, rack upon rack, shelf upon shelf, catalogue upon catalogue.

"Great," I told myself, poised with my fingertips on the swing bar of the door. "Finding the right floor alone will take a week." More, perhaps, because I had no idea what I was looking for.

Someone pushed into me from behind, and I allowed myself to be propelled into the main body of the immense edifice's lowest floor. I guessed I was committed. What else was there to do? I had promised Jason I'd find a way to help, and I was damned if I was going to look foolish when I met with him and the others tomorrow.

My first plan was to locate some basic information on the theory of what had happened in the gymnasium, and then anything which existed about Char, and his family. Of the latter I had little hope of finding much. From what Damon and Char had both implied, their actions had an impact on the workings of the world, but their existence was shrouded in obscurity.

If information was in the possession of anyone, it must be in a book somewhere. Had I been looking for the wrong things in books on the occult? I had always sought the kind of incantations and spells Hunt talked about needing to work magic when I had him as my instructor in the catacombs. But what if there was knowledge of a different kind floating around out there?

I went straight to search the computerized catalogues and, in doing so, placed myself as well in the center of the microfiche library stretching back into the older files which hadn't yet been translated into 21$^{st}$ century electronic storage. An hour later, I had found nothing of any value, and all my time spent trudging back and forth between the computer and shelves had yielded sore feet and calves, and no leads.

There was nothing either in any cross-referenced entry I could discover about a being like Char, or anything at all about demons which didn't sound like pure fiction. A lot of the speculative accounts contradicted each other, and very little of it resembled in the least anything Hunt had taught me about his own methods. Surely someone must have written honestly about these things. But every idea I hunted down lead into occult fiction, to a meager section of books on general occultism (mostly about cults, to be exact), and to obscure (and always absent from the shelves) treatises dealing obliquely with magic. There was nothing. When I asked at the information desk about the missing texts, I was told the titles in question had been deleted from the catalogue, or never returned, never replaced.

The entries I found in the various sets of encyclopedia were of as little use. Nothing struck me as true, for one thing. Most of the writing was scornful, or vague, or tied everything back into gothic horror. Vlad the Impaler. Elizabeth Bathory. Arthur Conan Doyle and Victorian fad psychics. The Knights Templar and the Holy Grail. Voodoo. My quest was a joke, it seemed, to science and academia. Not a surprise, really. Without my experiences of three years before, I would be as skeptical.

Another hour ticked by.

Then, I stumbled into my great find completely by accident. Switching to the actual archived paper files, for no other reason than my eyes getting tired of looking at the screen of the reference computer, I was immediately deeply awed by the collected years' worth of newspapers from around the world. Most particularly, I found myself opening the drawers for the Globe and Mail of three years before, wondering what was recorded there to replace every mention of the events at Westbrook Elementary School. Silently, I begged the labeled boxes to speak to me, show me the way.

The boxes were huge, holding the original newspapers unfolded and stacked one on top of another. I had to ask one of the librarians, a guy in his fifties without much to say, to help me get the right one onto a table, and then listened to the brief but explicit rules of handling. When I'd fallen over myself to his satisfaction to promise no harm would come to the historic documents, he retreated to his counter, leaving me with my past.

April was the start, and I carefully paged through to the day after everything got turned upside down. On the morning this edition was hitting newsstands, I was chained up deep underground in Char's catacombs, or else having my first disturbing interview with the man himself. Time passed without the benefit of suns or clocks down there, and it was only after I'd emerged from his realm altogether that I had any idea of how long I'd been gone.

So, front page? Not even below the fold. Nothing in the A section —everything Canadian was innocuous and none of the side bars mentioned either Jan's house-fire or the mysterious disappearance of several elementary school students. Nothing about a dead cop either.

Maybe the next day? Nothing there either, not in the A section or the local Toronto section either. But maybe the police had managed to suppress what had happened entirely, just found some way to keep it out of the papers for the sake of the oddness of it all. To let them try to figure out all the pieces that made these events odder than odd.

Then, on the weekend following, I found something—or rather, I found nothing. Under the heading NEWS OF THE WEEK in one of the sidebars, I found a blank spot. Nothing to explain it, just three or four column inches of nothing but newsprint.

Now, I don't have much of a sense of money, except as far as it extended to knowing that no amount of money could possibly entice me back to working in fast food again, but I had a pretty good idea that that much blank space represented a fair amount of lost revenue for the paper. It was not something that happened, ever. Sure, I'd caught places every now and then when reading a paper where an overzealous editor seemed to have accidentally chopped the last sentence or two out of an article, but too *little* type? Never.

Confused, but feeling that at last I was on to something, I went back to the librarian's desk and asked him about it.

At first, he didn't seem to understand what I was talking about, and came over to look, certain that I was misinterpreting what I was seeing. Then, I watched his eyes dart to the left—a sign of remembering, I'd read—and he said, "Yes, that's quite a famous week for the Globe. They left huge blanks spots in the paper." He glanced over to the stacks. "A couple of the other dailies as well."

I stared, then put a cautious finger onto the bare rectangle on the page. Here at last was concrete, outside proof of my power. I had done this. I had erased the past.

The librarian seemed rather underwhelmed by the discovery. "Anything else?"

I shook my head, and he went, leaving me to a cascade of other thoughts. Had people read about the blood on the walls of the gym, and then forgotten? Had reporters come and seen it, taken statements, listened to police press conferences—and then just. . . stopped knowing? My heart was barely beating. *I did this. Me.*

I thought about the librarian, the way his brow had furrowed before his eyes darted to the side. I couldn't be sure, but it was almost as if. . . as if the memory of the 'famous week for the Globe' had created itself on the spot, along with the notion that it meant nothing special. Could echoes of my power still be reverberating after all this time, the way I saw Jan start to remember, then forget again? Could something of what I'd done still be out there, still be operating, even after all this time?

Unable to shake the thought, I sat at a nearby Internet terminal, somehow miraculously unused, and called up a search on micro-expressions—that's what they were called—on Google and read. Eyes darting to the left was not about remembering; it was about inventing. Was this more proof that my magic had outlasted my ability to call on it?

I read on: in right-handed people, left meant creation and right meant memory, in general, with a normally organized mind, and, of course, if the theory was borne out in actuality. There was no way to really know.

I was totally going to cry if I kept on this line of thought. There was no way I wanted to think that my own power, sent out and separate from me, could still be working when I couldn't touch as much as a vague tingle of it in my pinkie. That would be monumentally unfair.

And to know there was no way to test this little kernel of possibility...

I put the newspapers back, after getting the librarian to photocopy the page in question so I had *some* kind of physical proof, even if it meant something only to me, and went back to the computer catalogue. There was nothing more the papers could offer me, I was sure, except more of the same.

Then, on a vague hunch, I watched myself type his name, not Char's, but the Hunter's. For Dale Hunt, there was no relevant mention. But for the Hunter, simply that, there were more than I could have imagined.

Everything here dated back to about ten years before Hunt became my grade eight teacher, and nothing came from that period three years back when Char turned my world upside down and then left me without a direction or purpose in life.

So. Here was where I would start. I took a pencil from the box on the table beside the catalogue and began.

Vancouver was the prime geographical reference. *Vancouver.* Finally, I was going to get to the bottom of the mystery of the Hunter. It seemed strange to me that all my interaction with the man added up to very little of his own life. He was of paramount significance to me. I wasn't all that significant to him. Statistically zero, probably. Here, in this story about events in Vancouver thirteen years ago, here would be the proof of that.

I was copying a dozenth date onto the slip of paper when I felt a breath of wind cross my ear. The chill in it made me drop my pencil. I saw a foot there, almost under my chair, and squarely on the corner of my jacket, and straightened, turning to look at the man standing behind me.

Hunt was wearing casual clothes, a nondescript outfit—except for the sunglasses. I couldn't see his eyes, and I had a feeling he wasn't looking at me but around to see if we were being noticed and remarked on. Me he didn't expect anything surprise-wise from.

Then his head tilted. He was looking at the computer screen.

"Vancouver," he said. "Not a particularly good period for me. Shall we?"

His arm swept out, a reserved indication of the location of the door. *No,* I wanted to say, *I'm not finished.*

"You want to talk?" I said instead.

His hand reached for mine, but it didn't touch me. Instead, it captured the paper I had been scribbling dates on. Deliberately, he tore the page into strips, then put the pieces in the waste basket beside the table. "You'll have to get back to this another time," he said.

10

Somebody Up There Likes Me

✪

Outside, he seemed to trust me less. His hand, big and leathery as I remembered from public school science class, came down around my forearm and clenched. The fingers met. "We're going for a walk," he said.

As he pulled me along, I tried to put together some bravado. "I was expecting you long before this," I said.

"Sue me," he said, scanning the street. Hunt was ever wary. I wonder who he thought might be following us. "I've had more important things on my mind."

If I'd taken him seriously, I would have been hurt. As it was, I understood Hunt well enough to know he was just defusing my statement with a one-upper of his own.

We went south, along Yonge Street. I had been this way many times underground, but couldn't remember seeing it by foot ever before. Usually, when in T.O., I stuck to either the strip around Bloor and Yonge, where the library was, or further south and west on Queen. Wellesley Street had been a subway stop name to me and little more.

It's funny how alone you can feel in a big city, even with tons of people around. It was nearing six thirty, and the streets were emptying, but there were still enough pedestrians, surely, that someone would be a kind, interfering soul and save me if I had the guts to call out. I didn't.

Hunt had a firm grip on me, and he was far more dangerous than any rescuer could be brave. Of that I was certain. Besides, I had been waiting a long time now for Hunt to show. Scaring him off would just delay progress, again. Although, and I tried not to remind myself, facing John Tamblyn square-on and bravely at the earliest moment had not in fact proved very useful.

He took me as far as a sunken cement park off Yonge south of College Park, not far from the police headquarters where I'd gone to confront Tamblyn—which I thought might be Hunt's subtle way of telling me he knew where I'd been the day before. But there was something more, something more personal. It gave me a sharp pain in my stomach when I realized what I was looking at. It had been here, or a shadow of this place anyhow, where I had sat in the Dreamworld to rest myself secure in an older woman's body. Only then, there'd been a fountain and a row of scrubby trees.

Funny. I had never really thought to chase down the places I had been in Char's dreaming kingdom. What would I find where Damon's apartment had been? I felt a perverse desire to wander back up Yonge to the Panasonic Theatre to see what sign there might be of the sleazy little basement bar where I'd found a job. What was it called? Mick's, that's right, after the owner.

Hunt had none of my sentimentality for the place, I supposed. Had he chosen it too because of my visit to Tamblyn? I couldn't ask, naturally. I would never get a straight answer out of him.

"Shall we?" he said, pulling me toward a bench.

The day was cooling, and I was glad I'd brought my jacket now. The hot spell which had ended the summer weather lingered during the daylight hours, but the nights were chilly. Fall was coming. Well, good. I didn't need any more reminders of summer. Hunt let go of my arm to allow me to put my jacket on, but he never moved his fingers more than an inch from some part of me. He couldn't possibly think I was dumb enough to run. I knew how cat-quick he was.

He was otherwise paying very little attention to me, which was infuriating. I hadn't kidnapped *him* from a library, after all. His focus seemed instead to be on the flow of people around us. I shivered, memories of the Dreamworld coming back. And something else came to me.

*Tamblyn.* Hunt had told me he himself would remember everything, in time. He had said nothing about Tamblyn. Tamblyn had had no idea his brother was alive. I had been inadvertently breaking news to him that was not just important, but shattering. No wonder my reception had been icy. For Hunt to have given me anything, specifically Arabella's ring, he would have to have been around more recently than Vancouver, thirteen years ago.

Hunt was thinking about the same person I was, it seemed. Interrupting my train of thought, he said, "You've been to the police."

"Uh-huh," I agreed. If he knew, there was no sense in denying it. My guess about his choice of location had been right on target.

He smirked. "You can't prove anything about me, you know. You won't even be able to find me unless I let you."

I laughed, mirthlessly. "I know that."

"Good." Hunt turned to me. "What were you doing there?"

I stared. "You know as well as I do," I said, sure he did.

"Let's pretend I don't."

I narrowed my eyes. What was this? "Tamblyn," I said, immediately regretting it. Something very odd was happening here—or was it just games? It had to be just games.

Hunt nodded, a wolf-grin spreading across his face. But his complexion seemed to have gone white. As if looking for a way to fill time while he thought, he reached and grabbed my thigh just above the knee. The big fingers pressed painfully into my skin.

"Hey," I said, trying to brush him away. I'd have no effect unless he wanted me to, so it didn't seem like any harm to try. I decided to move the conversation along. "Peter," I said. "What about him? He was supposed to—"

Hunt released my leg and stood. "No more," he said. It was a threat in itself. He left, walking west, vanishing into a maze of condos.

"What the hell?" I asked myself. I sat for a full half hour in the park trying to sort it out. What was my next move? What was Hunt up to? Eventually, I gave up. Hunt was always going to run his schemes above my head, and probably my only possible move was to play my own game, and to hell with him.

It was just before seven thirty by the electronic clock above Yonge Street, and Jan would be getting to wondering about me. I couldn't stand that hopeful gleam in her eyes every time she thought I'd been out late because I'd been with a friend. I would, I swore, be glad to share news of friends with her—if only she wasn't so astonished when I happened to have one.

I got on the subway at College and headed toward home, a near-repeat of the night before. I was going back to Westbrook without what I'd come into the city for. I probably should have gone right back to the library to continue my research, especially now that I knew where to find out more about Mr. Hunt. Frankly, I had run out of patience for the day. I was annoyed and tired.

On the Westbrook GO-train, I reconsidered—not about leaving downtown, but definitely about going home. So I stopped off at the strip mall near the subdivision and had a couple of coffees and a long think. By the time I made it to the house, it was dark, and my mother had gone out for the evening. A note had been left scrawled across a bank statement to inform me of this.

This was a good thing. It meant that she had a new boyfriend, and that freed me up from entertainment detail. Not that I did much, but at least her conversation would be filled with what she was up to, instead of querying me.

She was always after me to have a boyfriend. Stupid. What did she think I was? It would be nice if I could get my own head together before I started pulling other people into my life. She could have thought of that before bringing a baby into an impossible relationship with my con-man of a father. Why did people not think before they had kids?

I made myself a couple of sandwiches and hunkered down in my bedroom. It looked like she had been in again, *housewife Jan, straightening up and stealing away my dirty clothes.* You'd have thought, what with being an only child in a one-parent household, that I'd have had my fill of solitude before I was five. But no, I wanted my bedroom to be an impregnable sanctuary. Maybe it came of having been chained in an open corridor for a couple of weeks as my most treasured childhood memory.

I felt like such a complainer, lying there and eating and doing nothing else. I wasn't even really thinking, not with any particular direction, anyhow. So, it was kind of a surprise when I realized that I had fixated on one thing, one person, really. I was thinking about Jason Lawson.

I'd had a bit of a crush on him in grade eight. If I was to be totally honest, I'd have to say that it was probably bigger than a bit. A lot bigger. I would never admit that to anyone except myself, and that only quietly.

I remembered suddenly the secret he'd confided in me in the catacombs, when we sat hour after hour in our subterranean prison. He'd started in so reluctantly. He obviously needed both to tell me something that would make us even after the secret I'd laid on him, about my impossible power, and more, to tell someone about it and get it out in the open for the first time. It must have made it easier, opened the door, when I told him about Nick and my mom, and the screwed-up childhood I was too young to even recall. But I remembered every word he'd said, I think, about the way he'd suffered himself as a very young kid.

I'd never breathed a word of it to anyone, not that there was anyone really to tell. I think I'd even tried to bury the memory deep myself, just so I had something of him when all else was gone.

But you never forget, not something like this. What he'd told me was that an uncle, trusted implicitly by his parents, had often been given charge of both Jason and his older sister as a babysitter. It took Jason years to realize that something was happening to his sister every time Uncle Mike came over. He didn't really clue in that anything was even wrong until it started happening to him too.

By then, his sister was too screwed up to talk about it, and he only knew by her example that it must be something to be kept utterly silent.

The anger in him was frail, I remembered that too, as if he felt there was no sense in it, that any hope of justice was futile. We both cried, and never spoke of it again. I couldn't quite believe how strong he was managing to be down in the catacombs, imprisoned and helpless, until I reflected that he had, in fact, already been through much worse.

It was one of the things that made me care most about Jason's welfare. It was always on my mind when I saw him, because I knew without much doubt that he carried his secret as deep and as painfully as I did mine. I was pretty certain he'd never told anyone else, because it only came out reluctantly in the underground, and even then with a kind of tacit assumption attached that we might after all not be getting out of that particular situation alive.

It was probably also the reason that I loved Jason, as much as I felt I could love anyone, but was afraid to be too close to him. I knew that under the charisma and confidence lurked a very injured guy, and you never knew how someone like that might react. I wasn't worried about Jason dealing with an extreme or difficult situation. But, like me, I thought he probably didn't handle the ordinary all that well. It hurt that maybe he'd never told anyone else, and I'd robbed him of the knowledge that someone shared his secret.

I had a crush on him back in grade eight, but my feelings, although deeper than that now, were of a different nature. Because of the intimacy of what he'd shared, my crush had basically faded away to nothing during the time in Char's catacombs. I didn't really feel anything for him I could call "romantic." I would protect him, defend him, but I didn't want to be his girlfriend. He needed someone light and uncomplicated. We would bury each other in unvoiced past events.

Well, good. That gave me a nice, satisfied feeling, being able to write off that particular complication. I'd leave it to the probable real heroines of the day, Rae and Suzanne, to go riding off into the sunset. People like Maggie Stuart did things behind the scenes which got their hands dirty. They weren't meant to stand in the spotlight, modestly holding hands and smiling blithely while the cameras flashed.

## 11

## Teenage Wildlife

✪

The next day, and so sue me, I didn't feel like going in to school. So I didn't. I sat on the edge of the couch frowning and watching daytime television. Every now and then I would go to the refrigerator for something to nibble on, and remember I should be preparing for the meeting ahead after school. Somehow, I never got around to doing much more than taking out my notebook with the list of questions I hadn't answered at the library. Then, with the tick of the clock pressing its hands onward, it was time to go.

I biked, about the first time that year. The chain was a little rusty, but everything worked. The brakes didn't squeal at least.

The donut shop was starting to fill with the after-school crowd when I arrived, but no one from the group I was meeting. I took the coffee black—lots of people to impress today with my stoic coffee habits —and sat back with my notebook and a newspaper.

Aaron came in when I was in the middle of a leftover copy of the weekend comics, which maybe wasn't the best time to give him a positive impression of my intelligence. He gave me a nod of acknowledgment and joined me with a coffee and a couple of crullers, one of which he pushed across to me.

I must have looked startled, but he didn't remark except to say, "Now I get to read over your shoulder." I turned the paper sideways on the table.

Sitting there waiting, nibbling on sweet oily donut, I had a nasty little fantasy. The sight of Aaron so near to me made me think about the time when we'd been cellmates, and I wondered how he could have forgotten. So far removed from the feel of it, I hardly believed in magic myself, me who had based all life and angst on its loss. *What if,* I imagined, *I redecorated my room? I could have rock-textured walls, and a piece of foam for a mattress. Shackles from the walls, looped through big, metal staples. Then, Jason and Aaron would come over one day, and they'd see my room, and everything would come flooding...*

*Stop it, stop it.* I might as well dream about re-doing my room with mirrors, like the chamber where I'd lain to enter Char's Dreamworld, or all white like Damon's apartment. *Perverse, perverse.* I really knew just how to make nothing better and everything worse, didn't I? That wasn't a dream; that was just sick. *Sick.* Aaron's fair head tilted, and the blue eyes glanced off mine. Nice of him not to invade my thoughts, especially not at that moment. I don't know if I blush, but it felt like it might have been a distinct risk if he'd looked too intently.

"Turn the page?" was all he said.

*Aaron Scribner,* I decided, *was dangerous.* As if he'd had anything to do with the direction of my demented day-dreaming.

The rest arrived in a group. I was glad. It saved me from a repeated awkwardness, like I'd felt the first moment Aaron showed up. This was at least a single weird greeting, and some of the pressure was taken off me to be gracious.

I opened my notebook, the black leather one from the thrift store. Rae, I noted, had done the same, although in her case it was an iPad. Aaron looked almost smug. I wondered if I was reading him right. All I could imagine, looking at him, was that he was amused that I needed a pen and paper to keep my thoughts straight.

"First," I said, tightly. There were enough reasons to be on edge, but I wish I could say I was feeling it for any of the good ones. "The book."

"What about it?" said Scott sullenly. It was pretty clear he was here against his will.

"I need to know everything you can remember about it. Size, shape, writing—Aaron, I need to know what the language was and what it said, if you got down to translating any of it. Where did it first appear? And what, if any, feelings did you have about it?"

Jason seemed to consider this reasonable. "What order should we go in?"

I looked down at my notepad and turned to a fresh page. "Why doesn't Aaron start, and you all can just jump in if you want to add on?" If I'd meant to take Aaron down a notch by emphasizing his singular contribution to the ritual I'd interrupted, it didn't work.

Completely unabashed, he began. "Jason saw it first, when we were looking for something else in my father's library—"

"What?" I asked.

He didn't consider it important. "A history text. We wanted to check some facts." It wasn't, and I'd known it wouldn't be. Stupid badgering. *Shut up, Maggie. Shut up.* "It didn't look like something my father would own—far too Kabbalistic. He tends to dwell on economics in history, and something about magic or religion seemed... Never mind. Anyway, we took it out and looked it over a bit. The book —my impression was it was very old. The pages were stiff but not at all brittle. They were yellowed but legible. It was about this big—" he indicated with his hands "—and I would estimate maybe two hundred pages. I could be wrong about that. The paper was thicker than in most modern books.

"The cover was leather, thick, dyed a kind of blue-green. The places where the dye was scratched came up yellow, so I have no idea what kind of animal... Never mind. I don't know enough about that stuff to comment. Inside, the writing began on the first page and kept going almost without breaks through the whole book. The section titles were in the margins. Sometimes, there would be a little drawing or diagram beside the heading. The part I read from had something like this."

Rae passed pen and paper into his hands as if he'd silently asked her for them. Was there something going on between them? "There was a pentagram, and some letters and other symbols— then this arrangement of stars..."

He drew it all, and passed it over for me to see. Besides the pentagram, it meant nothing to me, but I recognized the characters from what had been drawn on the gym floor that day.

"We chose that particular section of text because the picture there was the least complex in the book. No other reason, I don't think. Jason?"

Jason shrugged. "It just seemed like the most interesting part."

That was curious. The book could have made them choose, but I didn't make that suggestion out loud. I knew how stupid it would sound, especially since I had nothing to back the idea up but a sudden inspiration. "What I want to know is how you knew what to do to make the ritual happen. How did you even know that's what the book was?"

"A manual for magic?" Aaron said. "Because that's what it said on the front cover."

I was starting to get some of the old anger back, what I'd felt when I came on them in the gym playing with fire. "So you decided to summon forces which were obviously beyond your control into a high school. In the middle of a school day. You didn't even look for a remote spot where the five of you would be the only casualties when something went wrong."

I was a little glad when no one rose angry in return to my harangue, although Scott looked like he was only just restraining himself. "Sorry," I grumbled. "I came to help, not to be stupid. It's happened, and now we have to stop it." It still didn't really explain how they'd known what to do. I wouldn't have had the first idea, and I had seen things like this before. How had they?

Rae said, "I want to know one thing, because I still don't understand." It would take a natural leader to be able to say something like that and not come out sounding apologetic or dense. Rae carried it perfectly. "What attacked us?"

"And how many more are there out there?" Suzanne added. She was looking not at me but at Aaron, as if help would naturally come from that place. She added, plaintively, "And what about the poor animals?"

I didn't appreciate being passed over for the role of trusted savior so I let them argue for a while on their own. Even Scott got in on it, though his bad temper hadn't lessened. What consensus there was was that they were—*obviously*—dealing with demons from some kind of Hell (that part was contentious— literal interpreters of the Bible and others unable to agree), which were intent on death and destruction. Suzanne, I started to learn, was quite a sentimentalist. *Poor little squirrels, poor little kitties.*

Something struck me while all this was going on, and in an effort both to end the bickering and to assert my own control over the proceeding, I said it. "There's one question we should be asking, the most important one, I think you'll agree." I didn't have their undivided attention, but I kept on. "Where are they now?"

Rae pulled her cheeks in with a hiss of air and nodded. "You're right."

The others quieted down, but hers was the only actual confirmation anyone had heard what I'd said.

"Okay," said Aaron, taking over my new business smoothly. "Any ideas?"

"Don't you think we got them all?" said Suzanne, more full of apprehension than hope. "Maybe except one little one?"

"No way." I could say it firmly. Maybe I should tell them about the Mr. Thurl and Aaron apparitions, impress on them that something was seeking me out too, and not in an indirect way like killing small animals. But that last was a better example. "When was the last time any of you cleaned up a dead squirrel?"

"Today," said Scott. His tone said, implicitly, *What are you doing about it?*

Jason said, "But Suzanne's right. There's been hardly anything, not like the first couple of weeks. Maybe they're not as strong as they were at first."

"Or there's fewer of them." This was my area of expertise, I supposed, although I hadn't really been making the point Jason stated. How could I have known the states of their death patrols? In any case, it seemed to be up to me to answer the question. "It's likely," I said, "that some of them will have just evaporated on their own, having lost control of their forms. But there must be at least one, and I would say more likely several, which have adapted themselves just fine to our world. There's many ways—" I broke off.

"Maggie?" encouraged Rae.

I closed my eyes, and then looked at her. I had meant to tell them about how I'd gotten rid of the one that looked like Aaron, but there was something I'd just thought of. All eyes were on me. This sort of time-wasting was pretty potent stuff. I hadn't meant to be dramatic, but if it was a skill I could develop—"I don't know *where* they come from, or what exactly they are. But we do know a few things. You know what they like. You saw in the gym. Heat and blood. The best place for one of these things to survive should be obvious." It was an inspiration, suddenly blindingly plausible to me.

Aaron was nodding, right with me and ahead of the others.

"Inside a human body," he said.

"Right." *What if they could stick around only if they found a person to hide inside?* I had no evidence this had, or could, happen, but the idea seemed so right. . . . Maybe I'd just figured out the key to the concept of demonic possession. *Maybe I was really, really full of it.*

Scott was the one who reacted most strongly to this suggestion. "This is bullshit," he said, standing. "I'm not going to listen to any more of this. No, man," he cautioned as Jason stood to join him. "No. I'm going. Tell me what you decide."

"Scott, wait!" I followed him out the door and touched his shoulder as he bent to unlock his bike.

He looked at me with murder in his eyes. What had I done to deserve such hatred? "Scott," I said, slowly and carefully. "Your little brother. I can't explain it—but I really care about him. I—don't want to see him scared or in pain or confused. You probably don't give a damn about what I want, but for him—I would do a lot for him. Okay?"

Scott stared at me, uncomprehending, for a moment, then went back to opening the lock.

"Scott," I said again, something of a plea entering my tone. I didn't stop it from coming to visit. "—Soren—" It was hard to say the unfamiliar name. "I need to talk to him. I really do. I wouldn't ask if it wasn't important, or vital. You want him to be safe as much as I do."

He made a vague gesture over his shoulder as if he was brushing me away, Maggie the pesky fly. Straightening, I was sure he would get on his bike and ride away without another word. But he said, low, through his teeth, "Maybe. We'll see."

That was it, but I breathed easier going back to the rest.

"You didn't convince him," said Suzanne. It was maybe the first time she had addressed me directly. Breakthrough? Something. Did she have something going with Aaron? Her eyes darted to him the moment they left me.

"No," I replied. "He was set on going. But I was really asking something else."

I had expected them to take that at par, leave me with a mysterious, unqualified statement. But Jason said, "What else?"

I shrugged. There was no harm in saying something. "I think someone should talk more to Soren." I had nearly bobbled the name again. *Peter,* I wanted to say. Little Peter, Prince of the underworld. Carrier of cool water for torn shoulders, nurse-assistant to Doctor Saunders, eagerly bounding to aid in the creation of a sling for my arm. Not suburban Soren Saunders, heir to the big family SUVs and media centers and carefully fenced backyards of Westbrook.

Aaron nodded. He was looking at me strangely. I would have loved to know what was going on in that crafty head of his. He inclined the piece of anatomy in question, the blond hair falling straight and limp over one temple. But he said nothing. Why didn't he say something? He was obviously thinking something. I wasn't keeper of the only closed-mouth at the table, and not the best one by far.

*Aaron Scribner, dangerous indeed.*

## 12

## Telling Lies

✪

The next step, I guessed, was to give them my take on the whole thing, but I was reluctant. I didn't want to share all my insights with them. I told myself this was a practical thing: I couldn't let them get too close to the truth, especially as it related to Hunt, for safety's sake.

And then I realized what I had been planning all along. I meant to interpose myself between Hunt and this group of people around me, to be the target of anything he cared to do. And it wasn't particularly out of a sense of generosity or protectiveness, not nearly so much that as a kind of greed. It was warped. Hunt, I intended, should have to go through me at every stage, and that way I would stay at the center of things. I didn't want to be left out.

"Mags?" said Jason, and I realized I'd paused too long.

I'd also completely lost the thread of my questions, not that we were following my list in any structured way. "Just thinking," I explained. I scanned my list for clues as to how to continue. "Right. Rae. No, all of you. Tell me about the ritual."

Suzanne was the only one who actually shivered, but there were signs of discomfort or outright fear on all of them. Even Aaron Scribner wasn't wholly immune.

Jason spoke first. "Aaron, Scott, and I kind of pieced together the whole thing from what we'd seen in films and from books. You know. A pentagram, the candles. We knew there had to be something in the middle and—someone... Who? Someone lit on the idea of matches."

"For the heat." I looked around the table. No one was taking credit for this. "It was Scott then?"

"I don't think so," said Jason, frowning.

"Maybe no one," I said.

Aaron, too quick as usual, jumped in. "Are you trying to say we were deliberately manipulated? The book got into our heads?" He looked around the table. "There was nothing in the book about what to do, I can promise you that."

"Something like that is conceivable," I said. "We have to keep the possibility in mind."

The fact they were scared was evident now, because no one crossed me on this point, or told me I was crazy. I was dealing with people who believed because they had seen.

"Don't be frightened, any of you," I said, trying to be reassuring. "This is all happening for a reason. I don't think even Hell, if that's really what we're dealing with, is totally random." It struck me, after it was out, as a completely stupid thing to say, but Suzanne at least seemed to take heart.

She nodded. "What do we do now?"

"First," I said, thinking fast. "I need that book."

Exchanged glances around the table. "Okay," said Jason.

I gasped. "Does one of you have it?"

"Yeah," said Jason. "Suzanne does, right?"

She confirmed this, nodding again.

I was an idiot. The Aaron Scribner-apparition had told me it was lost. All this time, it had been kept out of my hands by a simple lie. That was the purpose in sending the first creature after me, something weak which was probably already disintegrating, to tell me a lie which would keep me from examining the source of the problem. Damn damn damn! And, on top of that, I realized I knew a lot less about summoning and dismissing these things than I thought. If there was a reason for the demon-thing to come to me, it might have gone away on its own. So might have the ones in the gym. Was my involvement in this affair accidental, or premeditated? Who had suggested the gym as the venue for the ritual to occur?

I was scribbling furiously on the page in front of me, covering what I was writing with my arm. Around me, Rae and Jason tried to peer over and see what I was jotting. . . Was I leaving out enough of what I was sure of so that my notations would be incomprehensible? I hoped so. My writing was pretty illegible. . .

"Maggie?" said Rae.

"A minute." I kept writing. All this time, and the solution might be in that. . . "Suzanne," I said, not looking up. "Where's the book now?"

"At my house," she said.

"Aaron, have you looked in it for something to reverse what you did?"

"A bit," he said. For once he wasn't super-brain. "I can read the words, pronounce them at least, and understand the simpler ideas, but without a full translation. . . Even then, I don't think we'd know what each particular piece was supposed to do."

He was right, but there had to be a reason I had been kept away from the book. There had to be.

"We need that book, and we need it now. There's not a moment to lose."

"I live—" began Suzanne.

"I know," I said. I had my list. "Let's go."

✪

I don't know who actually vetoed my desperate suggestion, or how, but we didn't go to Suzanne's. I don't know what it was. Her family would be home soon, and she had basketball early in the morning, and someone else had a soccer game that evening—all sorts of little reasons. I wasn't swayed by the urgency of any of them, but I also didn't speak up emphatically. I found myself agreeing to Rae's bringing the book when we went riding on Saturday, and the meeting was over.

No decisions had really been made as far as I could tell, and we still were no further ahead on anything. I would have been more angry and bitter about the lack of progress we'd made, except that I was just as bad a procrastinator. So much time had passed already in my lazy folly; I'd let this be theirs, or be a hypocrite. I could only hope some of us would develop some momentum if events started picking up.

I began the ride home alone. The others, Jason excepted, were involved in some other planning of which I wouldn't be a part. Jason had left already, trying to get home in time for dinner.

Halfway down the block, I was hailed and stopped to wait for Aaron Scribner to catch up to me. I got off the bike and walked alongside him.

This wasn't precisely his quickest route home. I said as much.

"No," he agreed. I wondered why I was trying to push him away with questions. Maybe there was something he wanted to say.

But we kept going in silence. I had no idea what to say, and afraid that opening my mouth would throw out either more third-degree inquiry or something about how I wished he could remember how we had started to be friends, once upon a time.

He broke the deadlock. "So, what are you taking this year?"

Grateful for a neutral subject, I relaxed a little. "This semester, I have drafting, English, eleven math, and a twelve history, in which I am the only representative from our grade."

He chuckled. "That's tough."

"And I embarrassed myself royally the first day of class. Even the teacher doesn't want to have anything to do with me."

He chuckled again. "I'm surprised we don't have anything together this year."

Last year, we had shared both English and mathematics, but I don't think we'd exchanged a word. I almost said, bitterly, that being in the same classes this year would hardly have made a bit of difference, but bit back the words. I didn't want to blow the chance of having another conversation with him sometime.

"You?" I asked instead.

"French, phys. ed, twelve politics, and a spare. It's a bit of a joke."

Of course the politics course would be a breeze for Aaron. I'd been in a history course with him in grade nine, and for him, it was like air to a bird. "Get in any good arguments yet?"

Aaron made the kind of guffawing laugh I'd heard from him before, always in the company of someone who knows him well. I'd always read it as an admission that whoever tickled his funny bone had surprised him. It made me feel good.

"Yeah, you know," he said, non-committal, but in fine humor.

We reached the place where he had to either turn off or walk me home. He turned serious instantly, another quality I liked about him. "I want to solve this thing," he said, intensity back in the blue eyes. The sun was midway down the western half of the sky and glinted slightly orange in the corner of his glasses. "Anything you know, you can tell me. If you need something kept from the others, don't keep it from me. I can use discretion when I have to."

It was very kind of him, very nice. I nodded, lying agreement. "Of course," I said.

"Scott—you shouldn't let him bother you. Somehow he doesn't believe in... magic or whatever, no matter what he's seen. Also, he's got a problem when it comes to girls to begin with, and then— Well, Scott thinks with his heart and uses his brute force much more than his brain. When he gets an impulse, he doesn't check with his common sense before acting on it. So he can be pretty cruel sometimes. But he doesn't mean anything. We just ignore him when he gets like that."

I accepted this. I could see what he meant. I'd been at the wrong end of Scott's impulses a few times.

"Jay thinks a lot of your brain," he went on. "Just thought you should know. Maggie Van Helsing."

After that, I was a little embarrassed. He said goodbye in a fairly compressed fashion, and I waved awkwardly.

After he was gone, I realized we had made no plans for the next step, unless you counted me getting to see the book when Rae came to take me riding. I was not satisfied.

I should have, that evening, been able to relax and congratulate myself on getting through and being ready for the next stage. But I was moody by the time I got home. Now I was ready—and I couldn't really think of anything to do to proceed.

At least, I found talking to Mom easy. We chatted about the boyfriend, who was a repeater I gathered. I'd never met him the first time they'd gone out, but it had been years ago, possibly before I'd paid much attention to my mother's social life. It was a pizza night, which meant leftovers for breakfast, maybe even a slice for lunch at school, which was also a reason for celebration.

I spent a strange evening by the television after Jan went out with the new/old boyfriend for late drinks—I only half expected her home later. She was a big girl, after all, and even if I had no experience with certain things, I understood the concept.

What made the evening strange was deciding to revisit the painting I had done on the first day of school, the day the ritual happened and I lost a previously perfectly good hoodie. I had brought my whole meager portfolio downstairs from its hiding spot under my dresser, and it was now spread out around me on the floor. To it, I had added a copy of my list of questions, the contact list, and that intriguing photocopy I'd kept of the newspaper from the library with the blank spots.

*The painting.* This was something undeniable, wasn't it? I had started to paint this, before I ever thought that Jason Lawson and Aaron Scribner could be just down the hall, summoning otherworldly forces. It had to mean something, that either I had some kind of ability to predict the future—or maybe just that I could somehow sense what was happening without having to be there.

I didn't entirely trust my own memory, though. Maybe it came from having erased so many other people's in that one fell swoop three years ago, but memory felt fluid to me. I worried all the time that I was recreating my own memories to show myself in a better (or worse, depending on the day) light.

When I was thirteen, when everything went suddenly insane in my life, one of the first things I remember was starting to believe my dreams were coming true. I wished I had been the kind of kid to write dream journals, or—I don't know—at least to make a note on some scrap of notebook paper, when I had an odd dream.

But I wasn't, and even when everything was happening for the first time, I wasn't entirely sure if I was dreaming then experiencing, or just weaving the day's events back into my next night's sleep. I *think* I remembered one thing clearly enough though—that I dreamt one night about a black car that slowed behind me as I walked home, only to have that very thing happen the next day. It was like the most extreme kind of déjà vu, where not only did I have the feeling that I'd been somewhere before but knew exactly the moment when I'd seen it for the first time. That one time was not only a fact I believed set in stone as much as any memory can be but a touchstone that I returned to again and again, worrying it like a hangnail, sure that this at least was firm proof in the mundane world that *I was special.*

Or, at least, that once upon a time I had been.

I decided to pack up and sleep on it. The sooner I went to bed, the sooner it would be light again. Never mind that everything frightening so far had happened during the daytime. My imagination was going to get the better of me if I didn't get to sleep and soon.

✪

*I fall asleep quickly and deeply, and dream.*
*I'm flying again, and at first, it's as it has always been.*

*There's no sense of effort, no moment when my feet launch themselves from the ground. I'm just there, as soon as I'm aware at all of dreaming, and it is fine.*

*I am over Westbrook, the park on my right, the lake in the distance straight ahead. The air, cool and sweet, moves past me with the whisper of skin on a silk sheet.*

*Suddenly, everything is different. It's like the feeling of coming into the gym with the ritual in progress below, the feeling of wrongness juxtaposed with the familiar.*

*And then, I can't fly anymore.*

*All at once, my body is too heavy for the accommodating air, and I'm sinking. I don't fall; this is no sudden nixing of my flight by the laws of gravity. This is a deliberate rejection of me, and I take it very personally.*

*I fight to stay aloft, but every little gain I make, every effort to catch a rising updraft, comes at the cost of my stability. I'm no longer soaring like a kite, effortless and natural. I am ungainly as an albatross on lift-off. No thermal will support this too-corporeal form.*

*My toes skim the asphalt, my arms flail. I have lost the ability to fly, even in my dreams.*

It was still the middle of the night when I woke, not just with tears in my eyes, but outright crying. I had to stifle myself—not because I was afraid Jan would hear, but because I knew that if she did, she wouldn't come.

✪

The next day at school, I had to admit that there was a greater potential than I had previously considered for what was happening in the little group I'd attached myself to might spill into the broader community. That was because of Irene. My opinions, when it came to my potentially still-kindly grade twelve classmate, still weren't set. Since the first day of school, we had exchanged nothing-talk before and after class, but I was always deliberately distant, not wanting to commit to as much as a coffee after school or a longer conversation that would take us beyond the door of the room.

After homeroom, I grabbed up all my things as quickly as I could, trying to avoid a chat that could turn into a walk to our next classes. I felt like a shark: keep moving or die. Or in this case, make a friend I wasn't sure I wanted.

I took a slightly circuitous route to drafting, wanting to stay away from the main student body as much as possible and not wanting to get there early enough to go another round with Mr. Thurl. As I turned at an intersection into the automotive section, I saw something curious. No one but me seemed to notice the guy standing in the middle of the hallway, staring past where I stood and slightly over my head.

I slowed, and then realized that someone had just walked through his arm.

Not someone, then. Something. And only I could see it.

The guy, or whatever it was, grinned at me, and turned. It walked quickly through the sparse crowd, and I picked up my speed again to follow. It led me into one of Dief's more tortuous sections, one I was barely familiar with, and I felt scared. This was getting far too much like Char's labyrinthine underground passages. My legs were vibrating now, but I kept going. I was grinding my teeth together as I went, but that couldn't be helped.

The students had thinned to nothing, and the bell had to be no more than a minute off. I'd never make it to drafting on time, even if I managed to find a good route. But this was a much more pressing engagement...

I rounded a corner, right into a brick wall.

Nothing. No one. No *thing* either. Just me, late, and a demon-thing somewhere probably laughing its ass off.

"Maggie?"

My name was called tentatively, from somewhere behind me.

I turned. It was Irene, clutching her books and looking far too sharply questioning for my taste.

"What were you doing?"

I hadn't quite recovered any sort of composure, but I tried to shrug. She had to have *followed* me, all the way from class. There was no other way she could have ended up here, now. "I thought I saw someone I knew," I said. Lame reason, but I couldn't think of another.

"Right," she said. She didn't believe me at all. There was another moment's silence between us, then, "Hey, do you have plans for

Saturday?"

*My trip with Rae.* "Yeah, sorry." No follow-up from me, no question about what she'd had in mind.

She shrugged, as if it hadn't really mattered all that much anyway, and told me she'd see me on Monday in class.

I started to make my way to class, metaphoric tail between my legs.

I came to the conclusion on the way home after school that I was glad something, even something as big as escaped demons, had come up so I wouldn't have to spend time with Irene. Very uncharitable, but that was the way I felt. Someday, when all this was over, maybe I'd find out she was worth knowing. Right now, I just hadn't the time.

To be perfectly honest, I just hadn't the interest. Still, I couldn't get over the feeling I was missing something.

## 13

## Jump They Say

✪

Saturday dawned bright and sunny. Maybe I shouldn't say 'dawned' since I didn't actually wake up until well after ten. Rae was going to pick me up at eleven thirty, so that was lucky. As per my usual habit, I hadn't bothered to set my alarm for the weekend. This was the first time in living memory I had something to wake up for.

There was a note from Jan saying she'd be out with Harrison—that was the guy's name—playing tennis for most of the morning, and that they'd probably have lunch out. He was one of those expense-accounters, no question. Since Mom was from a company that did business with his, he could probably write off all their dates. Humph.

She'd come home last night, after all, but I hadn't heard her. That meant sometime later than one thirty, when I'd gone to bed. Either that or she'd snuck in this morning. . . Oh, I prayed this one would go well. Provided she was involved with someone—in other words, happier herself—she wouldn't bother me. I didn't even want to think about what would happen if I had to explain to her what was going on.

At twenty after, I started down the court to meet Rae. I had put on a pair of thick canvas pants and a hoodie, with a towel, a t-shirt, sports bra, and a pair of bike shorts in my back pack. That also contained, in a plastic bag to protect it, my black leather notebook and a pen. I meant this to be a working day.

I was undecided about whether I would swim or not. It had been years since I'd swum in company, three, actually, and almost as long since I'd swum at all. I didn't even own a bathing suit that would fit anymore. Having anyone see my scar would raise questions I couldn't answer and probably, almost certainly, couldn't stop myself from reacting to. If I decided to go in, the t-shirt would hide most of the scar, and the bike shorts would conceal everything else a *normal* teen-age girl would feel insecure about, especially around a girl like Rae.

But the important thing was to keep my mind on business, and an eye out for Hunt. I'd be spending some time with Rae, and it was vital we talked about the situation at hand. I sensed that she, alone maybe of all of them, would be conceivably. . . what was the word I wanted? Rae seemed like a good ally to cultivate, because she could be reasoned with and was enthusiastic. If she could be brought on side, she could help me with the others. Sooner her than even Jason. Besides, she had asked me out, not the other way around, so she'd already given me a head start.

I had just assumed Rae's mother or someone would be picking us up. It hadn't occurred to me that she had her own driver's license. The car, at least, belonged to her family and not her personally. I slid in to the passenger seat, smelling clean leather. Big car, over-sized Chrysler thing, but she handled it well. I should talk. I'd never sat behind the wheel of a car in my life. I wouldn't even be sixteen until October 26th, and Mom and I had never even broached the subject of whether or not I'd be getting my learner's permit after that.

"The book," I asked.

"In the back seat," she replied. She put the car in gear to take us away from the curb. I looked over. I could see a pile of blankets, but no book. It must have been underneath. *Good.* She was taking care to keep the thing hidden and safe. No telling who was around.

There was obviously going to be no time to look through it before we went riding. I would just have to relax and wait for my chance afterwards. It was easy to console myself; after all, by tonight the book would be in my possession and all its secrets mine to discover. I was the natural person to hold on to it, of course. Who else but Maggie, the Worker of Wonders? Maggie, the Demon Banisher? Maggie Van Helsing, Aaron had called me. *Hail Maggie, full of crap.*

We made small talk on the drive, little things about life and school. It was not too unpleasant, actually. Rae was easy to get along with, even if I wasn't learning anything about the situation at hand.

We left the city, started out into the countryside north of the GTA. My nose seemed very sensitive all of a sudden. The smells were heady—manure, hay, all the growing things. The leaves— I could swear I could smell them too, distinctly and intriguingly. I looked at Rae; she was smiling.

The stable where her horses were boarded, Merrymount, was also a riding school. Rae told me that her family lent them to the school for the better riders to use, and in exchange, she only had to come out a couple of times a week. Somehow, with the easy and casual chatter, neither of us brought up the book again.

Suzanne had been out a few times with Rae, I gathered from the stable mistress who asked after her. Feeling unjustifiably jealous, I hoped pathetically I'd be a better rider.

Walking into the main stable was magic. I'd never been this close to horses before, except maybe a pony or two at the Ex years ago. But everything seemed familiar. There were the smells, even stronger here, of horse, and hay, and leather. I welcomed the cats milling around my feet like old friends. And somewhere in the back of it all, I imagined something else, the scent of acrid tobacco and strong alcohol—brandy? I didn't say anything to Rae about that, in case it was someone doing something wrong. I didn't think it was fair for me to get them in trouble. Everything, even that, was making me feel wistful, and even a little sad.

I was to ride the bay, Caramel. Rae came to inspect the job I was doing currying her down.

"You're doing that just fine," she said over my shoulder. "You're sure you've never done this before?"

"Yeah, I'm sure," I replied. The horseflesh twitched under my hand as I patted Caramel's flank. "I'd remember if I had, right?"

"Then you're a natural," said Rae, and went back to Chocolate, the glossy brown mare she was brushing down.

The bridle and bit were harder for me to manage, and Rae thought it would be better if she handled them anyway, because I was still an unfamiliar person to the animal. I stood by Caramel's head, stroking the long, fine nose and the mane. Either Rae or the stable had kept the mane and tail hair free of snags.

We mounted, and I had the reins of a real horse in my hands. I know a lot of girls are overtaken by horse-love at some point in their lives, but I hadn't thought I would be one of them. I had thought myself insusceptible, but I was totally wrong. Being in the saddle was perfect. The leather under me seemed molded to my own shape.

"Caramel's not really a trail horse," Rae was explaining. "She's going to be a show jumper, but she's still young. Chocolate's the elder. We've had her four years. Caramel should follow along, but if she decides to be disobedient, tell her where to go with the reins."

I nodded. Warm horse against my thighs, I turned Caramel's head, and off we went.

Because Rae was an experienced rider, she was allowed to take me out of the enclosed field and onto the trails herself. I thought there shouldn't have been any problem, because she owned the horses. She told me that didn't make any difference to the stable mistress. Either you knew the trails and could handle a horse, or you stayed on the flat ground inside the fence rails.

It was a beautiful day. The temperature was comfortable, even a little warm for this time in early October. I heard birds singing, and everywhere there was the feeling of heat rising from the ground around us, like the earth was shedding its excess warmth in preparation for winter.

"Looking good, Maggie!" Rae called back over her shoulder. We rode single file, slowly to see the trees and what was left of the wild roses. There were apple trees as well, growing wild along the trails.

We went down into a section of densely foliaged wood, where the leaves had begun to turn but were yet to start falling, and where the sunlight came down in shafts. Caramel whinnied and Chocolate snorted in answer.

"They know what's coming," laughed Rae.

"Which is?" I asked.

"After the wood, there's the gallop. We get a nice flat stretch up to the creek. Do you feel up to it?"

I felt a surge of anticipation, much like what must have been going through the horse. "Try to stop me," I said.

"Great," said Rae. I could see her shoulders tense, then relax. We left the woods.

The trail disappeared. We were left at the side of a meadow. The sun was warm and the grass was golden. I was in heaven.

"Come on!" shouted Rae, and Chocolate surged forward.

I didn't have to do much more than give my mare her head. I could feel the ground through the pound of her muscles. The wind took my hair. I could imagine being dressed differently—like, I don't know, more formally. I could smell the brandy or whatever it was again. What a high it would be to ride like this at night, the power of the horse and me alone under the stars. . . Rae was somewhere, dropping behind, the flash of Chocolate's brown flank and the orange of her jacket disappearing out of my line of sight. It was Caramel, and me, and we moved as one.

I don't think I really noticed the fence, or the stream. I was vaguely aware of the explosion of energy under me and through me, and the way the world rocked in my vision. I pulled hard on the reins, and Caramel turned under me. Her muscles bunched under my thighs and she took off, fast. Then, it was me who was flying, not the horse. I rolled, never feeling myself hit the ground, and bashed into a tree.

Rae came hurtling off her horse out of nowhere, crouched down beside me and touched my head.

"Nasty hit," she said, eyes wide. "That was something."

Miraculously, although I had probably nearly wrecked her valuable horse, she began to smile, and then, when it was clear I was more winded than hurt, to laugh. She helped me to my feet, and we checked me over for bumps and bruises. Caramel stood patiently nearby.

I remounted, although the world spun as I did so. "Do you think I have a concussion?" I said.

"Probably not," she replied, staring into my eyes for a moment before swinging back up onto Chocolate. "I think you hit everything *but* your head. But we'll get you checked out when we go back to the stable. There's a nurse at the house. We'll see what she says. I still fall too sometimes, you know. But that was a good one."

We rode back quietly. I was trying to recapture the sensation which had come upon me just before I made that jump, as I was racing across the meadow. The memory was causing me to feel strange and subdued. The wistfulness I had felt in the stable returned full force. Horseback riding was having a powerful effect on me.

Back in the stables, that tobacco/alcohol scent I seemed to remember from the first time by the stalls was gone. Strange, that it was probably not unlike the musk that had so disgusted me in the office at the McDonalds, those sharp odours mixed with sweat, but here they had such a different effect on me. Maybe because this time, they were unconnected with a disturbing memory. Smell is supposed to be the most evocative of the senses. I hoped that every time I encountered this particular combination in the future, it would remind me of this day and not the other.

I was almost unaware of Rae's company. That had something to do with a sense of shame encroaching on what had been previously a fairly good humor. After the initial exhilaration of my spontaneous act, shock was setting in. I'd done something foolish, with a witness, and with considerable risk of damage to an expensive animal. I would have to apologize.

The anticipation of this detracted from the pleasure of currying Caramel down. I had explained to Rae I would rather see to the horse's comfort before my own. Mostly, I wanted to impress her with how responsible I was.

It was a pleasure, though. A glorious feeling, to run my hand along the satin flank of warm horseflesh, to follow it with the brush, to feel the occasional shiver that ran along her muscles when a fly landed.

Whenever I looked over toward Rae, similarly engaged with Chocolate, she grinned at me. It was almost conspiratorial. *See,* she seemed to be saying, *this is something nice we have in common.* It made me feel even more ashamed.

I finished going over Caramel's entire body and untangling a few stray burrs from her mane, and followed Rae to the end of the barn with my arms full of tack. As we got close to the bales of hay stacked against the wall by the racks of equipment, I heard a strange sound. My head whipped toward Rae to make sure she heard it too, then scanned toward the darkest corner of the stables for what was making it.

It was like a low shriek, like a tortured creature being pulled along metal or—I couldn't find a good analogy, but it was for sure something living, and in terror.

Something furry brushed past my leg at high speed, and I jumped, spilling everything I was carrying onto the straw under my feet. A yowl rose from behind me now, and more of the tortured shrieking from the darkness ahead. It had been one of the barn cats streaking past, I was certain, and I thought—*horrified*—that it might just be another barn cat in front of me still making that unearthly noise.

I motioned behind me to Rae, who was standing frozen with big eyes and a set to her jaw. "Are there lights for that corner?" I hissed.

"I'll open the window," she whispered back, taking a couple of steps backwards without letting her gaze move from the dark area ahead. She laid her armload of equipment down more carefully than I had and moved out of my line of sight.

Me, I had no choice but to follow my compulsion to move slowly the other direction, into the dark and toward that hellish squealing.

I closed my eyes as I passed from the light into dark to cushion my sight against the change of brightness. When I opened them again, I could see a smallish alcove, about the size of my bedroom at home, with a squared-off wooden post in the middle that supported the hayloft above. The walls were packed out with bales of hay two and three high. And deep in the shadows, in the corner of the room, was a huddled collection of cats of various colors and sizes, all with their backs arched as high as they could go, hackles raised, ears flattened back. The largest, in front of the others, was a mangy, multi-colored veteran of many fights with a torn ear and bare patches of fur. It was the one making the noise.

I took another couple of cautious steps ahead, firmly committed to interfering now. My head was spinning. I found myself thinking how good it was that I was with Rae today, not Suzanne. She wouldn't have waded toward this particular danger. She would have screamed and run away, poor little kittens in danger or no.

Was this, I wondered, the *thing* that had been destroying animal life around the ritual participants since that first day of school? And if so, was it as dangerous to humans as to other creatures?

The hissing cat shifted its wild gaze briefly to me, as if assessing whether or not I was adding to the threat. The other cats behind it seemed to take this momentary change of circumstances as a cue to run, and a mass of them suddenly dashed toward me and past into the main part of the building.

The yowling cat stood its ground the longest before dashing between my legs to safety.

But one of the smallest, a tiny one with the awkward proportions of kittenhood, didn't make it. Instead, it rose into the air, carried by nothing I could see. Whatever snatched it into empty space cast no shadow, made no distortion in my line of sight. The air was clear and still through to the hay bales. The kitten began mewing, frantically and piteously, its small voice without the grown-up authority of the other cat's. Red punctures appeared on its body, and then a line of blood opened up across its small nose.

My entire body was tensed almost past bearing; my legs were beginning to quiver. What now? This formless thing, would it respond to my telling it it was dismissed? Did it have the ability to hear me?

How could I know, even, if it was gone if I couldn't see it in the first place?

The kitten was wailing, twisting in midair, blood dripping now from various small puncture marks. I had to do something, both for it and to show Rae I was on top of this arcane game. But it was so much harder here than it had been when I was alone with the other apparitions I'd faced down. I had to succeed, had to stop this slaughter, because I needed Rae to like me as much as I needed to save the cat.

A shaft of sunlight suddenly cut into the space between me and the post, and I knew Rae had managed to open whatever window she'd been talking about. It was the worst possible thing, although I couldn't have known it would be beforehand. It blinded me entirely. I squeezed my eyes shut and threw myself forward into the shadow, hoping to pull the same trick as before to get my vision to adjust.

I bumped into the little cat in midair, feeling the wetness of its blood smear my cheek. I opened my eyes and was rewarded with a half-clear sight of what was going on.

The thing toying with the kitten raised it up above my head, above where my hands could reach it, to where I'd need to be in the hayloft or on a ladder to grab it away. If I even could.

Its pitiful cries were suddenly met with a matching whimper from below, from back in that corner where the group of barn cats had previously been cowering. I could barely see a little ball of fluff there, another even smaller, younger kitten whose presence might have gone completely unnoticed if it had stayed quiet.

The kitten in the air began bouncing slowly through the air toward the source of the second cry, and I knew I probably had only seconds to do something to save both of the animals. My mind spun, trying to enumerate what I knew, what I could do. Heat, and blood. That's what I needed to get the thing's attention. Heat I couldn't call on, but the other was inside me in abundance...

I grabbed both sides of the rough wooden post with my hands, and drove my head against it. Instantly, I was blind again, this time with pain, and I felt my own blood coursing down my chin and onto my hoodie. I felt the invisible tormentor's immediate interest electrify the air. The kitten dropped straight down to the barn floor, landing awkwardly with not quite adult four-pawed grace. It and the other straggler vanished, whether into the dark of the corner or into safety and the light I didn't know.

With me now a more attractive target, the thing attacked as I bent my head, trying to protect my face from its onslaught. It tangled itself in my hair, scratching the hell out of my neck and chin, as I crouched down, scattering the straw around me away from the dirt floor. I grabbed up something—maybe Caramel's bit—and scratched most of a circle around myself. Would this work without a star inside it? I could hardly think from the pain, from the numbness that seemed to be spreading from my smashed nose inwards into my brain.

I drew the five-pointed star to turn the circle into a pentacle, leaving myself in the middle pentagram of it. Drawing a deep breath, and hoping that Rae wasn't watching this part, I blew hard out my nose, dislodging a huge gob of wet and congealing blood, which I smacked from my palm into the center of the circle.

I felt the thing's attention slide from me to the far more concentrated treat in the circle, and almost thought I could see it as it disengaged from me and moved toward the offering of my blood.

Then, I jabbed the bit of metal in my hand forward, and completed the final arc to the circle. "You are dismissed!" I said, the sound thunderingly loud in my head but only a whisper in reality. There was a sucking feeling, as if the ground had become a vacuum cleaner for a split second, except I could swear that it was my breath and my actual life that was being tugged at. . . I heard Rae, somewhere behind me, draw a sharp breath, and call my name.

And we were alone in the barn.

"Maggie?" Rae said again. It seemed that she could tell as well as I could that the thing was gone. I felt her touch my shoulder with one hand. The other cradled the injured kitten.

"It's gone," I said needlessly.

"That was the bravest thing I ever saw," said Rae, and I think I either blushed or turned some shade of sickly pre-puke green, because she gasped and ducked in closer to put her arm around my shoulder.

"That hurts like a son-of-a-bitch," I said, reaching up gingerly to touch my nose, and suddenly we were both giggling. "Relief comes out in funny ways, huh?" I said, when I got my breath back.

"Can you stand?" asked Rae, and I tried only to fall back down on my ass the instant I tried to put any weight on my legs. I was shaking like crazy.

She smiled with concern. "You sit. I'll get some water, and then the nurse... You want to pass this off as part of the riding mishap?"

I let out a harsh burst of air. Time to start worrying about how to get my concussion checked out without alarms of *something's not Kosher* going off for the resident medic. "Oh yeah," I said.

✪

There was another half-hour spent with the nurse, after which she pronounced me *fine and ready for more frivolity,* as she called it. Chance of a concussion was in her estimation remote.

While she was seeing to me, Rae slipped back into the shadows of the alcove. I heard the hose running as she washed away the evidence of our occult encounter. I wondered what people would think if they discerned the faint scratchings of the pentagram on the floor.

I walked considerably behind Rae to the car, dreading the moment when I became vulnerable and told her I was sorry for earlier. It had taken me all of thirty minutes to stop feeling even so slightly a hero over the barn cat incident, and instead like a heel for what had happened during our ride.

"Rae—" I began. I couldn't look at her. The thing with the cats had distracted her, but I knew I wouldn't be able to just let my prior behavior go. She must be angry and hiding it. We had to get this into the open. "About what I did, about almost hurting Caramel, I'm so sorry. I had no business taking her over obstacles like that."

I looked over to Rae in time to see her smile broadly. What was that about? "No, I'm sorry," she said. "You wanted a challenge. You have ridden before, haven't you? I should have known you were pulling my leg. Oh, well, next time we'll really have some fun. And we'll take a more experienced horse for you. That's all it was, you know. Caramel just didn't know what you were up to. If you'd been on Chocolate, there would have been no problem at all. You gave her all the right signals."

I stared. "I really haven't ridden ever before."

"Then you're a natural," she said, easily. I couldn't tell if she believed me or not. "You have a good seat. It just looks like your muscles are out of practice."

My chest started to loosen up. I had been breathing very hard since deciding to apologize, but now I was relaxing again. "You think I can come out again sometime?"

"Sure!" She unlocked the passenger door for me, and went around to the other side. "Next time, we find a way to keep you unharmed for more than an hour, okay? So what now? Up for a swim?"

I nodded. It would be okay. "Or maybe. . ." I was thinking about the open cuts on my body. Like the last time I had been attacked by those invisible claws, during the ritual, my wounds were extremely superficial. Nothing but the nose had bled significantly, but pool water might still hurt. Or maybe, it would soothe my rising bruises. Somehow, I wasn't thinking at all about my far more pressing reason not to swim. Rae just did that to me.

On the way back into town, we chatted breezily this time, about horses, and competitions she'd ridden in, and I heard a blow-by-blow of what I'd done. I'd thought it was Caramel doing most of the directing, but according to Rae, it had been me. I'd jumped the fence at the edge of the meadow, then the stream. I'd convinced Caramel to turn and jump the creek again, but by that point, she was overwhelmed and basically just came to a full halt, dropping her shoulder so I literally rolled off and into the tree. It wasn't her fault either, Rae said. She didn't know any better. She was frightened, and so she disobeyed. She stopped, but I didn't, hence the leaves in my hair and the bruises coming up on my hip and shoulders.

We didn't talk about the other events at the stables at all.

She complimented me on my technique. I, quietly, gave thanks for beginner's luck.

## 14

### How Lucky You Are

✪

Rae's was a big place in the higher-end part of my subdivision. Most of Westbrook was pretty flat, but of course the expensive houses were built around the only interesting landscape we had. There was even a shallow ravine running along the back of her lot with a creek in it. I hadn't even known there *was* a creek in the area.

All this I saw on the tour Rae gave me of her family's property. From the front, the houses in this part of town looked squished together, but they had a lot of land out back which made up for it. The Kennies must be very well-off indeed.

The swimming pool had a raised deck around it. Off to one side was the changing shed, and beside that was the sauna. Tough, very tough life. Mom and I were living about as high on the hog as was possible on her salary, and we couldn't quite afford memberships to the YMCA, much less a pool of our own. Hardly any use quibbling about it though. Some people have. Some people want. And some people hang out with those who have and pretend.

We made Kool-Aid in the kitchen. The water looked inviting, and it would probably be my last chance to swim this year unless some kind of miracle happened. When I rubbed my fingers over my neck, I couldn't even feel where the cuts had been. Short of a slight tenderness in my nose, all the pain I felt was down to my time with Caramel, not what happened after. I guessed I could swim...

Following Rae, I went out to the changing shed in the backyard, cup in one hand, knapsack in the other. Totally uninhibited, she pulled her shirt over her head and a bathing suit down from a peg on the wall. I unzipped my backpack to take out my swimming things, and doffed my own shirt.

Then she saw the scar.

I hadn't forgotten about it, precisely. I hadn't been thinking about it either, although something like that is hard to forget. But it had slipped my mind in the excitement of the day—what with being asked to do something fun with someone I thought I could actually have as a friend, my sensitivity about it had gone all but unremembered.

The first I knew that Rae had noticed was when I felt her finger on my upper arm, tracing the white bulge.

I pulled away and picked up my shirt again. So much for fun. But Rae put her hand on my arm again.

"What? What's wrong?"

"I don't feel like swimming after all," I said. "I better go home."

She moved in front of me and I couldn't really look away without being very rude. "What, Maggie? Do you think I care if you have a scar?" She smiled, quite tentatively. "It's pretty impressive, you know."

If I hadn't had so many memories connected to it, I think I would have responded to her tact. But my face tightened up, and I felt that sneezing sensation come on which meant I was dangerously close to crying. The ache in my nose suddenly ballooned to fill my whole head.

Rae's arm slipped around my shoulder. "Maggie," she said seriously, almost darkly, "who did this to you?"

I was afraid to talk because I didn't want to cry in front of her. I managed, "It was a fight," which was true, as far as it went.

"Was it a long time ago?" she asked quietly.

"No," I said. My own finger moved up to trace it. The scar was jagged, wider some places than others, and puffy. Only the bone-white color suggested that it was fully healed. "Three years."

I could almost hear her calculating back.

"More like two and a half," I clarified.

"You were at public school with Jason and the other guys, weren't you?" she said.

"Yep." I tried to laugh, but it came out forced.

"Who hurt you?" she said again, quieter this time.

I said nothing for a moment. Here it was once more, temptation. "You don't want to know," I said at last.

"You don't have to tell me," she corrected. "But I'll listen if you'd like me to. Not that I'm not curious," she finished lightly.

"A magician," I said. Then, slowly, "a sorcerer. You wanted to know how I knew about the ritual, and how to stop it? Him. You want to know who hurt me? Him. You want to know something else? You are now the only person besides me left alive who knows about it." Barring Hunt, of course. Or—? A thought slipped through and out of my head before I could catch it. Paralyzing fear grabbed me. I had told. I hadn't spoken Char's name, but I had told. I tensed, waiting for the sky to fall in on top of the shed and bury us both.

Rae was silent, nodding. Then she said, "I guess there really are more things in heaven and earth. . ." She put a towel around my shoulders. I was shivering and I hadn't noticed until she'd moved to make me more comfortable. "We don't have to swim. Let's just go back inside."

I nodded.

In the house, we boiled water for hot chocolate. Since I'd gone on my coffee kick, I hadn't had much patience for it, but then, I'd forgotten how good it was.

Conversation was sparse until we were sitting in the big white living room on the leather sofa.

"Rae," I said, after a long sip, "what I said—it's not really true. I mean, I may have made something pretty ordinary sound more— dramatic. You know." She had been staring away, out the window. Now she turned to regard me. "I don't like talking about the scar, but it's not as big a deal as I made out before. It—" I was going to have to lie, a bigger one to cover up the truth. Why hadn't I had a neat little story ready? It was hardly likely I'd be able to go my whole life without uncovering my arms. "— It doesn't have anything to do with magic. Sometimes I get carried away. I took a bad fall off my bike, that's all." I laughed, still forced. "But I got you good, didn't I?"

She half-smiled, then laughed. She sounded partly relieved, but I thought I could sense that she didn't quite believe me. "You really had me going." She batted me with a cushion. "Don't joke about things like that!"

I bit back the bitterness rising in my throat. "Sorry," I said. "I'm out of practice in the practical jokes department. My timing, it's lousy, isn't it?"

"Your bike, huh?" she said.

"Clumsy me," I replied. "I'm not saying it didn't hurt."

"That? Could have fooled me," she said. She sighed. "You'll have to come swimming some other time, before we lose the weather for it completely. We usually close it up on the last day of September, but it's been such a warm fall. . ."

I took this as a cue for departure, whether or not it really was. "I had better be going," I said.

"Sure," she said, sounding a little sad. "I'll give you a lift."

We cleared away our cups and loaded them into the dishwasher. More little luxuries. "The folks should be home later tonight," said Rae. "It's not my turn on dishes, but I hate leaving a mess for them when they've been away."

"Where are they?" It was so natural to me to come home to an empty house it hadn't occurred to me to ask.

"Up at a wedding in Barrie," she said. "I wasn't really invited. One of those things where I could have gone to the ceremony but wasn't asked to the dinner. I preferred to stay here. Besides, we had to go riding."

I nodded, smiling. "Only child?" I asked.

"Youngest," she said, grimacing. "Of four. The only one who hasn't flown the coop. I hope at least that they're making all the mistakes I won't have to. That's the baby's benefit, isn't it?"

"I wouldn't know. Only child." I indicated myself.

"Terrible," she said. "I wouldn't give up having a big family for anything. We have thousands of relatives. It must be—lonely."

"Rae," I started. I was thinking back to Thursday, and the after school meeting. "Do you think Suzanne hates me?"

She smiled crookedly. "Don't worry about her. Suzanne gets a bit self-involved sometimes. You don't have to be nervous about her intentions, though."

I accepted this. Hadn't Aaron said something similar about Scott? I really wanted to follow my first question up and ask if she was going out with Aaron, or was interested in him since I still vaguely had that impression. But since I had no valid reason at all for wanting to know, I let it slide.

Rae surveyed the kitchen reluctantly, as if—I don't know—embarrassed? Wishing I could have some of what she did? "I guess we should be off," she said.

Then, she turned and fixed me with her strong, steady Rae gaze.

"Do you think. . . I mean, back at the barn. Did you get it? The thing that was killing all the animals?"

I nodded, non-committal, even while I was thinking more deeply about it than I had bothered up to that point. No, I didn't think I'd got that thing. Not in retrospect. The animals that had been dying around Jason and the others had, according to their reports, died without a mark on them. That was far from the scenario with the punctured kitten. I saw it in my memory, Rae sponging away its blood as I cleaned myself up, its little kitten mew sounding so much sadder than any animal I had ever heard before. I got whatever had followed us to the riding school, but it was far from over.

I couldn't keep the seriousness of my musings entirely from Rae. "I hope so," I said, but didn't tell her the progress of my thoughts. "All I know is I want to have a good long look at that book. I don't know what I can learn, but anything would be better than the next-to-nothing we know now."

It was the first time I think I'd used "we" to mean me and other people, in a sense that was at all personal or intimate. It felt kind of good, but I caught myself giving a silent and terse warning not to get too comfortable with the notion, or expect too much.

I put together my unused swimming things and walked around the side of the Kennie house through the gate in the fence to the front. Rae was standing by the edge of the driveway, her back to me and her head down, very still.

"Rae?" I said, walking faster. "Something wrong?"

She turned her head. There were tears in her eyes. "Look," she said.

A few feet away, in the grass, was an orange cat with a long stripped tail and funny short-clipped ears. Its eyes were glassy and paws outstretched as if it had been chasing something and had died frozen in the middle of the hunt.

"Another one," she said. "I can't—It's got to stop. We have to finish this."

"Get the book," I said, my voice dropping. "Let's go back in and find a solution."

I thought about putting my arm around her like she had me, but I couldn't. It seemed wrong, or at least I couldn't bring myself to perform the necessary action. By the time I had convinced myself it would be a nice thing to do, the moment seemed to have passed and Rae was walking to the car.

She unlocked the back door and reached over to the pile of blankets. She lifted these out, and I could see the shape of the book among them. "I hope you have more luck than we did," she said, coming toward me bearing her burden. I reached out and my fingers touched the edge of the fabric.

And everything started to move very slowly. Her feet moved, the blankets shifted in her arms. One moment, they held the shape of the book, and the next, like the book was a balloon deflating to nothing, they collapsed around her hands without anything inside. Rae sensed the shift in weight before I knew what was happening and her face filled with horror and disbelief. I reached toward her as she gathered the blankets closer to her chest, unable to hold on—and it was gone. I was too late. There was nothing left of it at all.

✪

She drove me home. I wasn't in the mood for talking anymore, and she let me stew.

Why? Why had it disappeared right when I was about to get my hands on it? Someone, maybe whoever had left it for Aaron to find in the first place, had snatched it away. But why wait? It could have been taken at the beginning of September when I thought it was already missing. It could have vanished while I was inside Rae's, or out riding, or anytime in the previous weeks. But no, it had disappeared while I watched.

There was only one way to look at it. If I wanted to be arrogant, I could say that the danger was in my being able to use the spells in it against whoever it belonged to. If I was realistic, it was obvious that someone was playing a joke on us. On us, but primarily on me. Whoever it was didn't want us to think it had been a conventional thief who had taken the book. And more, that someone probably knew how much it meant to me to get my hands on it, and was right now laughing at my anger and frustration. Yes, it was a calculated insult, and it had worked. I was furious with Rae for not having wanted to get down to work earlier, with Jason for not having talked about it earlier, and especially with myself for having fallen for the line fed to me by the apparition. This was a total cock-up, and on top of it, someone wanted to toy with my emotions.

Rae pulled up into my driveway. Seeing Jan's car was absent, I almost invited her in, but at the last moment decided against it.

She was a little more timid than I had ever seen her before, and I could see the unmistakable mark of frustration in her as well. "Heck," she said, hands on the steering wheel.

"Yeah," I replied. I tried to pass the problem off so I could facilitate our goodbyes. "Tough luck."

I slid out of the car pulling my backpack behind me. "Thanks again," I said. "I had a really great day— up to that point."

"Maggie," she said, leaning over the seat toward me. "What do we do? Should I call Jason and tell him what happened?"

"Yes, please." That would save me doing it.

"And then what?"

"Monday, Rae," I said. "Monday's soon enough."

"This is bad," she said. "We need that book. Don't we?"

I shrugged. There was a coolness in the day, and inside me, and I wanted a long, hot bath and some mindless novel or Youtube vids to relax me. "I think we have nothing to worry about," I said, and becoming sure as I said it. "I think the book will find us."

## 15

### Watch That Man

✪

As the missing car in the driveway had cued me, Jan wasn't home. Out with Harrison again, no doubt. His timing couldn't have been better; he was keeping her happy and completely out of my hair.

I made myself something to eat and went into the living room. It was surreal. Every time I thought of myself in Char's catacombs, I felt secure and right, like that was where I should be. Then, if I thought about school and home, that felt pretty okay too. Not particularly exciting or glamorous, but right as well. It was only when I tried to combine the two of them in my mind, magic and normality, that I ran into problems.

What was I going to do in the future? Where was my mother in all my plans? What would happen to Jan when I started pursuing magic? Someday, I'd have to chose, which meant another kick in the complacency for me.

Jan arrived home just before I went to bed. We exchanged few words. I was reluctant to talk a lot about the horseback riding for fear I would say too much, like I had with Rae. It was bad enough I'd talked about Char, even if I hadn't said his name.

Now, lying in the darkness, that forbidden name hovered on my lips. How long had it been since I'd given voice to it? Had I said it more than once, that time when I'd repeated it in his presence. "Char," I breathed. It still had a chill to it, that one staccato syllable. When he'd said it to me, *"Hunt calls me Char. . ."* I had felt a shiver of destiny. *When,* I had wondered, *would I have lived so long that my own original name was forgotten?* "Maggie Stuart" as a transitory thing. I could be, in time, anyone I wanted, or be like Char himself, beyond the point where a single name suited.

✪

The phone rang at precisely 8:05 am Monday morning, a time when Jan was guaranteed to be on the road to work and I was at least conscious, if not quite moving. Today, I was eating breakfast slowly while I did the homework I'd neglected the previous evening, forgoing the coffee I knew would just make me shake more. I seemed to be a bundle of anxiety lately.

"Hello," I said, not recognizing the number. Usually I left the phone to ring, since 99% of the time it was for Jan. Heck, let's just admit the truth—it was *always* for Jan. This morning, I'd answered solely because it was a 647 number that came up on the call display, usually a Toronto cell prefix, and I hadn't yet managed to ask all the players in my little drama for their cellphone numbers. A girl can hope.

It wasn't anyone I immediately recognized. "Maggie Stuart?" said a woman's voice. The use of my last name immediately negated the possibility of even a marginal friend. I instantly felt panic. What had I done wrong, to warrant some kind of official call? My first thought—the school has finally noticed my incredibly poor attendance. The office was out to get me.

I made a non-committal kind of noise, hoping that maybe they would think I was Jan and give me more information than they would if they knew it was the girl in question.

But the caller had already decided she'd got me. "Maggie, check the paper this morning. GT8, sidebar." And the line went dead.

I stood holding the receiver for a moment, certainty sweeping over me. Yes, it had definitely been Carla Szaba. Constable Carla. What the heck was she doing feeding me info?

I picked up the Toronto Star that Jan always got. I usually did the Sudoku if I'd left myself enough time in the morning before leaving for school, but besides the comics, didn't bother with much else. GT was the Greater Toronto section, peculiar to the Star, which got me thinking uncomfortably that Szaba actually knew what paper we got. That wasn't much of a stretch, really, given what I assumed must be the vast scope of police resources and the commonness of public taste, but still.

On the page in question, my eye was caught almost immediately by the name of my school. I started at the end of the piece and scanned back. It was all of an inch and a half of column space, but I saw the point instantly.

I wasn't exactly sure how far Square One was from here, even though I had been there lots of times to the big mall with Jan. It wasn't in Westbrook but nearby. I'd haul out the TTC map we kept stashed in a kitchen junk drawer by the phone to figure it out, or better yet just do a Google search. The gist was simple though. Dead body, middle-aged woman. Cause of death undetermined. Just like the dogs and cats and squirrels. The only bizarre note was that she'd been barefoot, her feet walked bloody.

The last line of the article read, "Mrs. Sanchez had been employed as a cafeteria worker at John F. Diefenbaker High School in Westbrook until her disappearance."

That sparked a faint memory of listening in on the cafeteria supervisor at Dief going ballistic over someone not showing for work. When had that been? Obviously after the sprained ankle and blood et al —that had been the first day of school, after all. Not long into September for certain.

And that led me to the memory of Aaron Scribner posing the possibility that the. . . things. . . that had escaped from the circle might just find the warmth of a human body a nice place to bunk down. Mrs. Sanchez, vanished from Dief. Dead for days and days in the parking lot at Square One until she'd started to smell and someone had bothered to call it in. No reason to think there was any connection to me, or the others, except for that cryptic call from Carla Szaba. Had she overhead something, listening in on one of John Tamblyn's calls? Or did she have other sources for mysterious information?

I clipped the article, then put the paper into the recycling in the garage. Let Jan be surprised I'd actually cleaned something up, but please, just don't let her notice that I'd cut something out. That was a conversation I definitely didn't feel like having. I was happy enough to have her think I didn't care much about anything. It was just—easier.

✪

I heard the screams, with everyone else in the wing during third my lunch period the next day. I'd returned to the area where I'd seen the phantom the previous Friday, just to see if it was trying to tell me something or if the purpose of its appearance had in fact just been to screw with me. I was closer than most people who responded, but then again, I also was more reluctant than most to leave what I was doing and go.

Once I had committed myself though, a feeling of urgency took over. I started to run, following the shrieks, down one truncated flight of stairs, around an odd-angled corner, and into the tech wing.

I had expected to somehow be connected with what was happening; my conceit would allow nothing else. But I'd also expected whatever link there was to be tenuous, perhaps even hidden from me. This was not the case.

The lights were dim in the hallway, with none of the overheads on, just sunlight sneaking in furtively from the half-buried windows high in the walls. The sense of deja vu intensified. What was I remembering? I recognized a few of the other faces around the stricken figure on the floor—none of the ritual circle, however. Or so I thought, until I realized who it was crouching on the ground.

Suzanne's blond hair was out of its usual ponytail, but she was instantly identifiable. I pushed the gathering crowd back to get through and knelt down.

She had stopped screaming, but continued to make jerking breathy noises, like she was still yelling but had lost her voice. Even I was asking myself why I was getting involved, I felt a surge of something—I hated seeing a person like this. The other people around weren't reacting sensibly as far as I was concerned. Why does no one know what to do in an emergency?

She was thrashing around. A couple of people tried to hold onto her arms. But she wasn't hurt, that was easy to see. She was scared. I can recognize that miles off.

I was close enough to hear anything she might say, but I also was loathe to take an active role this time. What could I do? It wasn't like I would be able to reassure her. The last thing I needed at this point were more lies on my conscience.

Moving in, I helped Suzanne to her feet. The crowd was hanging further back with each uneventfully passing moment. Whatever had scared her was not to be a matter of public broadcast. Over and over,

Suzanne was repeating that best of bluff lines: "I'm fine, really," and "I was just being stupid."

She recognized me as the person who'd helped her up as I released her arm. Her lips narrowed, but she said nothing to me. By this time too, she had retrieved her cellphone and was texting furiously. To Rae?

"I'm fine," she said again, still not for my benefit. "I got scared; I thought I saw something. But I was wrong."

"Suzanne—" I began, but she didn't hear me. Or pretended not to. The couple of people who'd first come to her aid were still hanging around, and her attention was on them, reassuring them that she was all right. No, she didn't need to go to the nurse's office; no, she didn't feel faint. *Thanks, and the next time you're in distress, I'm your girl.* That kind of crap. Very much the popular girl dispensing gracious words.

Aaron showed up, just as Suzanne finally got rid of the last of her well-wishers. I looked for the others, but apparently he was the only one of the original conspirators who would show. That meant I knew exactly who she'd been texting, before she'd barely got back on her feet. I stepped back against the wall, realizing I was unwanted but unsure of how to make a strong exit.

"What happened?" he asked Suzanne, with barely a glance in my direction. There was something about the way he looked at her, all friendly and concerned, that made my blood heat up. There must be something more than just-friends between them. Not that I cared. *No sir-ee.*

I missed the first part of the explanation, and only caught what she said last.

"And then," Suzanne was telling Aaron, "I saw a man, standing at the end of the hall. He didn't look like he was paying any attention, but I couldn't figure out why he was there at all. He wasn't looking for anything, or at anything. And then, I thought I'd seen him before. I can't remember where, but I know I did. It doesn't seem threatening, I know, but—it was just the way he turned in my direction and looked at me. Do you think he was. . . ?"

In league with, or one of, the demons.

"They can take corporeal form, or seem to," I said without thinking, or maybe only thinking as far as my own experience before lunch.

Aaron looked at me quizzically. "Inside someone's body? Or just on their own?"

I hadn't told them about the one which had appeared to me as Mr. Thurl—or the one which had looked like Aaron, down to the smear of blood on his glasses. The one that ran me into the wall was just embarrassing. Now wasn't the time, I told myself. "What did he look like?" I addressed Suzanne, ignoring Aaron.

"Average height, I mean not very tall," she said. "He had dark brown hair, or maybe black, very neat and pretty short-cut. Like a businessman would have it done. Pronounced widow's peak, slicked back, very Dracula." Trust her to notice a hair-style. "Mid-forties, maybe. I think he was wearing a kind of casual, dark suit, but it was under a black leather coat. Dark glasses too."

Hunt was keeping an eye on all of us, then. Who else could it have been? "He was wearing dark glasses, but you could tell he was looking directly at you?"

She stiffened, shrugged. I was being rude again. Oh, well. Sue me, Suzanne. I pressed on.

"Where did he go?"

"I don't know," she said testily.

I rolled my eyes. It was unintentional, but Aaron was instantly on my case.

"She's been terrorized, and you act like it's her fault. Come on, Suzanne. I'll get you a drink, and you can tell me about it."

"Yeah," she said, shooting me a glancing look that wasn't particularly inviting. "Let's bust a move."

I hadn't been specifically banned from following, so I tagged along toward the cafeteria, telling myself I was only going along to do some leg-work regarding the Mrs. Sanchez lead. The crowd had lost interest. Everyone obviously thought Suzanne had just been hysterical, which was partly true, or screwing around. I never would have screamed. I mean, I had already encountered three apparitions, worse than the one she thought she'd seen—well, maybe not the last, the one in the barn. But I had handled myself just fine each time, and her "demon" too, none of this panic and fear.

Aaron ignored me, but Suzanne kept casting little glances over her shoulder as we walked, me trailing behind as if I'd been going that way myself anyhow. She looked at least as afraid of me as she had been of the demon or whatever. I wondered if she seriously thought Hunt was a demon. Maybe in a sense he was. I shouldn't be too hard on her. She could hardly know any better.

I was trying to decide if I liked the look she gave me. Here was the awe I had been cultivating. *Maggie, consorter with the unknown, Princess of...* But heck, there was no respect there. I thought, if anything, she probably despised me. Either that, or just wanted me to get lost. It seemed like she didn't mind spending time with Aaron, in any case. I wish they'd make up their minds. Did they want my help, or not? Would they start ignoring me again as soon as this thing was settled?

✪

It was with a certain amount of relief I found myself leaving school just behind Suzanne at the end of the day.

Once my initial pique had settled, I'd been chastising myself all afternoon for my bad behavior. I liked to think of myself as anti-social, but not necessarily rude as I'd been with Suzanne, with whom I'd been reprehensibly unsympathetic while critiquing the actions of everyone else in the hallway unfavorably. I always thought of hypocrisy as one of my greatest pet peeves. It turned out that, given the opportunity, I was the hypocrite Queen.

"Hey, Suzanne," I called.

She let me catch up, but showed no emotion when I fell into step beside her.

"I hoped I could find you. I want to apologize. I was a bitch earlier. There's no excuse. I should have been more helpful. I—I've been there, right? Scared and confused."

She stopped and fixed me with a pitying gaze. "Maggie. Even your apologies sound like crap."

Her mouth kinked up at the corner then, and she rolled her eyes. "Look, don't sweat it. I just really want to know what happened, why he scared me so much, and if it was anything to worry about. You know, I kind of feel like I'm on the edge of all this."

We started walking again, and she continued.

"Like, I wasn't really part of organizing the whole thing in the first place, so somehow I'm immune from the effects. You know what I mean?"

I nodded. "Like your name is somehow not attached to it."

"Yeah. Like, even though there are dead animals around my place too, I'm not as involved, so if there's danger, it won't be aimed at me. Today was a wake-up call, and I hated it."

I found myself reaching my hand out to squeeze her shoulder. We stopped again in the road, other students passing without comment, isolated in our own little bubble of conversation.

"Suzanne," I said, with difficulty. I wanted to give her something, some kind of comfort, but I couldn't bring myself to actually mention his name. "I—I've been up against this guy before. We can't afford to underestimate him. I won't say there's no danger, because I don't know. But I do promise you this. Every time there's a chance, I will put myself between you guys and him. If I can't handle him entirely, at least I can maybe absorb some of the damage."

She tilted her ear to her shoulder as if trying to hear what I was saying in a different way. "If he's dangerous. . ."

"I don't know. He's not the one who's killing the dogs and cats, I'm pretty sure of that. And he's not one of those things. He's a real human being, for whatever that's worth. But he might understand why it's happening, and how to make it stop."

"You can't. . . What would you do, if you were going to get him to help us?"

I wasn't quite sure that had been what I was suggesting, that Hunt could be an asset, albeit a dangerous one. "I don't know if he would help. I'm not sure why he's here. He may not know why either." I thought back to Westbrook Elementary, and how Hunt had been drawn there by Char's search for me. "Maybe he became aware of us because of the ritual, and he doesn't quite know what's going on himself. But he'd never admit he wasn't right on top of everything, so we may never be able to figure him out."

She shook her head and we starting going again. "Man, it just gets more bizarre."

We were silent for a bit, as if that had summed up everything we needed to say to each other. Then Suzanne spoke again just as we reached the end of the street and prepared to go our separate ways.

"So, you'll tell everyone? About this guy?"

And I saw the mistake I'd made. "Ah, no. Actually. Probably not a good idea to talk about him in front of the rest of them. It should be our secret for now."

Because Jason, Aaron, and Scott knew Hunt in a different context, as our grade eight science teacher. If they remembered him at all. And because I wanted to have at least that much control.

Suzanne looked back at me once over her shoulder as she left me. I don't know what the look on her face meant: something milder than contempt but definitely nowhere near *like*. That was fair. I deserved worse, I figured. Just how was someone supposed to navigate friendships and cliques and all the crap that came with being a teenager? If Suzanne was less than warm, it mirrored my treatment of Irene. Is that what I was? The middle section of a pyramid of desirability, trying to climb to the next step on the heads of whoever came below?

There wasn't much use in hating myself, or examining the situation. There were more important things to think about. Dead animals. Lying to the police—or rather telling the truth where a lie would have been much safer. Hunt.

And as if my thinking about him had conjured him, there he was, standing across the street and a little ways down, very close in fact to where Suzanne had crossed only moments before.

Watching.

He gave a little smile and inclined his head. Hateful bastard. *I see you, Maggie May, and I know who your friends are.*

I realized I had no idea what the current state of affairs was with Jason and the others. Were there still animals dying around their houses, or was that a thing of the past? Was the *problem* Jason had first approached me about, in fact, a thing of the past? Or had we just changed one set of circumstances for a new one in which Hunt was the major player? I didn't know if I'd maybe want the animal-killers back, if that was the choice.

I hoped Hunt could see me rolling my eyes before I turned and went to get myself a coffee. I wanted an excuse to sit down and forget that my heart was racing, or at the very least, blame it on too much caffeine.

## 16

## Right On Mother

○

The next morning, I was actually running a bit ahead of time, so I thought I'd stop in early to Mr. Thurl's class and get caught up with my homework for drafting.

Mr. Thurl hailed me when I came through the door and invited me into the drafting office. The morning light was soft in the glass block windows, but the lights were on and dispelled any tangible memories of my interview here with Hunt.

"Maggie—have a seat."

I did, easing myself down as he pulled himself in behind his small desk and picked up a pen. He was concerned about something—that was obvious in the way he played with the pen and kept his eyes low. Poor man. My manner relaxed a bit.

"Maggie, we have to talk." He replaced the pen in the mug which held other writing implements—green overhead markers, blue drafting pencils, thin black pens for final sketches—and opened a binder. I remembered then that there was an assignment due from me today, one for which I had already received a two-week extension, claiming family difficulties. Of course he knew I didn't have it with me.

"I hate to say this, especially to a bright student. Maggie, you know I've been pulling for you. I know you can do the work, I do. And we both know you've succeeded when you've applied yourself. But you can't float yourself forever on potential and good intentions. At some point, the office is going to take a look at your attendance record, if they're not already concerned. We don't want that."

"Mr. Thurl, about the assignment. . ." I tried.

He carried on as if he hadn't heard me. Maybe he didn't want to.

"Maggie, you have to start coming to class. Just be present, and I know you'll pick up on enough to at least manage a pass. And who knows, you might just get turned on by something and find a reason to be here. Maybe you'll find something here you aren't getting. . . elsewhere.

"I'm not so concerned about the project as I am about you," he continued. He fixed me with his pale eyes. "You're having problems at home, aren't you?"

I tried not to register surprise, but he had caught me off guard. I had hardly seen Jan for the better part of a week. I could hardly think of one thing she'd said to me in the past month. If she'd upset me, it was more likely to be because of my mind-set than any friction between us. I was too preoccupied with everything else.

"No," I protested. "Everything's fine."

He pursed his lips in that annoying adult way that as much says, *"Don't lie to me, young lady."* I felt myself growing irritated.

"Look," I said. "I'm fine. Well, I'm not *fine*, but Jan and I are doing peachy."

"Maggie," he said, severely. "I haven't watched you through all these tough times to turn my back on you now. But you have to admit when there are problems, and you have to face them. More important, you have to talk to someone about what's going on in your life, and your plans for the future. I won't be able to pass you forever on your potential alone."

I was stunned, although I shouldn't have been. You try anyone's patience enough, it's bound to give. I guess I had never thought that that basic rule of human nature would apply to someone as generally yielding as Mr. Thurl.

"I think it's time I made some changes," I said slowly.

"That's a good girl," Mr. Thurl replied, and I felt him getting distant, as if he was already moving on to the next business of the day.

"No, I mean it." I was boiling. "Maybe it's time to look carefully at my timetable. Maybe I should have a therapy session every day until I can behave myself. Maybe I should commit myself for just a bit in some cosy psych ward until I can stop being a hassle for everyone."

"Maggie—" Mr. Thurl warned. "Calm down; I'm not your enemy. You're—"

"—your own worst blah blah blah, yeah I know," I finished with him. "I've got just about all the enemies I need right now, without pop psychology creating more, thanks very much."

The early bell rang, and I escaped without a backward glance. I wasn't sure if I was glad or furious that he didn't even call after me.

✪

At lunchtime, I reclaimed my place in the auditorium for some well-deserved utter solitude. After the scene with Mr. Thurl that morning I didn't want to become anyone else's pet project. I definitely didn't want to take a chance on running into Irene in the halls; I hadn't said a word or even looked at her since the strangeness between classes and my vanishing man.

I took my paints, but didn't get further than filling the water dish before I got bored, or distracted. Both, probably.

I wanted that book, and I wanted to talk to Peter. I wanted to make a difference, to make some progress on something in my life, and it really looked like that *something* was not destined to have anything to do with school. Please, let me succeed at *anything*. Nothing much else mattered.

✪

The next day, I skipped drafting, but actually made it to second. Irene shot me a half-smile when I got to class only a minute late. Feeling lonely and, more to the point, ashamed of the way that I'd been thinking of her, I risked my lunch hour privacy to say hi to her in the hall after class. Maybe it wasn't so much of a risk as a chance, since the previous day in the auditorium had depressed me more than I wanted to remember. And maybe she was more gracious about my rudeness than I deserved.

"Hey, Irene," I called, catching her at her locker.

Despite my anticipation that she'd be glad to see me, Irene seemed a lot less happy to wait for me than she had been closer to the beginning of the semester. Or it might have had everything to do with my brush-off after the running-into-a-wall incident. "Maggie," was her cool reply to my shout.

"What's up?" I asked. I leaned up against the locker beside her, keeping a sharp eye out for Jason or any of his cronies.

She shrugged and closed the locker, a brown paper bag now in her hands.

"Want to—" I began.

She stared expectantly.

I'd committed myself, I guessed. "I was going to sit under the bleachers for lunch. I've got some reading to do, but if you want just to go and sit—"

She shrugged. Good. Yes, good. I guess my company was as of little interest to her as hers was to me. Fine. Without anything else said, she followed me downstairs (and then up a stupid little jog— the school was frustrating me badly today) and out to the playing field where I'd staked out a new lunch spot in the shade by the playing field, tucked in under the stands.

Despite wanting to make some gesture to Irene, I didn't want her invading my sanctuary in the auditorium. I hadn't managed to swing a key to the costume room yet either, which testified to my utter inability to get it together this year. Last year, those sparks of bureaucratic wrangling had been my only real day-to-day excitement. Now I suddenly had magic circles and vanishing books and an encroaching past. No others need apply.

And that was it, really. We didn't talk, except when we compared notes on something that had happened in the one class we shared. I felt like I'd done something which should have, by all rights, been generous, and yet I felt awkward and quite hypocritical. She bored me, and I was boring to be around when I was with her.

I figured it said a lot for my feelings on the matter of Irene when I hadn't asked her to share my refuge in the auditorium, but had chosen neutral, meaningless territory instead. I was suddenly even more lonely than if I'd spent the time alone.

I'd have to find a way to talk myself out of trying. I went to the coffee shop after school, hoping I might run into Aaron, just kind of casually. Unless, of course, he was with Suzanne.

✪

*That night, I have a dream I seem to remember from my public school days: deja vu within a dream? At least, I'm back at Westbrook Elementary. That is, I'm there, but outside the high chain link fence surrounding the playing field. Inside its boundaries, I can see the entire school population spread out in recess activities. Some are playing basketball or four square on the tarmac. A group of other kids have organized a pick-up softball game with a stick for a bat.*

*By the size of the ones I recognize, I'm back further in time than my grade eight year, the last I spent at Westbrook. I see a few familiar faces—Tiffany, my grade two nemesis who teased me mercilessly about my near-silence in class, Bill Armistead who was one of Jason's cronies until they drifted apart in grade seven, possibly because Bill started smoking pot and stopped playing sports. I am scanning the crowd for those faces I really want to see: Jason, Aaron, even Scott. Circling the fence, I see them, over by the jungle gym. Scott holds the book under one arm, and his free hand holds Peter's. The smaller boy is just as I saw him in the Saunders' backyard, but the other guys are shrunken back to maybe grade four or five levels, before their respective growth spurts. In those days, I was about the same size as them, maybe even a little taller than Aaron. I got all my growth early.*

*I pass the place in the fence where, in the waking world, there would have been a opening to enter the schoolyard. Here, nothing. I feel a surge of fear, and fight against it. Maybe I'm not there yet. I keep walking, pulling myself along the chain link with my hand, but there's nothing but a continuous, unbroken fence. No gaps, no gate. When I reach the place where I expect the fence to end, up by the school's driveway, it goes on. I lean around the corner, and see it stretch unbroken to infinity.*

*Panicking now, I turn back the way I came and run along the fence, banging it with the flats of my palms, unable to call out. Beyond the fence, the schoolyard has shrunk to bring the group of boys I want most to join up close, the climbers just beyond where I stand separated from them by chain link. Jason! I am screaming, but nothing comes out. This range of fence too stretches away to vanish at last in the distance. I push my fingers through the links, wedge my sneaker in a lower diamond and lift myself up, meaning to scale my way into their company, but when I turn my face to the sky, the barrier goes up and up, right into the clouds.*

*I'm still frantically trying to get in when I wake, out of breath and about to cry.*

## 17

## Scary Monsters

✪

The next day, as I left second period on my way to one of my hidey-holes for lunch, Jason hailed me.

"Hey," I said, trying not to look pleased.

"You up for a lunch-time meeting, Mags?" he said.

I shrugged.

"You know where I live?"

I had the list in my notebook, of course, but I had never been there. "Kind of," I said, admitting as little to my ignorance as possible.

"The guys are all coming, so I guess we can walk over together."

I agreed and grabbed my coat.

It was a nice walk, just crisp enough to be invigorating. We talked about current films, which was also refreshing. I couldn't remember the last time I had discussed pop culture with anyone except Jan. I went to movies sometimes, but always on my own so I never really had the chance. It was easier, and cheaper, anyhow, just to download what I wanted to watch at home.

But when you're solitary by nature, movies can make you feel social even when you're not. Apparently, studies have found that people consider any face they see repeatedly as belonging to a friend, even if that person is on a television or movie screen. So I guess going to the movies was my way of having a social life.

All this was in the back of my mind as we walked and chatted, and I couldn't help imagining a future where I would maybe get a chance to go to the movies with Jason, or Aaron, or even Rae. Wouldn't it be great?

*Down, girl.*

Jason's place was nice, a long sloping driveway topped with a basketball hoop and a full-sized hockey net showing around the side of the garage. It was your typical suburban ranch, not unlike where I lived. From Jason himself, though, in his confessions to me in the catacombs, I knew maybe a little more than I would have wanted about what can go on behind closed doors in the suburbs.

Everyone was there before us; Scott apparently had the key, which he passed back to Jason as we came into the kitchen. It was a sweet little gesture of trust I hoped I might be able to offer someone someday, or be offered myself. It was ridiculous the kind of thing that made me misty-eyed.

We gathered around the island in the middle of the kitchen, a big wooden block counter that was waist-high on Jason and Scott, almost mid-chest for me, and somewhere in between for Aaron, Suzanne, and Rae.

They were all looking at me in an expectant way, as I unpacked my lunch as they had already done. I braced myself, and took my time, but when it became obvious they were waiting for me, I gave in. "What's up, then?"

Jason glanced at the others. "Do you want to tell us about your mystery man?"

"My—"

"Suzanne's mystery man, then," said Aaron, and Suzanne had the grace to blush slightly and look down.

"It's not her fault," said Rae, quickly. "She was really going to keep your confidence. It's just that he's been. . . following us around."

I must have looked shocked, because she hastened to add, "No, he hasn't initiated any contact. But he's been pretty obvious. Suzanne was just as obviously hiding something from us about it."

Scott, rolling his eyes, told me, "We beat it out of her, if it makes you feel any better."

I sighed, trying to grab a moment to collect my thoughts. "Uh. . ." *Great, Mags,* I told myself. *What an articulate response.* "I didn't mean for Suzanne to lie to you." *Yes, I did.* "I just wanted to protect you." It hadn't occurred to me that Hunt would show himself to any of the others. I felt, of all things, cheated. Like by letting them see him, he was being unfaithful to me.

"From. . ." said Jason, leaving the ellipsis big enough to see.

"He could be dangerous, or he could be nothing," I said. "I'm not sure he's involved, and even if he is, I don't know how or if it's important. The main thing is that he likes to make you think he knows more than he does, and he likes to intimidate."

Scott looked as me as if to say, *yeah, well, duh*. Or maybe, *like someone else we know, Mags?*

"I don't know if he's got anything to do with any of this. But I'm certain he's not harming the animals. That's something far less natural than him."

I saw, with reasonable disappointment, how little we'd actually accomplished since that first day at school. Not thinking about what I was doing, I fingered the ring, and made a snap decision, knowing even as I did that it was a terrible idea.

I reached to the back of my neck and unfastened the chain. "I have something to show you," I said, and drew out Arabella's ring.

Somehow, even without context, it was impressive. I heard Scott draw a breath, and Rae's eyes narrowed. The kitchen was bright, but the red stone in the ring glowed with more than ambient light.

"Wow," said Suzanne. I figured she'd probably be the most likely of the bunch to be able to put a monetary value to the piece on sight.

Aaron looked at me instead of the ring. "What is it?" he said, not the type to take something at face value.

"It's an artifact, of something like what we're chasing." That wasn't particularly accurate, but I wasn't about to repeat my mistake at Rae's of giving out a part of the truth I'd immediately have to retract.

He reached out for it, and I put it in his hand before I had time to consider the wisdom of the move.

And, horrified, I watched Aaron do what was utterly unthinkable for me. He put it on.

Because it was Arabella's ring, he could only put it on his pinky finger. He drew it past the second knuckle and held up his hand to see the stone in the light. "It looks. . . wrong," he said. "I can't figure out why."

My breath had stopped, I realized, and my heart was beating ten times too fast. What had I thought would happen? I only knew that when Arabella had worn the ring, she'd used it to deal death. I didn't know whether it could be used for anything else. All I knew was what it had done to Damon, consuming him from the inside out. I hadn't seen him die, but I knew he was past hope when Char appeared and banished me from the room. To put the ring on my own finger—it was not even possible to imagine it.

Aaron slid it off and handed it to Rae, who did the same thing. This time, my reaction wasn't quite as strong, but I still felt sick. What had I expected when I handed it to him? A ring is meant to be worn. How could he know what that would mean to me in the case of this particular piece of jewellery?

Rae said only, "Beautiful," before passing it along to Suzanne. Suzanne tried it on then handed it to Scott, who didn't. I held the chain limply in my hands. Suddenly, I wasn't so sure I wanted it back myself. Maybe I could get Jason to hold onto it for me, and he could put it back in the safety deposit box for me, so I'd never have to touch it again.

Jason reached out to take the ring from Scott, and I felt a weird electricity in the air. It had to be my imagination, but as Jason's fingers touched the gold of the band, I could swear. . .

"It's dead," Jason said, and turned the stone toward me. My stomach churned. The red stone was red no more. It was a matte, jet black, light-consuming, no longer shiny or bright. Dead was the right word. I had never thought of the ring as alive, although maybe that was the right word for it. It had never felt like an *object* exactly, but always something more, something with a life and a history. But Jason was right. The stone was black, and the ring was lifeless in a way I'd never seen it.

"What, is it like a mood ring?" Jason joked. "I guess I'm too cool for school."

Aaron reached out for it, and Jason passed it back to him. And the stone was red again.

Jason. I could hardly breath. Just like in the catacombs. Something about him. Something *in* him. It made him different.

Jason took the ring back and the stone blackened again. He laughed. "I'm feeling kind of insulted," he said.

I suddenly wanted this farce over. I reached out my hand and Jason stretched his hand across the island to return it.

Our fingers met with a palpable sizzle. The red stone flared to brilliance, just for a fraction of a second, and for that same instant I could swear that not only had the kitchen lights dimmed but the sunlight coming through the window had been momentarily eclipsed as well.

I gasped, and I think Rae did the same. Jason snatched his fingers back as if he'd been shocked, or burned.

"Wow," he said, "you have been keeping all the best tricks to yourself."

Aaron recovered quickly. "What the hell did you do?" he asked me, but I knew the truth. It wasn't me, it was Jason. Jason killed the ring, like he'd killed Char's magic ball, like he'd killed my powers when I held his hand in the catacombs. When the discharge of my power had been enough to shatter iron manacles and knock both of us and Aaron Scribner unconscious.

It was pretty clear that Aaron thought it was some trick of mine, something I'd done, that had caused the reaction. I knew better. It was Jason. Jason's *dampening*. If I had done it, it would have been a trick worthy of the way I'd behaved so far, keeping all the best secrets until they could be presented most dramatically. But this was unexpected and unwelcome to say the least. I had just proved that Jason retained whatever it was that made him so valuable to Char, while I had nothing for myself.

Then, realizing I couldn't possibly stomach my lunch, was suddenly not sure I could even keep what I'd already eaten down, I asked Jason where the washroom was. He followed me along the hall.

And he was there when I came out of the bathroom again.

"Pulling enigma on us, Mags. Don't know if I like that," said Jason.

"I don't like it either. I don't know what to do." I turned away from him, frowning. I wanted to say, *it would be a big load off my mind if I did—would you help me carry this burden like I'm helping you?* But I didn't. I clammed up.

"Maggie..." said Jason, warning. "I want you to be honest with me."

"If I could tell you, you know I would. But it doesn't really matter anyway." I hoped, at least.

Something in my expression must have warned him not to pursue the subject any further at that moment. Either that, or some boy-issue sixth sense was telling him I was going to burst into tears if I tried to say anything else.

Then, the perverse side of me took over. I wanted to lash out, punish him for still having magic, even if his power was just to negate whatever magic anyone, or anything, had.

"Jason. I know about the secret you carry."

Even as I said it, I knew I was going low, low like a snake on its belly. "Sarah, and then you. I know. And I will protect that secret with my life."

He looked at me at first with confusion, then something in his eyes morphed through wonder straight to panic. I had never really seen a person freeze before, not really. But he did. He froze, and I saw tears start to form in his eyes. In that instant, he went from confident, charismatic Jason Lawson to something with as much spine as a jellyfish. I jumped forward and braced him against the wall, because if I hadn't, he would have slumped to the floor.

"Jason," I whispered desperately. "I'm sorry, I'm so so sorry. I didn't mean to do this. I didn't mean..."

He stared through me, and I felt his pulse through his skin, beating like he was sprinting. His eyes were vacant; I didn't think he could see or hear me.

"Jason, please. Come back, please come back to me!"

A light kindled in his eyes and he turned his head to put me out of his eye-line. A thought occurred to me, and I felt even lower than I did for using his personal horror to divert him from chastising me. Had he even remembered this before? Had I just done to him what I'd done to Tamblyn, reminded him of something terrible that he'd been blessed to forget when I worked the magic on that bluff?

"I'm okay," he said, his voice steady. He didn't exactly brush me off, but he didn't use me to help him brace himself. I could actually feel the strength flood back into his legs as he pushed himself away from the wall. Then, he looked down at me. I felt smaller than usual beside him. He was at least a foot taller than me, but it usually didn't register. Now it did.

But he didn't say anything. He just stared at me, through me, as if willing me to vanish as he locked whatever memory I had awakened back in its dark vault.

"Jason—" I began again, but he shook his head. I had forgotten my previous nausea, but now it came flooding back.

I turned, planning to bolt toward the washroom. But just at that moment, something strange happened. It was like a blip in the corner of my eye as I turned my head, something behind Jason that caught my attention.

"What?" he asked, noticing my gaze go over his shoulder.

"On the shelf. . ." I said, and walked into the Lawson's living room. There were lots of knickknacks, and small objets d'art, and some books, some quite old. Typical suburban mishmash of chic and tack, I thought, but there was something I'd seen. *No, it couldn't be that.*

*Look*—I said to myself, but my eyes kept scanning. What had caught my attention so briefly but so urgently? And there it was. And then, there it wasn't.

"I saw it," I said, my voice going a little shrill. "The book. Didn't you?" Already, I was beginning to doubt what I thought I'd seen. Thought I'd seen. Right. Very large doubts.

"No," said Jason. His eyebrows came together in concern. He thought I was going crazy, didn't he?

"It was the book. On the shelf. Larger than a trade paperback, leather-bound, dark metal bands on the spine. This thick." I showed him with my hands. "Green or blue, almost black. Right? Tell me I'm right."

He shook his head, shrugging. "You're right. You know you are. Okay, you saw it. Where is it now?"

"Gone." I passed my hand over the shelf where I'd seen it. Now, I couldn't even tell where it had been.

That was pretty much the end of the lunch meeting.

## 18

## Repetition

✪

I'd managed to skip drafting the day after my little *chat* with Mr. Thurl, so after the abortive lunch meeting, I figured I had better go and see if I could somehow square things with him when I knew he had a spare during fourth. Thinking of trying to do the same with Jason just made me feel raw inside, monumentally disappointed in myself.

Mr. Thurl greeted me when I came through the door. He didn't look displeased to see me, but that vague expression was still there, as if he didn't want to give me his full attention. He ushered me into the office.

"Maggie—have a seat."

I did, conscious of the way history seemed to be repeating itself. I folded my hands in my lap and tried to look like a good girl.

"Maggie, we have to talk. I hate to say this, especially to a bright student. Maggie, you know I've been pulling for you. I know you can do the work, I do. And we both know you've succeeded when you've applied yourself. But you can't float yourself forever on potential and good intentions. At some point, the office is going to take a look at your attendance record, if they're not already concerned. We don't want that."

I nodded at appropriate intervals. It was, as they say, déjà vu all over again. Hang on—it really did sound like exactly the same spiel, didn't it? I was having a serious episode of been there, done that.

He kept on, and I was starting to get uncomfortable. "Maggie, you have to start coming to class. Just be here, and I know you'll pick up on enough to at least manage a pass. And who knows, you might just get turned on by something and find a reason to be here. Maybe you'll find something here you aren't getting... elsewhere."

"Mr. Thurl," I began, and stopped dead. In front of me, I could see Mr. Thurl's face, his blond hair and ruddy face. But he was also in the classroom, in the semi-dark, hovering just beyond the office door, a second Mr. Thurl. Sitting in front of me across the table, and also in the periphery of my vision, with a smirk on his thin lips. Just like the apparition of Thurl in the washroom, another escapee from the circle.

I fought to control myself, returned my focus to the man sitting at the desk in front of me. Mr. Thurl, unaware my attention had been taken elsewhere, filled the silence, oblivious to his döppelganger in the other room, shook his head sadly, waiting for me to go on.

I considered frantically, trying to keep my cool and not let on that anything odd was going on. Would Mr. Thurl even be able to see the other Thurl? Was this show just for my benefit? Were either of them real, for that matter? I couldn't square the moment with my memories of the last interview I'd had with Thurl in this very office.

And, more importantly, was I in danger? Should I go on with my charade of normalcy and resist the urge to rush through the door to banish the thing? If I could. If I had a clue as to exactly why I'd succeeded the times before.

I had begun to dig my fingernails into my palm. Mr. Thurl sat there in front of me, his double hovering at the edge of my vision, the room maddeningly normal with its trickle of sunlight through the windows, the obligatory teacher/screwed-up student interview. I could almost feel the thing's eyes on my back. I had to get out of here, one way or another. I had to get *it* out of here, away from Mr. Thurl, out somewhere I could try to take care of it.

"Mr. Thurl," I began again, interrupting whatever he'd begun to say about taking my present seriously *for the profound effect it would have in the blah-blah-blah...* "Look, I appreciate everything you've done, and are trying to do. You're my favorite teacher, and I think my only cheerleader in this place. Maybe that'll be enough, maybe not. But I need to think this out. I'll be here Monday morning, before the bell, and I'll make an effort, and then if you have time we can talk about it. But right now, I need to go... and think." I got up so hastily I almost knocked the chair over, and fled, closing the door behind me, hoping he wouldn't follow.

It was there, grinning obscenely. Any doubt I had about its true nature evaporated. Whether or not the Thurl in the office was the genuine article, this one was all hell-spawn.

Through the door to the office, I heard Mr. Thurl sit back, his chair creaking, and thought I might be safe to confront it for a moment anyhow.

"You are a pain in the ass," I said quietly, hissing and advancing on it. Caution to the wind, I was pissed off now and angry enough to be brave. "Didn't I get rid of a couple of you before? How many of you things are there anyhow?"

It retreated before me, red-rimmed eyes never leaving mine, and I pushed it toward the door, grateful it was doing what I needed it to.

Mr. Thurl called out from the office, "Maggie?" —realizing, I guess that he hadn't heard the door slam behind me so knew I was still in the classroom. I didn't answer, but the thing melted into the hallway beyond, right through the closed classroom door. I followed in a more pedestrian fashion.

The hallway was empty, classes in session all over the building and no one on the loose but me and my monkey. My extra Thurl lounged against the wall, the smile twisting its lips. I wanted to punch its smug face. My only real ally on staff, and this thing had stolen his shape—twice—and possibly destroyed my relationship with him. Although, in truth, I was just as much to blame for that.

"Tell me," I spat, stepping toward it. It scuttled away, still apparently cool but reactive to my movements. "What do you want? You might as well tell me, because I'm not getting it just from the bad-taste dress-up."

I don't think I really expected it to answer. The Aaron-thing had pretended to be normal, tried to fool me by just being Aaron accurately except for the red eyes. But this thing was anything but, an obscene mockery of nice Mr. Thurl.

"What do we want?" Its voice was a hoary whisper, as if it were more worried about being overheard than I. "We want. We want."

I rolled my eyes. *Great.* "Pathetic," I said out loud.

In response, it began to laugh, still quietly and with a cracked, painful sound. "Why don't you come down to play?" it said. "Down to play. Down, down, down. Deeper in is the only way out."

That seemed like something I'd heard before. "To the catacombs?" I said, coldness spreading through me as I said the word. "To the quarry?"

It laughed again. "Bring your bauble, your pretty. Bring your man." It smiled more broadly, something even more foul in the expression. "Bring the book, if you can."

I tensed, but I had to get what I could out of this encounter. Was I in danger? It didn't seem so. I was scared, but if it had wanted to hurt me, it had already had ample opportunity. It hadn't even blown my ordinary-student cover when it had the chance in the drafting room. And when did a little fear kill anyone?

"You said bring my man. Who's my man?"

I could guess at the rest. The book, the ring. And someone.

It leaned closer and I sprang back. "Touchy, touchy," it said, with something of the mockery I remembered from Arabella. "Touchy, like you want to be with your man. Like you want to be with him. Bring him. There's a prize waiting. A prize, and nothing."

"I really hate riddles," I told it, trying to hold my ground as it stretched out a ruddy hand. Even the calluses looked the same, just like the hand Mr. Thurl had just used in his office to pick up a pen. "You annoy me, creature. I banish you."

I don't know what I expected, but what happened probably wasn't it. Its two Mr. Thurl hands reached out and grabbed my shoulders, pulling me close. I smelt its breath, like an ice-swept version of my McDonald's boss's foul concoction of booze and nicotine, felt the chill in it on my lips. "We want this," it whispered, and vanished into mist, then nothing.

*We want this.* Nothing but that before it was gone. I was none the wiser, and my heart was beating ten times faster than it should.

✪

When I got home, I heard music and laughter filtering up from the finished basement. Down there was our nominal rec room, with the big TV and stereo. We didn't entertain much, Jan and I, and we were both more likely to use the little TV in the living room on the main floor if we were just watching the news or something, especially if we were using it as background while on the computer.

I checked out the front drive, and saw a red sports thingy in addition to Jan's sensible grey sedan. I had come through the shortcut at the back of the house, so I hadn't had any warning that we had company. It had be the Harrison guy. And, quite possibly, I would have to meet him.

If not, I'd at the very least be wondering all evening if he was planning on staying over. Grownup romance made me distinctly uncomfortable, probably even more than the teenage sort. I got that Jan was probably lonely for adult company (not that she took full advantage of mine, in contrast) but it was just a little freaky to have my mother bringing a date home.

I went to bed long before they did, after having managed to spend the entire evening in my room with the door closed, as insulated as possible from what was going on far below. Mom came up once to make sure I'd eaten something, then disappeared just as quickly back down to where they were, apparently, "catching up on some good TV." I hoped it wasn't one of those late night, creepy soft-core erotica things. And if it was, that I'd never find out.

✪

In the morning, there was noise from the kitchen and I knew I'd have to brave whoever was banging around with the pots and pans if I wanted anything to eat—or more importantly, a cup of coffee. I couldn't see if his car was still in the driveway. My only window looked out the side of the house at the neighbor's blank wall. It was Jan that had the front room on our floor.

The guy in the kitchen was fully dressed—thank goodness. As I watched, he finished selecting a frying pan and started making coffee. He was medium tall and lean-muscled with erect carriage. I remembered something about him playing tennis a lot when he and my mom were first dating; he looked like he might swim or cycle as well.

His smile when I appeared in the door was not particularly warm or friendly, although I could tell he was trying. "You must be Marguerite," he said. "Your mom's sleeping in. I thought I'd get the coffee started."

He'd started a heck of a lot more than that. The ingredients for some laboriously complicated egg thing were neatly laid out on the counter—finely chopped green onions, peppers, tomato, and minced ham along with a perfectly symmetrical mound of cheese. He'd just been making a row of eggs when I interrupted him, setting them out equally spaced on the countertop beside a clean white bowl. If this guy was any more anal, he'd have to forego solid food altogether in favor of consuming his nutrients entirely in capsule form.

"Hey," I said. "Harrison, right?"

I wanted to wander away immediately, but it would be pretty rude. Besides, I wouldn't get coffee if I did. I could put up with a little pseudo-bonding for caffeine.

"Does your mom let you drink coffee?" he asked, pinpointing the direction of my attention.

I hedged, saying, "I usually have a couple of cups a day. On the weekend, I mean. I think it's better for me than pop, at least."

He put out three cups, then started opening cupboards again. "Do you have a tray somewhere?"

"A what?" I didn't have a clue what he was talking about.

"I want to take your mom her breakfast in bed."

Oh. The penny dropped. "I don't know. Never saw one. There's a couple of bigger cutting boards by the stove though. Maybe you could use one of those."

He pulled out a painted wood thing from beside the stove, and seemed satisfied. I guessed it actually was a tray more than a cutting board, with gold and green paint on it and edges that curved slightly up. Who knew?

"Florentine," he said. "Your mom has great taste."

I shrugged. No one had said the words "your mom" to me so many times since my first day of kindergarten. This guy was giving me a creepy vibe. He was doing everything right, I guessed; I just wasn't taking to him.

"So, Marguerite," he said, going back to egg prep, "what do you have planned for the day?"

Nothing, was the truth. After the week I'd had, I was less than enthused about making plans. What a question anyhow. I supposed it probably passed for small talk, but I'd have been happier to deal with, *"Arrgh, matey, show me where your treasures are hid."*

"You know," I said. What would a normal girl say? "Going to meet up with some friends at the mall, maybe go into the city for a movie."

"Cool," he said, the word suiting him about as much as a pair of naked lady mud-flaps would have suited his sports car. I went from not liking him to really loathing him.

Then, he made it worse. He turned to me, and gave me that soft-eyed sincere look adults do when they want to impress upon you how much they're trying to connect with you on your level. "Your mom and I . . ." he began, then backtracked. "Your mother is a special person," he said. "I'd really like us to be friends, for her sake."

That was about as lame as anything I'd ever heard. "Sure, *Harrison*," I said, stressing the fact he hadn't bothered introducing himself to me. "That sounds great."

He smiled and took out the milk and put the sugar on the counter. How many times had this guy been in my house, to know his way around at least as well as I did?

"She's under a lot of pressure at work," he said. "You'll have to be patient with her."

Seriously—he was almost admonishing me. What had Jan said about me? That I was an ungrateful little brat with a nasty demanding streak?

"Patient, got you." I grabbed my mug from beside the coffeemaker, and poured myself a cup, ready or not.

He frowned with obvious disapproval. "She needs to be taken care of, and I think that's something we can both agree on."

"Sooner you than me," I said, snagging my coffee fixings and getting the heck out of the kitchen as fast as I could. What a moron. And, if my memory was right, this was the second, not just the first, time my mom had dated him. Did she remember the first time? Or was she repeating dumb behavior completely subconsciously?

Maybe, maybe I could be friendly enough though that he'd keep Jan occupied enough not to bother me too much. For a little room that way, I could probably manage to be almost civil.

I spent the rest of the day in my room, until mid-afternoon when I was sure he was gone.

19

Sunday

✪

Jan and I had a quiet night, neither of us saying much beyond the necessities. Still, it was kind of nice to have her around; it was the first evening in quite a while that Harrison hadn't been free. And it kind of proved what I'd said so glibly to Mr. Thurl—one of him anyhow. For the first time in a long time, Jan and I were fine.

I watched the late news by myself after Jan went up. Nothing exciting on the world front; the only thing of any interest was a subway fire in Toronto near Royal York station. That was something I'd never even imagined. Subways were like cruise liners. You knew there were accidents, but they seemed so safe compared to everything else. Buses and cars got in crashes all the time. An airplane disaster was uncommon, but highly publicized when it happened. But thousands of people travelled the subway every day, and I'd never heard about anything but a suicide every year or so. Even those seemed to be kept almost religiously quiet.

Jan came back down while the closing credits were rolling and I was trying to convince my bones to lever me off the couch to head upstairs. The only light came from the television. She came into the glow like a ghost in her white dressing gown. It was new, and silk, so either it was a present from him or *for* him. I would bet every time on the latter.

"I think," she said, "I forgot to mention the party at the Saunders' place tomorrow."

I looked at her. This was interesting.

"You probably know that from Scott," she went on.

I didn't. "We're not really friends," I said. *In fact, he can barely find the energy to be civil when I'm around,* I thought.

"I don't know if you want to come along. The invitation was open. I know it's not really your sort of thing."

"No," I said. "I'd like to." Very interesting. I'd wanted a way to get close to Peter, and here it was, the nearest thing I'd ever had to an actual engraved invitation. "Hold on—what was this? An all-neighborhood party call?"

Jan cocked her head. "No, Margaret Saunders and I used to play tennis together. I don't expect you to remember; it was a long time ago. Don't you remember that you and Scott used to be friends?"

This was news to me. "When was that?"

"We moved to the subdivision when you were five, and the Saunders family was living on Dunsinene, just across the backyard. You and Scott were the same age, and Margaret and I used to put you together all the time when we were playing tennis. I have pictures somewhere—"

"Maybe some other time," I said. With my luck, they'd be of me and Scott naked in a bathtub together. "But about the party—it would be okay if I went?"

"Sure," said Jan. "Margaret would probably be thrilled. It's been years since she laid eyes on you."

That settled, she gave me a kiss on top of my head and went up. I followed shortly afterwards. A party at the Saunders' house. Unless I missed my guess, Sunday might be my one and only chance to talk to Peter, a.k.a. Soren Saunders.

✪

Taking stock of my progress on the task Jason had set me later that night was rather dismal. It was getting harder and harder to pretend I'd made any progress. In fact, what progress I had made seemed distinctly negative. *You're cracking up, Mags,* I told myself. And where was the book? Was it waiting for me on some library bookshelf, just hovering there between a dictionary and thesaurus, waiting for its chance to vanish in the instant before I touched its cracked leather?

If I couldn't have it, I wanted a book of my own. I wanted something concrete, something I could hold like I held the ring, but something that offered more of a promise of action. The ring's magical properties were locked away from me, a secret I couldn't crack without the power I had given up.

Or were they? Tamblyn had reacted with recognition, with even a little awe, if I could read him right. Maybe the ring had had some kind of place in the world, some kind of history of interaction with human beings. Maybe its power didn't need me to be magical; maybe it could do something on its own. What else could explain his interest? There must be at the very least some extant lore about it, or it would have aroused no reaction at all. And what could explain Constable Carla's?

I took out my paints, but nothing came to me. Eventually, when it was obvious no kind of inspiration was going to strike tonight, I tucked myself into my bed and held the ring until I fell asleep. And I dreamed.

✪

*I sleep deeply, and fall into dreams.*

*In the dream, I'm on horseback again, but this time it's different. I know what I'm doing. The rasp of the chestnut flanks between my legs is as familiar as the touch of my hair tied back at the nape of my own neck. The horse and I breathe together, exhaling clouds of white into the cool air and then race through our own vapor, tearing it apart with giddy speed.*

*The world is quiet and barely light, some misty, chilly pre-dawn under a cathedral sky. I should be exhilarated by the run, intoxicated by the mad dash of the horse under me, flooded with endorphins from my own straining muscles. But inside, although I know I should be happy, I am dead and colder than the air around me. Why?*

*I pull up at the edge of a cliff, rough stone beginning where scraggly vegetation leaves off and only mist beyond. Faintly, I can see the ocean far below, hear it crash. England? The east coast of Canada? The view is achingly familiar, but I can connect it to nothing but itself. I linger, and the feeling rises in me that I must be gone. I can stay here no longer. The dream is evaporating as the cliff draws itself out to vapor beneath me. I find myself wondering if perhaps this is about to become another falling dream, and close my eyes. My last impression is, perversely, that I am wearing really comfortable boots. . . and I hit the bed.*

✪

Waking in the middle of the night, I flipped on my reading light and tried to put some of the ideas from the dream into pictures, because I'm no great shakes as a writer. Still, nothing came out the way I wanted it to.

Trying to hold onto the fading remainders of it, I fell back into sleep. Now, I was galloping through wild countryside, along the edge of a dizzy cliff. I had a heavy cape or cloak over my shoulders, fur-trimmed and lined. The smell was there again, that mixture of leather and brandy and sweat that was as familiar as my own skin.

It was night, cloudless and moon-lit. It was quite beautiful, except I had a sense of urgency totally out of proportion to anything I could see. Whatever was going on, I was excited and stirred. My heart beat fast; I could hear the blood rushing through my eardrums in time to the thud of my horse's hooves.

When I woke with the first buzz of my alarm, I was almost certain I could remember the horse's name. But by the time the snooze went off, it was lost, and I wasn't sure if I'd ever known it. Just another one of those illusions of dreaming, probably.

✪

It had been no sleep, really. I had managed not to worry about the disappearance of the book, or my upcoming subterfuge at Scott's house. But I had also managed not to rest; I could swear I was just as tired as when I'd gone to bed.

By two o'clock, I was going stir crazy and and was well and truly glad to leave the house. It occurred to me as I was getting ready to go out that I could have called Rae and seen if she was free, but that seemed a bit silly. Of course she'd be busy with her family today. She'd hardly have time for me two weekends in a row, would she? Also, I'd already slipped up once with her. I didn't want to take the chance of something else coming out when I spoke with Peter. *Soren.* Had to get that right—especially around his family.

Jan had dolled herself up in a peach party dress and makeup and was fussing around the house, looking for some nice way to wrap up a bottle of wine she was taking to the party. She was all business superperson lately; this Harrison guy brought it out in her, obviously. Peach was a terrible color for me, but I admit she looked nice. Not my style, but nice. Her hair was honey-blond, a long bob, where mine was brown and well past my shoulders, the color and texture a legacy from my father's side. In the summer, hers lightened to platinum—or maybe she had it done. My mother's beauty secrets were something into which I had absolutely no insight.

I hoped to look at least respectable. It was the least I could do when planning an invasion of someone else's private dwelling, and during a party no less. If Scott saw me looking just like normal jeans-and-hoodie Maggie, he'd know I was up to something. So I found a dress of my own, some thing I hadn't worn for probably four years. It was a little short now, but I had lost so much weight over my "illness" that it fit well everywhere else. It was really quite—I hesitate to say pretty when discussing something I liked. It was elegant without being too dressy, a pattern of tiny, unobtrusive flowers on a solid brown background, with gold piping around the cuffs and hem. There was no frivolity in the design, just straight long sleeves and a round neck, no gathering, no pleats, and no slits. A pleasant side effect was that my hair looked almost gold in comparison where it curled past my shoulders.

I tucked Arabella's ring on its chain well inside and under the hair. If my mother saw a hint of the silver around my neck, she'd be hauling it out, asking why I was hiding it and good god, where did I get such an expensive item of jewelery in the first place? Then, she'd jump either to the conclusion I was a thief or secretly engaged, and I didn't know what was worse. Maybe she'd think her Harrison had given it to me for safekeeping, for the time he could surprise her with it. That would be a whole shipping container's worth of worms opened.

Jan was surprised when I came down. "I thought you'd grown out of that thing," she said. "You look good." I had a vague memory that the dress had been a years-ago Christmas present from her. I'd unintentionally done something nice.

She gave me the ten second inspection, reserved for when I'd actually made an effort, and pronounced us ready.

As far as clothes went, I was. Inside, I was jumpy as a novelty

Mexican bean.

We walked, because it was close and a nice day. I was glad I had chosen slightly sensible shoes. I don't know how Mom managed. How did she actually walk in those heels? They hurt me just looking at them. Maybe they were actually comfortable. If so, I guessed it was a feature they saved for grown-up shoes. Kids were either expected to be in sneakers or just plain uncomfortable.

I hadn't walked along Fleance past Scott's house since the day I'd seen those pinkish eyes staring out at me through the fence. Now, instead of a deserted, work-day street, the curbs were packed with cars. Others were arriving as we approached, some carrying food or actual presents as well. Jan tensed a bit; I guess she hadn't thought about bringing anything besides the wine. I'm sure a contribution wouldn't be missed and wasn't absolutely expected in any case.

Margaret Saunders was hovering by the door greeting the guests. She had Scott's height and curly gold hair, even cut a bit like his, and towered over my mother and me. She did, however, seem genuinely glad to see us.

"Jan! I'm glad you came. And here's my little not-quite-namesake, only she's not so little any more. Marguerite, how are you?"

"Fine," I said. It seemed to me I could remember somewhere in the distant past this same effusive woman saying something in similar tones to a small version of myself.

Mrs. Saunders hugged me, and quite beside myself, I hugged back.

"Scott's not here right now," she went on, leaving her post at the door and leading us through to the living room where a buffet of snacks was laid out. This was addressed to me. She couldn't know, I guess, that this was *good* news, the best in fact. I tried to look disappointed.

"Oh well," I said. *Great, Maggie. Very convincing.*

My mother asked the question I wanted to, but wouldn't for fear of bringing suspicion on myself. "And the rest?"

"My so-called husband is outside, pretending to conduct a tour of the backyard for the three or four people who've expressed an interest, but really he's just shirking his host duties. The odious child is off with her grandparents—please never let on to Emily that I've called her that. I'm sure it's just a phase. Scott's off with his friends. He's of the age where he effectively rebels against being shown off, instead of just grinning and bearing it. I'm sure Marguerite can sympathize."

I nodded.

"What about Rebecca?"

Mrs. Saunders got a slightly sour look on her face that vanished so quickly I could only trust that I'd really seen it. "She's been going through some difficult times since she finished high school. You know the sort of thing. If I had a couple of hours, I'd regale you."

There was a kind of forced gaiety about the way she said it, as if her oldest child was actually in really deep trouble. It was as if she didn't want to burden anyone else, but the gravity of it was ever-present. And she changed the subject readily enough.

"And the youngest is around somewhere, but I doubt you'll see him."

Jan looked sideways at her hostess. "I didn't know you'd had another."

"Ah yes, but this one came the easy way. Haven't I told you about this? Has it really been three years since I've spoken with you at length?"

"At least that."

Three years. Warning bells went off in my head at any mention of that time. Mrs. Saunders was going on.

"It was the oddest thing. A miracle. It would have been spring, a little more than two and a half years ago. He just showed up, sitting on our lawn one day. We took him to the police of course, but Scott had gotten quite attached to him, as we all did. Eventually, when they couldn't find his natural family, we were allowed to adopt him. No one seems to know the real story."

So that was how it had happened. I wondered if Hunt had dropped him off the very night everything had ended. And if Scott's feelings for the little guy had continued over the end of his memory— that meant, didn't it, that other feelings could have carried over too?

*Don't get your hopes up,* I told myself.

The party flowed around me, but I had trouble making myself part of it. I tried, I really did, but after a few sausage rolls and raw vegetables, I wanted out. Mrs. Saunders had said something about a basement where there was a ping pong table for the young people and I wandered in that direction.

Downstairs, it was cool and quiet. The party had not spread down this way. I could have a few moments alone if I wanted, and I did.

The ping pong table was off the main basement room in a slightly smaller one with a cement floor. This first room was some kind of kids' television room, I guessed, complete with a Wii and the latest Playstation. Those would probably be Scott's. It was strange to be in a place where someone I only knew from school spent time. I couldn't imagine what I would feel if our situations were reversed, if Scott was snooping around in my house.

I thought at first I was alone down there. There was a big armchair facing the television and I set myself down in it and began leafing through the TV Guide. Then, just like that Monday when I had paused by the Saunders' curb, I caught a glimpse of white hair and a small body edged out of the shadows of the laundry room.

"Peter—" I said, the word catching in my throat, and the little blond head turned to look at me.

## 20

### Scream Like A Baby

✪

For a moment, there was an infinite tension between us. He, poised like he would dart back into the darkness behind him and disappear forever, and me, the vain hopes of three years perhaps resting on the next few words I said.

He had answered to his old name! Did this mean—but of course it did. He knew me. Please, please say he knew me.

What I didn't want, at all costs, was a repeat of our previous contact, with him running away screaming.

What should I say next? "Do you—" I said slowly. "I remember you used to sing. Do you sing?" My ears strained for sounds from the floor above. I couldn't be caught saying any of these things in front of witnesses. If Peter remembered, that was something to be saved and used some other time. I couldn't be caught knowing him. Not yet.

"Sing?" I said again. I did a few tentative "la–la–la's" and then stopped. I wanted him to remember me, not find out if he could still hold a tune. How old before a boy's voice changes? Was that beautiful soprano already gone? But no, he couldn't be older than ten, eleven at the outside. His voice wouldn't have changed yet, would it?

"Peter," I said.

He swallowed, the eyes which were colored only by swimming blood regarding me. He was either very frightened or very confused. But maybe he was neither, and I was forced to reconsider. Feet padding quietly on the thin carpet, he came toward me. Not really knowing how to respond, I put out my arms. Without pausing, he climbed up into my lap, still so thin and light, although not nearly so much so as I'd seen him in Char's catacombs. The Saunders household apparently agreed with him, and I was glad. He put one arm around my neck, and the thumb of his other hand in his mouth.

I sat very still and held on to him. He was so frail and small. Could it be that he was even older than I wanted to imagine, and only his size made me guess at ten years? Or was he younger than I thought? Ages got so screwed up when someone lived with Char. Damon looked twenty-five, but was older than I dared guess. But Damon was gone.

The door from the upstairs opened, and feet appeared on the steps. I recognized my mother's peach shoes and Mrs. Saunders' legs in long slacks. Peter was comfortable, a small, warm weight on me, so I didn't try to shift him.

"Look at that," said Mrs. Saunders, vastly content. "Soren doesn't usually take too well to strangers."

"He's very quiet," I said, not knowing how to respond.

"Soren's autistic," Mrs. Saunders said. "He doesn't say much, and when he does, it's hard for him to string thoughts together. But he's a wonderful addition to the family. Scott and Emily dote on him. For the first time, since he came, I haven't had to stop those two from fighting all the time."

Mom was smiling broadly, like an idiot. I could almost hear her: If only I'd had another child. Well, she couldn't have this one. I doubted if a little boy would somehow miraculously appear on her front lawn, and I couldn't see any of her begun-at-work relationships turning into anything more than dinner and sleep overs. Jan, like me, was too screwed up for anything else.

"Where did you get the name Soren?" my mother asked.

"Emily came up with it," Margaret Saunders replied. "We thought it suited him."

*Peter*, I said in my mind. *Not Soren, Peter. And he sings.* "Does he ever—" I started to ask it, but stopped myself. "—play with other children?" I finished.

"Sometimes," Mrs. Saunders told me. "We usually put him with children much younger than he is. Than we think he is, I should say. Without birth parents, we also have no idea of his birth date. We decided to call the day we found him his seventh birthday, so we celebrate every year as if we really knew."

"Maggie, are you coming back upstairs?" said my mother.

What I wanted was for them to go away and leave me alone so I could ask Peter some questions. But I didn't say anything to that effect, just shook my head. "I don't want to disturb him yet," I said.

The two women smiled and left. Mrs. Saunders took a case of pop from the laundry room upstairs with her, which I guess had been the original intention of their trip. As for little Soren Saunders, he curled closer to me when the door at the top of the stairs closed and his fingers tangled themselves in my hair.

"Hey," I said quietly. I didn't want to upset him by moving too quickly, but I was sure I had a very limited time before someone else disturbed us, and my chance was lost for good. "You remember me, don't you?"

No response. "Peter," I said. I turned him slightly on my lap to face me. "Peter. Swimming, you remember swimming?" Keeping him balanced, I mimed an overhand crawl.

He smiled.

"Swimming," I repeated. Then, "Scott?"

He opened his mouth, as if about to sing, then closed it again.

"Not in practice, huh?" I said. "But you remember. Maggie? Do you know Maggie?"

Peter hugged himself to my chest. A smile spread faintly on my face. "Oh Peter," I said. I was on the verge of tears. Someone remembered.

Softly, I began to sing to him, something I'd learned in school choir years ago, the tune I'd sung with him in the cave below Char's domain. He, without knowing the melody, had joined in immediately with soaring, beautiful harmonies. Now, with the memories stirring inside me, I was crying, couldn't hold back any longer. Sweet boy. He knew me, and he wasn't afraid.

So why had he run screaming when he saw me? But he hadn't, not immediately. There was a lag, a lapse. So what if the sight of me had triggered memories, like being with him did for me, and that led to the memory of something that made him run? And now, he was calm because he remembered the quiet time we'd had together in the cavern before everything went horrible.

But I had to press. I had to know what the 'red' he'd been talking about to Scott was all about.

"Peter," I said, pulling him away from me. "I have to ask you a question." I lifted him off my lap and slid down to the floor. He crouched down beside me. "Peter, you have to tell me. Red?"

There was no reaction from him. He looked at me, blinking away every few seconds and then back to me. "Red?" I said again.

One fine, white hand reached out and touched my wrist. "Red," I repeated. His forefinger tapped my skin once and came to rest. Red. What did he mean?

I had a thought, and reached up to my throat where the necklace was concealed. I slipped a finger under the chain and pulled, and the gold ring with its red stone fell over the front of my dress.

The reaction was not what I was hoping, to say the least. Peter tensed, staring in horror, and drew a huge breath. Then, he began to shriek.

I fled, racing upstairs, pushing the ring out of sight as I did. Even closing the door behind me didn't stop the sound. I bumped into Mrs. Saunders when I was almost at the front door.

"It's Pe—Soren," I said. "He started—"

She patted me on the arm. "Don't worry. It's not your fault. He gets excited sometimes. Is he still downstairs?"

I nodded dumbly and she was off like a shot in the direction I had come and at least as fast. No wonder they were protective of him. If I had had my power, I could have soothed him, taken away his fears, dove straight into his mind and found what was wrong. I could have done anything, and I would have done anything for him. But I didn't, and I couldn't. Helpless, but no longer panicked, I found my mother and told her I was going home. She was enjoying herself enough to stay put so I said goodbye. I had to admit, it was good to see her with old friends and so comfortable, even if the day had been pretty rotten for me so far.

Outside, the sunlight was bright. It was almost as nice a day as the Saturday the week before when I'd been with Rae , weather-wise at least. But it was a crappy day in every other way. I had confirmed something; Peter/Soren remembered me, and remembered the catacombs, but he obviously remembered Arabella's ring as well, and in terms so terrifying that he couldn't deal with even the sight of it. That meant I would have to be incredibly careful what I said and did around him, if I ever got to see him again. If not, I wouldn't be able to find out anything of value.

I also—but this I didn't want to consider because it was so low I'd even thought of it—wouldn't be able to use him to prove my wild story of catacombs and sorcerer to Jason and the rest, should it come to that.

And who should be out on the front drive as I exited the house but the whole load of them? The whole gang, except for Rae. Good, now I could distress the rest of them in a group. So much more economical. Jason, Scott, Aaron, and Suzanne. There was a car parked and idling at the bottom of the driveway, so they'd just driven from somewhere.

I didn't care to find out more. I was embarrassed at what I'd done, or at least at the reaction I'd had from Peter. I was in a worsening mood. All I wanted was to get home quick and hide until I had to come out again for school. Monday morning was disgustingly close all of a sudden, and I had promised Mr. Thurl I wouldn't skip. Monday would be soon enough.

I probably should have said something right then to Scott, but I expected nothing but condemnation for speaking to his brother without permission, without him there to supervise. There would be enough time for him to get on my case later. Not now.

I acknowledged them with a nod and swept past. I was still in very real danger of crying again, and that didn't suit at all my intended image of occult-superperson.

"Mags!" said Jason, quite a friendly greeting. Well, that would change when he found out I'd terrorized Scott's protected little brother.

"Tomorrow," I said, waving my hand vaguely. "I'll be at the coffee shop after school."

I said it like there had been developments over the weekend they should know about. That was a laugh. What had I discovered so far? The catalogue was pretty pathetic. That I could ride and fall off horses with great skill. That the sight of my ring, Aria's ring, made Peter scream. That, given a moment's discomfort about my scar, I could nearly spill the whole of my secret. That I could be so excited about a little attention from the more popular set that I was willing to treat someone like Irene with the contempt I imagined they'd previously aimed at me. I was a cretin and I knew it. If I went away now, perhaps I could find something, dig up some clue or useful fact, before tomorrow, because today I was a louse and an imbecile to boot.

Aaron, I saw out of the corner of my eye, started slightly down the drive after me, but something stopped him after a couple of paces. Scott's hand on his arm, probably. Division in the ranks would be a bad thing. It was not going to go well as long as Scott was actively working against me.

I walked the rest of the way home quickly. My distress had conveniently turned to fury, which was fine with me. It was probably just as well I was bad at blaming myself for things, or I would have considered the whole thing from ritual to Peter's shrieks my fault.

There was a strange car parked on our drive. I'd taken the shortcut up through the backyard, after crossing through the backyard of what I knew now had once been Scott's house, but had to come around to the front door because I only had that key with me. The car was waiting for me, a dark mid-range Honda something. Teacher/civil servant car.

The door of it opened, and a familiar figure got out, dressed in civvies but from the curling black hair to the neat jeans obviously that same Carla Szaba from the police station.

*Corporal Carla.*

"Corporal Szaba," I said. Names are important; use them if you remember them. My mother always said that about business. What was she doing here?

"Hi," said Szaba, smiling. Her manner was forced-casual. "Miss Stuart—"

"Maggie," I corrected. Where did I get the balls to interrupt? Had Tamblyn found something to arrest me for after all?

"Maggie," she repeated. "Carla." She held out her hand for me to shake. I did, thoroughly confused. "Can we talk somewhere? I have a few questions, if you have a bit of time."

"Not here," I said. Intriguing, but my mother would be home soon, and I didn't want to have to explain to her that I'd been down to the police station in Toronto to harass a detective. "The mall has a pretty good coffee shop."

"Sounds good." She pressed a button on the inside of the car door, and I heard a click as the passenger door lock opened. "I seem to live my half my life inside of coffee shops."

"Me too," I said, and went around to get in. *Curiouser and curiouser*, as Alice said. The police make house calls. Maybe I'd have something for the guys after all tomorrow.

## 21

## People From Bad Homes

✪

The coffee shop at the mall was a lot nicer than the one close to school, much more conducive to conversation. For one thing, it wasn't nearly as busy, especially late on a Sunday afternoon close to closing time. For another, it was less popular with students, which meant the chances of running into someone I knew were relatively low.

I mentioned this to Carla Szaba as we found seats and ordered our coffee, and could tell immediately she was not really inclined toward small talk.

"So," I said. "What can I do for you?" Hunt had taught me, mostly by example because I was always on the wrong end of the manipulations, to take the first line in a conversation and the last as well, if you could. Leave no advantage untaken. Always put the other guy on the defensive.

"Well." She said it like a complete statement, and sat back to stir a packet of sugar into her cup. Maybe she was as good at this stuff as I was trying to be. Finally she looked up and inclined her head with a smile which was more than a little unfriendly.

"I don't need to tell you you created a bit of a—situation at the station when you stopped by last week," she said.

"I guess not." I smiled back, trying to sound relaxed. I didn't yet know what the game was. I wondered if I should mention her early morning phone call prompting me to check the Star for the article on the dead cafeteria worker, but wasn't exactly sure how or why to do so. It was enough that I'd kept up the interest in the local section of the paper. If there was something to be found there that would eventually prove useful, I would be on top of it.

"Tamblyn's had your name circulated to various people in the department—nothing official, you understand, but he has a lot of pull. He's actually been into his office several times since you contacted him."

I laughed, quick and light. "So somehow I made him a little more conscientious? Instilled a work ethic in him?"

She didn't crack so much as an upward tilt of the mouth. "I'm glad you're proud of that." Deliberately she picked up the cup and held it poised before her lips. "Unfortunately, it doesn't make me all that happy."

What was this? It was odd, already, to have some plainclothes policewoman track me down at my house, but she was being pretty ornery without giving me any hint why. "What is this?" I said. Then, in a joking tone, "Am I under arrest?"

She answered quickly, which made me suspicious. This wasn't, I guessed, official. "Of course not."

"Why are you so interested?" I asked.

She refused to rise to the challenge of the question. Instead, she countered with that oh-so intimidating adult technique of accusal. "Young lady, I hope understand how much trouble you're in. You lied to a police officer, gained entry to a restricted part of the building under false pretenses, and wasted the time of a very special officer."

"Tamblyn?" I guffawed. "He—barely gave me the time of day." I had almost said something else, something about Hunt and Tamblyn's obvious terror of the man. Whatever slight reconciliation had happened after the incidents of the catacombs were wiped away now, with everything else. I gathered that present Tamblyn wasted very little affectionate thought on his estranged, presumed dead brother. Presumed, that is, until I had told Tamblyn Hunt was alive. No wonder he had freaked. Maybe it was like with my mother; some memories didn't fit, and now he had the clues to start to understand why. Maybe he hadn't even remembered about his ring until I'd pushed the fact of it in his face.

Szaba—it was hard to think of her as Carla when she was being so deliberately incendiary—had turned to another tack. "Look," she said, more kindly. "I don't want to badger you. I have some very serious questions, and I need straight answers from you. That's why I need to impress on you the gravity of the situation you're in."

*So you can hold a vague threat over my head,* I thought. I took a stab, the words out of my mouth before I even realized what I was going to ask. "What do you want to know about him?"

The blank look, begun with a flash of fear, told me I'd hit paydirt. "Detective Tamblyn is not the issue," she said, but I knew she was covering.

"I'll tell you what you want if you're honest about wanting to know," I said. "Level with me." I took a sip of my coffee, keeping her attention by keeping my eyes steady on her. "You have suspicions about him; that's obvious. You don't like him; I knew that when I first talked to you. What I don't know is how much you know—or suspect."

She locked her eyes with mine, then looked away deliberately. She sat back in her chair. I began to get nervous. I was again playing something far above my head. When would I get comfortable with this kind of thing?

Szaba frowned suddenly and shook her head, but there was a lightening of the mood I couldn't account for from her facial expressions. She had found whatever it was she had needed to go to the next step of her interrogation of me.

"Why don't you tell me what you know about him, then I'll be able to tell you what you're missing," I offered.

"All right," she said. I was surprised she'd agreed, but it seemed to be the opening she wanted.

She settled back into the hard-backed chair. "I assume you know what John Tamblyn does for the department."

I didn't, and almost tried to cover it up. But no, this was for me as much as her. "No, I don't."

She accepted this. "He's what we've dubbed our *Special Cases officer, Homicide Squad*. He deals with the cases that otherwise would close without solution. Often, his methods are—shall we say, not strict department policy. He has resources that are beyond the norm for usual police work. Not outside the law, you understand, but he has contacts we can't touch without him. But there are cases—"

I nodded. "Unconventional."

"Inexplicable," she upped, "and in need of resolution. The department turns its back where John Tamblyn is concerned. He isn't used often, and we're all supposed to give him a wide berth. If you do know him at all, you'll know that's what he prefers."

"Demands," I said, although I didn't know anything about his methods at all.

"And I used to ignore him for the most part. But then I got interested. I've seen some very strange things."

Tamblyn was doing magic too. I knew it. Or at least, his experience with his brother had made him valuable where Char-like beings touched the normal world. My way opened up again. "Inexplicable things? What do Tamblyn's methods consist of?"

She played with the coffee cup before answering, eyes narrow. "He does a lot of the standard wacky things many police stations do, bringing in psychics for missing persons and the like. He also disappears for hours into his office..."

"That's not so odd."

"Let's just say I might have overheard a few of his phone conversations and they're a bit outside the realm of reason." She stopped. "Can I see the ring again?"

It was my turn to sit back. "What do you mean, the realm of reason?"

"The ring," she repeated. "I saw it that day in the station, and his phone line has been buzzing about it ever since. I don't know who you are—"

I took a stab. "Vancouver? Has he been calling Vancouver?"

"You must know he was stationed there before he—"

"I know nothing. This is what I need. I'll tell you something you want, but you have to tell me about Vancouver."

"Then tell me!" She was vehement, her voice quiet but intense. "What is he?"

I shook my head. Her use of *what* instead of *who* opened a floodgate in me. "A man, a man as far as I know. But there's more than human beings in the world. He knows about the others, and he's been a victim in some power struggles before. He's been used in the past, so I guess I'm glad he's found a way to take what he knows and... He's just a man, but he's tied into a whole other world. I don't know how much."

"But how—no, show me the ring."

Slowly, I drew the chain from my dress, the weight of the ring slick and cold sliding up my neck. It repulsed me now. Since Peter this afternoon, it had become Damon's death, not a symbol of what I once could do and might again another way. Its red stone pulsed—no, it was still and translucently crystalline. I held it out to Carla Szaba.

"So that's what all the fuss is about," she breathed, more impressed than I imagined she should be.

"He's called Vancouver about it?" I asked. I replaced the piece of jewelry under my neckline, tucking the chain carefully away.

She looked at me quizzically. "Have you heard of someone or something called Aria?"

Shock must have registered on my face because Szaba's mouth opened with another question. I cut her off. "That can't be in the deal," I said. "Unless you tell me what you know. I can't—"

She eased off. "No, that's okay. It's Tamblyn I want."

"Then—" It was a big chance, but it wouldn't compromise me, or my secret. "Then check out the Hunter. That's where Tamblyn learned what he knows." It was part of the truth, and not enough to make me a liar. I stood. "That's really all I can tell you. I don't know anything more about Vancouver myself, only that whatever happened was about thirteen years ago. You have more access to information about it that I do, I'm sure."

She nodded.

"Only—" I said, "only, could we keep in touch? Could you tell me what you find out? I really need to know more as well. And I—" How much should I tell her? I decided on the mysterious tack I was taking with the rest of them from school. "There may be something strange going on around town."

"I know." She stood too. "Check out the Royal York fire when you find a paper. I will stay in touch." She gave me her card with her work number on it, then extended her hand. I shook. So grownup. My heart was starting to race. "You too. It's been—very illuminating."

We left the coffee shop together, and she offered to drive me home, but I told her I needed the walk and set out on foot. A lot to think about.

## 22

## Low

✪

Sunday night was a dead waste. I must have sat for a full hour in my room, that fabled contact list open on my knee, now with Carla Szaba's work number filled in, wondering if Rae would be glad to hear from me if I called. Wondering, actually, what I'd say in any case, and if I would even know if she *was* happy to hear from me. If she was distant or preoccupied, even if the reason had nothing to do with me, I'd only be able to imagine she'd heard about Peter's freak-out, and the inevitable blame Scott would place on me. I would feel lower than the proverbial snake's belly. I wished I had some kind of magic that could tell me if someone liked me, or at the very least what they were saying behind my back.

I wouldn't use it on guys, of course. That would be cheating, wouldn't it? Not a good way to start an honest relationship with someone, in any case. Would I use it to find out if Aaron had a little twinge of interest around me? If he and Suzanne were, as I suspected, somehow involved?

By bedtime, I had worked myself into a state of agitation that was only alleviated at all by my thoughts of Hunt. No matter how little it benefited me, at least Hunt still treated me like I was somewhat special. It might be the kind of special that got me hurt or worse, but I would take what I could get. Anything was better than just being lonely.

I went to bed and lay awake until I couldn't find anything else to obsess over.

By the time I got up the next morning, instead of feeling better because of the conversation with Szaba, all I could think about was what an idiot I'd been at Scott's. I had effectively put an end to ever being able to speak with Peter again. Even if Scott let me, I was terrified to consider it. And fear always puts me in a pissy mood.

Oddly, both Jan and Harrison were in the kitchen when I came down.

"This is a surprise," said Jan, with a big smile. "I thought you'd sleep in."

I stared blankly. Why would I sleep in on a Monday?

"Why don't you and I go to Swiss Chalet tonight," she said, giving Harrison an affectionate squeeze on the arm. "It's not home-cooked but hey, neither of us will have to do the dishes either."

The penny dropped. I wouldn't be seeing anyone at school today; it was Thanksgiving. That made sense of the over-the-top spread at the Saunders' house too—there was a turkey and fixings as well as the barbeque, but I'd hardly been in the mood to indulge. Embarrassed at having entirely forgotten, I forced a smile of my own and agreed. What Harrison would be doing instead wasn't broached, although that evening, it seemed to be something of a sore spot for Jan. She talked a little about his familial commitments, and I inferred that he was supping with his ex and two young children from a previous marriage. She tried hard not to show any emotion, but that in itself was probably a good sign of how much it bothered her.

✪

Tuesday, I made it in to school, determinedly on time, determined at least to fulfill my promise to Mr. Thurl. Sunday had been a bad day, yes, but I wasn't about to compound the problem by having to go to the office after arriving late, as well as losing Thurl's trust forever. That meant I had to be in school. Nothing would put Jan on my case like having her daughter threatened with expulsion.

In actual fact, I didn't have much cause for complaint. The interview with Carla Szaba had been—provocative. There was little I thought I could or should share with the rest of them, but here was an avenue for my exploration. I could tell them I'd made progress and not be lying.

Rae caught up with me in the hall as I was heading into drafting and mentioned that "we" were all meeting at the coffee shop after school, and I was grateful for her inclusion of me in that pronoun, even if I had seldom felt so apart from, well, just about everyone.

I ended up spending basically all day wondering what the fallout had been from my visit to the Saunders house, and what things Scott might have said in the wake of my disastrous encounter with Peter. Was that the reason for the meet-up after school? I pictured Scott looming over one of the formica tables intoning, "Maggie at least knows the reason I've called you all here today..."

Half anticipating, half dreading, I got too antsy to go to last period and, threat of an ignominious end to my school career notwithstanding, decided to hit the coffee shop a bit early.

With my coffee, I grabbed the paper and sat by the window at one of the little two-seaters. I left my bag on the other chair so I could screen potential table-mates.

I'd already read the comics when I noticed the paper was from Saturday. What had Corporal Carla said about a fire at the Royal York?

I figured I'd be looking at something that had happened at the venerable downtown hotel, so it was a surprise when, instead, I found out she'd been referring instead to Royal York subway station on the Bloor line. I had a vague memory of reading something about it in a previous day's paper as well. With luck, I'd either cut it out for my growing collection of clippings, or could salvage it from the recycling at least.

The article was at the bottom of page three. I had finished reading it when a shadow fell across the table. Looking up, I saw Irene's dark face.

"Hey, Maggie. Checking up on current events?"

Surprised at myself, I felt a surge of relief to see her. I didn't know if she was skipping or just had a spare last period. Another of the extremely long list of things I didn't know about Irene. "Yeah, something like that," I said. "You wanna grab some joe and join me?"

She shrugged and walked off toward the counter.

"I guess that was a yes," I said to myself.

And yes, it was. She left me to reposition my bag on the floor to make a place for her, then plunked herself down across from me.

"Lessee what you're looking so strange at," she said.

I handed over the article. She saluted me with her coffee mug and started reading. I watched, fascinated. Her lips moved as she went. Not like she was having trouble with the words, though. She mouthed the lines with the most brilliant animation, as if she was entertaining a child with a storybook. I couldn't help it. A big smile spread over my face.

She finished, and looked over at me with delight as she handed back the paper.

"Something strike you as odd about that little story?" she said.

I spread the article flat on the Formica. "I actually hadn't got through it when you came in," I said. Since nothing had jumped out, it was better to pretend

She waved me on, so I took a sip of my coffee and read.

The gist of it was plain enough. Early Friday morning, fire fighters and police had been called to a residential neighborhood in the west end of Toronto. I got through it once, and read it again just to be certain. I didn't notice a thing. But I wasn't about to admit that to Irene.

Fortunately, she explained, without my having to prove my ignorance.

"Why do you think the fire fighters weren't called to Royal York station, if it was a fire in the subway?"

I shrugged, and grinned, like I was in on it.

"You heard about Russell Hill? That crash on the Yonge Street line way back in '94?"

Vague memories stirred. "Some people died, right?" I shivered.

"Squeamish?" Irene said.

"I just don't like being underground," I said. "I don't like going below the surface of the earth. It makes me—claustrophobic." Brings back memories. And gives rise to embarrassing fantasies.

"Yeah," said Irene. "If God had meant us to go into tunnels, he would have given us mole-paws." She mimed a digging mole, hands scraping laterally at face level.

"They've got classy noses," I said. "It wouldn't be bad to be a mole."

"Except for the underground stuff, right?"

"Yeah, except for the underground stuff."

She picked up the paper again, and her coffee. "So what do you think? Why does this subway fire have anything to do with us?"

I bit my lip.

Irene flared. "Okay, missy, don't tell. I don't give a damn about your secrets. But you might find I'm a help, and not an albatross, you know."

The image of Irene's wonderful dark skin somehow blanching, and feathers sprouting all over her body was so ridiculous I had to laugh. She softened a bit, and rolled her eyes.

"There's a book," I said, and sighed. I was going to have to take her a little further into my confidence, I supposed. At least, as far as I felt wise.

"Yeah?" she said. "This anything to do with the crap that went down in the tech wing?"

I was surprised. "What do you know about that?"

"I don't know. Some perv walking the halls, hitting on a couple of the cupcake girls, and no one made enough of a fuss. I'da had the cops crawling all over the place."

I grimaced. "Where the hell are you from, girl?"

"What?" Her look soured enough to let me know I'd touched a nerve and she was determined not to show it. "Because I'm black I gotta be from some hell-hole of a US inner city?" Then she smirked. "Windsor. So, a few steps up from hell, but you can see it from there. You hear about this guy who was walking on the waterfront in Windsor? All of a sudden, he feels a sharp pain in his gut. Collapses right there, they rush him to hospital, think he's had a heart attack. Surprise, surprise, doctors pull a bullet out of his abdomen. Some idiot in Detroit firing a high-powered rifle in a shoot-out across the river, and one of the rounds got our guy in Canada. Wild, huh?"

"Man." I shook my head. "You are a sponge, Irene."

"Can't help it. Anything that comes near my ear goes in and gets stuck."

"I need you for Trivial Pursuit."

"Chick, my whole life is one big trivial pursuit."

I laughed. I was feeling very good, very relaxed. I almost said so, but that kind of off-the-cuff honesty still frightened me. Better to hope she figured me for relaxed without me saying so. That meant I didn't have to take the chance she'd want to get too close. Close and me were a bad combination. Obviously.

"The book?" she prompted.

"Yeah." How to do this? "It's kind of important I find it, and it has a habit of disappearing as soon as I find it. Maybe you could keep half an eye out for it." I described it, but I didn't say anything else. I didn't even so much as breathe the names of any of the other players. That had to be vague enough.

⸺ ✪ ⸺

We walked out into the sunshine.

"We need a map," said Irene.

We found one at the gas station down the block. "Okay," I said, trying to get to the right part of the map without unfolding the whole thing. "Here's the subway line. Where did it say the fire crews came?"

Irene gave me the intersection, and I traced the lines with my finger up, up. . . "It's nowhere near the station," I said.

"So it was on the tracks. They have escape hatches all over the place, you know, in people's backyards and stuff. I read about it. In the Russell Hill thing, people came out in the middle of some neighborhood in midtown."

"Yeah," I said, although I didn't know. "But this is, like, four blocks north of anything connected to the subway line. It's not near a station, and it's not anywhere near the track."

"What station is closest?" asked Irene, trying to get a look and at the same time to shield our illicit map-perusal from the store clerk, who had just noticed us.

"Uh, sort of Royal York, I guess, or Old Mill. Whatever, it's not on the way to anything except the GO line, and that doesn't connect to the underground in any way. Not in that direction."

Irene smiled, and helped me refold the map. "Ladies and germs, we have ourselves a mystery."

There was a loud throat-clearing behind us suddenly, and Irene turned her eyes to the ceiling, feigning innocence. "Hi," I said to the clerk who'd appeared between us. "This doesn't have what I need. Oh well. We folded it back right. . ."

He took the map from my hand with, I think, a bit more alacrity than really necessary. Irene and I fled from the gas station, holding back a completely inappropriate fit of giggles until we were out of sight of the clerk.

"Damn," said Irene, "that was kind of fun."

"Yeah," I agreed, out of breath. "No closer to understanding about the fire, I guess, but. . ."

"We could, I don't know, call the TTC."

"We could."

I don't know what perversity made me begin the old stonewall, but I closed down right then. Irene sensed it: I mean, you'd have to be completely out to lunch not to. Maybe it was that the others would be arriving soon, and I didn't want to give Irene any more information. Maybe it was that I wasn't used to having fun and doing mischievous things. Maybe I just didn't want to be seen with her.

"Right," she said, looking away. "I'll see you tomorrow."

Instantly, I was ashamed. "Yeah, unless you want to get a coffee. . . later. . ."

She shrugged. "Actually, I should get home. My mom'll be wondering where I am."

She turned, and seemed to be heading the same way as I eventually would. "Where do you live?" I said, realizing I was already planning to add her name and contact info to my famous list. No real reason; it just seemed like an important thing to do.

As it turned out, she was not that far from me, on a cul de sac I walked past every day to get to school myself. She gave me her phone number too, which I copied into my notebook, and we said goodbye. I headed back into the coffee shop, realizing I had managed, without conscious effort, to avoid any more mention of the book.

✪

Inside and feeling coffee'd out, I grabbed a Dr Pepper and borrowed the fat Toronto white pages from the bored woman at the counter. Another time when there were all sorts of reasons it would be nice if I had some mobile connectivity.

The pay phone was in an alcove off the main hall to the washroom, and I figured I wouldn't be disturbed there. Also, I didn't want anyone being able to call me back, so I wouldn't have used a cell even if I had one. *Subterfuge.* My time with Irene had instilled a bit of deviousness in me. I kind of liked it.

The main TTC switchboard number led me to an automated message, so I hit "0" repeatedly until I got a real person.

"Hi," I said, cradling my soda can like it would give me courage. "I'm calling from the Westbrook Gazetteer. It's a school paper? I was just wondering about the fire in the subway, because a lot of students in Westbrook take the train past that stop."

The woman on the other end had identified herself as Salla and had a pronounced accent but fine English. "I'm sorry," she said, "I cannot make an official statement regarding the incident. Perhaps you could call to this number..."

I wrote it down, dialed, and got another automated message. Hitting "0" didn't get me anywhere this time, so I waded through the six options, and chose the one that seemed most likely to get me to a human being. Two transferred calls later, I was speaking with a Mr. Hapcot, who apparently was qualified to speak about the matter.

"Yes, Miss—"

"Julliard," I supplied, flashing on a brochure Jan had brought home, trying to interest me in American college scholarships.

"Miss Julliard. The official statement, which was released earlier today, is not usually issued to lower school newspapers as a matter of course, but I can give you the gist of it. An explosion occurred late Saturday night near the Bloor line, leading to the evacuation of the Royal York subway station and interruption of service for approximately one hour. The ensuing fire was easily contained by fire fighters and emergency personnel, and there were no injuries."

I twigged to one word in his description. "*Near* the Bloor line?" I said. "Not on it? I noticed from the newspaper account that the location of the fire was four blocks north of the station."

"Uh, yes," said Mr. Hapcot, and I heard papers shuffling. "There is an emergency egress near the intersection indicated."

"But no subway line underneath?" I pressed.

He didn't skip a beat, so I guessed what he was telling me was no secret. "There's an abandoned section of track going north from midway between Royal York and Old Mill stations. It was a proposed line to Pearson International Airport which was started in the mid-80's but never completed."

"Really. Uh, how far does the track go?"

He shuffled again. "I don't really know. The plans aren't here, and I know the project was halted shortly after construction began. As to how far the tunnel extends, I really couldn't say."

I pictured the track leading off to the north from the Bloor line tunnel I saw when heading home. Off to the right and down into the earth. Heading north, toward the airport, but never reaching it. Burrowing down deeper into the earth, below existing Toronto substructure. Deeper underground. *Deeper in.* I shivered.

I wanted to ask him more, about the depth of the unfinished line, about access to it, but I had a feeling there was no more information to be had from him on this particular subject. Better to get what I could from him about what he did know. "Do you know yet what caused the fire? Was it a gas explosion or what?"

He coughed. "As far as I know, the investigation is still underway. It was a pretty hot fire, but it burned itself out quite quickly. No official cause has been released as of now. That's all I can tell you."

That had the air of finality, so I thanked him, took the spelling of his name for my "article," and said goodbye.

Tunnels. A chill traversed my spine from bottom to top in a thoroughly unpleasant fashion. Somehow, sometime, I knew I was going to have to go back underground.

## 23

## Big Brother

✪

Scott arrived first.

I was hanging around by the telephone, nursing my pop and vibrating anxiously. After the phone call, a coldness had settled into my bones. Every stupid thing I'd done during this whole messy time revisited my thoughts, from all the wasted time to the botched meetings with Hunt to the loss of the book. And, of course, I knew that I still had to deal with the consequences of my contact with Peter. With *Soren,* I meant. With Scott's beloved and over-protected little brother.

It was agony, hovering there, waiting, watching the curly back of Scott's head and wondering what would come first—the arrival of one of the others to deflect the brunt of Scott's anger, or the revival of that perverse streak in me that was just out of sight below the surface of my mind, spoiling for a disastrous fight.

Probably a good thing that the rest of them arrived simultaneously.

Just as I was striding over the table to take the best Scott could dish out in what I hoped would be true Mr. Hunt style, Aaron, Jason, Suzanne, and Rae arrived in a pack.

Scott caught sight of them before he noticed me.

Turning to look behind himself, catching the cue from Jason's line of sight, he frowned. "I hope you learned something useful," he said in the tone reserved for asking if a long-past-curfew teen had *had a good time.*

I sat, not trusting myself to say something off the top of my head. No one else seemed to be getting up for coffee or juice, so I took a couple of deep breaths, hoping someone else would maybe break the silence first.

In the end, we were saved by the bored counter woman stopping beside the table with her bad temper almost matching Scott's. "If you don't buy something, I'm going to have to ask you to leave."

There was a silent parade to the register during which I sat quietly and tried to think.

When they were all back and arranged around the table, I took out my notebook, playing for a couple of extra seconds.

"Well," I said, making it a statement. "A lot has happened since I saw you last."

Scott glared at me, but I had a way out and took it. I pushed the newspaper across the table between Suzanne and Jason, with the article about the subway fire uppermost. I got another few moments' grace as they all read the brief piece.

"You may notice," I said, "that the fire wasn't *on* the actual line, but a fair distance north."

"So?" said Scott.

I waited. In actual fact, I still had no idea what kind of connection the fire could possibly have with our dilemma, but I wasn't about to say so. If there was a connection, maybe one of the others would lead me to it.

"Fire," said Aaron. "Heat. Is that what you're thinking?"

I smiled at him with gratitude. It was as obvious to me as Scott's anger that Aaron, bright perceptive Aaron, knew I was bullshitting as surely as the moon moves the tides. He knew I was avoiding the issue of Scott's little brother with a smokescreen, and he was playing along.

"Exactly," I said.

Suzanne looked back and forth between us. There was no way he could like her, was there? She couldn't follow the actual conversation all that well, much less the subtext.

"I don't get it," she said.

"Neither do I," said Rae, but somehow her admission seemed less foolish than Suzanne's. "I thought all this stuff was happening just around the five of us."

Excluding me, I thought, then realized. She only really knows about the dead animals, on *their* lawns, Hunt, following *them*, the attack at *her* riding school.

"I need to do some more research. . ." I began, but Scott cut me off.

"More research? That's all we've been hearing from you since this thing *started*. You're full of crap, that's what I think. What did you say to Soren, anyhow? It took my mom like an hour to get him calmed down, and he still whimpers all night. He won't go outside anymore."

*The bluffs,* I remembered, *over Char's collapsed palace.* The sky above Peter, so unimaginably huge to a little boy who had never been anywhere but inside or underground. And me, reaching inside his head with a surgeon's delicate touch, and easing away his fear.

"He's regressed," I said, not really watching what I said. "He's remembering a time before. . . before he came to you."

I thought Scott was going to jump right out of his seat and grab me by the collar. He shifted, the energy surging in him almost visible, and Aaron brought his hand down on Scott's arm. The violence which had almost flared into flame banked. . . but I didn't know for how long. I realized I was half out of my seat myself, and felt Rae's hand on my shoulder, squeezing and comforting.

"Mags," said Jason softly. We all knew something very bad had just been avoided, and even Suzanne looked at me with caution. "What do you know about it? What do you know about. . ."

"Peter?" I finished. Scott stared, but no one said anything. It was like I had suddenly started speaking Urdu. Could they really be so dense? "Scott, your little brother. Peter," I finished, and only then realized I had made a huge mistake. "Soren, I mean," I corrected, but it was too late.

Scott was staring at me with murder in his eyes.

"It's not what you think," I said, frantically searching for anything I could say in the name of damage control. "I found out. . . just almost nothing, really, just his name, and that he doesn't have any family. That's it. Except you. You're his family. That's what matters."

He stared at me coldly. "And you will never come near him again.

"My brother's name is Soren," he finished tightly, then stood and turned his gaze on Jason. "She's nuts. Nuts." He turned back to me only briefly, and only to say, "I'm out of here. I'm not spoiling my last day here with any more of this useless insanity. You can count me out."

And Scott was gone.

No one followed him, although we all watched. I knew I was seeing the utter destruction of a long, long friendship between Jason and Scott, and one almost as long between Scott and Aaron. The absence, the sense of tragedy, was heavy in the air around us. I felt suffocated. I wanted to get out of there too, but what if I met Scott outside?

"I have to use the bathroom," I said instead, and got up.

✪

In the ladies' room, I started to bawl. It was the kind of crying that comes on so suddenly, with just a hint of tightness across the bridge of your nose before absolute torrents of tears. I cried and cried, first by the mirror and then moving into the stall in case someone else came in. I was there so long I was sure someone would, but the minutes passed, and, slowly, so did the fit.

I was splashing water on my face in a vain attempt to wash away the redness when Rae came in.

She didn't say anything at first, just let me splash and sob away the last of the tears. Then, still silent, she opened her purse and handed me her makeup bag.

I used a bit of foundation to calm the last of the redness in my face, and then she passed me a small bottle of Visine from the bottom of her purse.

I managed a small smile. "Thanks," I said.

"I do house calls," she smiled back, "any time."

I had a friend, and it was one that I wanted. I realized that all this time I had thought Rae looked on me much as I looked on Irene, as someone to be tolerated more out of kindness than affection.

"Better?" she asked.

"Sort of. I did a very bad thing back there."

She shrugged, not minimizing, but accepting. "He's been wound so tight. It's everything, the move, his sister..."

"Rebecca," I said, remembering Mrs. Saunders' vague mention at the party.

"She ran away a while ago. I don't think anyone knows where she is. So when he thought Soren..."

I got it. I nodded. "I feel so useless."

She smiled, sympathetically. "It seems so small, dead animals and all. Compared to what he's been going through."

I could have agreed with her. At least she didn't mention Hunt, or seem to share the feeling I had that something still bigger was coming, lurking just out of sight. Maybe there was something to the subway fire, some connection. It would be good to talk to Aaron about it. He seemed to bring out the problem solver in me.

"You okay?" she asked, and we both checked me over in the mirror. The Visine had done a pretty good job. Catching the drift of my thoughts, she grinned. "Boys never know you've been crying. It just doesn't occur to them."

I laughed. "I don't know much about boys," I admitted. "Or girls. Or conversation..."

"But you know something about magic," she said, serious. "And you're fun to hang out with."

A bubble of something that must have been joy started navigating upwards from some deep part of me that had seldom seen the light. She thought I was fun? She thought I was fun.

"Thanks," I said, "you too."

Then— "Hang on—the move?"

"It's somewhere in Quebec I know. I'm not sure if it's Montreal or Quebec City; I know he said but I can't remember."

"Scott's *moving*?" This was a bigger shock than Peter's reaction to my ring at the party.

As if she was reading my thoughts, she said sympathetically, "I thought that's why you went to his place yesterday. Because you knew they were moving."

I stared at her. "This is a disaster."

She put her hand on my arm. "Come on, Maggie. It's okay—we'll figure it out. You just have to tell us what you know. You've got news, right? We'll figure it all out."

We went back to the others.

Everyone seated at the table was staring at us expectantly as we returned.

Rae was right. There was nothing to do but tell them everything I could. I took the initiative. "Okay, here's the deal. The guy's name is Hunt, and Jason and Aaron and I know him. If you thought he looked familiar..."

"Mr. Hunt?" said Jason, "from Westbrook Elementary?"

I nodded. "He's a... magician, of sorts. He knows a lot of stuff. He can sniff out magic, and that's why he's here, I think. He knew you did the ritual, and he's looking for an angle. If he thinks you have the book, he's especially dangerous, because I think he'd do just about anything to possess the knowledge in it."

Aaron crossed his arms in front of his chest as if he could somehow hold the absent book to himself and protect it.

"And I don't know what's up with the subway fire, but I do know that these—things—these creatures. . ." *like Char,* "like the underground. And heat. So maybe they're down there, and got carried away keeping themselves warm. I don't know. But someone told me to look into it."

"Who?" asked Jason, and I took another deep breath. It was time to start being forthcoming.

"A police officer, called Carla Szaba. She tracked me down yesterday after I was at Scott's."

"The *police*?" said Suzanne, a little shrilly. A couple of other tables in the shop paused in their conversations to look at us.

I spoke even quieter. "I went to the main police HQ a couple of weeks ago. . ." it had been longer, I thought, "to see a guy who's a detective there. A. . . *Special Case officer.* He's connected to this stuff too." Probably not smart to mention he was with the Homicide Squad, if just mentioning the police had got a squawk out of Suzanne.

Rae was looking at me with huge eyes, full of curiosity and, I thought, a new respect. "How did you know about this guy?"

"Tamblyn?" Here was the crux, the place I had to be really careful. "He's. . . he's the brother of the man who's been following you all. Hunt. Our old teacher. But the thing is, Tamblyn didn't know his brother was alive until I told him, and he's, well, he's kind of pissed off with me and not too trusting."

Jason laughed a little, and said flippantly, "You're pretty good at that."

For a second, I was offended, then swallowed my indignation. He was right, and the others seemed to appreciate his lightening the atmosphere. "I guess I am."

Suzanne sighed. "So you've got the police half upset with you and half giving you information, you've got your old public school teacher stalking us, and we still don't know what's killing the animals."

"And I think there's something coming," I said, unable to keep that particular feeling to myself. Tons of information I had concealed, and now I wanted to play a hunch. "I don't know what, but I don't think these things would have stayed around if there wasn't a reason. I think they'd have gone on to torment someone else, or gone where the heat was more readily available. I can't imagine they'd stay with us for fun."

"Maybe they're looking for a way back to wherever they came from," Aaron said. "Maybe they need us to reverse the ritual, or they're trapped here."

I considered it. That was an idea that had never occurred to me before, and I wondered why, beyond my own desire to be special and at the centre of things. But no, there was the Thurl-thing in the hallway, and his demands.

"I'd like to believe that," I said, "but I don't think it's right. I saw one of them, and talked to it."

"You *what?*" A couple of them said it.

"It took on the shape of Mr. Thurl. You know, from drafting? It said I was supposed to bring something, the book, to it."

"When was this?" Aaron asked.

"Just. . . not long ago." He was looking at me now with the kind of severe intensity he usually reserved for his debate opponents. I can't say I liked it.

"What?" I said, trying to match his expression. "It was a successful encounter as far as I was concerned. I told it to get going and it did."

"How?" Aaron said. "You know how to get rid of them and you didn't bother to tell us? What if Jason, or one of the girls came up against one of those things?"

He didn't include himself, I noticed. Probably figured he'd know what to do, what with his superior intellect and intuition.

"Look," I said, standing, "that's all I can tell you for right now. I want to figure out what the thing meant, and when I do, I'll tell you. And in the meantime, *if* you run across one of those things, just tell it in the most confident way you can to *begone, you're banished.* That's all I did. It worked, but honestly, I have no idea why."

✪

Aaron caught up with me outside, and put his hand on my arm, much as he had to stop Scott getting up to pound me back in the coffee shop.

"What?" I said, more pissed off than I meant to be, maybe just trying to give him a little of the steel and ice he's shown me inside. He lifted his hand off my arm, lifted both of them in mock surrender.

"You can be very cold, Maggie," said Aaron.

"I have to stay in control," I replied. "That's just what I have to do. But –"

*You're very cold, Maggie.* It took a moment, I guess, for that particular cruel little observation to stop me dead. Me, cold? Just because didn't I get all gooey like Suzanne? It wasn't me that was cold; it was these guys. What hadn't I done for them? I'd obsessed over their problem since nearly the first day of term. I'd worried about them. I'd done research. I'd put myself in the firing line to keep Hunt away from them, and I'd let myself be laughed at by his brother. I was cold? Where was the friendship, the camaraderie, I was supposed to get out of all this? I give them everything I have to give, and then I get accused of coldness.

So maybe I hadn't been going out of my way to be all lovey-dovey with them, but that's my manner, nothing else. I hadn't exactly been exposed to the easy side of living with people. I didn't know how to make people like me. I definitely didn't know how to make them feel comfortable with me. But couldn't they just have been grateful for what I'd done for them? Couldn't they let me feel like a character in my own story?

I waited, then realized, horrified, that I was on the verge of tears standing there looking at him like that.

I had seen this whole situation as my lucky break, hadn't I? A crisis, I'm needed, and I get to make friends all over again with these great guys. But it wasn't going to happen. They needed my help, and to hell, I guess, with what I needed.

I didn't want to cry in front of him, so I did all I could: shrugged at Aaron, turned my back on him, and walked away to find somewhere to cry in private. What a big stupid baby I was.

"Maggie!" Aaron called after me, but the pathetic nature of my thoughts had done its trick and there was no going back to speech until I had time to calm back down. I waved him away without turning back. There. Let him think I was mad. In either sense.

Cold? I would have killed to have someone even notice I was about to cry, and to follow to hold my hand while I did.

It was only when I'd left him far behind that it occurred to me: Rae had done just that.

❂

For some reason, my brain didn't actually process what Scott had said until much later. I was home, running around my usual circle of futile thoughts. Jan was cutting vegetables for a stir fry. We occupied the kitchen in more or less agreeable silence. Then, like I was replaying a recording, I suddenly heard Scott's voice in my head. "...*My last day here,*" he'd said.

"Mom," I said, a sick feeling building in my stomach. "When are the Saunders leaving town?"

She kept chopping in even rhythm. "Hm, they should probably be gone by now. Elizabeth said Jim likes to drive at night, so the kids sleep most of the way. I thought you knew that was why they had the going-away party. I guess you've seen how Emily and Scott can be..."

"Gone?" I managed. "Do you know where..."

"Montreal, I think," said Jan. "It's too bad. I think I really reconnected with Margaret. It would have been nice to have a friend in the neighborhood."

She might have said something else, but I didn't hear another word. My feet took me to the back door, vague as a sleepwalker. "Mom," I said, whether into a lull or over her words I didn't know. "I have to—I'll be right back, okay? Don't wait for me."

I opened the door and was gone, sprinting over the back lot, through the neighbors' yard and onto the street.

My breath came in sharp pants as much from the intensity of my anxiety as my poor fitness level. At that moment, I felt like I could have easily run ten miles if it meant I could talk to Peter—to Soren—before he was ripped from my life altogether.

I rounded the corner onto Fleance and paused, panting hard, to catch my breath. For a moment, I thought it was too late: the Saunders driveway was empty, the house closed and dark. But then I heard a cough of motor as the SUV parked across the street from the bottom of the drive started up, and I saw red taillights, and a white face in the back window.

"Peter!" I screamed, forgetting again that he was no longer Peter, was no longer the Prince of an underground cavern in Char's realm, was suburban Soren Saunders, protected and adored autistic child of a stable, normal family. Brother of Scott and Emily and the troubled, missing Rebecca. Leaving town and slipping away, with his knowledge of my secret life, forever.

Did Emily see me? Did Mr. Saunders, looking in his rearview as he pulled away from the house on Fleance for the last time? I don't know, but Peter did, and his mouth opened into a big silent 'O' and his small white hand pressed itself to the glass. There was no screaming this time, no horror. I was glad of that at least, that my last glimpse of my hidden ally wasn't of a pale little face screaming and frantic. But then I saw the curly blond head beside Peter turn and there was Scott Saunders, catching sight of me, eyes narrowing, a look of the most naked hatred I had ever had directed at me with the exception of that of the Dark Man's daughter Arabella.

And that was where my mind headed as the taillights disappeared over the crest of the hill and towards parts unknown. *Montreal, I think.* And Rae: *Somewhere in Quebec. . . I can't remember.* My last potential connection with a friendly someone who remembered, someone who the final magic, the last rite, hadn't affected, it was severed and the chance was missed.

Instead, I had a slowly darkening sky above me, and the more disturbing encroachment of memories of Char, of sweet dark-haired Damon, of vicious, murderous Arabella with her cooing voice and fingers like stiletto blades. Instead of showing friendship to Scott when I could have, working to cultivate his trust, I could see now I had done everything wrong. I had pushed him whenever the opportunity had presented itself, and ended up upsetting his much-loved little brother. Had continued to behave in the most infuriating and pompous manner possible, in fact, until he and Peter were both beyond my reach.

*Bravo, Mags.*

## 24

## Quicksand

✪

At home again, I took all my "research" and spread it in a circle around me. The scariest piece, my strange auto-painting, I put directly in front of me, a meter from my bent knees. I meant to draw something new, but putting out paint and charcoal and a fresh piece of watercolor paper had no effect on my stagnant creativity. Giving up at last, I reached under the bed and pulled out of its hiding place a purple Crown Royal bag, and spilled its contents to the floor.

How long had it been since I had collected these items, telling myself it was so that I *would not forget* and had nothing to do with wanting a different way into magic? Chalk, candles, knife. The memory of Hunt's long knife, rusted and stained with the blood of who knew how many "experiments," made mine look cheap and virginal. I had bought it for its dark wood handle and wickedly serrated blade, the candles from an import company for their smell of distant places. The chalk I'd lifted from school.

Inertia is a powerful force, I told myself, but still I could do no more than pick up the charcoal I had meant to draw with, the tools of someone else's trade spread around me.

But slowly, as I sat, something began to occur to me. It crept like a thief into my consciousness. The painting, that scrap of paper with the pentagram and the evil eyes. It had been a premonition, of a sort. A warning of future events, in some vague sense, at the very least. And it had come, somehow, out of me.

The realization of the enormity of this discovery trickled slowly through me. *Magic? Me?* Some echo of Char's power still lingering? Most important, could I do it again? If there was ever a time I needed guidance, it was now.

I readied the charcoal, a black smudge already on my index finger. How had the inspiration struck the last time? I didn't know. I had been starting a drawing, with no idea of what I was going to produce. That was the way to begin.

The charcoal left a fluted mark on my clean watercolor page, then a second. What was I drawing? I rotated the page, drew another line, and tried to see the picture in it. I felt like a child lying indolent on a blue-skied summer day, imagining elephants and pirate ships made of clouds.

I sketched a few more lines, and a couple of vague shapes, but nothing formed. No hands took mine and led them. The experiment was, as far as I could tell, a wasted effort.

Finally, futilely, I threw the charcoal away and kicked the watercolor pad as far as I could across the room.

✪

*I dream, and this time I'm frightened before I'm aware of anything else at all.*

*I slowly absorb enough of the panic to take in my surroundings, using Hunt's old techniques of storing my power to do it—a little fear moved out into this finger, a bit into my big toe. Divide it, and you're strong enough to control the whole beast.*

*I'm in a cavern, deep and echoing. The walls are smooth but without the regularity I would associate with something man-made. It's like someone put an air pocket into a patch of non-homogenous rock and blew, like some mammoth glass blower, so that each part expanded differently, then warmed the whole thing up to let it melt, just a little. It feels unformed, unfinished, and somehow off as if I know something's wrong but can't place it.*

*And why am I so scared?*

*There's a lingering echo in the place—something that must come from outside of me because I haven't made a sound and yet I understand the special acoustics. It's a kind of rumble, and it's been all around me since I woke here, alway present but only now noticed. I listen, trying to get a fix on it, and realize, this is what is frightening me. This sound is the source of my now-growing terror.*

*The sound begins to increase, to intensify, as if given leave by my attention to it. I close my eyes, try to picture what's making it, what it reminds me of. The fear comes with a sense of dread and familiarity. I know, but I can't articulate.*

*There is a wavering in the echo, a feeling that I am hearing a sound with organic variety, a cresting and falling, peaks and... A laugh. A chuckle. That's what it is, and as I put a name to it, I hear it for what it is, with crystal clarity. A low, throaty laugh, delicious and relishing, and with it a remembered cruelty that takes my breath away. I sink to my knees, overpowered. The fear has surged from my extremities back into my core and fills my eyes, my temples, my guts.*

*"Poor little bug," I hear, the smooth, cunning alto turning me to quivering jelly, dancing with sharp feet on my head.*

*"Arabella?" I can barely say it, much less sound like anything but the terrified little girl I've become.*

*The laugh rings out, bouncing and echoing around me, an almost physical presence. "Can't you face me, little bug? Little pawn, little plaything?"*

*I shove a fist in my eye, determined not to cry, but sure I will. I say nothing. I can't trust myself. I have forgotten this is a dream.*

*"My father is finished with you, little bug. You have served your purpose for him. What's worse, being helpless, or finding out you never meant anything to him?" She chuckles again, this time reminding me of Hunt and his wild but too-accurate insinuations.*

*Let me keep my illusions,* I want to shout. *Let me pretend he wanted something more from me than to strip me of my powers, to save himself. I remember, as an unconvincing thread of memory, that Char did want something more, that in however a twisted and unconventional way, he had validated me. Someone needed me, someone wanted me to not give up. It was central to my personal dogma that the sacrifice I had made on the bluff was connected to the penance I had to do for destroying Char, and in doing so pushing away forever the one person who proved to me that Maggie Stuart was somehow* special.

*Arabella laughs again, the echos beating against me like fists on my body. I raise my hands to ward off the sound, touching nothing and feeling the blows rain unthwarted."Maggie, Maggie, Maggie," she chants. "Father's little Princess, torn and humiliated. Alone and ignored. What a joke you are, little bug. What a sight. A little more pressure and you'll subside into the earth, a stain in a crack."*

*I roll over, feeling her behind me, raising my hands to my face in case the attack I expect comes quickly.*

*A huge dark bulk confronts me.*

*An enormous shape, looming high above me, resolving itself slowly into something familiar but so wrong. . . A knee, a hip. A woman, long-limbed and clad in a mountain of black velvet. She is perfectly proportioned, but of titanic dimensions. A giantess lies comfortably on her side, raised on one long, white hand.*

*"Hello, Maggie, dear," says Arabella, leaning giant lips toward me. Each eye is as big as my hand. Amused at my discomfiture, she coos, "Do you still want to play?"*

*An enormous finger, as long as my body, inches its way through the air, like every deadly propeller on every runaway plane in every B-horror movie. I watch it coming and can't move as it arches, poised to flick me aside. Like an insect, like a little bug.*

*I know there is a reason I should not be worried, but can't escape the immediacy of the danger. I close my eyes. Here is the punishment, at last, for which I have been waiting for three long years.*

And I wake in the darkness, and this time I'm shaking so much that when I put my feet on the floor, my legs collapse under me and I land in a pile. Me, the Crown Royal bag, the chalk, the candles, and the wicked, wicked knife.

✪

I was fully conscious an hour before my alarm, and couldn't get back to sleep. Instead, I watched the sun slowly turn my curtains a pale pink and tried to distract myself from the memory of the dream.

In the kitchen, I read through the paper slowly, and found yet another article to clip. I had no idea if there was anything to the small collection I was assembling. Death, murder, disappearance. The common thread was that they were unsolved, and happened somewhere in the region. Beyond that, what could I really infer? Wasn't I just fooling myself to believe I was doing something the least bit relevant? It was probably just as futile as the "tools of the trade," the tools of a trade I had no business being in, and no idea how to enter in any case.

My thoughts were taking a very unpleasant course.

Arabella. My personal demon. But she wasn't real, I knew that. I had killed her.

And on that act and the rest of what I had done in the catacombs, I had built a belief system for myself that I clung to furiously, knowing it was perverse, knowing it kept me alone, but unable to see past it to anything better. I had learned to replay my time in the catacombs as some bizarre sort of moral lesson. I had been offered love, offered power. I had been offered a chance to join something vast and exotic, something that needed me as a part of it. Without me, Char could not survive, or would not, because without me he would be overrun by his children, by whatever had taken his wife. He was waning like a sick old moon, and I was his desperately hoped-for salvation.

What do you do afterwards, when you are the anointed hero, and you turn your back on your destiny? I killed my mentor, directly or indirectly wiped out his entire family, and took on more power than any human has ever dreamed of possessing. I was the thief, the betrayer, the traitor. It felt too simplistic to say Char was evil and had to be destroyed. It felt too much like empty justification to say Arabella was evil and I killed her in self defense. The truth was, as far as I could see it, without me, the balance of power might not have shifted. Without me, Arabella might not have been pushed to show her hand in such a sadistic way as to leave her brother dead.

I hadn't asked to be involved, but when I was, there should have been something I could have done to salvage Char's dynasty, something I could have done to preserve an ancient line I, in truth, knew almost nothing about.

I knew about survivor guilt. I'd read all sorts of literature on mental disorders, post-traumatic stress, coping with bereavement and loss. I didn't expect guilt to be the overriding emotion I'd have left after Char, after the catacombs. I didn't expect that I would be so worried I hadn't done the right thing.

Now when I looked back on the ritual afterwards, on the bluff above Char's ruined palace, I thought I could see what I was doing. I was trying to make myself feel better. In my own way, I was trying to assuage my guilt at wiping out Char and his family by erasing my mistake. Destroy the evidence thoroughly enough and you destroy the event, right? If no one remembered Char, no one could question what I'd done. I wouldn't have to think about it.

But guilt isn't killed as easily as a human being, or even as a being like Arabella. I used magic to kill her, magic to wipe away the memory of her in my circle of until-lately-friends, but the knowledge of what I'd done remained. I couldn't escape the guilt, and I couldn't escape the loneliness.

So I reinterpreted. I knew I was doing it, but I couldn't stop. It's survivor-redefinition. If you can't escape the facts, look at them differently. I did it so I could live with myself, so that I could go on as if the right things had happened. I tried to put my battle with Char into a less epic perspective. I was tempted to cast us as heroine and villain, virgin and evil seducer. That was attractive but shallow, and I didn't buy my own heroism.

So instead, I scaled everything back to its most human, microscopic level. Char had told me he wanted me to be his consort. I refused, and then killed him. I'd never even thought about what I'd done to Char as murder before. I obsessed about killing Arabella, but I'd done exactly the same to him. I, Maggie Stuart, constant whiner about how no one cared or understood, had actually stood on my own two feet and murdered a man who said he would be my father, or my lover, or my teacher. I had only to name the role, and he would love me beyond all boundaries of normal human affection. I, who cried about my absent father, ignored my suffering mother because her pain made me impotent to reach out, I who craved any sort of attention or affection, even the wrong kind, I had killed instead of allowing myself to be loved.

Now, who could love a killer?

## 25

### Station To Station

✪

I walked to school at a crawl, barely able to shift my heavy legs to move myself along. How innocent I'd been before Char, and how simple my beliefs.

It didn't help that so many of the memories remained strong. I couldn't erase what had happened with Arabella, the day she turned the power of the ring against her brother.

And I saw something finally that had escaped me before. Peter had been there, and watched every second as she did what she did. The red ring—but Peter had touched my wrist.

*Blood.* That's what he meant by 'red'. It was painfully obvious, now. It wasn't just Arabella's use of the ring that had traumatized him. Blood, inside Scott. Arabella's idea of a joke, playing a sick game of I-Spy with Peter. With Scott lying unconscious, Arabella had handed her long knife to Peter. Scott had been Peter's champion since he met him, his protector and knight-errant, although against a being like Arabella, it wasn't likely he'd ever prevail in any significant way. *"We're going to play a game called* Red. *Do you see anything red?"* And Peter held the knife by its blade, as if he had never seen one before, shaking so much I thought he'd cut himself.

Arabella, those slitted cat's eyes, the razor-sharp smile. Egging Peter on: *use it—use the knife. There's lots of 'red' inside him. Go on...*

Hardly strange that I'd forgotten about it until now, because at the time I was injured myself. Not to mention, at that moment, I was much more involved with trying to save Damon's life.

*Oh god.* I stopped dead, my legs refusing to work at all.

Damon, curled on his side, fists clenched into his stomach, the sweat beginning to bead around his forehead and lips, the dampness in his hair when I touched it. So much pain. *Damon*. Then I was back suddenly in his apartment in the Char's Dreamworld, feeling his arms supporting me as he carried me up the stairs to his bedroom, the gentle, chaste kiss he put on my forehead before retreating downstairs.

But that image, something which I admit had sustained me every now and then and kept me from total loneliness, was just as quickly replaced with the other image. Damon, the ring's red glow suffusing his body, his muscles spasming and twisting as he began to die.

Peter knew the ring, knew its power, and most of all knew the viciousness of the woman who'd wielded it.

*But wait*—if he could recognize it, did that mean that he retained his magic? Char had been using him to work magic through his singing. Did some essence of that remain?

*No, Maggie.* I told myself this firmly. *You will absolutely not use a little boy to get your way. Not for all the power in the world.*

Besides, even if I knew exactly where the Saunders family was going, it was probably more than my life was worth to try to see Peter again. If looks could kill, the one Scott gave me would have dropped me in my tracks. They were gone; Peter was gone. One more link to my past had dissolved.

Slowly, feeling crooked and twisted as if I had taken some of Damon's final pain into my bones, I turned and continued the labored walk to school.

And then, something snapped. Or I came to some decision, without conscious consideration. I saw a bus pull up to the stop ahead, and I was running to catch it. I wasn't going to school, yet again. I wasn't going to be responsible. I wasn't going to face Mr. Thurl's tacit disappointment today, or Jason, or Irene. I was running away.

I took the GO to the end of the subway line at Kipling Station, moved to the extreme east end of the subway platform and boarded the first car of the train that waited to depart.

Right at the front of the train, I rode in utter stillness, kneeling on the seat to face in the direction we were going, eyes glued to the tunnel ahead.

If there was any sign, any indication of the fire, I wanted to see it.

Coming up on Royal York, I intensified my gaze, looking left, to the north, and seeing nothing of interest. Past the station, same deal. I caught a fleeting glimpse of the descending tunnel where it curved away, and down, under the westbound tracks, and then nothing.

I decided to get off at the stop after the second line diverged from the main tracks, and ride back and forth looking for clues to what had happened here. Why had Carla told me to look at the paper for the story? The only reason I could think was that Tamblyn had said something, either to her, or during one of his overheard phone conversations. I would bet firmly on the latter.

I knew I wouldn't be able to get into the tunnel itself, not without some kind of official permission. There was no way I could count on being brave enough to break the law that far. Some kinds of civic obedience were just too ingrained in me. I have trouble jumping a turnstile much less sneaking down a tunnel.

We entered Old Mill station, and I disembarked. I walked up and over to make my way back to the west end of the platform and peered into the darkness of the tunnel. Nothing out of order, no sign that anything of note had happened.

Morning rush hour was only just winding down, but since I was now heading away from downtown, I was easily able to secure my front seat again.

The 'door closing' chimes sounded, and the train lurched into life.

We entered the tunnel, and this time, I thought I could sense something different. It wasn't anything I could put my finger on; nothing I could see or hear.

And then, I heard the driver, locked in his booth just to my right, swear loudly. At the same moment, I realized what was odd—I was burning up. The temperature in the car had shot up, maybe ten degrees, and the other passengers were loosening ties and unbuttoning collars. *No...*

The driver swore again, this time louder, and I felt a tremor in the earth.

The brakes of the subway train had already started to squeal hideously before I realized I'd left my seat. The emergency stop lever was in my fist; I was hanging from it, my full weight thrown into pulling it down.

Everyone was yelling now, some terrified, some angry with me, some confused and startled out of whatever morning fog they'd been in until a moment before.

The train shook again, more violently, and the door of the driver's compartment flew open. Inside, a large man with a big belly and white hair fought the controls. Something hit the roof of the train. We were slowing, the rising squeal of wheels on track deafening. I was glad the train wasn't too full; nearly everyone had had a seat, although those who did and those who didn't were equally involved in holding on for dear life as the careening car decelerated.

I was still gripping the handle of the emergency stop, afraid to switch my hold to something else for fear of flying across the car.

We shuddered to a sudden halt, and the train lurched backwards. I lost my grasp finally and hit the front window of the train hard.

A deafening crash echoed through the train, generated in the tunnel outside. I hauled my sore body up to the front window and saw nothing but dust.

Someone started screaming; others joined in and someone started yelling for everyone to *just shut up.* A crackling voice was speaking over the loudspeaker in the car, but as usual the words were unintelligible. I started to laugh, partly my standard response in such situations, and partly because I had often thought that the TTC public address system would be just this useless in a crisis.

And then, the dust settled in front of the train, and I sobered up.

There was no tunnel at all ahead, starting maybe twenty meters in front of where I sat. Instead, there was a wall of freshly fallen rock, and sparking cables, and a rush of water from a broken pipe.

I slid down to the floor between two rows of seats, and found myself shaking uncontrollably for what I silently told myself was already too many times today. My arms and legs felt bruised, but I didn't think anything was broken. I wondered how people in the other cars had fared, with far less warning than I'd had.

Another accident on the subway line, at somewhere near the same spot.

*But this time, I was here.*

And that was what I was thinking as the lights went out.

Train, tunnel, emergency lights, all doused. No flickering, just dead. An eerie silence settled over the car. I heard the driver speaking into his radio, and hearing nothing in return, no crackle of static, no nothing. We lay dead underground.

I don't know how long it was before people started moving

around. There was dust on everything, in my eyes, in my hair, up my nose. I hear sneezing, and someone's voice asking anxiously (and quietly), *Is everyone all right?*

I heard a whoosh like a flame igniting, but there was no light with it. There was a rush of air, hot against my face, sweeping by me and circling. Suddenly, I was back in the gym with Aaron's pale eyes going wide as the *whatever* escaped the broken chalk lines and attacked.

Someone somewhere far down the car flicked his Zippo. And screamed. Dark descended again.

Something was here with us.

I couldn't tell if it was one, or more than one. I tried to stand and was buffeted back down. Across the car, I could hear shouts and moans, confusion rising at the strange sensation of a hot wind racing back and forth across faces, shifting toppled briefcases, riffling hair and clothes.

But there were no screams, no indication that this thing or things were ripping and cutting like the ones in the gymnasium. I was knocked over again, but it felt almost incidental, circumstantial, like falling over on board a ship in rough seas.

And then, with the next pass, there was a change.

I felt a heat in the skin of my neck, and touched a wet place there where I was now, I thought, bleeding. And it returned.

I covered my face with my hands, backing into the corner, trapped between the seats. It came again and again, and I silently cowered, raising myself up off the dirty floor of the train but unable to do more than hunch into the nearest seat.

Claws raked my hair, my bare legs, my neck. The touch was light but unerring, each swipe turning me to protect some exposed part of myself, each finding bare skin and opening me up.

And still I made no sound. I heard the driver calling for attention, asking for everyone to stay calm. I fought to protect myself, and realized that everyone else, for the most part, *was* calm. I alone was under attack, hidden in the dark from help or scrutiny, by something no one would likely have been able to see in any case, and around me, everyone else was recovering.

Another unintelligible announcement burst out of the speakers above our heads, and I was suddenly free of the attack. I slumped against the seat where I had pressed myself vainly to avoid the invisible claws, and began to sob quietly in relief.

When the lights came back on a moment later, seeming too bright and painful, I was telling myself, *this happened because of you.*

There was no other way to look at it.

In the light, people looked strange and scared, really awake for the first time I had ever seen a group of commuters. There was a fine layer of dust on everything. People were talking, but my ears were full of pounding blood and I heard nothing. The driver had to pull on my arm before I turned to look at him. I heard him distantly,

"You pulled the cord?"

I nodded dumbly.

He patted me on the shoulder and went the door of the compartment, where he began to talk rapidly into his radio while surveying the dazed passengers.

✪

We sat in the car for an hour before transit officials came to escort us to the back of the train and through the tunnel to the platform.

First, we walked to the back of the train, led by the two TTC officials on board. That was okay—even a little enjoyable since for the first time, I was actually being told to ignore the explicit warning on the doors that *walking between cars is strictly prohibited.*

It was different when we got to the last car of the six and descended to the tunnel itself.

It might seem like hyperbole to say it was the worst moment of my life to that point, but maybe not by much. When the conductor gave me his hand to help me jump down out of the back of the train, I felt like my entire body had suddenly become made of tight metal bands under enormous pressure held together by only by the frailest of bonds.

It had never occurred to me, somehow, that to be in a subway train is to necessarily travel deep underground. Maybe it was because a lot of the track on the only section I rode with any regularity—between Kipling and Bloor—is actually aboveground. If you see sunlight every now and then, you forget about the parts where the sky is separated from you by dozens of meters of dirt and stone and concrete.

I was exquisitely aware of the live rail to the right of us. It crackled at odd intervals, as if it didn't want us to become too comfortable with its proximity. We were passed as we walked by TTC workers in hardhats, by police, by paramedics, by a multitude of other men and women heading back along the tunnel toward the wreckage of the tunnel and the scene of our near-demise. The conductors kept us between the two non-electrified tracks, and the rescue workers walked along the narrow raised walkway to our left. I would, I think, have liked to be up there and a little further from the live rail.

The distance between Royal York station and Old Mill was maybe the longest on the line between Kipling and downtown, and it certainly seemly like it. I, who had stopped a train, faced down an invisible kitten-killer and, let's not forget, stood up finally to Arabella, was utterly terrified the whole way.

It took everything I had to control the shaking of my legs. I know what it feels like to start to emerge from shock, and that was part of it. But far worse was the feeling of *being underground*, of being trapped in a world without sun, without escape, to be in the power of something I didn't understand.

The feelings had almost nothing to do with where I was, but where I had been. In Char's catacombs. Chained up, abused. Forced to submit, manipulated and stressed beyond anything a thirteen year-old kid should have to face. Alone, and on a path to become a killer where a stronger person might have felt instead like a hero.

We had to walk single-file, and I was the last in line except for the conductor behind me. My eyes adjusted slowly to the light provided by the slow swing of flashlights held by TTC officials, fire fighters, and rescue workers from Toronto's EMS, and the orange of the sodium vapor lamps and solid red signal lights at intervals along the wall. But the only way I could put one foot in front of the other was to focus on the dusty suit of the business man in front of me, to let my eyes fill with the pinstripes of its fabric, and fall into an almost hypnotic state where I could pretend that I wasn't here, in this tunnel, walking away from what had nearly been the scene of my death. And avoid falling into the memory of the only time in my life where I had really felt alive.

The mixture of sunlight and artificial light that greeted us when we turned the last bend before Old Mill seemed to mock me. *You silly, scared girl,* it said. *Afraid of the dark? At your age?*

But I was afraid. The driver, who had followed me all the way from the train, gave me a boost to the walkway leading up to a set of stairs, and from there to the platform. I walked the wrong way through a

"Do Not Enter" sign like those I'd noted so often at the end of the platform, and into human chaos. My legs buckled, and I felt his arm catch mine. A moment later, I was leaning against the wall, nodding that I was okay. I had made it.

Those in my car had suffered the worst, and paramedics swarmed over us to check us over before turning us over to the police and TTC officials.

The EMT guy checking me out was cute I thought, in his mid-twenties, with strong hands and a kindness that made me very self-conscious as he poked and prodded. He was perplexed by the cuts on my legs and neck.

"I don't get how you got these," he kept saying.

Remembering how the lacerations I'd sustained in the gym seemed to heal so quickly, I took a leap of faith. "My cat," I said, as if it had just occurred to me. "She really scratched me up this morning. I think I just got bruised from the crash."

Finally, he let me go, pronouncing me fit, although he remained unconvinced. I would go so far as to say suspicious. Then I was another hour giving a statement as the cops cordoned off the station and tunnel, and the investigators and bureaucrats moved in.

The driver had apparently given me credit for fast thinking when I'd pulled the emergency stop. That turned out to be a good thing; it kept me focused on what I *didn't* want to mention—the hot gusts of air, and the thing attacking me in the dark.

When they'd taken my statement, I collected my bag from the policewoman who'd been guarding all our personal possessions while we were looked over, and caught a glimpse of Tamblyn, talking to my paramedic. *Damn*. Tamblyn turned, following the indication of the other's finger, and looked in my direction.

I couldn't exactly run—although I did consider it—but I didn't exactly stand still either. I vibrated in place until Tamblyn reached me, shifting my weight back and forth like a jogger stuck at a traffic light.

"Well, well, well, Maggie Stuart." He positioned himself between me and the exit. Unlike a lot of stations, Old Mill only had one egress, so I wasn't going anywhere without dealing with him.

"Got to work on the trust, Detective," I heard myself say, and instantly regretted it. "Sorry," I covered quickly. "I'm... well, does scared begin to cover it?"

He turned to wave away the paramedic, who was hovering a few feet back.

"Miss Stuart," he started again, quieter, and motioned me toward a bench along the wall. We both sat, and I waited.

Tamblyn looked at me a long time, and then shook his head.

"No," he said, "I don't think you have anything to do with causing this. However, I don't think your being here is completely random either."

"I came because I read about the fire," I said quickly, without consideration. "The one on the other tracks."

He nodded.

"What happened?" I asked. "Was there an explosion? Was it a bomb?"

He grimaced. "Gas main. That's the speculation." He looked around, as if making absolutely sure we weren't being overheard, and continued, "I think it's something else. There was a cave-in, we know that much. It sealed the entrance to that *other track* you mentioned."

Slowly, I nodded. Sealed the entrance. And did it when I was there to nearly get crushed.

"Quick thinking," he said. "With the brakes. Driver said you pulled the cord, and that he'd barely had time to register something was wrong before you did. You probably saved a lot of lives today, including your own."

The shake was back, starting in my legs again, and this time progressing through my body to my hands and arms. "I don't remember doing it," I admitted, and something struck me. I *didn't* remember doing it—had it been me who somehow knew there was danger, or had something *made me* pull the emergency stop? *Magic...*

"I'd say you were probably due for some kind of civic honor..."

"Oh god."

"... but you're not the type, are you. Just like my brother. Keeping to the shadows."

I stared. His brother.

"Hunt," I breathed.

"We need to talk, Maggie," he said, and for the first time I saw concern in his eyes. "Why don't you come back to the station with me and we'll have a little sit-down?"

*Carla,* I thought, and suddenly wanted to cut her out of my relationship with Tamblyn. Such as it was. If I was to have direct contact with Tamblyn himself, I hardly needed Carla's help to keep an eye on him. And if I was able to speak directly with him, I didn't want to have to share what I learned with her.

"Not the station," I said. "Too many prying eyes, and Hunt may see us together."

"Okay," he said, agreeing readily. "Let's do it here."

26

Law

✪

*Here*, in Tamblyn's version, involved getting my suspicious EMT (who, I thought, was growing more suspicious by the moment), to bundle both of us up in blankets, including most of our heads, and walk us across the street to a waiting bus. He sat silently beside me while the TTC ferried us to Royal York station with a bunch of other weary travelers just trying to finish their trip. Satisfied that no one was taking any particular note of us, he had a few quiet words with a uniformed officer whose cruiser blocked the road in front of the station. Then, we ducked down an alley where we found a quiet corner across from the public parking lot, on the steps of a fire escape.

"That was so. . ." I said when we were seated, and then realized I had no idea how to finish the sentence.

Tamblyn's radio squawked and crackled with continuous updates. We listened for a minute or so to descriptions of the extent of the damage to the tunnel, to the re-routing of westbound traffic to surface routes, and then he switched it off.

Tamblyn was more as I remembered him from our first meeting on the bluffs over Char's palace today, wearing the trenchcoat and hat, the latter of which he placed on the bench between us as if marking out our individual territories.

"Well, Maggie Stuart," he began again. "A busy day today for you."

"Mr. Tamblyn," I said, feeling a surge of words suddenly fighting to get out, "*Detective* Tamblyn, I'm so sorry I told you about Hunt the way I did. It was cruel, but I wasn't thinking. It's just that. . ."

I stopped dead. What was I supposed to say?

"This is going to be difficult," I said slowly. "There's something I know that you've—you've forgotten. I don't know if I should tell you."

"Go on," he said, his voice gruff.

I took a deep breath. The levee I had damaged with my later retracted admissions to Rae strained to hold the flood of my secrets. Now was the time. Now I would tell, at least part of it. And since Tamblyn was already aware of so much of this *other* world I knew, it was hardly the same as telling Rae, or coming clean to any of the rest. "I met Hunt because he was teaching at my school. In Westbrook. He had plastic surgery, I gather, and he was looking for. . . for some magic something that was happening."

Tamblyn nodded. "We're both pretty tuned in to supernatural events. Hunt would go wherever something unusual was happening, or to any real practitioner who came onto his radar, just to see if he could get something for himself."

I waited. Tamblyn seemed to want to say something more.

"I'm not surprised he's not dead," he said at last, looking away from me. "Not at all. I never really believed it. He's too slippery, and far too good a conventional magician, let's not even mention his real abilities. I never thought he was gone for good. I just hoped."

Hunt, on the bluff, with Tamblyn at his side, the two brothers momentarily united in their aims and in a temporary alliance. And then, with a stroke of my hand, wielding a sharp knife. . .

"I used to. . . used to be able to do magic," I said. "Hunt taught me. And I made you forget. . . forget that you'd seen him again, that you'd met me, that anything that happened happened. You met my mom. You came after me, at least that's what I gather happened. I think you guys actually got along pretty well even. You were trying to save me, even if you don't remember. So—thank you for that, anyhow."

"And just *what* happened?" he said, and waited.

I bit my lip, and tried to decide what to say. In the back of my mind, I was imagining the strange energy of the investigation surging around us as we sat on the bench at the station, ebbing and flowing with firemen, cops, and transit officials. How much was I going to say now to Tamblyn? My secret seemed small again suddenly. Who would really care, after all, that I had been Char's chosen consort? It mattered to me, but it would hardly carry much weight with someone like Tamblyn.

"Hunt thought he could exploit my. . . abilities. But he was wrong. I lost whatever power I had. That's it. He went away, but he showed me how to make everyone forget what happened. You and my mom, Jan, you came after me. I don't really know how that happened, because... well..."

Of course Tamblyn didn't remember meeting Jan. What was I supposed to say? You liked her; she liked you. I almost thought there was something starting between you, despite my father's presence on that bluff as well. I sensed there could something nice between them; he was the kind of guy I thought my mom should be with, not a stiff like *Harrison*. Or a deadbeat like my dad, no matter how charming he might have been.

What hope was there for my mother and the detective now? My gift had untied their history into threads floating away on the wind. Nothing could bring them together again. *Changing the past,* I realized again, *was a heavy burden.*

Then, I finally understood what my mother was doing, when she stalked through the house on her strange, uncompleted missions. She was looking for the source of a memory. That sniff-sniff was my mother smelling smoke, something completely incompatible with her experience of her own history. No one but Maggie knew that the house which we shared had once been ruined by fire, ruined until I had used part of that final magic to fix it up the way it had been before Char entered our lives. No one but Maggie, and I hadn't even seen the damage, only knew about it because I had felt the effects of the fire when I reached out to heal it. But the healing was not perfect. There was a scar which remained, invisible, but which made Jan itch, whenever she was tired or otherwise susceptible to the seethings of her own subconscious.

I knew I should take this as a sign that hope remained, in however a perverse, upside-down way. After all, I had thought the final magic was complete and had utterly destroyed any chance of those pernicious memories returning to Jason, to Aaron, to Hunt even. Peter / Soren had put the lie to that notion.

Caught up in the past, I was telling the story in a way that made little sense, I thought. Making everyone forget was what had lost me my power. Hunt encouraged me to do it, which wiped me out. Why *hadn't* he found a better way to exploit me? All that effort to find me, train me, and manipulate my experience in Char's clutches. What *had* been his reward?

Tamblyn was looking at me steadily. He had obviously noticed the inconsistency, but he was cagey. He didn't know where my thoughts had gone, but he knew I was being less than forthcoming. Maybe he understood that I was editing as I went, I guessed, because he obviously had a lot of experience with that himself. Or maybe he just knew Hunt a lot better than I to take this kind of revelation at face value.

"So you lost your power, then used your power?"

I struggled to find an explanation that would suit both of us. I landed on a lie, and saw that it would do, although it would also restore my feelings of inadequacy.

"My power wasn't much," I said, "but what there was scared me. Hunt told me I could make everyone forget, and wipe it out, and I'd get to go back to being normal."

*Get to go back to being normal.* Tears started to well up in my eyes as I said it. A cruel lie, as cruel a thing as I could say about myself. Pretending that the lonely years I'd spent since Char's discovery of me had been my own choice, necessitated by fear. Pretending that "normal" was what I really wanted.

"Okay," he said, and there was a note of comfort in his tone as well as finality. I had satisfied him, I thought. Goddamn, how many times had Hunt pulled something similar, to have him so easily able to accept my version of events?

Then he leaned back and fixed me with his grey eyes.

"There is something you can do for me, and I think you'll agree you owe me. I was quite happy not knowing my brother was alive."

"What do you want?" I said, with a faint hope it would be something that would actually make me feel more useful.

"Show me the ring."

I breathed in. Carla had told me he'd been on the phone about it, and I should have remembered he was far more interested than he had let on to me in our last meeting.

I realized I had no objection at this point to showing Tamblyn the ring. Already, I had experienced a distinct sense of relief in being able to share at least a part of my burden with him.

That's when I felt a twinge, a hint that something wasn't right. I managed to keep my face stony, but inside, my heart skipped a beat.

The comforting weight of the ring around my neck on its silver chain was wrong. Something was different.

What I was feeling now, far too strongly, was a growing panic. What was wrong? I couldn't feel the weight of the ring against my chest. I imagined I could still sense the coolness of the chain on the skin at the nape of my neck, but it was all wrong.

I couldn't possibly reach up in front of Tamblyn to touch the chain. I had to get out of there, fast, before I panicked. I had to know if the chain was intact, but Tamblyn *could not know*.

"Detective Tamblyn," I said, forcing my voice to a steadiness I did not feel. "I have to go. I don't have the ring with me, or you'd be welcome to look at it. I'd very much like to know more about it myself. But now, I have to go. If you're not detaining me."

He looked at me intensely for a moment, until I felt the skin on the back of my neck crawl under the silver chain. I had to go—I had to know.

"All right," he said. "You did a good thing back there. I have no reason to keep you, and every reason to get back to the site of the cave-in. But I'm watching you, Maggie Stuart."

I nodded. "I don't mind," I said, thinking of Hunt. Thinking, also, of how Szaba expected me to return the favor and watch him as well.

"Watch your back," he said, his mind obviously in the same place, then, with no knowledge of just how damning he was being, he added, "Guard that ring with your life. Never let it out of your sight."

I fought to stay calm as we stood, shook hands in a professionally detached manner, and went in opposite directions.

I didn't have a clue where I was going, myself, just away from him. As soon as he was out of sight, I collapsed in onto a door stoop and put my hands to my neck.

It was gone. The ring was completely gone. The chain lay around my neck in two pieces, and if I was in any doubt about what had happened, a quick examination disabused me of any notion that it had merely broken in the accident.

Just below the midpoint between my collarbones, just where the ring had sat, was a vertical scratch running down to the edge of my bra. In the attack on me in the subway car, one of those invading claws had severed my necklace. And taken the ring. I had no doubt. I started to shake. The ring was gone.

I wanted to cry. First the book, now the ring. I had the distinct feeling someone was screwing with me. And that the games had hardly begun.

## 27

### Unwashed And Somewhat Slightly Dazed

✪

Needing something normal, I made my way back to Dief. That necessitated using the alternate surface routes the TTC slapped into place, with the subway out of service. It was nearly one when I got there, already partway through my first afternoon class. I made a quick visit to the washroom on the way into school to remove the worst of the dust from my clothing and make sure there were no bleeding cuts showing above my collar or on my hands. I felt like I was floating in a foreign world, barely able to hold myself to the ground.

Between classes, I looked for any of my co-conspirators, desperate for the salve of human contact. I even looked for Irene. I just wanted to say hi to someone, anything to return me to reality.

It didn't help that I could feel the lump of the broken chain in my pocket against my leg. How could I have put myself in a place where I at least suspected the things were hanging around, right where Carla had warned me to watch out?

I didn't find anyone until school was out for the day, when I caught sight of Rae's bobbing ponytail ahead of me in the hall, almost lost in a sea of departing students. I didn't manage to catch up with her until we were both outside.

"Hi," she said, stopping at my hail. She reached out to touch my hands, which again were shaking. "What happened to you?"

Relief flooded through me, such a strange feeling, to be glad to be outed. "There was. . . I went downtown to check out the fire, and there was a cave-in on the line. Maybe some kind of explosion."

"Oh my god, Maggie," said Rae, her quick eyes scanning me, and plucked a bit of debris from my hair. "Are you okay?"

"It was one of those things again," I said, pulling the collar of my shirt down far enough for her to see the quickly-healing scratch. "It attacked me after the train stopped in the tunnel. Rae. . . I don't know what to do."

She pulled me into a hug. "It's okay," she said, holding on tight.

For once, I didn't feel like crying. I basked instead, in Rae's kindness and care.

"You're coming over," she said in my ear, in a way I knew would brook no objections. Not that I was likely to make any. I wanted to be comforted, and I wanted to be with people.

We walked to her place, and this time, I got more of a feeling of what it was like to be a Kennie, not just the distant echoes I had experienced when I'd come with her to an empty house with my swim things and my secrets.

Both her parents were there, and two of her older siblings with their spouses and young kids. It was the oddest thing for me, to be in a house full of noise and laughter and fights and. . . well, love.

Rae's dad, who insisted I call him *Phil*, fired up the barbeque and, checking that I wasn't one of Rae's *carnivorously challenged* friends, threw on a couple of sausages and a burger for me, despite my insistence that it was probably more than I ate in two days.

We sat in the backyard beside the pool, and I declined Mrs. Kennie's suggestion that I borrow a suit and get in, giving Rae silent thanks as she rushed to deflect the idea. By the time Rae drove me home, I was full and relaxed and in a state of euphoria I thought I might never have known before.

"You are so lucky," I said as we sat on the driveway in her car, listening to a soft rock station.

She laughed. "Sometimes, I'd like a bit of peace and quiet," she said. "But yeah, they're a pretty special bunch."

I smiled sadly. I didn't want to make too much of my own less than exciting home life. "Mom and I live the quiet life," I said, and then, knowing that Jan wasn't home and probably wouldn't make it back for hours yet, I took a big chance. "Do you. . . want to come in? There's something I'd like to show you."

"Sure," she said, and turned the engine off, like this was something we did every day.

I led her upstairs to my sanctuary, the room where, I realized, no one but Jan and I had set foot during my entire teenage life.

That uncomfortable fantasy of remaking my private life to resemble my time in Char's catacombs jumped back into my mind. Only this time, I was picturing mirrors, curving to cut my bedroom into a perfect circle of infinite reflection. How could I picture that, and Rae, in the same breath? Someone like Rae, so perfectly suited to this real world, the one I never quite felt a part of. Maybe if Rae had been down in the netherworld with me, if Char had taken her instead of Scott Saunders for instance, maybe those mirrors would have shattered as I looked at them. Maybe he wouldn't have been able to transport me to the dream Toronto where I had followed Damon to his apartment and felt his kiss on my cheek. Maybe I would have been entirely safe, and entirely ordinary.

She looked over the shelf of books beside my bed, something I respected immediately. You can tell so much about people by the books they read and the music they listen to.

"I never read a lot of fairy tales," she said, running her fingers along the spines of my collection.

"I always think they're the basis of good storytelling," I said. "The essential ethical structures, and the whole range of good and bad."

"That makes sense," she said. "Probably make a good thesis."

Where I saw life lessons, she saw a Ph.D. Probably a good analogy for a lot of our differences.

"What about magic?" she said, like it was just another section of the Dewey decimal system.

"Uh—" She'd caught me off guard, I realized. I thought about Tamblyn's book, the one that looked like a cool relic from a musty bookstore, the one that I figured Hunt had probably re-appropriated after I worked my spell to make everyone forget, including the fact he'd ever stolen it. Did Tamblyn wonder where it had gone? Or had I erased the memory of it from his mind?

"I don't have any real magic books," I said. "They must be brutally hard to find. I wouldn't even know where to begin. All I can do is read stuff like this—" I lifted a copy of a Crowley book from the shelf "—and realize what complete charlatans most of them were."

She smiled sympathetically, as if my problem struck her as significant, and I felt that uncomfortable need to impress her. What did I have to show her, though?

Then, I took out the Crown Royal bag, and started my show and tell.

"Tools of the trade," she echoed me when I had shown her the contents of the bag.

She fingered the knife with distaste. My stomach twisted. This would be the way my obsession would be viewed by anyone who wasn't, like Hunt, already savvy to its oddness. Heck, to its *sanguinity*. No one wants to talk about blood, not even the people who thrill to ultra-violent slasher pics. Even in body alteration like tattooing and piercing, the idea was to *minimize* bleeding, not revel in it.

Then Rae laughed, for no reason I could think of, but it was a great, happy sound and so unlikely in a place like my room that I joined in. "Spooky," she said at last. "Sooner you than me. I don't freak at the sight of blood, but I think Suzanne does."

This seemed like an invitation to get closer, to bond with her over something that we could handle that Suzanne couldn't. But I realized I didn't know how far I should go, and figured I was likely to cross the line and say something very mean about Suzanne that would make Rae uncomfortable. So I kept my mouth shut.

"You know what we have to do?" Rae said, as if it was a natural extension of the conversation. "You, Suzanne, and I have to have a sleepover."

How had she got from blood to this? I had no idea. "That sounds great," I said, more to cover my confusion than anything else.

"I'll set it up," she said. "You good for Saturday night?"

I nodded. What did I do that could possibly pose a conflict?

Her smile quirked, and she touched the corner of my portfolio, which I'd failed to push completely under the bed. The question in her eyes was pretty clear.

"Uh, just some drawings."

Her eyes sparkled with sudden interest. "Really? You draw?"

I managed to stumble through a brief account of having started painting a while ago, leaving aside the possible influence of my absentee father. When she made a move to pull out the portfolio, I stopped her. "I really have a lot of homework," I said. "I should get going."

As if I was the visitor in this house, not her.

"Saturday then?" Her grin got bigger. "Cool. I better go. I'm actually due back for some family time tonight."

I walked her out. If *tonight* was for family time, what had I witnessed earlier? How could there possibly be some *more* intense kind of family event in the offing? *My ignorance*, I thought, *is breathtaking*.

Somehow, though, the idea of *family time* at Rae's was a little more frightening than imagining going back to Tamblyn, or even running into Hunt.

✪

Irene was missing from homeroom the next day, and for the next two days running. Was she taking a page out of the Maggie Stuart playbook? I decided she must be really sick, and wondered briefly if I should add her contact info to my list and find out if she was okay. It was an idea that slipped away almost as quickly as it had come.

I fought a constant battle whenever I thought of her. On one hand, I was embarrassed at my constant rude off-putting of her, but on the other, something in me was always trying to avoid any real connection with her. There was no earthly reason why I should waste my time with her, except perhaps that she was the only student at Dief so far this year who'd spoken to me without wanting something. Even Rae had only ever talked to me because of the ritual, and Jason. Probably Irene wanted something from me too. I just hadn't let her tell me what.

What was it with me and friends? I was too perverse, living too deep in the past to be much use to anyone, that's what I guessed. Like Jan, with her phantom smoke, living in a past no one else could remember or relate to. No wonder we were both the social anathemas we were.

And the worst part was watching the others making history with new people, finding interests they could share and exploring them.

Me, I had my ineffectual dabbling in the pseudo-dark arts, and my art, which was about as intensely private as a hobby could be, and not much else. I guess I really didn't have that much to share. So I couldn't blame anyone else for my loneliness, could I? And most days, I couldn't even admit I was lonely.

I would like, I knew, for Rae to be my friend. I wasn't sure yet about Suzanne; maybe I did and maybe I didn't. There was something too rough about her, and at the same time, too fragile. I didn't think anyone's ego would be safe in my hands, considering what I was capable of doing to my own.

And as for Irene, well, I really couldn't care less, and that was pathetic. I didn't feel invested enough to be even truly ambivalent. The person who seemed to want to be my friend was someone I could turn on in an instant, and the ones who didn't were the ones I chased. How did anyone live with that kind of unreliability inside her own head? To want, and not want, to be driven toward and afraid all at the same time. I wondered if this was what it would be like to be in love.

## 28

### Shopping For Girls

✦

I found another article in the Saturday Star to add to my growing collection of odd newspaper clippings. Someday I would definitely have to go through them and see if there was anything to them. It felt good to be doing something, even if I had no idea if it was useful.

Jan was far more low-key about the prospect of my spending the night at a friend's house than I'd feared. I guess I'd pictured her doing something intensely embarrassing, like putting *"Maggie's First Teen Sleepover!"* on the calendar in pink marker with lots of little hearts around it. Maybe she just grasped immediately that she'd be able to have Harrison over without interruptions or the discomfort of doing adult lovey-dovey things with her daughter just down the hall. If that was it, I was grateful—but I *really* didn't want to know.

I understood the concept of sleeping over much better than the thing itself. I had had sleepovers in my past, but it had been a very long time since Jan had set me up on one. And that's the way they'd always been: some friend of Jan's had a daughter my age, and I ended up at a strange house with some strange girl I'd met once or twice before sharing pizza and ice cream and a kiddy flick before bedding down in a sleeping bag on the floor.

It wasn't something I longed for, except in the way I longed for friends in general. It seemed like one of those icons of normalcy that was beyond me.

Jan dropped me at Rae's at seven o'clock, with a backpack and a sleeping bag. My portfolio of paintings was tucked carefully into the bottom of the backpack, held safely there by my change of clothes. Rae had made me promise I'd bring them. I also had an ancient green sleeping bag that I vaguely remembered using. . . once. . . somewhere. . .

Suzanne was already there, so I hung around in the foyer for a minute or two with Rae's dad while her mom went to fetch the others from the back den.

He said a few nice little nothing things to me, and I smiled and answered. I had been here three times now; it felt familiar, and that was quite pleasant. I was very nervous about being around Suzanne for an extended period of time, but maybe it would all be okay. Maybe I'd even have fun.

"Maggie!" Rae almost squealed. Suzanne was close behind her, but didn't even have much of a smile to offer. "We're all dug in—just ready to order pizza—right, *Daddy?*"

Rae's father raised his hands as if in defeat. "Anything you don't like, Maggie?"

I shrugged. "I'm good with anything. Maybe not anchovies."

"Ewwwww!" Rae trumpeted, and this time Suzanne added, "Gross. Please."

I followed them to the back of the house, where the Kennie's entertainment system dominated the entire wall of a room that looked out on the pool. Sleeping bags were stretched on the two sofas. They were into cans of Coke and a couple of bags of potato chips as well.

"You can have the recliner. It goes totally flat and I think it's bigger than a single," said Rae. "Unless you'd rather swap." I assumed she meant with her. It wouldn't be like Rae to put someone else out.

"No, that's good," I said, starting on my sleeping bag. I struggled with knots in its cord that probably had been undone the last time there was an Ice Age in this part of the world. Rae offered me a pop, and tossed me a DVD case.

"We're watching Twilight, but it's for, like, the twelfth time, so no biggie if you don't want to."

I hadn't seen any of them, but was indifferent. "Whatever you guys like," I said.

There wasn't a lot of conversation for the next few hours, at least not that I could get involved in. With Suzanne, Rae seemed to lose most of what I saw as her high intelligence and instead talked knowingly about shoes and designer bags and the latest celebrity hair and fashion trends. I tuned it out, but wasn't able to get quite enough into the movie to totally drown it out. If either of them noticed I wasn't contributing, no one said anything.

Finally, the pizza came and the end credits rolled so I was re-included as we divvied up the food and tried to pick our next film. I realized I hadn't seen a fraction of what Rae had on the shelves, and the satellite choices were completely overwhelming. We ended up watching a light romantic comedy, in part because it was the first thing neither of the other two had seen yet that Rae could find on the On Demand cable list.

The pizza was good, at least. My attention wandered during this film too; I studied Rae's profile surreptitiously, trying to discover just what it was that made her *her* and me *me*. Suzanne too—she was entirely captivated by the plot, or maybe by the costumes the lead female wore, for all I could tell. She kept up a sporadic commentary about what the women were wearing and which guys she liked the best, deciding early on that the secondary male lead was *far* cuter than the lead and they should have switched roles. I had no opinion, so I made some non-committal noise that could have been agreement when Rae turned to include me.

Unfortunately, the guy Suzanne liked in the film bore more than a casual resemblance to a grown-up Aaron Scribner, and that got me feeling a ridiculous, embarrassing surge of jealousy every time she said something about him. I had to find a way to ask Rae about that relationship, to find out, most importantly, if there was one. Not that I had any expectation of overcoming my nervousness to even admit I'd *like* to get closer to him. But the fact he'd entered my mind seemed to add him to our company, and once I thought about him for the first time, I couldn't stop.

"Hey! Let's call the guys!" said Suzanne, as the credits rolled on the second film.

"Awesome," said Rae, grabbing the phone off the end table beside her. "Who first?"

She looked at me, and I shrugged. All I could say was *Aaron*, and feel embarrassed, or say *Jason* and think they'd see right through me to know I'd rather have said Aaron's name.

"Aaron!" squealed Suzanne. "Wait—is it too late?"

Rae checked the clock on her cellphone. "Ten to ten. We're good. Just."

That was interesting. Aaron had a more controlling home life than either me or Rae, apparently. What would that make it like to date him? None of this sleeping-bag-in-the-recliner stuff, at the very least.

She was dialing before I could have any input, which was just as well. Even the fact he was momentarily going to be on the other end of a phone line made my cheeks feel hot. I was being ridiculous.

"You talk, Maggie," said Rae suddenly and handed the phone to me. I took the receiver but my fingers felt limp, and I had to bring the second hand up to make sure I didn't drop it. I heard a single ring, then a woman's voice, "Hello."

"Is. . . Aaron there?" I said, trying to keep my voice steady. Not so much so the woman, Aaron's mother presumably, wouldn't think I was some weirdo calling her son but so that Rae and Suzanne wouldn't have the least hint I was flustered. I suddenly felt like I might start hyperventilating, which was even more insane.

"One moment. I'll see if he's studying." I heard her footsteps receding as the phone was put down, and marvelled. Not only was she not shouting for him, but, if I was reaching the right conclusion, the fact he was studying might mean he was unavailable to take the call. Huh.

I heard the same quick footsteps returning a moment later. "He'll be right with you," she said. "May I ask who's calling?"

"Maggie," I blurted. "Stuart. Maggie Stuart."

Suzanne giggled, and I looked up at the other two girls, angry for an instant, but that evaporated immediately when I saw Rae's wide grin. She gave me a big thumbs-up, and I realized that calling Aaron might not have been all that easy for any of us. I gave a mock terrified grimace, and both Suzanne and Rae gratified me by laughing, hands over mouths to keep the sound muffled.

"Hello," said Aaron's voice suddenly. I hadn't heard footsteps; I guessed he'd picked up an extension.

"Hey," I said, feeling just cool enough to manage, "it's Maggie. And Rae and Suzanne."

I looked at the other two as Aaron answered with his own "Hey," and then I continued, ". . .uh, we're having a sleepover and I don't have a clue why we're calling you."

Rae and Suzanne broke down in hysterics, and Aaron guffawed over the phone line. "Yeah, sleepovers do that kind of things to girls. Or so I've heard."

I laughed now myself. "Seriously, though. Does this mean that somehow you're *not* studying on a Saturday night? I'm kinda disappointed, Scribner."

He laughed again, longer this time. By now, Suzanne had apparently fought down what shyness she'd begun with and was holding out her hands for the phone. I passed it over, and she started chattering animatedly with Aaron. Whatever he was saying was making her laugh; that was clear at least. I'd lost my chance. If it had been a chance, that is.

Rae came closer and tucked her arm through mine. She squeezed, and I felt her warmth and affection. How could she do this, so easily? Be the supportive and generous friend who makes everyone feel a part of things, even misfit Maggie? I smiled at her, and she leaned closer to whisper, "Let's get ice cream. They could be a while."

I wanted more than anything to tear the phone from Suzanne's hands, make Aaron laugh myself, listen to him joking and happy, but ice cream was the offer, not Aaron. I nodded and followed her out. The tears were a lot closer now. They'd been threatening all night, but now I thought I might be running out of strength to man the barricades.

I didn't want any boy to have this kind of power over my emotions, especially when he was undoubtably oblivious. It was something I didn't understand about human interaction, not one little bit. I had cried so many nights over Nick, my long absent dad, when I was younger, as soon as I was old enough to know there was a space in my life only he could have filled. But Nick never knew; he didn't know his daughter felt that pain and longed for the one person who could ever be her dad.

Rae had the bowls out by the time I reached the kitchen and was going for the spoons and the freezer near simultaneously from what I could tell. "Did you get lost?" she said. The tone was a hundred percent joking, but it ripped something open inside me.

"Maggie?" she said quieter. She dumped a pair of ice cream cartons on the counter and put her arm around me. "What is it?"

"Nothing," I said. My throat tightened around the word.

"Suzanne can be a bit preoccupied with herself, but she does mean well," said Rae, taking a stab that, I guess, wasn't that far off the mark. "She tends to forget there are other people around, especially when there's boys..."

She smiled, urging me to join her. I shrugged and picked up a spoon, hoping I looked more detached than I felt. "What do we have here?"

Rae put her hands to her face. "I almost forgot the best!" She twirled back to the freezer and rummaged for another container. "Mint chocolate chip, strawberry yogurt—not as blah as you might expect—and. . . my favorite and possibly yours, Rocky Rocky Road!"

She wrenched the top off the last, grunting as if imitating a carnival strong man. "Me like Rocky Road! . . .unless you're allergic to nuts?"

"Only the institutionalized kind," I said, and she grabbed a spoon of her own while pushing the bowls away.

"I don't know why I even bother with the pretense," she said, and we dug in.

Suzanne pranced in a moment later, motioning to Rae for a spoon of her own. "Gotta go," she said into the phone. "We've got *ice cream!*" She handed the phone to Rae as she hung up: a real princess move, I thought. *Put this back for me, serf.*

"Rocky Road!" she squealed and stuck her spoon into the middle of the carton. "Oh man—do you remember that first time out in back?"

Rae laughed, hard, joining Suzanne in a peal that threatened to get right out of control. "*Someone*, no names mentioned, dumped a whole scoop into the pool." She directed this at me, letting me in on the joke I guessed. "The ice cream melted away fine, but we kept finding floating bits of nuts all night."

"It was pretty sick—and by that I mean *gross*," added Suzanne, but mostly to Rae.

"Sounds like it," I said, focusing more on the coldness of the ice cream than the story. It was doing a good job of cooling my cheeks down and making me feel more in control.

"Do you want to call Jason too?" asked Rae. "There's no curfew to worry about there, not on a weekend."

I shrugged. The call to Aaron hadn't exactly been a thrill as far as I was concerned.

"We could talk about what to do next," said Rae. This was a little rich as far as I was concerned. We hadn't come up with much in the way of ideas face to face. How could a phone call when everyone was acting kind of goofy be any more productive?

"You know what I want?" said Suzanne, and this time it was actually to me. "I want to brush your hair."

I reached up. My hair was down to mid-ribcage now, brown and pretty well straight. Like on most days, I had it pulled back in a simple ponytail. "Okay?" I said, unsure. I didn't get the thrill.

"Cool!" she said, and ran out of the room, to get her brush I presumed. Rae put all three containers of ice cream under her arms and motioned me to follow.

Back in the den, Suzanne was pushing a chair into the middle of the room. "Madam?" she said, and indicated the chair with a sweep of her arm. I guessed we were playing. . . *salon* or something. I hadn't played like a girl with other girls in so long I was surprised there was anything like this in Suzanne's repertoire. Girls our age still played games like this? Or was she just being facetious?

I said rigidly and Suzanne pulled a couple of combs, a bunch of hair pins and elastics, and a fat round brush out of her baggage. "I don't know if you can use that kind of brush on my hair," I said. I only ever used a flat-backed brush.

"No, it's good," she said, and started in.

I knew we were in trouble almost immediately. A few strokes in, something caught and I felt a sharp tug. My scalp wasn't so sensitive that it hurt exactly, but I still found myself saying, "Ow!"

Rae jumped up, and came over to examine the situation. "Eeesh, it looks tangled," she said, and reached out.

Ignoring both of us, Suzanne gave another couple of strokes that just cemented the brush more firmly into my hair. I realized the brush was wrapped multiple times by my hair—Suzanne tried extricating it by first pulling it straight out from my head, and then rotating it, which only served to lock it in tighter.

Mrs. Kennie chose that moment to appear at the door. "Everything okay in here?" she asked. I had my back to the door and couldn't turn my head without pulling out half my hair, not with Suzanne holding the brush with a death grip.

"Fine," said Rae, and even she sounded a little strained for once. I could almost hear Mrs. Kennie give her the hairy eyeball. *Sure you're okay. I heard that yell. Why do you think I'm here?*

But instead of following up, Mrs. Kennie came into the room just far enough to pick up the ice cream containers. "Rae, really. You couldn't just choose *one* flavor to melt?"

She vanished back out of my line of sight with the ice cream, and my composure slipped. "Just. . . get it out," I said, but to Rae. I didn't want Suzanne even looking at my hair again.

"Hang on," said Rae, and I felt her fiddling with the brush. "It's stuck good."

There was a sharp stab of pain as Suzanne tried to take the handle of the brush back, and I'd had enough. "Oh, forget it. Leave it alone! Don't touch me."

I grabbed the handle away from them for myself. "I'll do it." I fought with the brush for a minute, but it was impossible without being able to see what I was doing. I burst into silent tears. Anger was in direct conflict with the absolute need to make sure Mrs. Kennie wasn't drawn back by any unhappy noises I might make. Rae was radiating intense sympathy and longing to help; Suzanne looked like she might cry too, distressed and totally uncomfortable.

I almost liked seeing her that way, after the way she'd monopolized the call to Aaron. "I guess we're even for Hunt," I said, and stormed out to the downstairs bathroom, quietly of course.

Even with the mirror to help, I couldn't find where one strand of hair ended and the next began. The whole thing had become a rat's nest. I guessed I might be lucky, if this was only the first thing Suzanne had had planned for my head. I began tugging and testing, trying to unweave the mess from the brush.

After about five minutes, I heard Rae's tentative tap on the door. "Maggie? Are you okay?"

*No,* I wanted to shout. *I've been humiliated and experimented on, and all I want is to go home except that would necessitate passing by you and Suzanne and I can't handle that right now.*

She tried the door handle, but I'd locked myself in. I tried to answer but all that came out was sobbing.

"Oh, Maggie, please don't cry. It was an accident. Suzanne feels terrible." *Good. Let her.*

"Maggie? Do you want some help?"

I didn't answer still, and I heard Rae give a big sigh. "Okay, I'll leave you alone. Just come out when you're ready. I know Suzanne wants to apologize."

I heard Rae's footsteps retreating, and then nothing but the distant sound of the television. They must have felt really sorry, to go back to the TV so quickly.

Gingerly, I took stock of the mess of my hair. The brush was caught in the full length of it, hanging at shoulder height if I released the handle. I didn't think it looked like it was going anywhere. *How do you turn this one into a positive, Mags?* I asked myself, and there was no ready answer. Maybe there were styling products or something else I could use to extricate the brush. Even if I did, how much of it would be broken and damaged? *A lot,* I thought. Amazing how little had been required to wreck what had taken me ten years to grow.

Under the sink I found the kind of supplies you'd expect in a half bath with no shower or tub: extra deodorant, floss, toilet paper, bathroom cleanser. Nothing to help me with my current dilemma.

Except maybe the scissors.

I'd never realized how proud I was of my long hair: despite the blah color and lack of body I'd really liked it and how it looked on me. My eyes welled up as I held the blades open in the unforgiving light. I didn't just want to hate Suzanne right then; I wanted to punish myself. I was stupid for coming here tonight, an idiot to imagine I could fit in with girls like Rae and Suzanne, and even stupider to imagine I would *want* to when I came to know them. I didn't want all this shallow fashion talk and feeling horrible because someone else got to talk to a boy and I didn't. I wanted to suffer. I wanted to feel pain. Maybe that would make my shame and anguish go away.

I raised the scissors.

✪

After it was done, I curled into the corner of the bathroom with the scissors still in my hand. I'd flushed the excess hair, even removing every strand from Suzanne's brush. I had no idea how much time had passed, only that there was no sound from anywhere in the house now. For a while during the time I was cutting, I'd heard Suzanne and Rae on the phone again, this time with Jason, I guessed. There was some giggling and laughter, a little more subdued than we'd been earlier with Aaron. *Thanks, guys,* I thought, *for being so immensely considerate of my feelings.*

Now, it had to be midnight or later. I'd fought with myself all the way to not turn the scissors on more than my hair. I hadn't cut myself before, although in the days and weeks after I returned from Char's realm, I'd been tempted again and again. The pain of feeling so different, so removed. Something about its intensity called out to be countered with an even more present physical pain. I thought I understood long-distance runners after that, thinking that the only reason to put your body through that kind of stress had to be to cover up something just as intense inside.

At least, that's what I thought. I couldn't run because my body didn't seem to like that particular exercise. The summer before last, I'd taken to riding my bike for hours at a time, crying all the way. In time, the immediacy of the emotions started to fade, and I settled in for a lifetime of low-level sadness and loneliness.

I hadn't felt so intensely hopeless for a long, long time. Part of me abhorred the feeling, but another perhaps larger part was all too comfortable with it. *Maggie, lost and lonely. Maggie, the Queen of the Underground in Permanent Exile.* I could only fight the feelings so far because I had no better status quo to replace them with. When I was miserable, miserable felt like all I'd ever been.

Finally, I couldn't sit any longer. Despite the misery, or maybe as part of it, I was dog-tired all of a sudden. I tried to calculate how to sneak back into the den, pack up my stuff, sneak out of the house and walk home. How long would it take me, tired as I was and at this time of night? Would it even be safe? Hunt was out there and, for all I knew, watching.

I unlocked the door to a darkened hallway. Rae had left a small nightlight on, enough to find my way. I let my eyes adjust before going into the den, and felt fatigue descend on me like a lead blanket. Short of calling a cab, which I had no money for, or waking Jan—provided she was even home and not taking the opportunity to spend the night at Harrison's—I had no way home that didn't require me to walk. And I was sure now that I was way past able to do that.

My eyes felt raw from crying. I thought the headache I'd developed from the combination of tears and hair-pulling would probably keep me awake all night, but I'd barely slid my aching body into the sleeping bag on the recliner before I was fast asleep.

✪

Kitchen clatter woke me, and for an instant as I came to, I thought I was home and just about to encounter Harrison again, maybe in duplicate like I had with Thurl. I didn't know what time it was, but I was used to waking no earlier than ten on weekends, and it seemed probable that the Kennie family rose earlier than that.

The way the ends of my hair brushed along my collarbones as I sat up reminded me of the part of the past dozen hours that wasn't a dream.

I grabbed the ends and pulled them down, just to see how much damage I'd done. I must have hacked off more than half the previous length. I remembered how much I'd cried at the hairdresser when the one inch I'd agreed to having cut turned into three.

I couldn't even imagine going to the washroom to check what I'd done in the mirror. And how could I face Rae, or even Suzanne? Maybe I could just pack up my stuff quietly and slip out the patio doors before they knew I was awake.

But if I did that, what would happen to getting rid of whatever they'd released from the circle that day? What would happen with Hunt; what would happen to my relationship with Jason or with Aaron for that matter? What would happen to the one ray of hope I'd had in my life since Char left it, my possible reconnection with the part of myself I'd thought lost for good.

I might feel I hated Suzanne, or like I was disappointed in Rae for not sticking up for me when Suzanne wrecked my hair. I might be pretty sure now that whatever I felt about wanting to get to know Aaron a little more was not only unrealistic but just a path to more humiliation and disappointment. But what option did I have but to try to find a way to cope with my anger and my sorrow?

Even as I worked this through in my mind, my eyes started to leak. I couldn't help it. I hated to cry, but there was nothing I could do to hold the tears back.

But as quickly as they'd started, they choked themselves back again. The impulse, the desire to cry was now stronger than ever, but nothing would come. I wanted to give myself over to misery, put off the inevitable next step I would take, whatever that was. Running out the back door and straight home to lock myself in the room seemed like the best, if not only plan. The question was, could I actually force my sad brain to come up with another option?

Before I could get further in my thinking, I realized I was halfway to the door, my stuff still spread out around the recliner I'd slept in, on the way to the kitchen. *I'm insane,* I told myself.

I came around the corner into the kitchen, expecting Suzanne and

Rae would be making breakfast, or perhaps waiting for breakfast to be made for them. But there were no parents present. There was cereal and milk, and orange juice poured into glasses. Place settings for three, in fact, and they hadn't started eating. They were waiting for me, which made me feel somewhat ashamed of having planned a back-door exit.

But that wasn't what stopped me in my tracks. What made me freeze in the doorway was the sight of my portfolio lying between the neat place mats, opened to the picture of the ritual circle and the eyes I hadn't painted.

At first, my instinct was to be outraged. I got as far as feeling my stomach clench along with my teeth—but then I saw the looks they turned to me. Rae's eyes were hollow, haunted, and Suzanne had bit her lip hard enough to press the blood out of it.

Rae's fingers traced the pentacle circle, the question clearly enough implied. I cleared my throat.

"This is what I was painting on the first day of school."

"I saw the date," said Rae. "You painted what happened."

"No," I said, to clarify, wanting to give them the real story, no deception for once. Here was something real, that made me afraid. Something that might be easier to carry if it was shared. "I mean I was in the middle of doing it when I heard the noises in the gym. I had almost finished it. That's the absolute truth."

I took the picture from under Rae's hand. The eyes, their black lashes and the glint of watery reflection, still made me cold.

Suzanne's brows drew together, but she didn't say anything.

Rae's hand shook as she took it from me and traced the lines of those cold grey-green eyes with a finger. "How could you have known?"

Then, Suzanne nudged Rae, who went back to the stack of paintings and drawings, and spread them over the countertop until she found what she was looking for.

I'd chosen a very motley collection of subjects, I saw when all the sketches were laid out. I had started drawing about a year after the whole 'incident,' as a sort of therapy for myself. I'd been a pretty good artist in Char's Dreamworld, and it was a fantasy of mine that I would be good eventually out in the real one as well.

For two years, I guessed there wasn't much: about twenty-five pieces of paper of various sizes. Ten were pulled out of a watercolor book I'd been given for the previous Christmas with the paints. The rest were on slightly water-rumpled pages from a dollar store sketchbook.

I'd done a lot of the usual girl stuff, I suppose. There were a couple of attempts at a dragon, and a castle with surrounding countryside. There was a bunch of still-lifes, mostly things around the house like the tree out front. One was a boat I drew from a distant memory of my grandparents' cottage on the East coast. There was even a unicorn, or at least a horse with skinny legs and something that was supposed to be a horn sticking out of its forehead. Another was nothing more than a series of color washes, intended to capture the sunset I was watching at the time.

I'd done a lot of figures as well, mostly women, but a couple of men. One of the latter was a magician of some kind. I might have been trying to draw Hunt, and, failing, took the sketch in a totally new direction. I couldn't really remember, but it might have been something like that.

But the one which Suzanne was tapping to draw my attention was the first watercolor I'd ever done, the same day I got the paints. It was of a woman's face. The expression on her face was kind of crafty, kind of catty. The smile was more of a smirk, knowing and cruel. I had been thinking, as I painted, of a sorceress, some kind of High Priestess of a blood cult. The watery gray-green eyes stood out in the pale expanse of skin against the wild, black hair. They were, in fact, exactly the same eyes that had appeared on the picture I had done the day of the ritual.

Rae looked from me to the painting and pointed from it to the one in my hands. No wonder they were so freaked out. A shiver ran down me as I picked up the two pages to compare. There was no doubt. To a stroke, down to every bubble in the pigment, they were identical. No wonder I had imagined the eyes were painted in my style. If a color photocopy had been used to transfer the image from one picture to the other, it would have been less exact.

I had, to this point, studiously avoided any mention of my own powers, any hint at all that magic could be something accomplished without Hunt's paraphernalia. This wasn't the time, or the place. What I was telling Rae was enough, I thought, and not for my sake this time. It was enough that she'd already seen the foundations of her version of reality shaken. A little at a time was all any of us should have to cope with. I knew I was right about this. She'd already taken in enough for today.

So I said, "I don't know," which was true, but not really the whole truth. I suspected that I had been controlled by something, when I pulled the emergency stop on the subway, when I painted those eyes and that pentagram, and when I had found the words to banish a demon. But I could hardly tell her that, not when I thought I might just be losing my mind.

## 29

## Always Crashing In The Same Car

✪

Irene was in class on Monday morning. I smiled at her, but she looked less than thrilled to see me. "Nice hair," she said, and there was a not-so-subtle opprobrium in her voice, as if she thought the only reason I could have for cutting it was to be more like the popular girls. Or I was projecting. God knows I was good at that.

I had managed to convince Jan that Rae had a friend who cut hair, and I'd given her a chance to try out her skills, just to avoid any real comment on my *choice*. She'd fluffed the ends critically, and said something about having it evened out by her stylist, maybe for my birthday.

*That* was something I hadn't given much consideration to, although it was fast approaching. I was an October 26th baby, born at ten minutes after midnight five days before Halloween. Another way I'd just missed out, I'd often thought. This year, it fell on a Saturday, so I'd be able to spend the day on my own, which was usually all I asked for. I didn't like birthdays much; they'd often been less than special occasions on which Jan struggled to do something that I would enjoy and succeeded mostly in showing just how little she knew me.

This year, I'd turn sixteen. That was supposed to be something of a benchmark, something of a special age to reach. I figured I better get ready to be disappointed. Then, if anything nice happened, I could be pleasantly surprised even if it wasn't much.

Was Irene the kind of person I would invite to celebrate my birthday with me? Was Suzanne? I walked out into the hall after homeroom with the former, silently musing about friendship and how high school made it seem so. . . dirty somehow.

"I was sick," Irene said, when I asked about her absences at the end of the previous week. Her tone was noticeably cool, and for once it seemed like she was the one trying to get away from me.

"Man, that's terrible. You better now?"

"Yeah."

I hovered, not sure what to say. *Kid on the phone who doesn't know when to hang up.*

"Actually, I wasn't sick," she said at last. "I was doing some stuff that took me a couple of days to figure out. I have something you want."

At first I was confused. Then, "The book?"

"Meet me after school, if you're curious."

How could I not be? But the dynamic between us was all wrong, all screwed up, probably thanks to my rudeness. What if there was no way to heal the rupture, and she actually did have the book? It only peripherally occurred to me that I was being one of those people I professed to hate, the ones who only interacted when it was to their advantage.

✪

We walked together down the road from school and into our mutual neighborhood. I hadn't seen any of the other guys, and felt antsy, anxious. I would have to call Rae as soon as I knew the score. My mind flashed back to the thing that had taken Thurl's shape in the drafting room, and its words in the hall. "Bring the book..."

They had the ring. But maybe we'd have the book.

I wasn't even thinking in terms of resolving the situation or sending the creatures back to wherever they came from. I wasn't for once even thinking about regaining my lost power. Just like on the cliff above Char's palace, I realized, I just wanted to give my friends their old lives back.

"You're sure," I said, to break the silence, "that it's the right book?"

She held her hands about a foot apart. "This big, green leather cover, real old, and it showed up on a shelf in the library where it didn't belong. Not English, although that's not a big deal."

Not a big deal. Right. This was getting weirder. I could buy that Irene had somehow come across the book; I could even believe that she had managed to hold on to it when I hadn't. But that it had revealed its secrets to her, even in part, was something it made me sick to contemplate.

I caught a glimpse of the top of Irene's binder where she had written her full name.

"Solomon," I said. "That's Jewish?"

She looked at me with annoyance. "There are black Jews, you know." We had paused, just at the end of the cul de sac where she lived.

"The book," I said, realizing. "Aaron. . . Scribner, he said he could read it a bit. He saw it. . . once. . . before. . . He made it sound like it was something you had to be. . . something that was hard to read if you weren't. . ." I sounded like an idiot and Irene seemed to know it.

"Hebrew." She nodded, smirking just a little as she shared the secret. "That Scribner is a prig. He's not the only one in the world who knows it. I may not be doing classes every week like I used to, but I'm not totally ignorant."

"Hebrew," I repeated. There goes Maggie for a total fool. Here I was blaming the Aaron Scribner apparition for misleading me about the book, and the real one had done it too, very neatly, just like I had been doing about Hunt. He'd told me he had a pronunciation key and a dictionary to help him with the book, and still I had believed we were talking some arcane, forgotten language instead of something I would have access to as well. Score one for Mr. Scribner, and dock Maggie for letting him get away with it. *Hebrew.*

"Not modern Hebrew, so I have a lot of trouble with it. But enough of the words are similar so I can get some sense out of it. I wouldn't be surprised if I understand a lot more than him. He probably just figured out how to sound out the words and looked 'em up online. . . Do you want to see it?"

This last was said impatiently, naturally enough. If I was her, I wouldn't understand why I was stalling either. After all, I had been trying to get my hands on the damn thing for long enough.

"Where is it?" I put as much plain excitement into my voice as I could. Hide the part of me that was just plain pissed, at her, at myself, and more than anyone at Aaron. Give her that much consideration.

She led me inside and into the kitchen. "Downstairs." I started to get excited. She flicked the light switch, and led me down the stairs past the basement door.

This was very different from the Saunders' half-finished rec room or the cosy TV room downstairs in my house that neither Jan nor I took much advantage of. The Solomons' was unfinished, a bare concrete floor and a single naked bulb hanging from a wire in the middle of the room. There was no drywall even; the room was framed and some of the insulation was in place, but that was it. A washing machine-dryer set sat in the corner beside a heavy double sink.

On a shelf made of a two-by-four and a couple of metal L-braces were candles and matches. Irene led me over to these, saying, "There's no socket in the back room."

She lit one, and so did I. I felt like I was entering a ritual even as I took the match she passed me, much more so than I had even on top of the bluff doing real magic with John Tamblyn bleeding all over the flat stone in front of me. Of course. That was my nature—my nature then, in any case. Suddenly numb and stupefied, I followed Irene into the black archway to our right, shielding my candle as she did from the cool draft that met us.

The house was pretty old, I could tell. The basement, past the arch, was lined with stone, not concrete. It had been laid and not poured. Irene was explaining.

"This is one of the oldest sites built on in the area. The first house they built here burned down, maybe fifty years ago, but it was already almost a hundred years old. They put up this one on the foundations, but it wasn't on the same plan. So the basements doesn't quite match up. There's places where the walls are hollow between the old one and the new one, and there's these little access panels where you can almost crawl in. It's pretty creepy."

I could agree to that, even though I didn't say so out loud.

I brushed my hand over the exposed wood of the house's frame as I walked, as much as anything to give me the feel of something solid and real, and drew my hand back with a start. Amazed, almost stunned, I looked at a point of red growing on my fingertip.

"Damn, a nail. I should have warned you," said Irene. "Lots of things sticking out of these walls."

"Don't worry," I managed. *Blood.* No magic without it. *No great magic without it*, I had to correct myself. Hunt's training had warped everything I saw.

She led me down a corridor of maybe fifteen paces, and the surrounding air got steadily colder and damper. On the right, we passed a small doorway, black and drafty. All I could tell for certain was that the level of the floor past that door dropped somewhat, and, my mind filled in, probably to a dirt floor. This set me shivering. I didn't dare examine closer, or even think too much about it. How could Irene live here without going mad?

The corridor ended in a small room with a small window, set high up in the wall and so dirty it was merely a yellowish square and let no discernible light into the room. Then, I held my candle up as she was doing, and nearly laughed. In the corner, completely foiling all my frightened notions, was a big, white water heater. Ideas of literal skeletons and vengeful ghosts quickly fell aside. It was still creepy, yes, but here was proof of modern and very normal activity here.

Irene motioned me behind the water heater, and I moved in close to her.

And there it was.

And that sense of anticipation rushed right back.

"I put it the only place I knew my family wouldn't be looking," she whispered. "No one comes down here unless there's a flood or a power failure." She sounded spooked. So the awe wasn't just something I was feeling. "Here at least I could protect it properly."

I was beside myself, quite literally, in that floating way you get when something shocks you right out of your skin. I could almost imagine standing a couple of feet away from myself and Irene, a witness to my own amazement.

On the ground lay the book, tucked in between the water heater and the wall in a depression in the floor where the concrete sagged. But protected it was, or at least in the only way I could have thought of, and in a way I would have been afraid to attempt for lack of knowledge. Surrounding the heavy volume, its cover dark green with dancing yellow highlights in the dim light from our candles, was a line of chalk, a circle. Just around the edges of the book, I could see the white lines crossing through the circle and forming a five-pointed star. At the places where the star touched the circle were the melted stumps of five red candles.

"Why red?" I asked when I could find my voice. I'm sure the pause seemed much longer than it really was.

"That's what we had," she said, practical as I was beginning to understand she was.

"And what did you use to seal it in there?"

She grinned, bobbing her head. "Just this thing my gramma used to say to me when I was going to sleep. Either it worked, or you were wrong about someone taking it every time you show up."

My heart leapt, my whole chest clenching. This was it—she was right. I was, it seemed, excited almost to the point of apoplexy. Here was the book which had been avoiding me with almost apparent malice. Irene had outsmarted it.

I grabbed her hands spontaneously, eyes burning, and instantly, passion surged through me. "Irene," I managed. "You are great. We may have a chance after all."

The corners of her mouth turned up sardonically. If I had thought we were on the same page, here was the proof I was mistaken. "We? Look, Maggie, this thing is dangerous. You've pretty much proven you know less about it than I do, and definitely less about keeping it in one place. I'll tell you what, let's just let me keep it safe until *we*" and she made the word a mockery of my shallow pretense of friendship, "can figure out what's going on."

I blew a long breath out between slack lips. This was not going as I had envisioned, with somehow Irene making a miraculous transformation into my Igor, my faithful sidekick and helpmeet. I had, just for a moment, felt like I was the star of my own story, and the euphoria that had started to build when I saw the book wedged in its mystic circle behind the water heater burst like a ripe sore.

"You might as well tell me everything," she said, and it sounded like an order.

I figured I could tell her a little, and made up a hash of the bare minimum, about the ritual and the things that escaped from the circle. About Hunt, about the ring, about my suspicions about what was happening in the subway tunnels under Toronto, I said nothing. I even resisted the temptation to tell her about my heroism in the explosion, knowing the only reason I wanted to was to gain a little respect from her cold eyes.

At the end of my recitation, she was silent.

"Come on, Irene, Aaron and the guys and I have been looking for this thing for weeks. It's *killing* animals. We have to try to reverse whatever they did and return whatever got out to the place it belongs."

"And where would that be?" She sniffed. "You don't know a damn thing more about this book than I do, and it would be irresponsible of me to just hand it over and watch it dissolve into the ether again. Because that's what would happen. It doesn't want to be with you. For whatever reason, it's happy here."

I wanted to mock her endowment of the book with a personality, but a shiver had gone through me as she said it, and I realized I had no trouble anthropomorphizing it just as she had done. It was a beast. It hated me. It was toying with me, teasing me, enjoying itself at my expense. It was as much a part of the destruction wrought in the wake of the ill-conceived ritual as whatever was on the loose thanks to the secrets locked in its pages.

"Look," I said, more emphatically, "the only way we'll end this is by studying the book. We can't do that if you're controlling all access to it. Okay, here's a compromise. Why don't Aaron and I come over later, or tomorrow after school, and we can examine it here? You're obviously a good guardian for it." I was gaining steam as I went, the idea sounding better and better to me as I voiced it. "What do you think? You call the shots, I can live with that."

She stared at me, the contempt and ridicule so evident in her eyes that I felt my cheeks redden. For a moment I thought she was nearly too apoplectic to speak. "You—" she said finally. "I got you so wrong. From the start. You want to hang with the popular people, that's fine. But don't behave as if you're any better than me. You're no beautiful person. You're just like me. It's so stupid—sad." She rubbed a clenched hand along her thigh, as if waiting for me to vanish, or for the urge to hit me to fade. Then, she rolled her eyes, maybe pissed that I wasn't taking the get lost hint, and said, "Get out of here, Maggie. There's nothing here for you. I'll do this in my own time, my own way. The bunch of you have screwed things up bad enough already."

"You don't know—" I began, but she cut me off.

"I can't do much worse, can I?" she said, and waved me out of the basement.

We didn't say another word as she followed me up the stairs and out to the driveway. I tried to come up with some kind of cogent argument, but she had slammed the door before I realized I could think of nothing at all to say.

✪

It couldn't have gone worse, and I couldn't have gained less from what should have been at last a victory. Now, to get what I wanted would require a campaign to rekindle her interest in me, which I had done everything in my power since the first day of school to reject. And I wasn't even sure I was up for it. Could I be so false? Worse, was I exactly what she said I was, a girl from the lower echelons of the social strata who got a little too dizzy from a bump in status? I realized that the biggest problem with my past and future dealings with Irene was that she made me ashamed of myself. Even through my own obviously kinder eyes, I looked like a complete bastard.

To my greater shame, I was hardly off Irene's street before I had decided on a way to use this new development for a completely ulterior purpose. By the time I made it home, I had slipped my phone list out of my backpack and my fingers were all but dialing Aaron Scribner's number in the air.

He answered on the second ring. "Hello?"

"Hey, Aaron, it's Maggie," I said, and felt myself reddening. This was pathetic. The most momentous thing that had happened since that first day in the gymnasium, and all I could think about was how jealous I'd been when Suzanne spend so long talking to Aaron on the phone at the sleepover. The fact that he'd initially just annoyed me this year was barely an afterthought any more.

"Maggie, hey," he said. He didn't sound awkward or embarrassed. He sounded as cool as ever, maybe even a little more distant than in his hello, before he'd known it was me. Or was I really reading too much into almost nothing.

"Something has happened," I said, not quite knowing how to broach the subject now that I had him on the line. Irene's name would not be mentioned, obviously. "I know where the book is."

I could hear the interest kindle in his voice, so maybe I hadn't been wrong before. "Yeah?"

"Getting our hands on it—well, that might be another story." *Yeah, it involved manipulating or bribing or otherwise convincing a senior that a bunch of grade eleven students should take over possession of a magical artifact.* And unless I was very much mistaken, it was the first time that Irene had ever laid eyes on one, or even believed something like it existed. I knew how impossible it would be to wrench a treasure like that away from me.

"Where is it?" he asked, and then immediately, "Damn, Mags, you made pretty fast work of that issue."

There was a lightness in his voice now that was almost flirtatious—although yeah, I was probably reading too much into it again. "Danke," I said. "I try to be at least occasionally amazing."

He guffawed, that laugh I had started to like so much. "So, what's the plan?"

That was something I hadn't thought through at all, but I wasn't about to say so. "Leave it to me," I said.

There was a moment's silence on the line. Then Aaron said, "Maggie? Still there?"

"Yeah," I said. What on earth could I say? "Man, I thought I was never going to lay eyes on that thing without it running for the door."

He laughed again, and I felt a little more comfortable. "You said it. I guess if opposites attract, that means that you and that book have a little too much in common."

I laughed now, but I considered that seriously. "That would be interesting," I said, a little quieter. "Maybe we'll develop a theory of supernatural physics along the way."

"Hey, Newton was just as interested in the paranormal as in all the boring stuff he's famous for," said Aaron, and for some reason, that was exactly the encouragement I needed to sit back in my chair, open a Coke, and relax.

An hour later, we were still talking. I could hardly believe the subjects we covered; I even found myself slipping in a reference to Aleister Crowley and found that Aaron knew exactly who he was, at least in broad strokes. The stuff he knew about sports was outside anything more than my most general knowledge, but I really enjoyed his analogies between sports positions and, for example, the composition of the federal government. He had me laughing out loud frequently, and I made him laugh almost as much.

Finally, I heard a female voice faintly in the background on his end, and he excused himself, saying that his mother was complaining about having the phone tied up. His frustrated sigh telegraphed so clearly over the line I could picture the exact expression on his face.

"I'll go," I said. "I don't want to be on another family's hit list as the 'bad influence' friend."

"There's got to be a story or two in that," he said. "See you soon,

Mags."

He hung up. I drained the last sip of my now-warm Coke, and wished he was right. The truth was, of course, that the only time I could have ever been considered an influence on the lives of anyone my age had involved him directly, and Scott, and Jason, in that forgotten time. Then, I'd been the worst possible person for them to know, inadvertently dragging them deep underground and into the most terrifying unknown. Keeping Aaron on the phone until it annoyed his mother was relatively mild in comparison.

I realized I was smiling, broadly and dumbly. Aaron Scribner was fun to talk to, and he had talked to me. I might have contrived an artificial initiation of the conversation, but after the first moment, it was just fun. I felt, well, almost normal.

It was still light outside when I opened the front door to check the mail. There was still no sign of Jan, and I was more grateful even than usual when I saw the official-looking envelope from my school mixed in with the flyers and bills.

Bracing myself, I opened it at the kitchen island. It was as bad as I'd expected. I was on notice that my absences from class were nearing the number that would get me kicked out of a couple of my courses with an incomplete on my record. And I wasn't far from mandatory suspension for the same offense, which seemed a little insane to me. *I've been missing so many classes I will be forced to miss more?* Right. That makes sense.

I carefully shredded both the letter and envelope, left the rest of the mail where I usually did for Jan's perusal, and slunk off upstairs.

✪

*That night, I dream about walking in a misty field. I know my shoes—boots?—are wet, either with dew or with previously fallen rain. I think I can even smell the moisture in the air.*

*It's dark, except for a thin sliver of moon that hangs high in the sky. I can barely make out the sharp edge of the field, and beyond it, the ocean.*

*The wetness of the air has a salt-tinge to it, and I breathe it in deeply. I'm almost home. I could reach into my fingertips and be there instantly, but I want to walk. I want to be alone.*

*Into my fingertips? It seems natural to think it, but I'm not sure what it means. I picture myself making the tiniest little gesture, barely a flick of a finger, and harnessing an iota of some huge reserve. Of power. That's what I'm dreaming about. The power I've lost.*

*Hunt taught me to picture it divided into manageable, tiny packages, discreet and minute, spread all over my body like work-stations on a huge internet network. Fingertips, toes, the hairs of my head, each prickling with the potential to make something incredible occur.*

*So why am I here, in this field, damp and calm, with the energy I've lost forever tingling in my carpals and tarsi and scalp?*

*I'm smiling, loving the sensation, loving the solitude, dancing a few steps in place with my only partner, the silver moon above. This is what it means to hold power, a place where I am wholly, thrillingly, myself.*

*And then I feel a nudge, nothing much at all, just a tiny little bit of pressure on my insides. It's gone as quickly as it comes, but then it's back, more insistent. What is it? My extremities tingle in response, in warning. I am alert suddenly to something beyond the field and the moon, beyond the world in which I stand. I am alert to a world that is just outside all of those things, a place I have locked away with the strongest walls.*

*Walls, locked. Not the right words. Some place that isn't in this reality at all, that doesn't exist in the same way. I picture the attack on me in the subway, the attacks on all of us during the ritual in the gym, the way the kitten was lifted into the air in the barn. I can see what is there, doing the ripping and tearing, and at the same time I can't. It's not my eyes that are doing the seeing but some other organ of perception altogether. I remember what it was like feeling and using my power for the first time, where it was like some new eye or ear had opened to a new sense I'd never even knew existed.*

*I know that I am sensing a danger beyond comprehension. I know that something is happening that I must stop before disaster occurs. This is my doing, this bulwark, this wall. I erected it, and it is failing, and that too is my fault.*

*I wake, and the images stay although the idea I ever understood what was going on in the dream seems an impossibility.*

○

Over coffee (after Jan's departure, naturally), I checked, as I had faithfully since the subway fire article Carla had pointed me to, the local section of the Toronto Star. In particular, I read every sidebar beside the major articles, scissors in hand.

I was not going to be caught out this time. I was going to figure out if there was something happening, some odd pattern that was affecting more than just our little corner of suburbia, and I was going to figure it out without Irene to clue me in.

I had become slightly obsessed for the first time in my life with the newspaper Jan had delivered every morning; if she noticed my sudden interest in the Greater Toronto section of the Star, she said nothing about it, probably just rejoiced that her money was being well spent. After Carla's first call, I'd actually gone out into the garage and sorted through almost a month's worth of old papers, back to the first day of school.

There had been nothing substantive. But I really didn't know what I was looking for, and the brief paragraphs or two the less important stories received in the paper were, I though, barely enough to sink my teeth into. I had clipped car thefts, robberies, high speed chases, and animal attacks, not entirely sure what I thought I might be looking for.

Because of my vigilance, I thought I might actually have something new to tell Jason and the gang, but I was unsure if I had really detected an actual pattern or something I wanted to see because I expected it.

There were upwards of a dozen clippings in my collection today, sorted into relatively neat little piles on the kitchen table. I'd borrowed a bunch of Jan's envelopes to keep them separated into my nominal categories—murders, missing persons, animals, accidents, and the just plain bizarre. Moving aside the most explicable, I was left with a bunch of disappearances and unexplained deaths, but there was something that nagged me about my final grouping.

Looking in the kitchen drawer nearest the telephone, I found an abused map of Toronto and spread it out on the table. I grabbed a pack of raisins from the cupboard, figuring I could do breakfast and research at the same time. *Okay, here we go.*

Starting with the earliest article, I placed a raisin on the map where the incident referred to occurred. Then, splitting the fruit between the map and me, I moved through the rest.

Yeah, there was a pattern. Almost perfect, and nearly inescapable. Maybe I'd uncovered more than I'd expected.

With the exception of a couple of pieces that I'd been pretty dubious about in the first place, and one piece that didn't fit at all, the raisins lead neatly across the map from Westbrook to the place where I'd discovered my preternatural urge to pull the emergency stop lever on a subway car just before a major cave-in.

I picked up the offending article that ruined my neat pattern. It was the very first that Szaba had drawn my attention to, the one about the cafeteria worker who'd nearly walked her feet off on her way to her death close to Square One. And there, I saw my error. No, the line of incidents didn't move exclusively east only to jump back to the western edge of the city once and then return to the previous plan. My cafeteria lady had been discovered long after her death. She had probably died at a time that placed her demise right in the inexorable path of destruction and death wrought by what we'd released.

I realized I was thinking of the culpability for the ritual as mine as well as the rest's now. What had changed? Just that I could no longer see what had happened as unconnected to my presence in the lives of Jason, Scott, and Aaron. I hadn't found the book, or decided to see if I could make it work. But without me, why would the book have been on Aaron's dad's bookshelf? Without me to taunt, who would have targeted them?

Because I was the common denominator, not Hunt, not Jason, not little Peter. And I had seen myself manipulated, doing things I only believed I had chosen to do. How could I blame Jason and the rest anymore for making the decision to open that book and start reading the words? How could I know that they ever would have without something acting on them the way I'd felt it act on me?

And here was the thing itself, working its way across the GTA, hopping from body to body. Mrs. Sanchez, forced to walk until her feet bled, ditched like a piece of litter in a remote corner of a parking lot, covered up partly with cardboard so people had walked by her for days thinking she was homeless, not murdered. Mrs. Sanchez, then Jerrold David Norton, a custodian at Square One. A businessman called Trevor Rapplings who vanished near the site where Norton's body was discovered, and was found three days later closer to the 427 and the West Mall. And another, closer again. Seven disappearances, five bodies. Two unaccounted for, but I was sure they'd be found soon. The last, a man who worked for the TTC on track repair, who'd vanished the day of the explosion I'd been present at. Not found in the tunnel, assumed to be the sole fatality of the cave-in buried in the rubble, even if no one had an answer to why he'd been there at the time.

But all just as Aaron had guessed, and I'd followed his lead. Something, using the heat of human bodies to leap-frog across the GTA into the depths of the subway system. Underground.

This was not happening. There was nothing in the world that would possess me to go underground, not into the bowels of the Diefenbaker sub-basement, a place that I'd shunned entirely although it made a decent shortcut for lots of savvy students. I was hardly capable some days of going into the more subterranean and unlit corridors of Dief, in the first basement level, the half-underground one in which Hunt had surprised Suzanne. Even that couldn't help taking me back to memories of Char's catacombs. I'd had panic attacks in underground malls for months when I'd first started going into Toronto on my own a couple of years back, and although those had subsided, that mysterious *even deeper* subway extension where the first fire had occurred gave me chills that wouldn't stop whenever I thought of it.

The information was undeniable though. I was going to have to share it with someone, and I was going to have to admit the possibility, the horrific, terrifying possibility, that at some point, this adventure would take me back underground.

## 30

## Cracked Actor

✪

I thought it might be a good idea to call Rae immediately and let her know I had something of value finally, but my real desire was to call Aaron. My nerves were on fire when I thought about dialing his number. And yeah, it was probably a better idea to call him than Rae, and would likely yield more applicable suggestions, but I was far too nervous. I didn't want to take the chance of *not* being able to repeat the easy fun of our last conversation. Besides, I told myself, trying to pretend I was being rational not afraid, maybe the forbidding Mrs. Scribner had rules about people calling Aaron in the morning too.

So I folded the articles and the map together, after replacing the raisins with stick-on binder hole reinforcements from a roll in the drawer, and hid the lot under my bed for later. I added Carla Szaba's and Tamblyn's business cards to the growing pile, after copying their contact information carefully into my black notebook. There was no guarantee I would see anyone today at school, and the last thing I wanted was for Hunt to find me with that batch of evidence on me.

Hunt. It was amazing how he was still lurking in the back of my mind as the ultimate boogeyman, but I'd seen no sign of him for so long. I kept meaning to ask if any of the others had laid eyes on him, but never seemed to remember to do it when I was actually talking to them. Maybe that was a good sign. Or maybe Hunt sightings had become so common that no one even thought much about them any more.

✪

I ran into Rae and Suzanne at lunchtime, and was very glad to see them both. For the first time since I had started high school, I went to the cafeteria and sat down with... with friends to eat.

I didn't even mind. In fact, I kind of liked it.

I kept one eye open for Irene, thinking that if I saw her, I would feel even in my own eyes like *the enemy*. I had gone over to the cool girls, and it would sit with me a lot better if Irene wasn't there to spark any feelings of guilt and shame.

Suzanne looked suitably abashed when I sat, trying a little too hard *not* to look at my new short 'do, but I rose to the occasion with a magnanimity that surprised, well, probably mostly me, by saying, "Don't sweat it. We're even for Hunt, I guess."

Rae solidified the truce with one of her blinding smiles, and a compliment about how well it suited me, and some of the awkwardness seemed to be salved, at least for now.

"We've got to get together after school," Rae said, after a little small talk. Then, she answered the question I had again forgotten about asking. "You know how that... man...has been following us?"

Of course. Hunt.

"Yeah, well," Suzanne took up the thread, "He's only following Jason now."

Jason? I hadn't seen him all day, or yesterday either. Except for hearing Suzanne and Rae giggling with him on the phone at the sleepover, he'd kind of vanished from my life for the past few days entirely.

"I can't get over the feeling he's in danger," Suzanne said.

I looked at her intently, wondering if there was at last something to a statement of hers. "Why?"

She rolled her eyes, offended at my tone. "It's more than just a hunch," she said. "It's because of how he's doing it. Jason told me he just hangs around, right, like he did before, but he seems to, I don't know, be guarding him or something. It was threatening before, you know, but now Jason says he actually feels better when he can see him."

That was new. "Okay," I said and we made plans to meet after school Friday at the coffee shop. In the meantime, I toyed with the idea of skipping the afternoon to compose my thoughts, and then remembered just how close I was to mandatory suspension for my absences to date. I went to class.

⊛

By Friday, I had had lunch with Suzanne and Rae three more times, once including Aaron, and had seen Jason just long enough to ask if he was okay and receive a standard-issue boy-grunt in return. Were we okay? Now that I'd built up something of a rapport with Suzanne and Aaron, had I lost the guy whose friendship I valued most?

Ten minutes into a lecture I could barely follow for preoccupation, a kid came to the door with a note from the office. Jan was coming to get me, something about a family emergency. I couldn't imagine what that would be, but it was not without precedent. Once, I had been pulled from school because she had a Friday afternoon off and decided to treat me to ice cream and a matinee. Every now and then, the erratic nature of our relationship worked in my favor.

I walked across the playing field to cut through a parkette to where she was supposed to pick me up, trying to put myself in the mood for a surprise. The parkette was a tawdry little thing, bordered by the visitors' parking lot, the field, and the backs of a bunch of run-down townhouses. It was fenced on two sides and full of mature maples. A good place, in fact, for meeting someone like Hunt who didn't want to be seen unless he had decided to be.

He was there, leaning against a tree, blocking my way back to the playing field. I had the uncomfortable feeling he'd been there for much longer than I wanted to know, waiting with some deadly intent.

"Maggie Stuart," he said, smiling the shark's grin he saved for games.

"Mr. Hunt." It was vital to be at least as cool as he was, otherwise I was lost before I began. "Hunt," I said, the way I'd addressed him in the catacombs.

His mouth twitched. Amusement? This was it, this was what had fooled me previously. I had thought he knew very well what had happened between us when I was in grade eight, and he had not led me in any way to believe otherwise. This, this attitude of his, it was time to call it for what it was. I had no idea now what he remembered of our previous time together, but I was willing to believe it was close to nothing.

"What is it, Hunt?" I asked, weary and not amused.

He approached carefully, familiar in menace. "You have something

I need, Maggie May." His voice was all conversational ease. *My old nickname*. He had called me Maggie May back in Char's realm. Did he remember after all? Was he torturing me consciously? No, he was probably making a joke out of my name, I realized belatedly, the way he had before. Same man, same reference. Just coincidence, not memory. And he'd called me the same thing in public school, so maybe that part of his memory was intact.

He jumped in before I could say anything. "I've come back. Aren't you glad to see me?"

*Don't answer,* I warned myself. "We have to talk," I told him. I was even more glad now that I'd left the newspaper clippings at home, so I could decide whether or not to tell him about them myself. I didn't think he was above going through my bag with or without my permission.

Come to think of it, I didn't think he was above breaking into my house whenever he felt like it and finding the things I'd cleverly hidden by stashing them under my bed, the first place *anyone* would look. And I'd never even thought about it before, so I'd never looked for evidence he'd been there. As far as I knew, he'd been into every aspect of my life a dozen times since I'd first seen him in Thurl's office.

"You didn't tell me you were happy I came," he said, same smile, moving in closer.

I decided it was time for my own gloves to come off. Strange, how I had been more scared to call Aaron this morning than I was to face Hunt down now. "There are some things, very important things you don't know," I said. He'd listen, and weigh, regardless of what he pretended. This I had to count on. "I want to tell you the truth about the gap in your memory. I can tell you what you want to know."

He laughed, very quietly, his hand moving to cover my upper arm on the side with the scar. I was suddenly confused. The scar—how could he know about the scar if he had forgotten everything else? It couldn't just be some kind of lucky guess, could it? It didn't make sense.

And in the moment of my hesitation, Hunt had an arm around my throat and dragged me out of the parkette into someone's backyard, and from there onto a rough dirt path leading down to the run-off ditch below.

*First rule,* I told myself, as he increased the pressure on my neck. *Run—don't let the attacker get a hold on you. If he catches you, you're lost.*

Not Hunt's rules this time. This was an echo from the unit on rape we'd done in gym class last year. Which I had failed. I struggled, fought as hard as I could against him, but I couldn't break his grip. My lungs began to burn, and even if I could have brought myself to scream, I was past being able. He had twisted my scarred arm around behind my back. I was helpless, and he knew it. He was good.

He released me just long enough for me to get my breath. We were in the woods now. There were no houses that I could see; the trees hemmed us in. The air was thick and cool, cold even for this far into fall, and I could almost imagine my own breath leaking out in jerky puffs. My eyes were full of tears. Trees surrounded us on all sides, and there were enough leaves left that no one would see us unless they were right on top of us.

We'd descended a ways on the path, far enough that I knew screaming wouldn't carry up and out. And we were only about a minute's walk to Dief's lower car park, down this very path, at the end that would be entirely deserted at this time of day. Wrong, wrong, wrong. I was a goner. I had been so stupid. This was it. I wanted to cry out, 'Why?' I wanted to blurt out apologies. Playing with fire, with such a dangerous man. *Why?* Not to him. To myself.

His hand, quick and brutal, reached around my neck as I paused, stunned by my own tears. Again, I couldn't get away. Fingers stained with his lifetime of questionable deeds ripped open the neck of my shirt and tore at my throat.

I staggered back under the onslaught, and he grabbed my arm to keep me upright, and within striking distance. "Where is it?" he hissed.

Now I was more terrified. I tried to draw away, something horrid and poisonous seething in my belly, but he pulled me effortlessly into a choke-hold.

"Where is it?" he whispered, the fingers of one hand dragging the skin of my neck as if trawling for treasure on my epidermis.

I couldn't speak, couldn't even scream even if I thought it would do any good. My stomach had twisted itself into knots and I could hear the beat of my own heart, blood pounding in my ears.

Rougher now, he wrenched my right arm against my spine. His other hand went flat against my breastbone, and I felt a quiver that I was not accustomed to, something I'd known only once before in my life, across a desk in a McDonald's. Sexual panic.

He cursed me under his breath—I don't know what exact form the cursing took but its venom was plain from his tone. Then, the hand removed itself from my chest. I had almost no time to be grateful before his arm, prickly with coarse hair and sweat, smashed across my throat and I was fighting for air. *This is it,* I thought blackly. *I've let him too close—and now he kills me.*

I started falling, my legs turning to useless sodden things under me. I could see the ground, at a very odd angle. Then, blinding headache—lights—and nothing.

✪

The first thing I thought was that if I had wanted to sleep, there were better places than the floor to do it.

I came to slowly, in blossoms of black and white, wondering what could possibly have possessed me to lie down on my bedroom floor to sleep. The floor part, at least, I had right, but the ratty, odorous carpet was definitely not home.

I stirred—and he was over me, straddling my body, one knee tight beside my stomach. He wrenched my arm.

"You're awake now, huh," he breathed. My voice caught in my throat. I was stripped down, to my undershirt and my panties. He had done this—he had undressed me. He had—*babble in my head*. I wasn't even wearing a real bra, just a thin sportsbra under the undershirt that made me feel worse than naked. Spittle bubbled on my lips and I couldn't stop. My breath came in jerks, through the bruised windpipe.

"Stop crying," Hunt ordered, and gave the arm another cruel yank, bringing me around to face him. "Pathetic," he whispered, his thin lips twisted. I could see it; he was right, and I started to cry in earnest.

He threw my arm away from him. *Disgusted.* I lay shivering. The room wasn't too cold, but it was definitely cold enough. He crossed to the other side of the room; I had just enough time to imagine I could escape—even into the chilly autumn afternoon in my skivvies—when he came back with the rope.

It was textbook Hunt, but I couldn't be very appreciative. I was feeling a little too—uh, exposed—for that. This time, his knee went right into the small of my back as he wrenched my arms up, and proceeded to bind my wrists and ankles while I remained completely immobilized. Textbook, because he could have done all that while I was unconscious, and chose to wait until I was witness to my own humiliation. Somewhere in the process, as he continued in his rough way, I found myself with my face nearly against his crotch, and that started the panic again. I would have done anything to release myself from the sexual anxiety, to feel only the fear for my life, but I couldn't. He took so much care to touch me, to tousle my hair when I was finally bound; even the scrape of his boot along my side made me shiver obscenely. I knew I was in greater trouble than just situationally if my sick mind had such a facility for translating dire physical circumstance to something erotic.

"New haircut," was all he said during the entire ordeal, and I was glad I wasn't facing the right way to see whatever smirk he accompanied the statement with.

When I was bound to his satisfaction—he made quite a show of tugging the knots, just to prove how useless an escape attempt would be—he stood back, hands in his pockets, as if to admire his handiwork. I couldn't help imagining myself as some kind of 50's heroine in a sexploitational Stone Age film, trussed up on the hero's floor as the spoil of the hunt. Spoil of the Hunt, really. He was so cool, as if he'd done this exact thing so many times it was routine. I didn't know, of course, that wasn't the case.

And then there was the whistling. It had gotten on my nerves down in Char's Catacombs, and it was just as bad here. Tuneless, and inexplicably menacing, if I have to explain my fear beyond my obvious helpless state.

He spoke finally. "So, it's up to me to break the silence. I guess I won't have the pleasure of hearing you beg. Not yet, anyhow."

I stared up, neck crooked uncomfortably, eyes locked on him as I supposed they must have been from the moment he stepped back to admire his handiwork. It was the first time it had occurred to me that I could, perhaps, unnerve him a little. It wasn't something I would push, naturally, but it was some small consolation. Now, if I could just manage to get out of here, preferably with my virginity intact—

The fact my sixteenth birthday was fast approaching seemed like the ultimate irony. Was this the way I would end up in compliance with that dubious statistic my disgusting boss had quoted at me across his desk at the McDonalds? *Lose your virginity by sixteen, or be a freak.*

What a thought for an old teacher to evoke!

He knelt by my face, and brushed two fingers across my jaw. The move was so sudden and so intimate, I flinched, nearly rolled away in my haste to separate my skin from the electricity of his touch. This made him laugh, which started me crying. So much for the unintentional—and small—victory of forcing him to speak first.

"Maggie May," he said, definitely amused. "You're not really my type. Believe me, anything I do is for pain or expediency. Besides—and this is the truth—if I wanted you that way, you would come to me of your own free will, begging for me to touch you." It was so much like something Char had said to me once—but at the same time carried a raw sexual quality that the Dark Man's invitation lacked. He poked my scarred shoulder with one finger, and laughed again when I couldn't control my reaction. "What conceit!" he chuckled. "You're one for the *book*, Mags, that's the God's honest truth."

He stood, and levered me up with a hand under my arm. I balanced on my bound feet, using his body to keep myself upright. I felt like a fool, but the sexual wariness remained. Here I was, all prepped to fight the wrong battle; I knew it, and yet my emotions were so far down that wrong path. It was the most vulnerable I could imagine being, to be afraid of a sexual advance and to be, because of that, so clouded as to not have any idea what he might really be planning. Maybe that was a blessing.

He chuckled, and I was pretty sure he knew exactly how uncomfortable he was making me. "Wouldn't you prefer a boy your own age, darlin'? That Jason Lawson is awfully tall, dark and handsome... or what about the intellectual Mr. Scribner?"

I must have blushed. Cheeks burning, I could only try to meet Hunt's eyes as he wrenched me around to face him. I must look like a mess to him, suddenly overheated despite the coolness of the room. He must have thought I was terrified.

Or at least, that's what I hoped. It was bad enough remembering that Hunt had undressed me with no intention beyond making me as frightened and vulnerable as possible. To imagine he knew my heart was too grim to bear.

Hunt twisted me around and let me fall into a worn armchair. I sank into it with even a little relief, comfortable—relatively speaking—for the first time since he'd crushed my windpipe. Even sitting mostly on my hands was okay. "So," I began, "is it time for us to have our conversation? Where are we anyhow? Is this your secret hide-out, and now I can never leave?"

He dropped into the equally worn sofa across from me. From the thickness of the cushions, I guessed it contained a pull-out bed. Between us was the grubby, matted carpet on which I had come to, bordered by a stretch of uneven hardwood. Hunt's bachelor flat, perhaps? Somehow, I'd always pictured him with more decorating flair.

"Haven't decided," he said, replying. "Don't get me wrong. I hate killing little girls. But sometimes, when you don't think you're getting enough of the truth, you don't mind hurting them a bit."

I laughed. I didn't know where I found the guts to do it, but I managed. It even came out with a bit of bravado. "Hunt," I declared, to draw him back, "I *want* to tell you what you need to know. I was willing to even without this little charade, so why don't you give me my coat at least and something warm to drink? You should pay your heating bills."

This amused him further. I realized suddenly why I was feeling so out-of-body—it was because the whole situation was desperately familiar, and it wasn't until it struck me what it resembled that I understood. This was the way Hunt and the Dark Man had sparred, except with me now in the Hunt role. It had been his method, as far as I could tell, pretending he wasn't afraid of Char, to keep him guessing, and amused. *Sauce for the gander.*

"I'm not exactly running a Holiday Inn here, as you can probably gather. And I gave my butler the week off." He steepled his index fingers and considered me. "Information."

It was the order I had been waiting for, and put me in mind of the demands I had made on him during my stay in Char's domain. Maybe I'd be more forthcoming.

"Char," I told him, savoring the blank, guarded look that fell over his face to hide the unmistakable beginnings of surprise. "He's dead, although you might not know it. I'll save how he died for last, because you won't believe it."

And with that, I began. I stinted on some of the information, but I laid heavily into his own former interest in me, and especially into his training. Maybe he would be stirred to imagine I had been, at least for a short time, an apprentice to him.

When I finished with the account of the final magic, in which he himself had directed me, he stood. Reaching up to a bookcase that held a jumble of junk, he extracted a felt bag not unlike the Crown Royal bag I had myself under my bed. He set it down on my lap, grinned and peeled back a section of the shoddy carpet to allow him access to the bare boards below. Bare boards on which he'd painted a complex diagram that included my old friend the pentacle.

Now I struggled a bit, because in my mind I could hear his voice, clear as a bell. *"Any ritual of a certain size needs blood."* Only, last time it had been Tamblyn willingly supplying the, well, the magic ingredient. This time, there were only him and me in the room, and I couldn't see him deigning to open one of his own veins.

He seemed to take more than a little pleasure in using my lap as a table for the bag as he undid its ties and extracted ten nubby white candles and then the long, cruel knife that had haunted my dreams for all these years. It was rusted along its length where it was chipped, as I'd remembered. What the hell was it made of? Wasn't everything made of stainless steel nowadays and all but impervious to corruption?

But then, the knife didn't look like it was newly purchased, like the one in my Crown Royal bag. I was a poor imitator of Hunt's style with magical tools. My knife was impressive, but in a very basic way: *Ooo, big knife.* Hunt's called for use. It called for blood.

He was still smiling as he came close and locked eyes with me as he drew the knife across my breastbone, just under my left clavicle. The blade cut easily through the undershirt and stretchy sportsbra, and stung. So, so sharp, unexpectedly for all its dull and rusty looks. The cut he made started oozing immediately; I felt the wetness of my own blood on my skin and the coolness of my skin where the fabric that had been between Hunt's knife and me flapped down.

It didn't expose anything really, nothing that would have got us an "R" rating in the entertainment world, but I felt entirely vulnerable. How could he make me feel more violated, short of a real violation? The blood was running freely—I remembered the way he seemed to know exactly how deeply I should cut Tamblyn in order to keep the blood flowing but not put his life in danger—and soaked into the remnants of the straps of my underwear.

Still looking into my eyes, searching them for my reaction I guessed, he took each squat candle and rolled it in my blood before placing it on the floor. Then, finally, he took his eyes away from mine and began to chant.

I didn't understand a word, but I figured that *this* at least wasn't some old dialect of Hebrew. It was altogether more guttural in some places, and more sibilant in others. It seemed to change the thickness of the air in the room, as if the words were sucking away the space between us and filling it with fibrous, cloying threads of sound.

I remembered how Tamblyn had passed out while Hunt instructed me in the magic I used to send the forgetting spell out over the world, but I had no such luck. Instead, the minutes stretched by while my blood dropped and dried, while Hunt chanted, while the candles guttered and flared, all in that thick, dense atmosphere where sound had become an almost physical thing.

Then the candles were out, and I saw they had burned almost to nothing, leaving nothing but ten nubs each crowned with half an inch of black wick. There was a *whoosh* sound that passed through the room, taking the oppressiveness with it and, as if a window had been opened and uncurtained, the room suddenly became emptier and brighter.

Hunt stood, and stared for a moment into the space between us, as if he needed a moment to examine something that perplexed him. Without a word, he left the room. Several minutes passed, and I heard the whistle of a kettle.

He returned with two cups of instant coffee, mine laden with milk and sugar, exactly the way I liked it when I wasn't trying to look tough. He knew what I took, but such attention to detail no longer surprised me.

He pushed me forward to undo the ropes around my wrists, but made no move to untie my feet. When he had put the coffee mug into my hands, he bent to my ear and whispered, distressingly sensuously, "Run and I kill you, story or no. And I won't even cry if my mug gets broken."

The coffee was not bad, and the milk was fine. I had half expected, when he'd made the concession, that I would find brown grit in tepid water finished with chunky cream. I sipped slowly, like a condemned prisoner trying to stave off execution by lingering over my final meal. He allowed me to drink in silence, and even threw my coat to me to cover my bare knees when the warmth of the coffee set up a new barrage of shivering.

When I had set the mug aside on the arm of the chair, he looked at me, bird-intent, and said in a conversation tone, "What, fifty percent?"

I stared. "What?"

"Of your story. Fifty percent true? Zero? Ninety? Are you keeping a lot back, or just a little, wee bit to use for bargaining your way out of this room?"

"It's all true. Wasn't that what the bell-book-and-candle show was all about?"

"Right." He stood, and for a moment as he lingered in front of me, I thought he'd hit me. If I was right, and he'd used some kind of magic to check my veracity, he was still having trouble believing the evidence of his own senses. No wonder he was so—unsettled. Eventually, he just took the coffee mug. "Lesson one," he reminded me, "you move and I —"

I cut him off. "Lesson one, trust yourself first, and no one second."

That wasn't quite right. Lesson one, blood and magic. Lesson one, Hunt is his own man. Lesson one, from every terrible cop show I'd seen on television, always let your backup know where you are.

He stopped. "That's vintage me," he said. There was a note in his voice I didn't recognize, possibly because he was letting me know he understood that I was being at least partially truthful.

Then, he seemed to relent. "Tell me again about the cat in the barn," he said. "In detail."

I guessed it was nitty-gritty time. He was fact-checking. I went through the whole thing again. When I got to the part about drawing the circle and dismissing the thing, he stopped me.

"That's it," he said. "What's wrong with this picture?"

I frowned. "It worked. How I don't know. Isn't that your department?"

"Tell me again," he said, giving me the proverbial hairy eyeball.

I had no idea what he was getting at.

"You were in the circle," he prompted, "and. . ."

"And I finished it, told it to get lost, and it did."

"Really." He sat back down, leaning forward, head resting on his hands.

What was I missing here? What was the flaw he obviously saw in my story? I had told it just like it happened. It was intensely frustrating that something I was being entirely honest about had struck him as a lie. "There was this—crazy feeling, like someone was trying to suck my insides out through my skin. Just for a moment, after I told it to take a hike and before things came back to normal. That's all. There's nothing more."

"A sucking feeling, huh?"

I was getting a little pissed off. "Yeah. It was pretty uncomfortable for a second or so. Like being on a ride at the fairgrounds you didn't really expect to be so tough on your body. And then—just like I said."

He regarded me, and I felt my scalp prickle. Had I missed out on something in that moment in the barn myself? Had I done something I wasn't supposed to do? But then, maybe it had something to do with Arabella's ring, the ring I no longer had. Was Arabella's ring somehow responsible for my success getting rid of the demons? But no, the first couple of times I had dealt with them, it was just me. It had to be something else.

"Okay," he said at last. "I'll admit it. I just don't know. But there's the matter of the book, and that's my price. For letting you go. *It* comes to *me*." he finished after a pause, when I must have looked blank. "And then there's that pretty ring of yours.."

I looked at him steadily. "It's gone," I said.

"I know," he said, in the same cool tone. "But when you find it again, as you know you will. . ." He left the thought hanging. I will what?

He reached down slowly between my legs, and my elaborate tensing made him chuckle. "Really not my type," he repeated, amused, and slashed away the bonds around my feet with his ubiquitous knife.

✪

The conversation was almost civilized after that.

"Tell me about the other book," I asked, "the one I remember from the ritual you taught me, it was yours?"

"Was John's," he corrected. "I didn't know how it had come into my possession. I assume I must have stolen it from him at some point. Can you perhaps illuminate me on that one, sweetheart?"

I couldn't, but I sat still and stoney-faced, staring at him. It was the only revenge I could think of at that moment. Only softly in the back of my mind did a small suspicion form that somehow this theft was connected to Corporal Carla's interest in the detective. Something I'd have to think more on later. Right now I had to stay in the present, with Hunt.

"That's very good for enigmatic, darlin'," he said at last, unknowingly echoing Jason the day of our abortive lunch meeting. "But I'm not going to rise to it. I have a feeling my actions are at least as mysterious to you as they are to me. At least in that particular period of my life."

I regarded him for a moment, the salt-and-pepper hair I remembered so well from my elementary school days showing not a bit more grey, the widow's peak over his forehead not a notch receded from where I had seen it last. He seemed not to have aged, while I was almost all the way through the changes of puberty and, although no taller, had become just a tad more recognizably a woman.

"What about the green book, the one they used?"

He smiled. "Now, that's a wonderful piece of arcane literature."

"And you gave the book to Jason. . . knowing it would somehow make its way to me."

"I gave it to them," he confirmed. His eyes flickered away, and I knew he wasn't telling the whole truth.

I looked at him closely. A suspicion was forming in my mind. He knew too much about the book to have never held it in his own hands, but something was wrong. He was lying. "You didn't give us the book," I hazarded. "You wouldn't have."

He laughed. "Darlin', that's the last thing I would have wanted. If it had been mine, there's no way you or yours would have ever got your grubby little hands on it."

"You gave it to them. But you didn't want to," I blurted, guessing. I remembered what I thought I'd experienced on the subway train. "Something like that would have been your prize, even if you didn't know how you ended up with it. Something controlled you, made you do it."

"Nothing *controlled* me," he scoffed, as if to say, *what could?* "I was blackmailed. By someone who wanted your little friends to do just what they did. I admit, it was a pretty sweet plan: give a piece of powerful occult literature to a bunch of boobs who couldn't possibly have known what it was capable of. . ."

I wanted to cry. I wanted to badly, and I didn't really care if he saw, but my eyes were painfully dry.

Then he made it worse. "Although when I heard it was circulating, I hoped that you would know about the book. Would desire it. Would lust after it. Would crave its secrets to the bottom of your. . . heart." He smiled, no warmth in the expression. "Do you?"

Of course I wanted it. Three years of hunting for arcane knowledge had got me *what*? Notebooks filled with scrawled writings of unprovable supernatural phenomena, recipes for spells that I hadn't even had the heart to attempt—recognizing them for the garbage they were—occult symbols and diagrams, names of angels, and demonic alphabets to memorize so that I might, someday, be able to find some truth in the chicanery. It was rubbish, all of it.

He leaned in and touched my face, and I cringed, unable to stop myself. It wasn't that I found him repugnant, not exactly. But the shiver he sent through me with his words and the brush of his fingers? It felt like enough to make me explode.

"You want it badly, don't you? And I will do everything I can to stop you from having it. How do you like that, Maggie May? How do you like the destiny I am writing for you?"

Inside, I was seething, molten. He was right. I had never been in love, but in my imagination, it would make me feel like I did when I was doing magic. That's what my dream about Damon had been about, as much as a desire for affection. I wanted to feel powerful again.

He grinned, as if he knew just where his words had taken me. Maybe he did. If not, he made an all-too good guess.

"It's what sex is to most people," he said, "what they think they're getting from sex, at least. Or ambition. Satisfaction. Winning. But we know the truth. It's the ability to move the earth, that's what we really want. The capacity to overcome nature through simple desire.

"Now what, Mags?" he asked, dropping onto the sofa across from me. "I suppose some quid pro quo is in order, and it's not like I don't have a lot that you want."

I wished I still had some coffee left to prevaricate before answering. There was a lot I wanted to know, but what would he tell me?

"Jason thinks you're protecting him. Is something going to happen?"

He laughed. "What a thought. My altruism is legendary."

But I glimpsed a bit of surprise as he answered my question, like I had again necessitated that he lie to keep me in the dark. I decided to move to another subject, but I thought I could probably also give Suzanne credit for telling me something *très* interesting.

"Those things, the demons..."

"No such thing, Maggie," he said, "Not in my experience anyhow, not the way you think. But there are a lot of beings that, shall we say, lack a conventional corporeal existence. That's what you and your little friends released."

"And you wanted them to?" I cried, ignoring the automatic lumping of me with the culpable parties in that case. "Those things are killing everything they can."

"Not my problem, Mags."

There was something else I needed to follow up. "How? How could you have been blackmailed?" I said, but I knew without him saying, without me even knowing what it meant. *Vancouver*. Something about Vancouver had been enough to convince him to give up a book he lusted after even as he held it in his own hands.

"You want it back," I said, dropping the question he wouldn't answer. "The book."

"I do," he said. "I was too late to stop you from performing the ritual that released those things, but..."

"We find ourselves on the same side of the equation."

"For now. And only just."

I stopped myself from shivering, but only just.

## 31

## Under Pressure

○

After letting me dress (turning his back more mockingly than as a salve to modesty), he blindfolded me, making a big joke out of it, and led me down a back staircase to his car. He told me to lie down in the back seat, and not to sit up *or else*. He was laughing as he said it, as if he wanted to show me just how much pleasure he was capable of taking at my expense. I didn't know if the *or else* carried a serious threat, but that was hardly the point: I'd learned long ago with Hunt that no matter what I did, he would react in whatever way would throw me furthest off guard.

After what I'd just been through, and despite the coffee, I had no energy to tempt him to some new kind of response. I lay quietly.

We drove in silence for five minutes or so. We seemed to be turning more than necessary, as if Hunt was somewhat worried I'd be able to figure out where his hidey hole was by backtracking our route. I guessed he didn't know that was the least of my preoccupations.

Mostly, I was thinking about Corporal Szaba. Had he said something about his *book* on the telephone or in some email she'd intercepted? If she was spying on him, I was sure she'd have the resources to do the latter as well, even if he was careful and already wary of surveillance. Who better than a cop to ferret out the secrets of another cop?

I needed to process what I'd learned, and try to guess what further misinformation I'd received. It was ironic that I'd tried my hardest to be honest with Hunt and tell him everything, and he probably believed me as little as I figured I could trust him.

The brief feeling of detente I'd had with his bringing the coffee had handily evaporated, and I was left even more certain that this was a dangerous man. And worse, I don't think he'd really believed a word I'd said. Not about our previous involvement, at least. He didn't believe he'd asked me to erase his memories. I could hardly believe it myself, in retrospect. He must have had an angle.

Finally, he said, "You can sit up now." I moved upright, and felt his hands on the blindfold. "Take off, Maggie May. We're done for now."

We were back in Westbrook, at the GO station. I guess he figured it was more fun to make me take the bus the rest of the way home. I wondered if anyone at school had noticed I was missing for the last part of the day. Probably not. Talk about crying wolf; even if I'd vanished for the afternoon *without* a note from my mother, my absences were hardly remarkable.

He drove off, and I realized I hadn't even bothered to take his license number or note the make and model of his car. "Gold four-door sedan" was all I'd be able to say by way of report. Some investigator I was. I couldn't even manage the mundane, much less the supernatural.

I went into the station, found fifty cents in my pocket, and dialed Rae's number from memory. Not having a cellphone had never sucked more. She answered on the first ring. It wasn't too long after the end of classes, but it *was* enough time for them to have made it to the coffee shop without me.

"Rae—" I began, but as soon as she heard my voice, she broke in.

"Maggie, Jason's gone!"

The panic in her tone was contagious. "What do you mean, gone? Where did he go?"

"We don't know," she said, words coming faster and faster. "He was there in third, and Aaron saw him in the hall on the way to fourth, but he never made it there."

Sort of like me. But I knew where Hunt had been at that time, so he couldn't have have anything to do with Jason. And *unlike* me, people would notice Jason's absence.

"Did you check if he went home? Or check the coffee shop? Maybe he was sick or something."

"Nothing. He's just gone! I come to fourth from the opposite end of the school—if he'd left the building, he'd have had to go right past me. If I didn't see him, and Aaron didn't see him pass in the other direction…"

"And he's nowhere in between. . ."

"That's where we're at. Aaron called his place after school, but no one's there and he's not answering his cell. It's not even going to voicemail."

*Bring your man.* Even when the apparition had first said it to me, I'd thought of Jason. Not Hunt, not Aaron, nor one of any number of adult men I knew, although of course the pool of selection was small. I had immediately thought the thing was talking about Jason. And now he was gone.

She was still talking. "Then when you weren't at the coffee shop after school, we thought something had happened to you too. . ."

It hit me then, hard. We were being decimated by attrition—we'd lost Scott already, then the ring, and then Jason. The book was located, but out of reach as truly as if it were still in the wind. We were losing; we had lost all the accouterments required for the game, and two of the key players, and we had no more idea than before of what we should do. Tears welled in my eyes then, and I felt two fat ones roll down my cheeks, for Jason, and for me.

Embarrassed, I could only speak in a strangled way: "I'm—sorry. Oh, God. I'll . . . Rae, I'll—I'll come to you as quickly as I can. I have to do something first. Can you get everyone to the coffee shop in two hours?" She agreed, and I fled, to catch the GO and get to the only person I could think of who might be able to help.

✪

Tamblyn's door was closed, but I could see the light on under the door. I had come up the stairs with an empty pizza box and had thus evaded both suspicion and Carla Szaba, whose desk was at the far end of the hallway from Tamblyn's office. Knowing his rep, I wasn't surprised they stuck him out of the way. I was just grateful that whoever "Officer Smith" was, he was hungry enough when I got the desk to call up that he accepted the unordered pizza as a stroke of unexpected good luck instead of with suspicion. I hoped he wouldn't be too disappointed when it went AWOL before reaching him.

I put the pizza box down against the wall outside his door and breathed deeply before knocking. My stomach was doing crazy things, somersaults and bungee-jumping flings.

"Yes?" He sounded surly. If I wasn't so scared, I probably would have walked away right then. But fear can be a very perverse thing sometimes, and my fear was goading me forward. I was more afraid to be a coward than I was to go on.

I tried the handle, but the door was locked. *How surprising, Mr. Paranoid,* I thought, and heard him shuffling papers before he stomped to the door.

The expression on his face was about what I expected, as soon as he realized who it was. I jumped in, before I lost all my nerve, or puked on his shoe or something. We'd struck a kind of truce in the subway incident, but I guess that didn't extend to me showing up unannounced at his place of employment.

"I want to lodge a complaint. I mean, report a crime."

He tapped his foot, arms crossed. "That's a new one."

I pushed on. "Kidnapping. I want to report a kidnapping."

"Whose?" he asked. There was no hint of interest in his voice.

Suddenly, I realized I didn't think I should tell him about Jason. It wasn't the right time, and he wasn't the right person. I wanted Hunt, not his brother. Or I was just chickening out, afraid to make this real by telling someone in the police about Jason's disappearance. And besides, what if Rae was wrong, and there was some normal reason for him missing the end of school? It would destroy my already fragile credibility with Tamblyn, and we might lose him as an ally when it really counted.

"Mine." It came out very small. "I was. I'm back now."

I was blushing furiously, as he motioned me forward into the office. He stepped around the desk after closing and locking the door. I hovered across from him, again acutely aware of the lack of a second chair in the room.

As preamble, I stepped up to the edge of the desk and held out my wrists. Hunt's ligature marks were still clearly visible, the twists in the twine making a diagonally striated pattern of red against the skin.

"I didn't do this to myself," I assured him, since I didn't know quite how poor his opinion of me might be.

He leaned forward to examine my wrists, not touching me. I could feel his rising distaste hanging between us.

"My brother," he said at last, and sat back. Now, he wouldn't even look at me.

"How do you know?" I said.

"Not because he was a boy scout," he said, then relented, knowing, I guess, that his meaning had escaped me. "People tie distinctive knots, depending on where and how they learned. My brother in particular."

"Been there, huh?" I said. It came out more flip than I had intended, and I braced myself for some fallout.

But Tamblyn merely leaned back in his chair, hands behind his head. "So, we're both victims," he said. "I'm not like most people, Miss Stuart. I don't get all upset because a particular victim is a child. I lack most common sentimentality, so don't try to appeal to some misguided sense of outrage. Besides, in the ways that matter, you aren't really a child, are you?"

I said nothing, but it was like he could see into me, like he could see me the way I saw myself. Of course I wasn't a child, as far as I was concerned. I had been born old. Later matters hadn't helped that particular part of my self-image.

"Well, me too," he said. "I was exposed to more of life by the time I was ten than most people have to see in a lifetime. He's older, you know. He was using those knots on me as long as I can remember. And this too."

I moved forward in my chair. Tamblyn, with the air of a reluctant showman, unbuttoned a sleeve of his shirt and rolled the cuff to his elbow.

The skin of his forearm was a mess of white lines, the scars of long-ago ages of abuse. I stopped breathing as he turned the arm to show me the scored underside, including one thin keloid I knew well, because I'd seen Hunt cut it myself and watched it bleed.

"And a few years ago, three to be more exact, I found this."

I knew what it would be. He untucked his shirt, unbuttoning it to the middle of his chest, and lifted his undershirt. Across his ribs, stretching from breastbone to below his heart, crossing and intersecting older white scars, was an intricately carved pattern, less healed, more red, newer. At the centre of it was a pentagram, echoing the pattern Hunt had carved on the floor in his room. Flesh or wood, it was all the same to Hunt when he had a knife in his hand. My lust for my vanished power extended to envy of his indifference when choosing a canvas for his designs. Tears welled to the corner of my eye, and I reached quivering fingers toward these particular lines on Tamblyn's skin, made when I *could* work the same kind of wonders as his brother.

"I did it," I said in a tiny voice. "It was me."

My fingers brushed his skin and I felt the electric twinge between us. If he had been reluctant to touch me, I knew why.

"You," he said. His brows furrowed slightly.

"Not him," I confirmed. "But he. . . he showed me how."

I felt the tears spill, first out of one eye, then the other. *One for me, one for Tamblyn this time,* I thought. I made no move to stop them or wipe them away. "I'm so sorry. But I think. . . I think there was a good reason."

He pulled his arm away, and rolled his cuff back down, re-tucked his shirt. "That's one of the terrible burdens of it," he said at last. "There often was. Or seemed to be."

He sat back again. "Once you start using it, the magic can be extremely seductive. It begins to make demands. It wants to be a part of your life. It wants you to practice it."

I thought of my books at home, the stash under my bed, the portfolio with the stubbornly intriguing paintings. That knowledge I wanted, desperately. *So I could, eventually, become just like Hunt.* Wasn't that what I wanted? My eyes lingered on Tamblyn's skin, and the story it told.

"I knew something had happened," he said, "something I didn't remember consciously. Because of the fresh scar. I knew it had to be him. But as the years went by, and nothing else happened, I tried to forget, to imagine I'd done it to myself in my sleep or some ridiculous thing like that."

He handed me a Kleenex from the box on his desk. "I don't hate you. . . Maggie," he said, using my first name at last, although with difficulty. "He's a hard man to avoid, if he wants to use you. He can be impossible to say no to, because he gives you impossible options."

Opening a drawer, he pulled out a business card and handed it to me. "This has all my numbers on it, including my personal cell. You understand that I can't file an official report about what happened to you. You're going to have to live without justice. But I know, and I *know*, okay? So take your comfort in our common pain. That's all I can offer you. That, and the card. If you need me, if you have to have me there, *I will come.* You understand?" He stood and ushered me out. I paused for a moment at the door to the stairs, but he motioned me on, and bent to pick up the pizza box leaning against the wall. "I'll take care of this," he said, and I didn't think he just meant disposing of the garbage.

## 32

## Together Alone

✪

It was a strange trip back to the place from which Hunt had abducted me. So much had happened in so short a time. Despite the fact I'd taken action—if you could call my abortive trip to see Tamblyn that—I felt like I was playing catch-up in a seriously effectiveness-challenged way. I hadn't even verified Jason's disappearance, much less taken the time to think anything through.

As I rounded the corner to the coffee shop strip mall, I could see Aaron, Suzanne, and Rae standing there. It felt like a million years since I'd laid eyes on any of them. Funny how time flies when you're being strangled, kidnapped, embarrassed…

I tensed, and imagined Hunt giving a little derisive snort to ridicule me. Could I be that transparent, to be so obviously crushing on Aaron and so stupidly aware of the exact distance he was standing from Suzanne, the nearness of their hands? *Was* he with her? I felt so idiotically out of my depth. I knew nothing, nothing at all about dating, about attraction.

Aaron turned, and instantly I knew from the paleness of his face and the way his eyes gleamed that what Rae had told me at least was true. Jason was gone, and they were certain of it. This was no false alarm. He was gone.

"Anything?" I asked as I joined them.

It was Rae who answered, and I could see her face was drawn as well. It looked as though she'd been crying. "We don't know who to go to," she said, quietly, a dreadful stillness about her. "We can't go to the police, not yet."

"What could they do anyway?" Suzanne added, a statement.

No need to mention at this point I had already tried that, and chickened out. But should I mention my own brief captivity?

Aaron was close to anger, I could see, and not like in class, not just the passion and assuredness. He restated what Rae had told me on the phone. "We thought they got you too."

Rae finished perhaps unnecessarily: "It's like I said. Jason's gone. Vanished."

I could hardly form the words. "I just saw Hunt. Well, about an hour and a half ago."

"Jason is missing," Aaron said, his voice very tight and dangerous. "Mr. Hunt? If you saw him, all that means is that he didn't take Jason." He turned to Suzanne. "Maybe Jason was right. Hunt *was* protecting him, right up until the moment he. . ." And he looked at me. Blaming me.

No one asked me what had happened to me. I became self-conscious about my itchy, damaged wrists, and pulled my sleeves down to hide the rope marks.

Suzanne's eyes started to seep, tears rolling out from each corner. "I keep thinking about the birds. Then cats, then dogs."

She didn't have to say more. I knew they were picturing Jason lying somewhere, on a lawn, on a driveway, in a manicured back lot, not a mark on him, but still as the grave. That would have been the perfect moment to tell them about the lunch lady, the article in the paper to which Szaba had drawn to my attention. Instead, I decided to sit on my knowledge a little longer.

"I think I can get the book back." I said it, but for a moment, I wasn't sure anyone else had heard.

Then Aaron turned on me with all his intensity, and a good measure of anger. "*Jason* is gone. I don't think any of us are particularly concerned about the book at the moment."

I looked away so they wouldn't see my shame, or the fact that, although I felt like a total bastard for caring more about myself than their friend, I really was in desperate need of security, which I believed could only be found in the pages of that mysterious volume. There was the mad Hunter to appease. Without the ring, only the book would do. And because I'd been so secretive, they didn't know enough of the truth about Hunt. And I had lost them Jason. Lost *us* Jason.

"What about the police?" said Suzanne. She looked at me. "Don't you have some kind of person there that knows you?"

That was either an understatement, or barely enough to describe my current status with Tamblyn. "We can't go to them," I said with all the finality I could muster. I pictured myself returning to Tamblyn after only a bare two hours had passed to report a second kidnapping. No matter how good an idea that might be, I realized I couldn't possibly take the embarrassment calling Tamblyn right away would cause me. Now I wasn't just a detriment to my so-called new friends, I might be damaging our chances of finding Jason just because I was afraid to damage my own pride.

✪

None of us wanted to be alone after that, although maybe they could have done without me just fine. Since Rae's parents were out for the evening, we decided to head over there and try to make sense of what was going on.

Aaron seemed to need to spend time in a corner of the yard comforting Suzanne, leaving me and Rae to go into the kitchen to put together something for us all to eat. At last we had a solid problem to concentrate on, but what could we do? Jason's parents would just call the police if they knew he was missing, so Aaron had called and made it sound as if Jason was staying over at his house. There were too many potentially awkward questions in that approach. We'd bought ourselves a day, but was it a good thing? Should I have told Tamblyn after all? Quietly, I ran the idea by Rae. I left out the reason I had refused to consider it in the first place.

"It's complicated enough, without bringing in the police," she said, the last thing I'd ever thought I'd hear from someone as apparently law-and-order as Rae Kennie. Then she laughed nervously. "I mean," she said, "what exactly are we supposed to tell them? We never reported anything leading up to this."

"Bunnies, birds. . ." I supplied. I flashed guiltily to the cache of newspaper clippings under my bed. Maybe it was time to bring the others up to speed. I figured my credibility was at such a low ebb any regard would be welcome.

"Yeah," she said. "I think that's the right thing to do. But it means it's up to us to find him." I heard her voice catch, and she voiced the question that should have been first. "Do you think. . . what you and

Aaron said about those things going *inside* people. . ."

"Rae," I said quickly, "they want him for some specific reason. If it was just for a host, they could have taken anyone, right? They want Jason specifically, so they won't hurt him. I'm sure we'll hear something soon."

My mind started to race. Just what did Jason have that they wanted? I suddenly had a suspicion, but I couldn't share it with Rae without telling her everything.

In the catacombs, Jason and I had held hands when he, Aaron, and I were chained in our prison. We had all noticed that magic seemed not to work consistently on Jason the way it did on others, including me. Our idea was that maybe there would be some kind of reaction between the power surging through me—dampened by the shackles that encircled my wrists—and the negating effect Jason had evidenced, something powerful enough to free us.

The resulting explosion almost took the roof down when our fingers touched.

I thought I'd killed both of them. I could recapture the feeling of panic without much effort. My desperation had driven me straight into Char's arms.

You aren't likely to forget something like that.

"Rae," I said cautiously. "Remember what I said about doing magic with spells and blood and all?" As if she was likely to forget. "Well, some people just have the ability to do magic without all that. . ." *people like me, once.* "They can just, you know, do it. What if that's why they took Jason? Because he has some kind of ability, and they want to use it?"

There was a small silence as she thought about it, and then Rae shrugged. "It's as good an explanation as any." *Poor Jason.* I thought again about his secret, and the hidden part of him, not the power-dampening thing, but that injured place of abuse and horror that I knew, maybe alone of all his friends.

It was absolutely the wrong time to think of myself, but I suddenly couldn't bear the not-knowing any longer. "Rae," I asked. "Suzanne and Aaron. . . are they. . .?"

She looked sharply at me, and if I could have felt stupider, I would have descended to the level of protozoan intelligence. "Are they what? Going out?"

I didn't even nod. Maybe she'd think I wasn't asking that question after all, that I was talking about something far weightier, more serious, and above all more relevant. But she just shrugged, seeming to let me off the hook.

"For a bit earlier this year. It didn't exactly go anywhere, but they still talk a lot. I guess it's good to stay friends and all."

Instead of feeling relieved, I felt dumber and more tense. "Oh, okay. I just wanted to know if there were any, you know, complications."

If Rae bought the weak justification, she wasn't letting me know. "It's more Jason and Suzanne, if you want to know. I don't think either of them are really admitting it yet, but they've got a lot in common and you can see the attraction."

I couldn't, not even a little. What did she mean by commonality? It had to be the sports thing, I guessed. I wondered if Suzanne knew anything about Jason's darker side, about the secrets he held. Would that even make a difference around someone as preoccupied with herself as Suzanne? I wondered, would someone like her be actually good for Jason to be around, someone who didn't have heavy, complicated memories and hidden damage?

Was I feeling a little jealous of Suzanne even though I'd realized that my feelings for Jason were no longer of the romantic sort?

"Maggie?"

I'd missed something Rae had said. She had the door of the refrigerator open and was obviously waiting for a response.

"Sorry?" I said.

"Above the sink. The plastic glasses, if we're going to eat outside. We don't have glass near the pool."

I remembered that from the Kennie family barbeque, and my first time at the house with Kool-aid in plastic tumblers in the changing shed. I reached up to pull down some cups for us, and realized as I put them on the tray Rae was assembling that I'd put out five. It seemed right, so I left the extra one.

I carried the tray, and Rae a bottle of Coke and the big Brita filter from the fridge. She opened the sliding door for me and ushered me into the backyard where Suzanne and Aaron had seated themselves at the same table where I'd enjoyed the picnic with the Kennie family such a short time before. This gathering, in direct contrast, was anything but joyous.

Rae doled out the plates and we all helped ourselves to bread and cold cuts, eating in silence, each caught up in our own thoughts. When we were done, I noticed that both Suzanne and Rae had turned their focus to Aaron, as if waiting for him to tell them what to do next.

Perturbed, I started to feel more and more annoyed as the uncompanionable silence dragged on. No one was looking to me for answers. Instead, Aaron was being treated as if he alone held any authority on the current mess. Was it just some obnoxious deferment of control to whatever man was in the room? Why was no one treating *me* like I could offer solutions?

It wasn't like I didn't have information or ideas. Well, information anyhow. My wrists still ached where Hunt had bound them, and I could feel the itch of dried blood on my sternum where he had cut me. Here I was suffering for them, and they didn't have a clue.

I'd gone to Tamblyn too, risking possibly greater complications if the police took an official interest in what was going on in Westbrook. Maybe that was more foolhardy than brave, but I'd done something at least. What was Suzanne doing except lapping up Aaron's attention, gazing at him with doe eyes, and begging to be comforted when she should really be showing some backbone at last?

Aaron put his elbows on the table and steepled his fingers against his lower lip. The portrait of a genius in deep thought. It was really starting to get up my nose, but what could I do to drag the focus back to me and gain some respect?

For some reason. . . no, for all the old reasons of secrecy and perversity, I couldn't tell them about Irene's possession of the book. All I'd be willing to say was that I had an idea of where it was, and how we could get our hands on it. Besides, I'd successfully kept the information from both Tamblyn and Hunt. It would be nothing short of shameful if I blurted it out without any pressure on me at all.

Although I was trying hard *not* to focus exclusively on Aaron the way the other two did, I found myself noticing that his eyes looked less bright than usual. He was tired, no less than I was. Aaron, I thought, had had some of the fight taken out of him by Jason's disappearance. And no wonder. Any time now, the Lawsons were going to start to wonder where their son was. The logical place to start looking was with his known friends. Aaron was already the centre of the biggest lie we'd told yet.

Funny how it seemed easier to me to have lied to the police than to

Jason's parents.

*Funny how easy, period, it was for me to lie.*

"Okay," sighed Aaron finally, and that broke the dam. We all seemed to relax; even I sat back in my chair for the first time.

"I'm really worried about Jason," he said. "Do you think. . . I can't help thinking that we're going into the subway after him. I heard about the cave-in, from Rae. She said you were there."

Caught off-guard, I shivered. "Yeah. . ." I hovered on the verge of telling them about the ring, and stopped myself. "What are we going to do about Jason? His parents are going to know something's wrong when he doesn't come home tonight. Is he one of those responsible guys who calls when he's going to be late, or will they assume he's okay until morning?"

Rae and Suzanne looked at Aaron.

"I think I might be able to work a bit of subterfuge," Aaron said. "Pretty sure he doesn't have plans for Saturday, so it wouldn't be too unusual for him to stay out late or even end up at my house. So I might be able to call his folks in the morning and play for another day. We haven't had too many sleepovers that last two nights in a row, but it's not totally a first."

"And they're not going to wonder why you're the one calling?"

"Ah," he said, "But that's the beauty of my plan. My intimate knowledge of the Lawson parental routine leads me to understand that Mr. and Mrs. play tennis Saturday mornings, and with luck, I'll be able to leave a message on the machine. I can do a pretty fair Jason, if I'm not pressed to converse. The other thing in our favor is that their machine is about twenty years old and as far as I know they've never replaced the tape."

I laughed. "Okay, sounds good." I wanted to tell him how brave I thought it was he was to be willing to make the gamble, but of course I said nothing.

When we had talked through everything we knew, and come up empty of suggestions on how to proceed, we decided to call it a night. Suzanne burst into tears, but I think we all felt the same way.

We moved in a tight group through the subdivision in the direction of Suzanne's house into the gathering gloom.

I had tried briefly to comfort her, remembering the salve of Rae's kindness on the day Scott left, but was less than effective. Probably a combination of how Suzanne, apparently suddenly uncomfortable about *everything,* kept trying awkwardly not to focus on my hair, and the way I hadn't exactly forgiven her for the necessity, no matter how much I was beginning to like my new look.

Rae stepped in, and the two of them walked hand in hand, leaving me to trail along beside Aaron.

Suzanne was composed again, but her shoulders were tight. I hated that everything I ever said to her seemed to be wrong, but what could I really do about it? My mindset was returning in the tension to its old perverse patterns. Once words left my mouth, I shouldn't really be held responsible for their effect, right?

I was just about to say something to Aaron—what I didn't know—when I realized there was someone familiar lurking by the side of the road. Did I say lurking? He was lounging, that was a far better way to describe it. Our little group came up alongside where he stood, leaning against a tree, and I saw Suzanne stiffen even more. No wonder, considering the fright he'd given her before. *Hunt.*

In all his smirking glory. I guess you could forgive me for trying to get a glimpse of his eyeballs; the swagger of Hunt and the arrogance of the demons were pretty much indistinguishable.

"Hi," I said, feigning a casualness I didn't feel. "Mr. Hunt. Do you know everyone?"

Rae took a baby step closer to me, pulling Suzanne with her, just enough to spark my realization that I really did like this confident, well-adjusted fellow student far more than I envied her. I felt more than ever that I wanted to protect her, from Hunt, from demons, and from myself if I had to. With Rae in the environs, it was a lot easier to be around Suzanne and to wish for her welfare as well. Still, despite Rae's revelation of the status of her relationship with Aaron, there *had* been something between them, and who really knew what it had become except the two of them?

Hunt grinned his most wolfishly at Rae. "Hello, darlin'. I hear you're quite the ball player."

He extended a hand, and Rae shook it as if she was putting her hand into the famous snapping lion's head of Roman Holiday. When she withdrew it again, I saw her glance down, counting fingers, maybe.

"And Suzanne, of course. Sorry if I gave you a start, sweetheart. Just remember, only demons vanish when you tell them to go to—"

As if he hadn't so recently scoffed at my mention of demons. "Hunt!" I burst out. "Is there a reason you're here? Because if you're just looking for a game, there's an arcade at the mall. None of us are in the mood to play."

"How odd, Maggie May." He turned his grin on me, and I shivered. "I do value our quality time, but the game is bigger than that, isn't it, Mr. Scribner?"

*Mr. Scribner?*

Hunt gave a little indication with his chin to Aaron, effectively shutting the rest of us—and by that I meant *me*—out of the equation.

And there he went again, turning to Aaron and redirecting both the focus and the conversation away. In addition, I found myself flashing back to Hunt's squalid little room, shivering in my undies as he trussed me up. Worse, I was all too aware that he had just made it clear to anyone who didn't know my history with him that I was a secondary player in this little drama, and that Aaron was the shining knight who would save the day. And Aaron obviously was taking his role very seriously. Even as I found myself cringing, moving in closer to Rae the way she'd moved to me earlier, Aaron seemed to grow an inch, imbued by some kind of weird instant heroic stature. *Savior in a box.* Why could Hunt do this to me so easily, make me a mouse, when I had almost been a Queen?

*Almost.* Well, no mystery then, really.

Aaron put a hand on his hip and the other to his chin as if weighty decisions required a particularly thoughtful pose. It irked me that Hunt seemed to produce no fear or uneasiness in him. I would have liked to believe that this was only because Aaron didn't know what I did about our former teacher, but I had a pit-of-the-stomach suspicion that Aaron was actually brave enough to possess full knowledge of Hunt's past misdeeds while remaining calm and resolute.

"Mr. Scribner—" Hunt said then, and put a hand parentally on Aaron's shoulder. I could hardly believe it. He led Aaron aside, leaving us girls standing there like prize hogs at a fairground ribbon ceremony, dumb and totally helpless.

"What the—" I said under my breath, but Rae just nodded acceptance of way the we'd been relegated to the verge.

"I know," she said quietly. "I don't like it either, but after all, Aaron is the one who's been negotiating with him."

I blanched. "He—what? He has?" I blurted.

"Didn't he tell you?" asked Suzanne, as if it was of no importance whatsoever. "You know he was Aaron's teacher back in public school—"

"Mine too!" I said, but it was like she didn't even hear me. What's more, Aaron had only had him for science; Jason and I were in his actual classroom. What had happened since Jason had gone missing, when I had been trussed up and then made to feel like the only reason Jason had been taken at all was because I had been monopolizing Hunt and leaving Jason unprotected?

"—so he came to Aaron with what he knew about those things that got out of the circle. I don't know how he knows what he does—"

"I could tell you something about—"

"—But he's been really helpful, I guess, especially when Aaron told him about the book."

"The book. Hunt was—" . . .the reason Aaron found the book in the first place. . . "Hunt wants it back. It's his, or at least he used to have it."

"No, I don't think so," said Suzanne. "At least he didn't say anything to Aaron. He just wants to make sure those things don't hurt anything else."

"I'm sure he does," I said, but even through my sarcasm, I saw that an intense sorrow had crossed Suzanne's face, the pain of *the loss of a dozen bunnies*, you might call it. I felt sorry for her suddenly, that she could be so concerned for a handful of dead animals that she might completely miss the big picture. Then, I realized I was a little envious too, of her empathy. What part of me had so withered that I was barely aware of sadness at death?

"Don't blame Aaron," said Rae. "I should have mentioned it. He came to Aaron to apologize, and they got talking. I guess he's been keeping an eye on the school since the ritual. He—knows things."

Oh, he did. He certainly did. *Apologize? Don't make me laugh.* "Look, you two," I said. "Let me set you straight about a few things. One, Hunt is a dangerous man. He talks a good line, but he is in this for himself. No matter what he says, he will only help us as far as it furthers his own plans. Anything else is a crap shoot. And the book? He was the one who put it where the guys found it. That's how innocent he is in all this." To *apologize?* That was total bull if I'd ever heard it.

Rae looked at me piercingly, as if she could see through every lie I'd ever told, as if she had suddenly realized I was just like I had described Hunt. "Have you had dealings with him too, Maggie, more than you said before? I mean, I thought you didn't know anything more about him than you told us."

Crap. Talk about playing a hand badly. I'd forgotten for the moment that I was supposed to be nearly as ignorant of Hunt as they were—or rather as ignorant as I had *thought* they were. I was supposed to have offered full disclosure. I rubbed the raw skin of my wrists, still hidden under my cuffs.

"Yeah," said Suzanne, something between disgust and a note of betrayal entering her voice. "Aaron told us about Hunt, from the start."

"Well, he didn't tell me," I exploded, with much more vehemence and hurt than I had intended to show. A short distance away, I saw Hunt and Aaron look up from their whispered conference.

I felt like even more of a heel than I had before as I continued, hardly lowering my voice, "Okay, so maybe I haven't told you everything. I thought I could protect you if you didn't know every sordid detail." I indicated Hunt, who looked up with what I can only describe as an expression of amusement, with a wildly thrown arm.

Finally I lowered my voice and leaned in to Rae. "Especially him! You don't know what he wants, and whatever he's told you, he's not here to help us. How am I supposed to take care of you if you're not completely honest with me?"

That effectively stopped the conversation. When I looked around again, Hunt was gone, and Aaron was walking back to us slowly with the weight of the world showing in his step. He put his hand on my arm with a gentleness that shocked me.

"You okay?" he asked, as if he really wanted to know.

I nodded, and felt a curious heat in my cheeks. I turned away so he wouldn't see me blushing.

Aaron must have thought I was still mad. "He'll contact me soon," he said. "He's going to help us get Jason back."

✪

We did a kind of pseudo conference-call that evening, with Rae as the go-between, relaying information between the rest of us. I had a huge urge to talk to Aaron on my own, to see if I could ferret out what

Hunt had told him. Not for any reason of my own emotions. Of course not.

I suspected he had been completely honest with me, that Hunt had said very little and had given him no clues I didn't already possess. Maybe I was projecting to imagine there was something to be gained from pressing him. I was furiously jealous Hunt had confided *anything* to him, and especially angry about the way he'd done it. Now especially, when my former mentor had a better idea of what I'd once been able to do. I mean, I hadn't explicitly laid out what I'd meant to Char, but even the knowledge I *had* revealed should have counted for something, right? He always seemed more than capable of filling in the blanks.

I decided that my next step would have to be an assault on Irene's, to retrieve the book, and because I knew in my heart that the merest brush of my hands would send it scampering back into the ether again, I would have to confide in the others. Or, at least, in Aaron.

"Rae," I said, holding the phone to my ear while I doodled pentagrams on a page of my notebook, "I think I should call Aaron." I was hyper-aware of Jan in the living room below my room, watching television in silence. It was odd she wasn't out with Harrison; I had kind of got used to having the house to myself most evenings. He hadn't been over here much after the first couple of times, possibly because of his abortive attempt to bond with me.

"Okay," she said. "You guys are the strategists. I guess that makes sense. Will you call and tell me what he says?"

As if the real contribution would be his. "Sure, Rae," I promised, feeling unappreciated and not nearly as good as I'd thought I would. I was feeling something else too as I hung up. If I had been startlingly jealous of what I thought might be some kind of romantic thing between Suzanne and Aaron, totally unsupported though that idea might be, it was nothing to what I felt thinking about Aaron's relationship with Hunt.

"Rae?" he answered the phone.

"No, it's Maggie," I said, waiting for his disappointment to register even over the phone line.

But he surprised me, which I was starting to understand was par for the course. "Good," he said. "We need a plan, don't you think? I'd like to put some ideas out for how to divvy up some tasks for when and if Mr. Hunt contacts me."

It was a good idea, and I said so. "You're not going to cut me out of the action," I cautioned, trying to make it sound like a joke and figuring I'd not quite succeeded.

"Would that even be possible? No, I'm sure that whatever happens, you'll go with me."

With him. Oh well, it was a start. "And Rae and Suzanne?"

"I can't see Suzanne in a fist fight," he said, and it was my turn to laugh, imagining it. "And Rae is probably going to need to stick close to her to make sure she doesn't freak out. So we're the two in the horror flick who go up to the attic to explore, and they're the ones who make a run for the phone down the road."

*Or we're even dumber, and decide to split up.* "So everyone who's watching our movie is yelling at you and me not to be idiots and just get out."

I had hoped for a guffaw, but I was disappointed. Was the situation just too serious for his trademark laugh, or had our relationship shifted to where he was less than enchanted with me?

"Yeah," he said, "Mr. Hunt isn't going to put himself in the path of whatever it is that took Jason. That much I can infer."

He was right about that, I figured. Hunt wouldn't do the dirty work when he could manipulate someone else into doing it for him. The part I really hated though was that Aaron seemed to think that he was Hunt's primary contact, and that I would be tagging along. As if he was the one that Hunt felt worthy of imparting secret knowledge to. As if I hadn't had all those sessions with Hunt deep under the old quarry north of Toronto where he trained me in the basics of using my power.

"Aaron," I began, thinking that I had to do something to raise my stock in his eyes, "I've been doing some research into a series of strange disappearances and apparent murders in and around Westbrook. I think it's time we talked."

"Okay. . ." He drew out the word. I could almost see him looking at the clock. It was after ten o'clock now, and if that was the cut-off time for him on the telephone, I could only imagine what his formidable mother would say for him going out at this time of night.

"It should be tonight," I said quickly, pushing, suddenly eager to prove that I could work on him even more effectively than our old teacher.

A long pause, and then he said, "You really think so?"

"With Hunt lurking around like your evil shadow, I think the sooner the better. And I can't do this over the phone." I felt a twinge, and I wasn't sure if it was because I was thrilled that I might actually get to spend some time with him alone or that I was aware that I was manipulating him as basely as Hunt had ever done to me.

"Okay," he said. "But it'll be hard for me to get too far from the house."

I snorted, being unnecessarily cruel now—*Aaron Scribner is scared of his mommy*—and suggested we meet at the bus stop at the corner of the crescent he lived on.

"Half an hour," he said, "I think I can make it by then."

Would he crawl out a window, or were his parents even now heading to bed, and be deeply asleep in time for him to sneak away? I remembered something about a dog from our captivity three years back, a dog Damon had killed, but I didn't know if the Scribners had replaced it. I was putting Aaron in an awkward position, whether or not he was risking being caught because of a barking dog or not. Mrs. Scribner certainly hadn't sounded like a woman who was used to being disobeyed.

And what was the point, really? I could have asked him to meet me tomorrow just as easily. But it wouldn't have given me the same sense of power. And that, truly, was as pathetic a reason as there could be. It was only as I hung up that I realized what I'd agreed to tacitly—no, that I'd insisted on. I was more certain than ever that the path to Jason lay underground. The fire, the cave-in, and the trail of bodies all led there. I guessed I was resigned to it now, no matter how much it terrified me. Maybe *because* of how much, knowing my own perversity. We might be hoping that Hunt could narrow down the search area, but all roads led, so to speak, underground.

And I was pushing to be included in a plan of action that would put me into the worst possible environment for me. Wouldn't it be better to insist I stay with Suzanne while the resourceful and determinedly *not* neurotic Rae went with Aaron? On sober examination, there was no doubt that it was.

But I wasn't Maggie Stuart, Princess of Pain for nothing. I packed up the newspaper clippings, slipped them into my portfolio—it was time Aaron got a look at those haunting, evil green eyes I hadn't painted as well—and set out, shivering, into the night.

## 33

### Up The Hill Backwards

✪

He beat me to the rendezvous point, not surprising since he was so much closer. But he had a deeply worried expression on his face, and I guessed it wasn't just about his mom.

"I don't think I'm going to be able to keep this going long enough," Aaron said as I braked my bike and swung my leg off.

"Jason?" I asked.

He nodded. "I already fielded a call from his mom, just after you called. She won't try again tonight, but some time soon she's going to get my mother instead of me, and we'll be busted."

I nodded. "Can you invent a third party or something, someone whose house you're both supposed to be at?"

He snorted, frustrated. "Scott's the only one who would have fit that bill, and he's a little out of the sleepover loop in Quebec."

Not to mention that if we were unable to finish everything up over the weekend, there was no way that Aaron's mom would even consider an imaginary sleepover on a school night.

"I wish we had another long weekend to work with," said Aaron.

"So we could have Monday as well as the next two days to. . .what?" I said. "Resolve this whole bloody mess." I smiled, and he grinned back with what was probably a reflection of just how overwhelming it felt to me. "Okay, then. If we gotta get it done, we'll get it done."

He laughed then. "You wanna share some of that 'power of positive thought' mojo?"

"I don't think I even have enough for myself," I said. "Damn, but I suddenly find myself wishing I did heavy drugs. . ."

"Yeah." Aaron reached out his hand for the portfolio I had half-removed from my backpack. "What's this?"

"Our demon. A bit of an itinerary, I think," I said. I led him to the bench inside the bus shelter. There wasn't any breeze to speak of, but I had a sudden horrific vision of all those pieces of newsprint and my so-called works of art blowing halfway across the neighborhood. "I guess it's been body-hopping, just like you thought. The animals weren't its only victims."

For the first time, it came down on me like a heavy weight, that people had died. Yeah, it hadn't managed any casualties when I was on the subway—unless you counted that TTC worker who'd vanished, but I thought there was a darker reason for that—but it wasn't just birds and squirrels and the occasional orange cat that had died for this thing to do what it was doing. There was Mrs. Sanchez, and the others. And I wasn't nearly so prosaic about animals caught in the crossfire either when I was directly confronted by it, as I had been on Rae's lawn after our trip to the stables.

"Here's what I think," I continued, as he paged through the articles and traced the places of incidence on my map. "We've been dealing with a bunch of. . .of things. Whatever they are. The little ones tried to stick around by killing small animals. But one or more of these things have a bit more intelligence or craft or whatever. And one, some big nasty, has figured out not only how to survive by jumping into human hosts but has been on the move, deliberately."

Aaron nodded. "Hunt said something like that, but not nearly as cogently." His finger tapped the place where the most recent body had been found. "The subway. You were there, right, where the cave-in happened?"

I recapped for him what I'd been told about the aborted subway line stretching north toward the airport. "But the access has been sealed; the explosion did it."

He rearranged some of the other papers and drew out my painting of the pentagram.

He shivered as he raised it up to examine it in the light from the streetlamp near the shelter. It was hard to remember that it hadn't been him standing in the aisle of the auditorium with the splatter of blood in the corner of his glasses when I'd first seen those eyes, that it had been something else entirely. It was hard to remember it had been so damn long ago. Now the weather was starting to turn. October was getting cooler; fall was in full swing. My birthday was coming, not that that ever made a splash for anyone, including me. Would winter take down the last of those nasty things that hadn't managed to get somewhere warmer? Would all our problems be over if we just waited for the first snow—barring of course the *thing* that was too smart to be caught out in the cold. Barring the one that had ripped Arabella's ring from my neck, that had taunted me so effectively with my own incompetence and ineffectualness?

Aaron had said something I only half-caught. "He what?" I said, frowning.

"Hypnotized me. Only a few times. He had me remember the things we talked about, so I got as much out of it as he did."

I bet he did. No way did Hunt let Aaron remember everything that came out under hypnosis. No wonder Hunt had kidnapped me. He wanted verification of things Aaron didn't know he knew. Now, a lot of what Hunt had said to me during my abduction made more sense. It made me feel a little dizzy, figuring that Aaron's subconscious had actually buried more about our prior relationship than he realized he knew.

But what else was Hunt doing when he had Aaron under his spell? And was it just hypnosis, or something more—supernatural? Did I dare ask Aaron to check for cuts he didn't remember receiving, or would have Hunt have covered that with some kind of post-hypnotic suggestion? When it came to Hunt, I would probably never know. But it was disturbing. How far could I trust an Aaron that Hunt had hypnotized?

Deep in thought, I jumped as a pair of headlights swept over us from a car making a U-turn to pull in beside the bus shelter. *Hunt,* I almost said. As much as I wanted what he knew, I wanted to be left alone with Aaron far more. It was bad enough Hunt had injected himself into whatever relationship I would ever be able to have with this guy. No matter how much time passed, I would have to remember that Hunt had purposefully, deliberately spent time with Aaron.

"Maggie Stuart," said the figure that emerged from the car. Despite the fact I was nearly blinded by the headlights in my face, it was plainly not Hunt. It was just as clearly Mr. Thurl, my drafting teacher and erstwhile ally.

"Hey," I managed weakly.

Mr. Thurl's face coalesced out of the brilliance. His mouth was set and his eyes hard. It was the most angry I had ever seen him.

He dismissed Aaron Scribner with a brief glance. There was no reason for him to know Aaron, for Aaron to even have spent much time in the tech areas where Mr. Thurl taught. To him, Aaron was not one of the school's top students; he was just a boy that Maggie Stuart was meeting in the middle of the night.

"What the hell do you think you're doing now, Maggie?" Mr. Thurl's voice was low, the tone aggressive. I shrank further into my jacket. "Do you know how much I've gone to bat for you with the administration over the last week? I was hoping that Mr. Philps would take the weekend to reflect on your file, but I'm starting to feel a little used, Maggie."

He took another step and motioned for me to come over to the sidewalk, away from Aaron. "You know how close you are to failing the semester—or maybe you've forgotten? The absences and the incomplete work are pretty hard to get around. But I was hoping that you'd prove yourself willing to get yourself under control. I've really tried to impress on you the importance of showing a better attitude."

I wanted to throw back into his face that it was his idea—at least a few times—that I go home when I seemed too stressed to cope at school. Not that I could blame him for just how far my lax attendance had got, but wasn't it something he'd actually encouraged at first?

He sighed, but it was as much an angry exhalation as a frustrated or defeated one. "When Mr. Philps reviews your impending suspension on Monday morning, I'm sorry, Maggie, but I will no longer be there to defend you. Get home, Maggie. And maybe you want to take some time over the weekend to figure out what you're going to do with your life if you don't get back into high school."

Without giving Aaron the merest acknowledgement, Mr. Thurl turned back into the bright headlights of his car, and it drew away from the curb.

Aaron was still on the bench in the bus shelter. I clamped down on my impending tears as well as I could, and joined him to start putting the papers we'd been looking at back in the portfolio. I hadn't even shown him the second painting for him to compare the eyes.

"Are you okay?" he said, and I was almost angry for a moment. That was the kind of thing a person says when they want you to say yes, so that they don't have to deal with you.

"Let's just concentrate on Jason," I said tightly. I had to get away from there, as soon as possible. I wasn't going to be able to hold back my tears for long, and I would not let Aaron Scribner see me cry.

## 34

### Over the Wall We Go

✪

The last thing I said to Aaron before saying a taut goodbye and biking off into the dark was that we had to get the book, and it had to be soon.

He agreed, and when I explained that it was something that needed to be done under cover of darkness, he jumped to the conclusion that I meant sometime within the next few hours.

Okay—so I guess I wasn't completely forthcoming with Aaron. But hey, I mean, I'd just suffered a betrayal of my own with the whole Hunt thing happening behind my back. I know, really I do, about two wrongs not making a right, but sometimes it feels so good to be obstinate it's just irresistible.

Also, if Aaron knew what we were really doing, I was pretty sure he'd try to talk me out of it. At the moment, I was not convinced I had the strength to stand up to him or anyone else. This particular campaign was utterly vital, but that didn't mean it would be hard to sway me from my purpose. I had proved that enough times to myself.

So, not a word about the comfortable suburban ranch we would be breaking into before dawn being Irene Solomon's house. Nothing about my strained friendship, or about Irene's contribution to my understanding the language of the text. It was more, for once, than me trying to maintain a fragile element of mystique. I needed my secret because without it, I had no leverage. I had no faith in my ability to con Aaron into helping me otherwise. The truth, I thought, could not possibly be my friend.

I arranged to meet him back at the bus stop at four a.m., and pedaled away, feeling pressured from all sides. I shouldn't have said yes to him that easily, especially because there was no way I was going to feel comfortable about breaking into the basement of Irene's house while she and her family slept above. I didn't like the fact that Hunt was calling some of the shots, without my awareness of exactly what he'd told Aaron. And I should have said *something* in my defense to Mr. Thurl, if only to show Aaron that I could stand up for myself.

But instead, if I wasn't just suspended indefinitely from school by Tuesday afternoon, I might actually be in jail for break and enter. This was not the way I had pictured my little meet-up with Aaron going. In fact, it was a good argument for just how dangerous, not to mention humiliating, it was probably always going to be for me to like someone. If I hadn't been weak enough to act on the impulses of my ridiculous crush, he wouldn't have known about my upcoming academic discipline. I also probably wouldn't have reminded him about the book, setting us up for rushing into a situation where we could get into deep, deep trouble with the police. Maybe even deep enough to stop us from being able to help Jason, deep enough to take both me and Aaron out of the mix and put Jason's fate into the hands of Rae, Suzanne, and Mr. Hunt.

There was no way to stop myself from bawling as I biked home. Not even halfway there, I became so blinded by tears that it was too dangerous to keep riding. I dropped my bike on the grass verge by the road and collapsed on the curb to cry.

If I had felt pathetic earlier in the evening, that sensation was nothing to what I was feeling now. I was so stupid. What an idiot, to jump gaily from the things I was finally getting a handle on—my understanding of the creature we were chasing, the knowledge of the book's location if not its possession—to an entirely new and impossible set of circumstances.

Only when I had cried myself dry-eyed and headachy did I realize where I was—right at the corner of Irene's street. That had to mean something, if I was to believe that anything could go right ever again. I pedaled slowly up the court, aware of the funereal silence and empty feel of the street. Subdivisions could feel deserted and isolated in the middle of a sunny day. How much more silent could they feel in the middle of a fall night?

There was no station wagon outside Irene's house on the drive. The

Solomons had an open carport instead of a garage, so that was surprising enough. The shadows were dark and thick, so I laid my bike down under a tree and padded as quietly as possible up to the house.

A piece of paper protruded half an inch or so from the mailbox. Careful to be utterly silent, I lifted the mailbox lid and removed it.

*Gerry,* it said in hand-printed caps, *away for the weekend so please put the papers between the doors. Closing the cottage!*

I held the page for an endless moment before replacing it just as carefully and quietly, although I guessed it was less important to be stealthy than I had thought. We had just—finally—got lucky.

I did a little more recon at the Solomon house, feeling more confident and eager to prove to myself if no one else that I was moving past the evening's earlier developments. I identified the window to the basement room where the book was kept, but could only see it through the Solomons' backyard fence. Aaron and I were in for some climbing in a few hours.

At least, there were vines and a couple of nearby trees that would make the process possible, if not exactly easy. My stomach was in knots, but this time it was as much excitement as nerves. By sunrise, we'd have the book. I hoped.

✪

My alarm went off at quarter to four. Jan hadn't arrived home by the time I'd returned home to doze for a few hours, but I'd put the clock under my pillow anyhow. I'd slept in my clothes, so it was the matter of a few seconds to be ready. Jan's door was still open when I hit the hall, but I took the precaution anyhow to pile some pillows in my bed in a vague "Maggie shape" and close my door, just in case she arrived home while I was gone.

It felt ten degrees chillier than when I'd been out before, although I put that down to the comparison between outside and my nice warm bed. No matter; with any luck, I'd be back there within the hour.

I had already decided that—no matter what—I would not touch the book. That meant making Aaron the one who actually entered Irene's house, but so be it. The book's aversion seemed specific to me, and we didn't have enough going for us to take any chances.

He met me at the corner of Irene's street, and we both stashed our bikes half a block away under an overgrown hedge. We'd be more maneuverable on foot up close to the house. I had brought an old cloth shopping bag for the book, and handed it to him, explaining my theory on why I should not be allowed too close to it.

"You make it sound like it's got something personal against you," he whispered, and I nodded.

"It's just better not to take any chances," I said. "Are you okay with going inside?"

"Yeah," he said. "Whatever it takes."

Hooray for Scribner practicality.

"What is this place?" he whispered as we worked our way up the court, sticking to the shadows.

"The important thing is that no one's home," I said. "Doesn't mean we can be loud, but at least it improves our odds of getting in and out unnoticed."

Aaron took that in stride. I pretended to myself that I was just loathe to mention Irene because it would just cause a lot of pointless questioning, but the truth was I was still pretty embarrassed about the scene in her basement, and the cavalier way she'd dismissed me. No matter how reasonable her viewpoint seemed to her. But I was the one who'd suffered in Char's realm, and then suffered worse with all my secrets. What did she know about magic, besides what I'd told her?

Besides, I wasn't entirely sure how Aaron would take the news we were breaking into the house of a fellow Dief student, despite there being no particular reason he'd ever come into contact with her. Best to just avoid the subject altogether.

He gave me a boost up to the tree nearest to the fence, and I experienced the same guilty thrill I got whenever I accidentally came into contact with him. It was pathetic, but nice at the same time, and god knew I didn't get a lot of pleasant physical contact from Jan or anyone else.

It wasn't too hard to get over the fence and into the backyard, although I didn't like how exposed we were between the fence and the near wall of Irene's house. Despite the fact that there were no houses around whose windows offered a glimpse of our movements, I felt naked. The moon had risen since my earlier recon, and our shadows were stark and black against the lawn.

I took the roll of duct tape and the other things I'd brought out of the shopping bag, grinning at Aaron as I did so. "It's all yours from this point on," I whispered.

We worked silently to cover the entire window with the tape, then Aaron gave it one good hard tap with the brick I'd picked up from our garden back at home. The window shattered silently, leaving the glass clinging to the tape. I used a pair of pliers to remove the remaining shards from the frame, and cleared away as much of the excess glass as I could see. Then, I lined the frame with a piece of heavy canvas from the garage, taping it in place to protect Aaron from any rogue glass, and gave him a thumbs-up.

He put his mouth so close to my ear I could feel his breath tickling me. "I don't want to know how you're so good at this," he whispered. I was glad it was night; I was sure I was blushing, just like real heroines don't.

Aaron leaned in through the window, then I guess decided that it would be easier to slide through feet-first. He dropped to the room below, and I remembered the creepiness of the dirt floor, the incongruity of the white water heater, the flicker of the candles.

Amazingly, as I lay on my stomach to watch him, I could see a flicker coming from the dark shadows behind the water heater. Irene must have renewed the candles before leaving town. I guessed it wasn't like it was a particularly dangerous thing to do, in a basement with nothing flammable around except the book itself and no stray breezes to worry about, but it suddenly gave the operation an uncomfortable organic feel. Irene had been there, probably not too many hours before. And she'd be back at the end of the weekend when, I was sure, she wouldn't have too many doubts about who'd been into her basement to steal the book away.

"What do I do?" hissed Aaron in my direction.

The mechanics of actually removing the book from its circle were not something I had even considered. Was I putting Aaron into some kind of danger by having him do it?

"Blow out the candles and make a gap in the outer circle," I whispered back. I crossed my fingers. Had I just told him to do something reckless?

But the candles went out like candles usually do, and his finger made a clean break in the chalk circle without any kind of occult fuss whatsoever. He put the book in the bag, grinning up at me.

His excitement was infectious. I rolled my eyes at him, smiling broadly. But the smile left my face when he turned to pass the bag up to me.

"I can't!" I hissed. "Just, I don't know, toss it up here."

"Maggie, it's in a bag. I think it should be fine."

But I drew back from the window. Into my mind came the original Arabian Nights version of "Aladdin." I hadn't read the story for years, but it used to be one of my favorites. All I could think of was the moment where the evil magician, who has been posing as Aladdin's long lost uncle, tricks him into handing the magic lamp out of the pit he has sent the boy into to retrieve it. "Give me the lamp," he says, "and then I'll pull you out of the hole."

But Aladdin is suspicious. "Pull me out first," he says, "and then I'll give you the lamp." Infuriated, the magician waves his hands – and buries Aladdin alive.

Caves. Underground. Magic. No wonder the story resonated with me. But this was Aaron, and it was me standing in the magician's place, saying not "Give me the lamp," but "Don't pass me the book!" In case it vanished again.

I hauled myself awkwardly to my feet and jogged half-bent over to the fence. I could hear Aaron hissing quietly behind me, the sound swallowed up by the distance and the wall of Irene's house. But I found what I was looking for quickly and returned to the window. Through it, I extended a long, thick stick I'd located under one of the trees.

Aaron wrapped the cloth straps of the shopping bag around the stick and guffawed quietly. "You are too much, Mags," he whispered.

My hands shook as I drew up the stick with its burden, dropping both as quickly as I could on the grass beside me. Aaron hauled himself out of the window with catlike boy-grace, and shouldered the bag. We had done it. The book was ours.

✪

He went up the fence and swung himself into the tree before reaching a hand back for me. But something caught my attention—I scanned the deep shadows of the backyard closest to the building, unsure what I had noticed.

"Maggie!" Aaron whispered.

"Just a moment," I said, and skirted the edge of the fence in its shadow back toward the Solomon house.

She stood by the wall, between the fence and a flowerbed, her dark skin luminous in the moonlight, the expression on her face stoney and hating. Irene.

For a moment, we just stared at each other.

"We need it," I whispered, even though we didn't need to whisper any more. "You won't understand, but it is seriously important that we have it."

I heard her laugh, humorless and angry. "That's what it's always about, isn't it, Maggie? What you need. Well, screw you."

I took a step away, back toward the tree and Aaron and safety. But it felt like I should say something so I said, "I thought you were out of town."

She laughed again, just as coldly. "Ironically, they think I'm staying with you. You owe me for a window."

She walked away. Maybe it wasn't an actual death, like the cats and poor Mrs. Sanchez, but I had just killed something as surely as if I'd wielded a knife. I wouldn't justify it; there was no way I could take back or apologize for the hurt I'd just caused. It didn't seem like enough to say it was necessary to have the book. I knew exactly what I'd done up to that point with Irene—used her brain, dismissed her friendship, and blocked her from participation in either my daily life or what she must have seen as my attempts to get closer to the *popular* people. There was no justification, and there was no escape from just how badly I had treated her.

Thanks to her, we had the book; without her, who knew if we'd have found it in time to have a chance to save Jason? And I had treated her like crap, like an imposition at best and an impediment at worst.

Holding back tears for the second time that night, I crouched low and ran for the tree and Aaron.

## 35

### As The World Falls Down

✪

Now I felt the urgency I hadn't before. Not only were we battling the clock to get Jason back before his family noticed, I had to assume that Irene might just do what I was scared to and call the police. No more was this just a secret held between those of us who only wanted to rectify what had been done in the gym on that first day of school; we had now crossed a very clear line of legality into crime. Now, I could worry about getting nabbed for B&E, not just expelled.

Aaron held up a hand as I joined him on the ground in the neighbor's yard. We ran, crouched low, although the damage had really already been done. As we did, he scooped his cellphone out of a pocket and answered it in a breathy whisper.

I caught his side of the conversation, but it didn't tell me much. Who was calling him at this time of night?

He hung up as we reached the bikes. "Hunt," he said.

I breathed deep. "Why?"

"It's time, he says. He's texting detailed instructions."

Somehow, I knew that our retrieval of the book had to be the reason for his call. He must know. He must be spying on us, by natural or arcane means.

So we'd become Hunt's creatures after all, and unfortunately, there was no better option available. "Aaron," I said, "when it comes to Hunt—you don't know how twisted he can be. I know this seems like the only way, but it doesn't mean we should even blink until Jason's safe."

"You've seen this flick."

"Every single variation. He has an angle. Even if he seems to be helping us, every moment we follow his instructions, we're acting for his benefit. We just don't know how yet."

"But if it gets us Jason—"

"Yeah," I agreed. "Just—keep your eyes open."

"All right." We started to walk with our bikes; I figured wherever we were going and whatever Hunt said, I would have to follow along with whatever Aaron chose to do. "So Hunt says we need to gather up some specific things from our houses—flashlights, water, that kind of thing—and be ready to go at five am."

That gave us all of twenty minutes. "And then what?"

He tapped his phone. "Instructions to be issued at a later time."

I grimaced. This was ridiculous. "Water, flashlight. . ."

"Layer our clothes. He says we might have to deal with extremes of temperature."

I knew; I was trying not to let myself process it, but I knew. He was sending us underground.

"He said to get to the corner of Dunsinene and Donalbain. I assume he's coming to pick us up." The intersection marked the midway point between Aaron's house and my own, which Hunt obviously knew.

"Just us?"

Aaron nodded. "He said it would be good if you came with me."

*Came with him.* As if it wasn't a for-certain thing that I would be included. It was all I could do to grit my teeth and pretend I wasn't offended.

"So Rae and Suzanne wait to call for backup."

"That's about the size of it. I can text Rae so that she gets the message right when she gets up. She said she'd check in with me first thing."

I trusted Rae to be sensible and methodical with whatever instructions we left for her. Aaron would have his cell, but cellphones wouldn't be of much use to us underground, and I couldn't imagine that tracking us by the GPS of Aaron's phone would be possible either. I had no idea how that was done, in any case, or if it could even be accomplished by civilians like us.

"Will your tame cop help us?"

The idea of Tamblyn as tame was pretty laughable; I wasn't Hunt after all. "I get the feeling he's on standby without us even having to ask."

"Good. . ." There was a long silence. Maybe he was calculating as I was the unlikelihood that Tamblyn would be able to do anything for us even if he were willing.

So I continued, "Look, Aaron, Tamblyn knows Hunt, and he would tell you just like I'm going to. Don't trust a thing he says. He's in this for himself. He doesn't give a damn about us."

There was a short pause, and then Aaron said, "Yeah, I figured as much. But he's going to lead us to Jason, and that's all I care about."

That was the point, after all. "Okay," I said, and threw my leg over my bike. "See you at five."

✪

The house was still dark when I got home, but Jan's car was on the drive now. This was potentially bad; depending on how long she'd been home, she might be dead asleep or still awake enough to hear me come in. Somehow I had to make her think I'd just got up myself instead of that I was sneaking in.

I set my bike against the side wall of the garage and crept around to the back door. The key made an unforgivingly loud click in the silence of the night, but I hoped it would be quiet enough not to catch Jan's notice.

I locked the door behind me, a much quieter action, but as soon as the door was shut, I heard a sound I would never have expected.

Silhouetted in the darkness by the meagre light coming through the kitchen blinds, Jan was sitting in the dark at the breakfast bar, sobbing.

I froze. There was no way she wasn't aware of me, no way at all that she hadn't seen me come in. But she said nothing, just sobbed louder as if to demand my attention.

My mind was on my tasks, and the clock ticking down fast toward five am. The big flashlight with the extra batteries was in the kitchen drawer, so I'd have to pass right past my mother to get it. Same with the bottles of water in the fridge. I wasn't worried about my clothing; I'd already layered up for our nighttime raid of Irene's. Aaron was going to put together the other items Hunt had demanded we pack, so I just had to remove the unnecessary bulk from my backpack—the sketchbook and news clippings—and grab the other things.

What was I supposed to say, to do? My mother, crying, obviously just having arrived home. What the hell was happening here in the dark, and was it in any way connected to my own current preoccupations?

"Mom?" I tried softly as I got close to her. "Mom, I'll be back in a minute, okay?" Better to run upstairs and hide the portfolio while I tried to make sense of this new development.

I checked the answering machine on the way past; no new messages, so that wasn't what had made Jan cry. On a different note altogether, I was surprised to see October 26th as the date. Hallelujah. Ten minutes past midnight, as I was standing at a bus stop getting dressed down by my former favorite teacher, I had turned sixteen. And as far as I could tell, Jan had absolutely no idea.

It didn't matter, right? How could it, with everything else going on? But Jan didn't have occult armageddon on her mind. She wasn't battling the ghosts of her past and the fears of the present. What did she have to cry about? I wouldn't cry, not now, not when I'd half expected this birthday to be no more remarked upon as any other. Sure, you only turn sixteen once, but still.

For once, I wasn't about to cry. Instead, I just felt deflated, disappointed, as I slid the portfolio under the bed as far as I could push it. I also loaded a few medical supplies into my bag from the bathroom cabinet. Following Hunt's orders had often caused varying levels of bloodshed in the past and I wasn't going to assume this undertaking was without risk.

Back downstairs, I approached Jan tentatively and put a hand out, fingers stopping just short of her shoulder. Then I thought of all the nights I'd spent crying silently because her assumptions about why I was miserable often just made the situation worse. Here, I was entirely out of my depth. I wanted to scream, *What are you doing? You, who never takes care of me, want attention for yourself? Why should I do ANYTHING nice for you?*

Ignoring the fact that, if anyone deserved to be upset at this moment, it was her newly sixteen year old daughter.

"He's gone," she said at last, as I watched the clock on the oven click over another minute toward my five am deadline. "I don't know what I did wrong."

Harrison. Dumped her. Everything made sense except what she expected me to do about it.

"I can't deal with this now," I said. *Or ever.* I figured that leaving the house by subterfuge was not only impossible but pointless. What would she care that I'd left, except that I wasn't there to comfort her? I felt the anger rising in my stomach. *Good. Use it. Finish what you started on the first day of school. Save Jason. Force Hunt to help you so that you aren't sitting in a dark kitchen some number of years from now, wailing because your boyfriend showed you the curb.*

"I'm sorry," I said, and broke for the back door, angry, hideously disappointed in myself, and feeling like the world's biggest weakling. She was so mired in her own tragedy she didn't even ask where I'd been, or where I was going in the middle of the night. Not that I was surprised.

✪

I didn't think I should take my bike in case Aaron was right and Hunt was coming to pick us up, so I jogged all the way to our rendezvous point. I did a bit of crying en route, which lessened the knots in my stomach. I hoped that it would remain dark enough that Aaron wouldn't see my red eyes. To have him think me as much of a weakling as I considered myself would be unbearable.

He had arrived there first, also sans cycle. His backpack was bigger than mine, stuffed more full as well. The sky had lightened almost imperceptibly. Wherever we were going, it was likely to be light before we arrived. If it was to descend underground, would doing it in the light of day make it worse or better? I could feel the usual panic rising in me as I thought about tunnels, making the inevitable connections to Char's catacombs and all that entailed.

"I guess I might not be able to make that call this morning to Jason's parents," he said. "Rae's got his phone though. I'll tell her at least to text them during the tennis window."

He got out his phone and started composing a text to Rae, while I watched him and watched out for a car that could be Hunt's. *Gold sedan, unknown license number.* Dunsinene was the main thoroughfare for our neighborhood so even at this time on a Saturday morning, there was a little traffic. But I think Aaron and I were equally surprised when a Beck Taxi pulled up at our corner and stopped.

The driver lowered the passenger window. "Scribner?" he said.

Aaron exchanged a glance with me that indicated he was just as surprised as I was. Hunt was accomplishing this particular duty at arm's length, I thought, which made me very concerned about what he might be doing instead of picking us up.

We hopped in and the driver swung out into Dunsinene, heading for the nearest major intersection. Neither of us questioned the driver about where we were going; I guessed maybe Aaron felt as awkward as I did to ask the driver where he was taking us. That would be undoubtably an uncomfortable conversation.

He dropped us a few blocks east of Royal York Station in Etobicoke, probably less than a five minute walk from where I'd sat with Tamblyn after the subway explosion. When Aaron pulled out his wallet, the driver waved him off. Prepaid, by Hunt I assumed. Aaron's cell buzzed as we got out, indicating a text message. "Hunt," he confirmed. He scrolled and scrolled as he read. A pretty long message. Aaron's face took on a puzzled look.

"What?" I said. Was he going to read me the text or not?

Aaron took out a compass from his backpack, and frowned again as if confirming a surprising fact. "This way," he said, and led the way along the subdivision road where we'd been dropped, roughly parallel to the subway line, but veering away again from Royal York and the station.

"There's lots of escape hatches along the subway line," I said, using Irene's info as if it was my own. "Maybe he wants us to go to one of those."

Aaron scanned the area. "I think you could be right," he said. "Don't you think they'd be able to be opened only from the inside, though?"

That didn't take much thought. "Hunt will make sure we can get in."

We found the hatch, like a manhole on a squat concrete pillar rising about eight inches from the scrubby grass in a vacant lot. Aaron glanced at me, almost as if he wanted me to wish him luck, then heaved at the edge.

It was heavy, but it moved, opening up on stiff hinges to reveal a cylindrical hole like a sewer opening, with a ladder down the side. Fortunately, the smell wasn't that of a sewer. Aaron set down the backpack and took out a large ziplock bag. He removed a flashlight from it, and a folded piece of paper.

"The instructions are a little cryptic," he said apologetically, but he made no move to hand me the page.

"Can I take a look?" I said, trying to keep the exasperation out of my voice. Now I was mad. Yeah, he'd just received a long text from Hunt, but this paper was something he'd obviously received before and just hadn't said anything. When had I been excluded from "need to know?"

"Sure," he said, but, instead of giving me the map, handed me the flashlight.

Not wanting to deal with the fact he'd misinterpreted me, I took the light and aimed it down the hole.

Far below, I could see a dimly lit, flat, concrete surface, and some pipes, nothing more.

"Looks like a tunnel," I said, hoping my tone conveyed how unsurprised I was. Duh. A tunnel. Of course.

"Good," he said. "I guess I should go first."

I shrugged, and he settled the pack firmly on his back and swung into the hole.

When I had joined him on the ladder, I glanced back up at the circular slice of sky above us. "I guess I'd better close the hatch," I said, not relishing closing us off into the dark at all.

Below my feet, I saw Aaron's blond head nod. "Yeah, don't really have a choice."

It sounded like he was trying to be brave. *Good,* I thought. *Me too.*

I reached up and pulled down the cover. And the darkness became dense.

Aaron shone the flashlight up at me before we continued our descent, careful not to get it right in my eyes.

"You okay?" he said.

"Yeah. Just—let's get this over with. I don't like doing anything Hunt tells me to."

Which wasn't quite true, because he'd previously saved my life by telling me what to do, although indirectly. I didn't like it, though. Hunt's plans made me nervous. You never knew who was going to get hurt, and I figured that part was kind of immaterial to him, as long as he got what he wanted.

The ladder took us right down to the level of the tunnel, which, we saw, was actually lit by sodium globes at fifty-foot intervals. We wouldn't really need the flashlight, at least not yet. Aaron switched it off, and went to one of the globes to check his mysterious paper.

"Aaron?" I said. I pointed at the wall near the ladder.

There, in chalk, was a funny squiggle I recognized from somewhere, and an arrow. "I think this is from him."

Aaron came over, and motioned me in the direction it pointed with a grim smile. Hunt was already here. I didn't know if that made me feel better or worse.

## 36

## The Tunnel

✪

We made quick progress for the first five minutes or so; the tunnel was damp but not smelly, the lighting adequate. Maybe being underground wouldn't be the trauma I'd feared.

Every couple of minutes we'd find one of Hunt's little squiggles, just to let us know we were still on track. Aaron and I didn't talk much. I found I'd forgiven him for keeping the map or instructions or whatever from me. That was Hunt, not him. Not as much, anyhow. What exchanges we had were limited to the kind of pathetic small talk I usually defined as "situational:" *"Hey, that's a lot of rust." "Look at that drip!"*

It would have been risible if I hadn't been a participant. Strange how hard it was to talk when you had a lot you wanted to say.

First, of course, I wanted to say something nice to Aaron, tell him I enjoyed his company, what I'd had of it, and that I'd like to spend some more time with him. If that was okay. And he wanted to too. And. . . Of course, any fantasy conversation I had in my head went quickly into hysterical inarticulate babbling.

And when the conversation I was having in my head had petered out into nervous compliments or pleading to be liked, I would get defensive and go on attack: *Why didn't he tell me more about his interaction with Hunt? Why didn't he trust me? Why wouldn't he let me see the map?*

I didn't know which way an actual conversation would go, and was apprehensive about starting one—after all, if I couldn't have a sensible interaction with Aaron in my head, how could I do it for real? So I walked, and stayed mum.

Aaron stopped at another chalk scribble, holding up his hand for me to do the same.

"What?" I said.

"This is where it gets really specific," he said, and frowned. He paced off twenty steps further down the tunnel, and looked to his right.

With my help, he opened a heavy door in the tunnel which led us into a dank stairwell. This time, we climbed up a dozen steps to another door and out. . . onto the tracks. I heard him chuckle in surprise. "The next stage in our adventure, I guess," he said.

"Oh, this is not good," I said. The claustrophobia and fear that hadn't been triggered by the first tunnel were firing now, softly but insistently. Maybe it was due to the fact that the last time I'd been in a subway tunnel on foot I'd just barely survived a catastrophic cave-in.

Aaron checked the text, and his paper. "This is right," he said, but he sounded unsure. "We turn left, stick to the left hand wall, and walk another fifty paces."

I didn't like this at all. The left hand side of the tunnel was the furthest from the live rail at least, and the one where there was a ledge for maintenance workers to follow. It was wide enough not to feel like we were on a dangerously narrow path, but had no rail and, I imagined, not a hell of a lot of clearance from the side of oncoming trains. I looked up the tunnel in the direction we were supposed to be walking. "What time do the trains start running?" I asked.

"No idea," said Aaron. "But this is exactly the time we're supposed to be here."

I didn't like that one bit. "Okay, let's get going."

He counted, I followed, feeling like I was doing a balancing act along a tightrope. I was a little dizzy, which I put down to repressed memory. If everyone else could have them, why not me? There must be lots of details I couldn't remember about my time in Char's clutches. It wasn't enough just to admit I was scared out of my gourd wondering when the westbound to Kipling would show its headlights in the darkness ahead.

There were a few sodium lights along the upper part of the tunnel wall, but they didn't give off much light and were widely spaced. Both Aaron and I were using our flashlights, but they didn't help much either. And I was far more concerned about keeping one hand bracing myself against the concrete of the wall than aiming my light effectively. The various openings and irregularities we passed were something to focus on, so I could think less about our possible imminent demise. I kept my eyeline up, on the back of Aaron's head, and listened to him count out loud.

We passed a signal tree, requiring us to skirt out a little further over the tracks. And then, we'd reached fifty paces. "That's it," Aaron said.

I jutting my head—*what?* "Uh, that's it? That's *what* it?"

He checked again, then checked his watch.

"Did Hunt have you synchronize your watches?" I asked. His annoyed expression told me they had. I tapped my foot against the wall, leaning back so I felt a little safer. "So—we wait?"

At my back, the signal tree switched with a click from solid red above and below to flashing orange. "Uh, Aaron?"

"Run!" he said.

I heard the rumble of the subway before I saw the reflection of its lights. The whole tunnel seemed to shake. I wasn't sure if I could run, but I turned, edged myself as quickly as I dared around the signal tree and started to race back the way we'd come.

There had to be safe places to shelter from a train—I knew I'd seen the alcoves lining the subway tunnels from my perch at the front of the car when I was riding back and forth looking for evidence of the fire. But I hadn't examined any of the ones we'd passed as we'd come along the tunnel, so who knew which were big enough for two and which were just a *literal* dead end? This was insane. We passed what looked like a good-sized alcove on the other side of the tunnel, but I was damned if I was going to stop and suggest we make a mad dash across, *in front of an oncoming train,* just hoping we'd make it in time and it would be big enough to shelter both of us.

I remembered seeing workers standing on this same ledge, waving their flashlights to let the driver know they were there. Logically, there must be room to stand pressed against the wall and have the subway cars pass safely in front of us, but our panic was blind and irresistible. Could we reach the place we'd entered the tunnel in time, get the door open, and get to safety? What the hell was Hunt—

My right hand, skimming the tunnel wall, met a void. Without considering what I was doing, I darted into it, grabbing Aaron's arm and pulling him after me. He fell against me, pushing me hard against a rough stone wall that didn't seem to be part of the regular tunnel architecture. Seconds went by, the shaking and noise and light all cresting, and the train hurtled by our refuge.

I knew a TTC subway was typically six cars long, but it seemed to take forever to pass. And after it had gone, the thunder of its rumble fading away, I realized I had stopped breathing entirely. I pushed Aaron off me and took a deep breath.

"That complete bastard," I said.

Aaron chuckled. I peered toward him in the darkness in disbelief. "What?"

Then I saw, as he pointed with his flashlight. The alcove we'd discovered had a very narrow inlet, less than three feet wide. We'd both somehow missed it on our trip up the tunnel. It was just luck we'd found it on the way back—or maybe Hunt knew something about human psychology that we didn't. Maybe he was just willing to play with our lives as casually as placing a sports bet.

The opening I'd pulled Aaron through was rough, irregular. It led through a thick wall, maybe four feet of brick and concrete, to the stone wall I'd fallen against. Aaron shone his flashlight around the small cave created by the opening, and showed me a tunnel leading off to the left—call it north—and down. It was probably eight feet high and after starting off a lot more narrow, seemed to open out after a short bit to somewhere more than six feet wide. It wouldn't be entirely claustrophobic. Beside the opening that led into this new tunnel was a chalk sign, a curvy arrow pointing downwards, and a big, ugly smiley face.

I pointed my flashlight near enough to Aaron's face to see his laugh had been anything but pleased. He looked as pissed off as I felt. "It's thrilling to be manipulated by the best, isn't it?" I said.

He looked at me sharply. "I guess I should have taken you more seriously about him."

I shook my head. "Hunt is whatever he wants to appear. Most of the time, I only make points around him by accident. So—what's next?"

He steeled himself—it was interesting to watch him visibly shift gears and get himself under control—and took out the paper.

"We're at the end of the text," he said, "so we've just got the notes he gave me earlier."

I held out my hand. "Can I see?" This time, he passed over the paper with no fuss, so I guessed that his earlier apparent unwillingness to share had really just been a jump to judgement on my part. Hunt's printing was meticulous and precise, littered with diagrams and arrows. It was like he'd deliberately made it as intricate as possible so it would be hard to figure out exactly what he intended us to do.

"This is what confused me before," said Aaron, pointing to a curvy arrow that matched the one on the wall beside us. "When we stopped out in the tunnel, I was looking for that sign. I didn't know he meant us to nearly get run over by a train to find it."

"That's Hunt for you," I told him. Now that the immediate danger was past, I felt a grudging admiration for Hunt's planning. That had to have been the first westbound train of the day. There was no other way for him to have been sure it would be on time. And with no apparent back-up plan, he must have been pretty sure we'd do exactly as we'd done. I shivered.

"Shall we?" said Aaron, waving the flashlight toward the opening. I handed the paper back to him, having been unable to make any more sense of it than he had, and Aaron folded it away in to his backpack. I drew a deep breath, and followed him in.

## 37

## Subterraneans

✪

    This tunnel was worse, a lot worse. It was narrow and rough, more like something cut by grave-robbers trying to sack an Egyptian tomb than something built for repeated use. I never could watch those shows on television, where the intrepid archaeologists shimmy on hands and knees through crumbling tunnels, not knowing if they would hit an impasse around the next corner or if the walls would disintegrate suddenly and bury them alive deep inside a monolith of solid stone. They freaked me out. I'd never even made it through "Raiders of the Lost Ark," and that had nothing to do with the snakes.
    It didn't help that, as I trailed after Aaron, pretending to be okay, my hand dislodged small stones and chunks of rock from the wall. I couldn't make any progress without the wall to lean on, but touching it kept its potential fragility constantly on my mind.
    If you asked me how long we navigated this tunnel, I couldn't tell you. An hour, ten minutes. It was all the same to me. I was trapped in an eternal moment of fear, and it could have been no time or forever and it would have made no difference to me. What had seemed from the hole in the subway tunnel wall to be a good and passable route felt like an internment waiting to happen. Even if the sky was falling, I would rather be outside, not under tons of concrete and rock.
    Aaron used his flashlight to sweep the way ahead of us. I'd put mine back in my pack, not trusting myself to manage my balance and an additional tool. I kept my eyes fixed to the dancing beam, because that way I could at least convince myself to put one foot in front of the other.
    As we walked, there were little falls of stone from the ceiling of the tunnel, like random showers to remind me to be terrified. It made for a

dusty atmosphere around us, and particles of stone danced in the beam of Aaron's flashlight. At one cascade, I must have given some kind of gasp because Aaron turned around and touched my hand.

"Are you okay?" he asked. I could barely see his face; his flashlight was pointing downwards between us.

"Not really," I said. I hoped that being honest wouldn't make my fear even more obvious to him, but what else could I say?

He squeezed my hand and looked right into my eyes. "Is it being underground?"

I nodded. "Totally. I'm entirely freaked out. I'm not good with. . . this. Subterranean, Morlock stuff. I'm 100% Eloi."

He laughed, quietly as if any loud noise would bring the roof down. "We'll be back in the sun soon. Trust me."

Hunt was the guy who usually told me to trust him; it wasn't a happy reminder of just who was calling the shots down here. Yeah, Aaron might think he had an inside track, an edge, because of Hunt's instructions, but I knew better. Whatever we were headed for, it was crafted for Hunt's benefit, not ours. I felt even more at a disadvantage than I had at thirteen, which was amazing because I knew so much more now. Maybe that was exactly the problem. Innocence is not a thing itself, but a lack of experience. I was too experienced to believe that everything would be okay.

"You good to go on?" he asked. I nodded, and he continued. "I didn't want to say anything, but you probably need the hope. I just started to feel a little breeze coming from up ahead. Just a little freshening in the air. It might be nothing, but we might be almost out of this tunnel."

I gave him a faint smile. Even hitting a cavern or something would be welcome. Even if we had to go back into a tunnel after that, at least it would be a respite from the constant, aching fear.

He squeezed my hand one more time, and we went on.

Soon, I started to notice what he already had, a little chill of movement in the air around us, coming from somewhere in front of us.

Aaron drew in a deep breath. I saw him nod to himself, confirmation that yes, there was some chance that we were at the end of this leg of our nearly blind journey.

"Are you okay if I turn out the light for a moment?" he asked, and I jumped, as if he'd physically startled me. "Close your eyes before I shut it off, and then open them slowly."

I knew what he meant; it's a good trick to force your eyes to adjust to different light levels quicker. Me, I thought I'd be best off just keeping my eyes closed entirely. Would it be worse if I became aware of just how dark it was down here?

I closed my eyes, and saw the hint of the flashlight through my closed eyelids—before it went out. Total blackness. Total, utter dark, and we were miles from anyone who knew us, far under some Toronto suburban street. There would be no access tunnels here, no way to emerge unexpectedly in someone's backyard or urban park.

In the double darkness of the tunnel and my own eyelids, I heard Aaron make a small noise of satisfaction. That little sound gave me just enough courage to open my eyes.

I didn't really expect there to be light to show us we were coming out of the tunnel, but after some more time, there was. It wasn't much, just a faint, faint glow making an oval of grey against the black.

"The egress awaits," he said. "Ready?"

I nodded, and he turned the light back on. Faint illumination ahead notwithstanding, the flashlight definitely helped.

✪

We reached the end of the tunnel much sooner than I had anticipated, based on what I remembered about the size and shape of the grey blotch ahead. Aaron too was surprised; we went from picking our way along to bashing together as he stopped abruptly, flashlight beam illuminating the edges of a ragged tear in the stark wall ahead. The tunnel had narrowed quickly in the last dozen feet, and now it was clear that the exit from this section of our route into whatever lay beyond was more like a vertical tear in the wall than a proper opening.

Aaron shone his light up and down, then said, "It looks like we'll have to squeeze through one at a time, without our packs."

I shivered, hoping he didn't notice. "What's through there?" I asked.

He put his head right up to the opening and shone the beam cautiously through, first just at the ground then higher and around. I almost expected him to come back with that immortal whisper of Howard Carter's as he first gazed into the antechamber of

Tutankhamen's tomb— *"Marvelous things..."*

"A cavern," he said, "pretty good size. Can't tell how far back it goes. The flashlight's not strong enough." He unshouldered his knapsack and made to hand it to me.

I jumped backwards, raising my hands. "No way, no way in hell."

"What?"

I pointed, as if the bag was full of snakes. "The book?"

He didn't say anything for a moment, as if trying to decide if it was important to humor me this time as he had at Irene's. "Okay."

Instead, he took my pack as well and pushed them both through the hole. I tensed, thinking (not without reason I thought) that this might be another one of Hunt's plots, here to separate us from the book, but he seemed satisfied with their safety. Then, he put the flashlight between two fingers and wedged himself into the space in the rocks. "I'll go first."

That was fine with me. I closed my eyes tight as he turned sideways and slipped through into the unknown, so that I didn't have to see the flashlight's happy little beam vanish for the time it took him to get through the opening. *Easy as pie,* I admonished myself. *Hunt doesn't want to kill you. The subway train near-miss was just his idea of a joke. If he'd wanted you in mortal danger, there were a million easier ways.* I put out of my mind the quick thought that flashed through it—that if Hunt *did* want to kill us and make sure our bodies were never found, this was as good a place to dispose of us as any.

"Okay," said Aaron, from the other side of the crack in the wall. I opened my eyes, and was rewarded with the sight of Aaron in his own flashlight beam beyond the tear. "So far so good. You'll be fine; you're even smaller than I am. No problem at all."

I took a moment to brace myself, then felt around the rim of the fissure for sharp edges. Trying not to think of doomed archaeologists, I slipped through.

My feet landed on irregular but stable ground. Immediately, I felt the breeze pick up. The freshness of it brought home how claustrophobic and stale the tunnel we'd just exited had been. There was no dust in the air, as there had been before, and the ability to move away from the rock walls was a great relief.

"What now?" I said, wondering what part of Hunt's paper had covered this particular stage.

"Stay close to the wall, see if we can find another tunnel, I guess," said Aaron, which was what I probably would have figured we should do, if I'd been in any state to think clearly. Even though we'd gotten out of the previous tunnel, I was still scared nearly stiff, and there was no reason to think we'd made it through the worst yet.

"Uh, can I help you?"

Aaron whirled while my heart caught in my throat. I tried to fake some kind of ninja readiness, but I'm pretty sure it wasn't a convincing act.

A couple of dozen feet behind us was one of the tallest, skinniest guys I'd ever seen. His hair was a crazy rasta-blizzard of tight reddish curls, and his glasses, at least in this light, made his eyes into flat mirrors. Tangled in his curls was a miner's light which gave a steady but directional beam, pointing low. I guessed that was how he'd gotten so close without either of us noticing.

I moved a little closer to Aaron, but I didn't really feel threatened. The guy had a huge, happy grin on his face, which of course would be a great tactic if he really was a demon coming to kill us. But I just couldn't feel scared somehow. After the initial startle, I was just curious, and a little glad to have someone else join us at that moment, truth be told.

Still, it didn't hurt to be careful. "Take off your glasses," I said, trying to muster a tone that was commanding but not too confrontational.

"Sure, man," he said, and whipped them off dramatically, Superman-style. "You got a favorite side?" Grinning even more broadly, he turned his face first one way then the other. "I'm ready for my close-up!"

"Maggie—" Aaron had a warning note in his voice as if any evidence of odd behavior was irrational and therefore dangerous.

I shushed his concerns, grinning myself now, and shone my light up into the guy's face. "What's your handle, Randall?" I said, thinking he might appreciate the rhyme.

He tilted his head coyly and coughed, then said in a lower, more manly tone, "Bob, ma'am. I run the public transit in these parts."

I flashed my light in in the direction he'd pointed. The beam picked out a decrepit handcart that looked mostly rebuilt from scrap and garbage sitting on a length of track that vanished into the darkness.

I felt Bob's hand suddenly on my shoulder, and tried unsuccessfully not to flinch.

"Watch out for the ghost train," he whispered. "It's almost got me before. Dangerous down here. You and your sherpa should stick with me."

I looked over my shoulder at Aaron, who was indeed pretty laden down with my stuff as well as his and tried not to smile too much. "Hey, Gunga Din," I said to Aaron, "we can share the load."

Aaron didn't seem nearly as amused by Bob as I was, and a lot more suspicious. He grunted as he passed me my pack. I wondered if we were having leadership issues. Not that I hadn't felt put out since the beginning of this leg of our journey, what with Hunt pretending to Aaron that he was his friend and confidante and that I was—well, nothing.

I snapped Aaron a crisp salute. No use making him feel uncomfortable. "Do you care to interrogate the... Bob, sir?"

Aaron sighed. "Hi, Bob," he said, as if he'd just decided he'd been rude before. "Ghost train, huh?"

Bob shivered and looked over his shoulder, back down the inky tunnel. "That's two. You say it three times and it always comes. So..." He put a long finger to his lips and replaced his glasses.

"Where to, sahib?" he said, this time to Aaron. I shouldered my own pack. I guessed acknowledging Aaron had set it in Bob's head that he was leading this expedition. I'd just shut myself down and out, again.

"Oh," said Bob, smacking himself on the forehead. "I almost forgot. I was supposed to give you this."

He pressed a folded square of grubby paper into Aaron's hand, and something cold and hard into mine. I knew instantly what it was, but I had frozen as soon as I felt its stone touch my palm with the same weird spark it had generated when Jason had passed it to me at our abortive lunch meeting. Arabella's ring.

Aaron unfolded the paper and held it out to me. His face was grim; I'm sure mine matched. In Sharpie, a squiggle that we both had seen a few too many times in the last hours already—Hunt.

Not able to talk about it, not even wanting to try, I put Aria's ring into my pocket. I hoped that Aaron had been preoccupied enough with what Bob had given him that he hadn't noticed him hand something to me as well. The master manipulator had nudged us again. I had to keep remembering that whatever we did down here, Hunt had his hand in it. That meant that nothing was simple, and that nothing would be easy.

✪

Bob led us to the handcart. He offered me a hand up but I pretended I hadn't seen and jumped up on my own. Aaron let him boost him, but then, he was carrying about twice as much stuff as me. I wished I'd insisted on taking a look through his pack or at least checked out Hunt's inventory. An advantage isn't an advantage if you don't know what it entails.

"I think we'll go stealth today," said Bob, when we were settled on the milk crate seating he'd added to the cart, and took up a position behind us at the pump handle. He flicked a switch and a much stronger light flared into life at the front of the cart shining a good hundred feet down the tunnel. Whatever he meant by stealth, it wasn't about traveling in the dark. That was fine by me.

He started pumping away and we moved off smoothly into the tunnel. There were only two tracks here, not three, so this tunnel had never been electrified. Who had built it? Was it indeed the remnant of an aborted TTC project? Or, like Char's palace north of the city, had it been excavated for one purpose and one purpose only—to house a entrance to the Burnt Man's world?

"I got a pretty good motor in this thing," said Bob as we set off. "Dozen horses, five liter engine. We grab diesel for it when they park the old service vehicles—some of them still aren't electric. Good thing; if there's one thing a Citizen knows, it's how to siphon. We'd be screwed if we needed to steal the electric." He laughed. I could almost hear the capital "C" of the word "citizen," and the way he slanted the pronunciation so it was almost "City-zen." Was that some kind of accent thing, or was it supposed to tell me something? I didn't think a lot of Toronto's average "city-zens" would have a clue about using a siphon hose to steal diesel. What did he mean by service vehicles? City maintenance vehicles? Did they run on diesel? And if so, where were they parked that Bob and his friends had access to them? Just how big was the network of two-track tunnels underground?

I motioned to Aaron to hand me his compass and saw that, as I'd thought, we were traveling more or less north with a bit of a bearing to the west, the direction that track to the airport headed initially. As to how far or how fast we were going, I had no clue. And not having any idea how far we'd actually travelled in actual crow-flying distance before

Bob had found us, it was not feasible to make any kind of guess. Rae and Suzanne would have no idea at all where we were, or where we might emerge. And until we got far enough above ground to hook a cell signal, we couldn't tell them. It was funny how modern gadgetry was failing us entirely, while the ancient technology of Aaron's compass was still giving us accurate information.

Bob had launched into a chatty travelogue as he worked us down the tunnel. He might be skinny, but he was obviously in great shape—no shortness of breath or any sign he was exerting himself. That might be a sign he was something less than natural after all, but I figured it was owed more to the fact he spent all day jaunting around on a handcart. I had tuned out the first part of his monologue, but started paying attention now, as Aaron squeezed my hand and looked at me with comically opened eyes.

"This is one of our first and greatest tunnels," Bob was saying, "dating back to the glory days of possibility when the great excavators moved through the earth to cut out a route for the normal, non-ectoplasmic subway trains to wend their way northward to the then-two terminals, or so was the intent. But lo, the municipal government changed and the plan was abandoned. But thank god, eh?"

I looked over my shoulder. Bob was grinning broadly. "Why's that, Bob?" I asked, playing along.

"Because without those plans being scrapped, where would the Alterna-City be?"

There he had me.

Aaron seemed to have sunk into thought—or maybe he was just trying to avoid the air of madness Bob had brought with him. It seemed like it would be up to me to keep the ball rolling, so to speak, with Bob. "What's that?" I asked. "Where the City-zens live?" I said the word as much like I remembered Bob doing it as I could.

"Exactly!" He seemed delighted. "I knew you'd get it. Where the City-zens live. We're going right through Alterna-City Central, but you probably won't see anyone."

"Bob," I said, because as far as I could tell, we were still going down a tunnel with no more than two or three feet of clearance a side and nothing looked like it was capable of hiding a Playstation much less a whole city, "Alterna-City, is it. . ."

"We're not there yet," he said. "But you won't have any doubts when we get there. It's a pretty awesome place. I've been there... almost seven years myself. Running the transit for five."

This was getting weirder and weirder. Hunt's insertion of himself into it was the worst part. He'd understand whatever it was Bob was talking about, and it was obviously separate from whatever scam he had going with Aaron and me. How many other plots did he have running at the same time? Just who *was* Hunt, come to that? I'd had that hint of a scandal of epic proportions in the Vancouver reference I still hadn't bothered following up, even with access to the Internet at home. Maybe I really didn't want to know. I would do anything for a route back to Char's world and my lost powers that had nothing to do with Hunt and the uncertainty and danger he represented.

"Mags," said Aaron quietly, taking my arm. The tunnel made a gentle corner, and opened out suddenly into a huge cavern. The light of the handcart was lost in its depths. To each side of the tracks, the ground fell away down steep hills like the worst ditches in highway history. We were traveling now on a raised abutment in a rocky plain. I couldn't see the roof above us any more, or the sides of the place. What I could see was hill after hill of garbage and refuse, dotting the plain and stretching into the blackness where the handcart's light couldn't reach.

"If it was just me here," said Bob, getting back into his tour-guide voice, "all over Alterna-City, you'd see the scattered lights of our civilization, the cooking fires and awesome LEDs of the City-zen housing." He leaned over confidentially to me. "LEDs are the most awesomest thing, huh? Never have to replace the bulbs; we grab a few packs of watch batteries and we're good for a year. Not like the old days." He sighed dramatically.

Looking out more discerningly, I could see places where slender columns of smoke rose from some of the hills—those fires he was talking about, hastily banked to avoid our notice? Somewhere in the darkness I heard splashing water, like a fountain or running stream. And on each of the hills, I could make out what seemed to be dwellings constructed of the same garbage and cast-off mix that Bob had used to furnish his handcart. People—lived here.

Aaron had his look of most intense concentration on his face. After looking intently at both sides of the tracks, he turned to me with wonder. "Just from what I see, even if there's only one person living in each of these places, there's a population of several hundred."

Bob ducked his head between ours. "Lots more than that," he said. "Especially in the last ten years. People went black market, then even that wasn't enough. You start off homeless, this place is the way out. No worries about the weather, and the cops never roust you. You get a chance to live however you dreamed it."

"What about laws?" asked Aaron. Of course.

"You don't wanna know," said Bob ominously, then laughed. "Yeah, there's laws, but we only figure them out after something bad gets done. If it's bad enough, you get thrown out, back into the Up-world. We figure part of the reason we're down here is because people up there'd rather look at law books than at people, so we reversed the whole shebang."

I laughed. "Sounds pretty sweet to me."

Then, suddenly, I saw something on one of the mounds ahead, near to the track. "Bob! Stop!" I called out. My voice, louder than any noise we'd heard since coming underground, seemed to fall flat into the dark void around us, as if sound would only travel where there was light as well.

Bob threw a switch and pumped a couple of times, reversing the cart into a full stop.

Aaron half-rose, trying to see what had made me call out.

"There," I said, balancing myself upright on the seat. "Can you see it?"

He peered into the darkness, sweeping the place I was pointing to with his flashlight beam. "That looks like. . ."

"Scott's jacket," I finished for him.

Behind us, Bob leaned forward. "Tall kid? Blond curly hair?"

"Yeah," I said cautiously. Bob knew Scott?

"And a cute little blond guy with long-distance eyes?"

That was about as apt a description of Peter/Soren as I could imagine. "They were *here*?" I asked, unable to keep my voice from rising.

"Few weeks back," said Bob, nodding. "Asking a lot of questions. Couldn't help him, but I think he got what he was looking for."

"Maggie?" said Aaron.

I shook my head. "I have no idea what he would have been doing down here, or what on earth would have possessed him to bring his brother with him."

Bob laughed, as if I'd said something ridiculous. "That kid was never his brother."

A much deeper shivered passed down my spine. I realized that I was no longer thinking about how scary it was to be underground. There was something going on that had far graver implications than my irrational fears. I had never really trusted Scott; I saw that now. Especially since he'd been the only one of us, out of the ones who'd been taken to Char's lair, that had spent significant time with the most dangerous person I'd ever met, the one that I had killed. Arabella, the Burnt Man's daughter.

"What now?" asked Aaron, and I was hardly able to feel the pleasure I normally got out of anyone deferring to me. He reached out, but the jacket was too far to grab.

"Hey!" said Bob sharply. "Leave that alone. The guy who owns that now traded for it, fair and square."

"Traded what?" I said, just as sharply.

"Dunno, something from the archive."

"Bob," I said, trying to keep my voice calm, "what's the archive? Can we see it?"

He shrugged. "Don't see why not. We'll go right by it, although I didn't get any word about it either way. But you can't take anything, unless you have something really good to trade."

I fingered Arabella's ring in my pocket. That was something I wouldn't trade away, for certain.

"We just want to take a look," I said. Cross the black market trading-post bridge when we came to it.

"Okey-dokey," Bob said, and looked from Aaron to me and back again. "Shall we ferry on our merry way?"

He turned the switch back to the forward setting, and we were off again.

Bob was silent now, no more travelogue, as if by stopping in his city we'd suddenly stopped being tourists. We were coming to the far cavern wall, and the plain was rising again to the level of the tracks. Ahead, I saw the mouth of another tunnel, this one bigger than the one we'd been in before the Alterna-city cavern. There was an unexpected regularity to the shape of it—it was scalloped, like the edge of a fire, with sharp points sticking up and out of the profile. I had never seen anything like it before. If it was man-made, it was of a design that was completely foreign to anything I'd ever seen either with my own eyes or in books. That's when I knew that we were about enter a place that, like Char's catacombs, had been built with something other than machines and human labor. We were entering the lair of the beast.

As we slid from the relative roominess of the cavern of Bob's City into the next tunnel, I grabbed Aaron's arm. "Aaron—I have Tamblyn's private cell number and I never even thought—I never talked to Suzanne and Rae before we came down here. They don't have his number."

"Rae's smart; she'll know what to do," he said.

I knew he was right about her intelligence, but as to knowing what to do—did any of us?

## 38

## Let Me Sleep Beside You

✪

This tunnel was different. As Bob switched off the headlamp of the hand cart, we saw just how true that difference was. I tightened my hand on Aaron's arm, and Aaron covered my hand with his. It was a sign of just how unnerved we both were that I didn't even worry about what he might think, and he didn't seem to notice how strong his grasp on my fingers had become.

He wasn't looking at me, but like me, was fixated on our surroundings. It wasn't just the stones: the walls themselves were rippled and undulating like nothing I'd ever seen. It wasn't like they were carved at all, or what you might expect from some natural force like, say, the wind or water. I compared the seemingly random patterns to other characteristic natural ones, like the ripples of sand made by underwater currents, or the distinctive rounding of water-worn stone. It wasn't even comparable to what might have been left by hurricane firestorms that might have melted stone in their path, like lava flows.

No, as I had observed at the entrance to this section of tunnel, it was like flames had shot up, etched the stone in their profile, and vanished again, so that the whole length of tunnel might have been carved entirely in a single outpouring of immense power. That was the only thing I could possibly imagine, a fire that was so hot it didn't melt stone but merely evaporated it at a touch. I wondered if Aaron was making similar observations, and if so what he'd come up with as a reasonable explanation. Or if he realized, as I was starting to, that no reason could reason through what we were seeing.

"How do you tell if something is artificial," he said suddenly into the quiet, "or if it's just made by something beyond your current understanding of nature?"

That summed it up perfectly. I wasn't sure I had anything to add, so I treated his question rhetorically.

Although Bob had turned off the cart's lights, we were not in darkness. In the walls around us, a myriad of warm, bluish stones gave off a faint but consistent glow. It was enough to see each other, and to see down in the direction we were traveling much more distinctly than we had with the brighter, harsher electric light. Bob's silence felt almost reverent, and Aaron and I both were caught up in it.

Were they naturally luminescent? Something created by the creature we were chasing? It was funny, but all the time we'd been down here, I'd focused much more on just following directions than I had thought at all about our ultimate goal. We were getting closer and closer to the thing that had walked poor Mrs. Sanchez to death, bloodying her feet and abandoning her body like refuse. We had to be heading toward it; otherwise, none of this made sense. The Thurl-apparition had told me as much, that it wanted us to come, to bring *my bauble*, which I took to mean the ring that Bob through some unknown agency had returned to me, the *book*, carefully wrapped in Aaron's backpack, and *my man*– whether that meant Jason or Aaron or even Scott now seemed to make no difference. If it was Hunt, I had not control over whether or not he would show up on his own. If I thought about it, it seemed he might; Hunt liked to lurk, but he liked to be close, even if you didn't see him. His use of Aaron as a backdoor spy showed that pretty clearly, as if there'd been any doubt.

And so we travelled on, heading steadily northwards as well as deeper down. *Deeper in, the only way out is deeper in.* That seemed to be the theme of all my interactions with the non-natural world. You can't extricate yourself until you go right to the heart of the matter.

Like the last time, when I'd been dragged into Char's clutches, I didn't know if I wanted to be extricated. Or rather, I was attracted and repelled in almost equal measure. I didn't want to lose my connection to this other world which felt *so right* in so many ways, but how much damage to my friends and that normal world would I tolerate? Could I really have severed all my relationships with anyone who lived in the sunlit, non-magical world in order to enter this altered, foreign one? I would have said yes in a moment, but then, I had never really stopped to calculate the cost.

Beside me, Aaron seemed to have had enough at last of holding onto me. He twisted his wrist and checked his watch. I took what I wasn't sure was a hint, but my insecurity around him made me remove my hand from his arm at the same time.

"What time is it?" I asked. Hours could have gone by, or minutes, since we'd been underground.

He gave an enormous yawn before answering. "Almost ten am. No wonder I'm tired. We were pretty much up all night."

Now that he'd said it, I felt fatigued from head to toes. "You said it," I replied. "Anything in Hunt's note about getting in a nap?"

He guffawed, the first time I'd heard that sound in a long time. "No, and no Arrowroot biscuits either. Although. . ."

He reached into his pack and brought out some sandwiches in plastic baggies. Mine was ham and cheese. "Scribner, you are a marvel," I said, and happily stuffed my face. Bob took a couple of sandwiches when offered and did an amazing job of pumping the hand cart one-handed while mawing them down. For a few minutes, silent and eating, I was actually relaxed. Maybe all I had to do to be comfortable underground was to spend some time doing banal, common things like eating and drinking. Maybe not, but it was a start. The sandwich went down fine, and I felt the knots in my shoulders and stomach release a little for the first time since I'd heard Aaron say the word "underground."

Aaron put the empty plastic bags back in his pack, and Bob, wiping crumbs from his shirt, announced, "Almost there, kidlets. Next stop, the archive."

The light up ahead brightened and the tunnel this time, instead of ending, opened up gradually until it seamlessly became a rather triangular cavern. Its walls were made in the same pattern as those of the tunnel, except here the fire-etching stretched up and up and up until the ceiling of the place vanished in a blue glow. I didn't like to look up, because it reminded me of just how far underground we now were. If the ceiling of this cavern disappeared into those heights, we were a lot deeper than we had been under the station.

From this cavern, several tunnels led away through funnel-like openings. I was putting together a disturbing picture of the creature whose powers had made this place, standing here in a small pocket in the rock, then blasting away in direction after direction to form those other exits. And straight up into the blue nothing.

The tracks Bob's cart ran on ended in the middle of the cavern, but there was another line heading down one of the radiating paths. I wondered where it went, and how Bob was able to manage moving the cart from one track to another. What he really needed was a turntable, like they used with big trains in the heyday of steam. Did those still exist now, or did they only live on in miniature in Tommy the Tank Engine play-sets?

Aaron asked, "Where's this archive, Bob?"

Bob jumped down from the cart and pointed up. Now, I saw what seemed to be a ladder of sorts made by the crenelations of the wall, leading up to a small opening maybe fifteen feet above the surface of the cavern floor. "Don't worry," he said, leading the way, "It's an easy climb. Not like some around here."

I didn't really want to think about having to do aerial monkey-work, adding even more danger to the mix. I always hated movies where the heroes had to navigate some narrow bit of rock or rickety bridge over an endless abyss. The only thing worse than being underground was being faced with the possibility of falling *further* underground, right?

Aaron went up first, and he made it look so easy I was comforted a bit. Bob seemed to notice my hesitation. "Seriously, it's a piece of fine chocolate cake."

He didn't seem inclined to go up himself, so I put my hands to the wall and hoisted myself up.

He was right—the climb was no big deal at all. The stone felt vaguely buttery under my hands, smooth and just a little soft to the touch. I didn't want to think yet about how it might be more difficult going down, so I kept my face turned to the stones and put one hand and foot after the other.

Aaron gave me his hand to pull me up the last couple of feet, but I took it more out of wanting the feel of his strength than because I needed help. He smiled and tilted his head toward the small cave beyond the opening in the wall, obviously excited. "You have to see this," was all he said, and led the way.

This was something I could not have imagined. Maybe seeing Char decked out as an old-time professor, sitting at a desk doing paper work like any normal man should have prepared me for this. But, like Aaron, all I could do was smile.

"This is so cool," I said.

The cave wasn't big, about the size of my room at home. It reminded me of artist renditions of how the Library at Alexandria might have looked, or an ancient dove cote like I'd seen in photographs of medieval castles. Each of the four walls was dotted with holes, each holding not a scroll but a single sheet of newsprint. The alcoves seemed to be about as deep as an average newspaper page, and that's what they all held. I went to the nearest wall and slid a page from its hole.

It was yellowed but supple, not crumbling like I might have expected. The humidity must be just right to preserve paper, I thought, although whether that was by luck or design I couldn't guess. The page I'd chosen randomly was an article from the *Globe and Mail* from 1953, August the 10th, and was about a house fire in Rosedale in which three children had died.

The next I picked out was from June 18th, 1993, and talked about a man sentenced to the Don Valley Jail for various offenses including house-breaking and the theft of several valuable antiques.

As I worked my way along the alcoves, I could see no rhyme nor reason as they say for the selection of articles, or their organization. Aaron, starting on the opposite wall, seemed to be having no more luck.

"Do you get this at all?" I asked him.

"If you mean why these pieces and not others—no, not one bit. Maybe we just need to see more to get the pattern."

"Or there really isn't one," I suggested. "Maybe it was created by Alterna-City people like Bob. A lot of them seem to be about crime and kind of societally-marginal events. Maybe it's a record of things that happened to or were done by people who live down here."

Aaron went silent, holding the next piece he'd pulled from its spot. He seemed to be reading it more than once. "Maggie—" he said finally and handed it to me.

I went totally cold, as if the paper itself had been sub-zero and had frozen itself to me and sent icy liquid through my veins. It couldn't be. The date was from the spring of my grade eight year, and it was about the bizarre findings at Westbrook Elementary School after an assembly which none of the students could apparently remember.

I looked at the alcoves all around us with new eyes. Somewhere up there in one of those little cubbyholes, I was sure, we would find an article about a police constable—was he a sergeant? I couldn't remember—killed in a Westbrook suburban home. That cop was left to die in his own blood by Arabella while Scott Saunders watched. I'd got that information from Scott himself in that brief moment of detente between us when I was recovering from the slice down my arm.

These were the articles that had been missing from the papers I had seen in the Toronto Reference Library. Were all of these pages the same —incidents that had happened, but had been made to vanish from common perception? Were these events that someone—someone like me—had erased from everyone's memory? And maybe this archive was the only place where you could find the truth, where you could discover what had been yanked from your mind and replaced with a satisfaction that nothing was missing. If you didn't know to come looking for missing pieces of the past, how would you ever know what you didn't remember?

Aaron was gazing at me, knowing that I was holding something back. "I'll tell you everything I know," I said, "I promise. But please, can we get Jason back first? If I start talking, I'll probably collapse into a puddle of emotion."

He nodded slowly, not liking it but willing to accept it. Then, looking beyond me, he motioned to me to follow and walked past me. Below, I heard the motor of Bob's hand cart chug to life. I ran to the opening above the cavern floor below just in time to see him vanish back down the tunnel that had brought us here, without a single glance back.

"Bob's gone!" I said, but Aaron didn't seem worried.

"I think that's what was supposed to happen," he said. "Look at this."

I joined him at the wall, and saw what I hadn't noticed from the angle I'd been looking that direction before. There was an opening here, and a path through the rock beyond. It was dark, no friendly blue glow, but Aaron got out his flashlight and aimed it through. It was passable, regular, and curved downwards out of sight. On the wall just inside the opening was one of Hunt's chalk scribbles.

Then I saw what had drawn Aaron over here first: around the opening was a band of carving maybe three inches wide forming a frame and lintel, like around a regular door. My breath caught, remembering the small back door of Char's throne room which had been carved with a multitude of tiny faces. This was work of the same hand, or in the same style at least. There were faces here too, of every age and ethnicity it seemed, with every expression from joy to terror. Between them, unlike on that other frame, were fruits and leaves. I saw dozens of different fruits, none repeating as far as I could tell, and all sorts of different kinds of foliage. It was, as Char's had been, a wonder. The only carving I had ever seen that compared was in pictures of Rosslyn Abbey in Scotland, which I'd investigated after the whole *Da Vinci Code* thing and this work was so much more delicate, or at least didn't have the same ancient, worn look of the carvings at the Abbey.

Aaron and I exchanged a look, and I could see he was as full of awe as I was. It was incredible and breath-taking. And it had left both of us entirely speechless. We took our time with the border, running our fingers over the little faces and the fine renderings of flora and human fauna. Finally, he took a deep breath, as if it was the first he'd been able to manage since we began our examination, and gestured toward the path forward.

I nodded, and he shouldered his pack and led the way, flashlight bobbing, both of us still tongue-tied.

✪

An hour further in by Aaron's Hunt-synchronized watch and we were both walking like the living dead.

"I've got to crash soon or I'm just going to collapse," I said. The walls and the floor of our tunnel were relatively smooth, but not exactly inviting. I would probably have to be even more fatigued to choose this as a bed, especially given the close confines, but I was running very, very low.

"Yeah," said Aaron. He pulled out the grimy paper Bob had delivered.

"Still nothing about our reservations at the Holiday Inn?" I asked.

He guffawed. "Not a damn word. I never thought about adventuring being so exhausting."

"Yeah, something they left out of the manual." I stumbled then, and went down on one knee. "Crap."

Aaron helped me up. "This is getting slightly ridiculous," he said. "How far down do you figure we are? And how much further do we have to go?"

Questions I had purposely avoided asking myself. Hunt, if he could see us, would be loving this. "Maybe he didn't figure we'd be up all night before he sent us down here. He couldn't know we'd be zombies by this point."

He nodded, but I figured he was as unsure about this reasoning as I was. I no longer believed Hunt left anything to chance. Or at least, he knew when to hold 'em and when to fold 'em, so to speak. He knew how to bend the odds to obey him.

"Maggie, look!" Aaron, pacing just ahead, had got a look around the bend in front of us. I took the few steps necessary to bring me beside him, and looked—not to mention sniffed—in wonder.

"I'm starting to get bored of surprises," I said.

We had somehow made it to what apparently was part of Toronto's sewer system. "Terrific," I said. "I love the smell of rotten cabbage."

At least the tunnel was bigger now, although a lot more treacherous. Our old windy descending tunnel had been dry and smooth; it had deposited us on a dirty, damp walkway that stretched into the darkness left and right, alongside a canal of filthy, stinking water. It seemed to me that the level was a lot lower than capacity, and entirely stagnant, as if this sewer was no longer part of an active system.

"Which way?" said Aaron. Good question. He shone the flashlight both ways and I saw nothing to distinguish one from the other. He took out the compass and humphed. "South southeast, or north northwest. We can't even go mystical and head toward Mecca."

"Coin flip?" I suggested. "Last refuge of the indecisive?"

"Good as anything," he said, and dug in a pocket. The flashlight beam danced erratically, and I caught sight of something on the wall.

This time, it wasn't a chalk scrawl from Hunt. It was something far more pedestrian. A light switch. Laughing a little, I depressed it with my thumb. Aaron started—I probably should have warned him—as a row of sodium lights flared to life, but only to our left. Aaron used his flashlight beam to pick out a couple of the caged lamps to our right, and we saw that the bulbs had all been shattered.

"That's a good enough sign," Aaron said and I had to agree. Despite myself, I was feeling just a modicum of pleasure at having solved another of Hunt's little tests. If tests they were. Was it really a test if someone knew you so well that he could accurately guess the limits of your deductive abilities and plan around them? I should probably feel more manipulated than proud.

"Okay," I said, "next leg of our travels. And Scribner? I know you're tired but try not to fall in. I don't know if I'd even *want* to carry on with you if you smelled as bad as that canal."

✪

We made a series of turns, always following the lights. Aaron had turned off the flashlight to save the battery (he said he had spares, but my terror of being stuck in the dark didn't allow me to count on that—and of course, with all of Jan's distress, I had entirely forgotten to pack mine) and I must admit I was rather impressed at the amount of time and thought Hunt must have put into marking our route. Breadcrumbs might have done just as well, and not involved smashing hundreds of lightbulbs. I didn't want to put too much thought into another alternative—that Hunt had used magic. That would just make me envious. So I concentrated on the more practical implications of the trail he'd left, thinking it was probably a good thing this tunnel didn't seem to be in use; replacing all those bulbs would mean an awful lot of hours at a city worker's salary.

And then, we hit a dead end. I must have been on a serious second wind, if not a fourth, because coming around this corner and seeing a blank, brick wall in front of us took every remaining breath of air out of my sails. "Oh god, no," I groaned. There would be a way forward, certainly, but it would require us to figure out another one of Hunt's little games. And I was just too damn tired for that. "Aaron, I swear. . ." I began, and stumbled forward. Something caught at my foot, and I went flat out on my face. Tripped, again. Clumsy Mags. Not only did I look like a total klutz in front of Aaron, I—well, I looked like a total klutz in front of Aaron.

He rushed to give me a hand, and then removed it before I had a chance to take it. "Maggie," he said, wonder and anger vying in his voice.

He used the flashlight to pick out the length of a trip-wire anchored across the cavern. "Terrific," I said. "Hunt has a taste for prat-falls."

And then, I caught a glimpse of something to my left, something I wouldn't have seen but for being flat on my wounded pride, not to mention my knees. "Aaron. . ."

Near the edge of the canal, under a jutting lip, was an iron lever. I got up and went around the end of the canal to the walkway on the other side, and reached under the lip for it. "Watch out," I told Aaron. "Don't know what this is going to do."

I pulled, and the lever moved smoothly. As it did, a section of the wall opened up at the end of the tunnel, effortlessly, barely requiring effort on my part at all.

"Holy Scooby Doo," said Aaron. "This just gets better and better."

There were no sunny sodium lights past this new barricade. It was pretty clear we had returned to a section of our journey that had nothing to do with the work of city planners. The new tunnel was high, with a raised walkway in the middle sloping down sharply on both sides, like we'd be walking in a roadbed between two drainage ditches. "Interesting," said Aaron. The "ditches" were dry, but they had crusted salt stains up almost to the level of the center walkway, as if they had flooded many times in the past.

"We're in opposite world," I said. "First a drainage tunnel with walkways on the sides, now a walkway with drainage ditches."

"Yeah, looks like," he said. I could see the clever Scribner brain playing with the idea, tugging it apart to tease as much information as possible out of what he was seeing.

"Good to go?" I asked to reorient him to the task at hand.

"Absolutely," he said, and handed me the flashlight, waving his arm like a ringmaster ushering in the first act at a circus.

"Thanks a lot," I said, but took the light and started walking.

And immediately fell on my face again.

"Son of a bitch!" I screamed. It was the loudest noise I could remember making in years. Maybe forever. My voice echoes down the tunnel, and got caught up in Aaron's attempts to muffle his laughter. "Not funny, Scribner," I said, and then repeated, "Son of a goddamned bitch!" because I'd just caught sight of something, again.

Aaron was inspecting the trip-wire Hunt had rigged to get me this time, but I drew his attention to a glimmer of light low on the wall, down deep in the drainage ditch. "I think it's another tunnel," I said, and stayed flat on my belly to shine the light down to inspect it.

What I saw was an opening big enough to easily accommodate either of us with our packs, and without fear of getting stuck. It would be easy to lower ourselves down—and I could see a flat floor beyond that didn't look as if it was some tiny ledge or other hidden danger.

"I'll go first," said Aaron.

"Yeah, you do that," I said, a little sulky but mostly mocking myself. "It's totally your turn to do a face-plant."

He smiled, and slithered down into the opening.

After a slightly unnerving period of silence, I heard him call out, "Mags, you're not going to believe this!"

I turned and lowered myself after him. It was easy, and it would be just as easy to get out, which I saw was the point. This wasn't a tunnel; it was a cave. An oil lamp burned in an alcove, providing more than sufficient light. On the far wall of the cavern was a wide shelf, and it held blankets and pillows. Miraculous, and more beautiful than anything else I could have imagined. By the shelf was a small table with a set of covered dishes and a pitcher. Glasses and actual cutlery completed the set-up.

"This is insane," I said, but for the first time since we'd come down here, I was smiling broadly and unreservedly. "I don't think even the Holiday Inn caters caves."

Aaron laughed. "I don't know if I want to sleep or eat first."

I smiled at him. "Five minutes ago, I would have said sleep, a hundred percent. But I think I smell burgers. . ."

✪

I was right, and we dug in. The table itself was warm, which in turn seemed to keep the food at a good temperature. The cavern seemed a little steamy, like a sauna on low, but it was nice on my muscles after all our walking and clambering.

We sat on the cavern floor with our backs to the sleeping shelf, and stuffed our faces. Food had never, ever tasted so good. We didn't speak. At first, I thought it was just about the hunger and the fatigue, but there was something else. Elephant-sized. I sat shoulder to shoulder with Aaron on the ground, our shoulders brushing every now and then. Was he as conscious of the contact as I was? Was he thinking too about the sleeping arrangements, about whether one of us would, so to speak, take the couch?

When I'd scarfed the food Hunt had left us—I assumed it was him, and if not, I didn't want to think about it—and drank about a pint of water, I excused myself to find a quiet place above to pee. It wasn't as big a deal as I thought it might be; the drainage ditch provided a perfect place, and by using the other side, I figured I wouldn't unintentionally urinate our sleeping quarters. Aaron went after I returned.

While he was gone, I found myself examining everything in the room with almost fanatical attention. Here's my backpack. Here are my dishes. There is the oil lamp. I stood with my back to the entrance, but not quite looking at the blankets. Time was running out, but for what I wasn't quite sure.

I heard Aaron behind me slither back into the cave. Then, nothing. He must be standing as still as I was. Who could speak to break this silence? How on earth was I supposed to turn, to look at him, when he'd be able to read dangerous thoughts in my eyes?

"Maggie—Maggie," said Aaron behind me. I felt his hand brush my shoulder and then come to rest there. Tentatively, then more confidently, the fingers squeezed.

In that moment, I became completely indecisive and very confused. The room, despite the warmth coming from the table beside me and the steamy heat hanging in the air, seemed to cool suddenly, even though I could feel sweat beading on my brow. My mouth was doing acrobatics, trying to pull itself into the beginning of a word. He had rendered me speechless.

Slowly I turned. He was backing away from me, hand still on my shoulder, and I was compelled to follow. His eyes behind the lenses of his glasses seemed very deep, and I couldn't meet them for more than a split second at a time. Fortunately, he looked to be having the same problem.

I couldn't remember being more uncomfortable in my life. This was new, this whole situation, and I was—what was I? What was this?

The backs of his legs touched the shelf and he sat, pulling me after him. And then, his arms were around me as much as mine were around him. I buried my face in his neck and hair and felt his breath on my cheek.

His hands were tight on me, one still holding my shoulder, a powerful tension running through the fingers into me. What were we doing? I had never even thought. . . At thirteen, it would have been much easier. I was almost sure. He smelled good, clean through the sharpness of our mingling sweat.

"Maggie," whispered Aaron in my ear. His breath tickled me and my mouth smiled, even though the rest of my face still seemed on crooked. He pulled away from me a little, pulling more of his body comfortably onto the shelf. I wasn't sure if this was an implicit invitation to join him or the beginning of disengagement. *Did* I want to follow him? Was it the right thing to do? His hand remained firm on my shoulder.

And me, I was warm all over, and shivering anyhow. There was a trickle of ice running straight through my insides, from the place his fingers touched the nape of my neck down through the centre of my stomach and down my legs. No one—I had never—but of course not. I'd never even been on a date, and my only other brush with this kind of thing had happened across a desk in a fast food joint and made me feel nothing but hideously dirty. And that was only if you didn't count Hunt stripping me down to bra and panties, which I didn't, not for a second.

If I could lock away visions of Damon through my thirteen year old eyes hidden in my older girl body. . . and even Damon hadn't had this effect on me, not like Aaron in this moment.

I could suddenly hear Jason in the back of my mind: *Eesh, Mags, sometimes you think too much.*

"Maggie," Aaron said again, low and throaty. I slid in beside him, daring to go just a little closer than before. He said, "This—it doesn't—I mean, I don't want to be so—"

A disclaimer. It sounded almost like the beginning of an apology, or at least a tactical withdrawal. He didn't want me to get the wrong idea, and I had only been starting to put together what that might be. His arms were warm, but I felt that my skin had gone icy against him.

Then, "oh, god, Maggie," he whispered, and everything was all right again, my apprehensions swept away. I was nervous and tense, but it was a good kind of tense, a good kind of nervous. I wanted to tell Aaron that, for the first time since I'd known him, I wasn't afraid of him. For the first time, I felt like. . . But it was unnecessary, after all. For once, I didn't want to be in control.

I felt his hand move from my shoulder down my back. I was perspiring, all pretense of cool gone. His touch sent a thrill through me. Then his hands moved around me and started to lift my hoodie over my head. I thought better of it, but I didn't resist. Part of me wanted to stay guarded and safe, but part of me, the far more insistent part, sent a hand roaming under his shirt and along the warmth of his back.

I helped him with my top, and then I was in my black undershirt, arms bare to the shoulders. And I realized that I had exposed a lot more than a bunch of teenage girl-skin.

"Ouch," said Aaron, his lips near my skin. "That's quite a—" He put a hand on my scar, negotiating the thickness of it.

"Aaron," I said shakily. "Maybe this isn't such a good idea."

"Whatever you want, Mags," he said. His blue eyes, through the reflecting lenses of his glasses, stared into mine, questioning.

"There are a lot of things I should tell you," I said, hesitantly, but a lot of them seemed irrelevant now. I had wanted the past to give me a history with Aaron, with Jason, with Peter, even with Scott and with Hunt and his brother. But what was happening now, what had already happened this school year, no one could take that away from us.

"Like what?" he said.

*Like what?*

All those little fantasies of mine, all the dreams of the glories and adversaries of my past, were signposts to this conclusion, including the one in which I'd imagined myself tossed screaming into the looney bin. That one, in fact, was particularly perverse.

You see, no one—and on this I would have staked my life until a few moments ago—would ever take me seriously enough to put me away, or even believe I was really sick. The perverse part was that I would have loved the attention. That's also what made it a fantasy instead of a nightmare.

Besides, choosing to stay silent about it—apart from being a great breeding ground for fantasies—meant *martyrdom*. Martyrdom was, of course, a Maggie Stuart speciality. Well, no more. At least, I could go as far as I had with Rae. I'd revealed something to her, no matter that I'd taken it back, and the world hadn't fallen down. I guessed I could go that far with Aaron.

"I was in a fight. It was a magic fight. I used to have powers—amazing powers. This scar—it's because of them. I was in a fight."

"You said that," he said.

"I know. It was with a magician, a sorcerer, who was very powerful and who had me prisoner. It happened during grade eight."

"I can't remember you missing much school." He laughed, just a little.

"Think back," I said, pleading. "It was in the spring of grade eight.

You must remember some of it. That cop you read about—he was killed at Scott's house. Scott's house. You maybe could— if you tried— After all—" I lowered my eyes. The time was now or never. *You were there*, I meant to say. But I couldn't. Not after keeping silent for so long. I'd hated myself for letting so much slip to Rae, and I wouldn't let myself get caught in it again. Maybe someday, like Hunt, Aaron would start to remember. Hopefully, he'd remember the good stuff first. Maybe we could go back to the archive even, and I could show him all the missing pieces, the proof of what I said.

No matter how little my secret mattered, there was still the reason I'd done it, to protect those who'd been through the same hell as I had from their memories. Could I put Aaron through that? I remembered suddenly, for the first time in years, the way he'd looked when he talked about his dog, the one Damon had killed. I could picture his face so clearly, the haunted look that remained throughout the rest of our time in the catacombs, after he came back from Char's testing ground. The specifics of that I hadn't even had time to fully hear, but what if that was enough to destroy him even now, three years later?

"Maggie?" he asked. The atmosphere had settled down, away from the sexual mood of so few minutes before. His hands were still on me, one around my waist and the other caressing the scar, but there was no urgency, just warmth.

I embraced him, pulling him close. His muscles tightened on me. "Please—" I said. "Let's get out of this, and then if you still want to know, I'll tell you everything."

He put a gentle kiss on my neck. "It's a deal," he said in my ear. In response, I could do nothing more than press my head against him and close my eyes, feeling the brush of my eyelashes over the fabric of his shirt. It occurred to me then that he was just as nervous and unsure as I was, that we were both vulnerable in this moment, and that it was okay. My first kiss from a boy, not on the cheek or lips, just a few inches from my horrible scar, and the sun hadn't yet set on my sixteenth birthday. It wasn't losing my virginity, but it was something, I supposed.

We arranged the blankets and pillows, turned down the wick on the oil lamp, and then we lay down together, wrapped in each other's arms. Aaron had pulled off all his tops but his undershirt too, which I guess made us even and me a lot more comfortable in my half-nakedness. His breath was in my ear, warm like his skin. I felt like I was coming to a normal temperature finally. Inside, I was shaking. Just for tonight, maybe we'd be able to feel safe. Tonight, we could hold back the world. I hadn't been this physically close and comfortable to someone else, ever. It was good.

"Aaron," I whispered to him. He rolled slightly to look at me. His blue eyes were steady on mine and hardly flickered away when he reached up to remove his glasses. Whatever I was going to say, whatever I'd meant to say, evaporated. Instead, I smiled, and he grinned back.

"Yeah," he said quietly, not really an answer but just an agreement to all the things neither of us were going to say. That this was nice, and comfortable, and that we were both really scared and needed someone right then. No, more than needing *someone;* we needed each other. I needed him. His arms shifted, pulled me closer, and like that, wrapped in a secure, happy embrace, I fell asleep.

## 39

### Lady Grinning Soul

✪

We woke to the harsh cry of an alarm.

I bolted upright, dislodging Aaron's arm, thoroughly confused about where I was and how I'd got there.

He sat up more slowly, laughing quietly. I punched him in the arm. "Stop it," I said. "Not funny."

I reached for the source of the noise and found a small travel alarm clock on the ledge beside the oil lamp, turned it off, and turned up the lamp. It had *not* been there when we'd fallen asleep.

"He was here," I said, turning to Aaron who'd found his glasses and replaced them on the bridge of his nose. "Hunt."

It was creepy beyond measure to think of Hunt sneaking in while we slept, while we slept in each other's arms. Hunt, who was the only other male in the world to have seen me in my undershirt: even creepier. My agitation must have shown on my face. "It's okay," said Aaron, touching my leg under the blanket that still covered most of us.

"It's what happened," I replied. "We don't really get to chose what's okay and what's not down here."

I turned and put my legs over the edge of the shelf. "Everything's like a game to Hunt, even when the stakes are really, really high. He just —likes it that way, I think. He can't help himself. Like. . ."

Like pretending he hardly knew me, and making Aaron the centre of attention. I couldn't say it, not so much because I didn't want to disabuse Aaron of the notion, but because it would only look like I was bragging about my own importance.

". . .like the way he's doling out the information, a tidbit at a time. Notes and texts, never letting us know, or giving us the option to chose."

"I have to admit, if he'd laid out the entire thing for me, all this underground stuff, the city in the tunnel—I don't know if I'd have bought in. Definitely would have had more suspicions about whether or not he could be trusted. I don't think I'd have believed a word of. . .of this." He indicated the cavern with his hands.

"That's the point," I said. "Hunt is really good at gauging people's limits and even better at finding the right buttons to press."

Aaron slid in beside me and looked me right in the eyes. "What are your buttons, Mags?" he said. "Or is that another thing I have to wait to hear about?"

There was no good answer for that. Not one that wouldn't make me look like a very bad friend. Or worse, like I was deliberately manipulating him for my own ends. And that was a question I needed to ask myself: was I manipulating him? Was I treating Aaron just like Hunt always treated me? Or was I better than him because I knew when I was lying, and felt horrible about it?

Or did that just make me a conflicted, unhappy person?

"I promise," I said. "Anything you want to know. As soon as we get Jason back. Only. . ."

I waited for him to prompt me to continue, but he only looked at me with his blue eyes behind the lenses glinting in the yellow light from the oil wick. "Only," I said at last, "I think you'll probably think I'm nuts. If you don't already."

He guffawed. "Maybe it's not even a detriment down here."

I could easily give him that point.

✪

We toyed with the idea of cleaning up the cavern to put it back as we found it. It was a little too surreal to imagine who might be arriving to pick up the dishes—for all the jokes about a hotel underground, I had had time to think about the appearance of our comforts and had come to about the only conclusion I could, and one I didn't want Aaron thinking too much about. There was that table that had stayed warm, and the fresh food. Not to mention the sheer bulk of the stuff in that room. I had a sneaking suspicion that if I lifted the blankets where we'd slept last night, I'd find one of Hunt's pentagrams chalked there with the greasy leavings of candles at its points.

Who knew? Maybe for Hunt, cleaning up the mess was just a matter of a few words. And possibly, a few drops of blood. *There's no great magic without blood,* he'd told me. I'd seen it. If he had magicked up some bedding and a hot meal for me and Aaron, was that even big magic? Was it something he could do without even breaking a sweat—or someone's skin?

I didn't know if there was some kind of prohibition against using his own blood in one of his spells. I didn't know much, in fact. Was it just inadvisable, because blood-loss tends to make one, well, light-headed? Or did the magician and the blood-donor, willing or no, have to be two different people? The more I knew, the more I realized I hadn't even scratched the surface of Hunt's most basic actions.

I wondered if I should take the alarm clock; I didn't have a cell phone like Aaron and it might be useful to know the time. I grabbed it off the shelf, meaning to check the time. Instead, I checked the date. October 26. It was, and would be for a few more hours at least, my birthday.

That stopped me for a moment. How ridiculous and pathetic was it that a girl doesn't even realize it's her birthday until she accidentally notices the date walking by a calendar? How insane and sad is it that a girl's mother hasn't so much as mentioned the event in the days or weeks leading up to it? And how much worse, really, if the birthday in question is her so-called sweet sixteenth?

It was crap; I thought I'd already dealt with this disappointment the night before. Yes, Jan could be a terrible, unaware mother. Yes, I'd kind of cried about it already. Yes, there were more reasons than usual for my emotions to be in flux, with Aaron half-undressing me and nuzzling my neck all night. I was purposely telling myself my own recent history in the most unflattering light possible. Perversion again; I *wanted* to make myself cry. Only then, I seemed to think, could I get myself past what I was feeling.

This was just about the most... I didn't even have a word for how I was feeling. Betrayed? Abandoned? Just plain let down? Remembering Harrison and his smarmy admonition in kitchen that morning to take care of Jan—that really took the cake. I was even happier with myself that I hadn't taken the time that morning to comfort Jan in her meltdown. Of course, it was just another unavoidable, focus-pulling moment that put poor old Maggie out of the frame. It was probably the best possible thing for me to be lost forever underground in some Alterna-Toronto, because obviously the few and far-between benefits of being a teenager, like someone to care you'd just turned sixteen, were not about to be visited on sad, lonely me.

I kept my face away from Aaron's until I had my emotions under control. Fortunately, Aaron was apparently oblivious as he dressed, went through his backpack checking and rechecking his supplies against Hunt's list, and finally looking around the cave for anything that might prove useful in our unknown future. Well, good. Let one of us imagine we were in some control of what we were headed toward.

"Mags?" Aaron had finished pushing things around and folding things to his satisfaction, I guessed. I slipped the travel clock into my pocket, since unlike Aaron I had no watch, and nodded my readiness. For once, I hadn't cried, or even come close. Maybe that was progress.

The other shock was how completely I'd lost track of time. When I looked at the travel clock as I put it away, I was shocked to see it was nearly eight at night. We'd slept for hours and hours. And all the time we'd slept, Jason was a prisoner.

Before we lit out, Aaron at last showed me the page Bob had given him, which was really no big deal since we'd done everything it said already. Back in the tunnel, on the raised walkway, there was nowhere to go but ahead, and no way to do it but one step at a time.

We shouldered our packs, and set out.

Soon, it was apparent that the blue glow that had lit Bob's terminus cavern was emanating from the walls around us. At first, it was just a speck of blue here and there, but as we continued, more and more of the surface was covered with whatever it was that made its own light. Aaron shut off the flashlight and we continued by the glow.

The further we went, the more selfish I felt about being such a baby about my birthday.

"Aaron?" I said finally, after we'd walked a long time in silence. "I was thinking. About those other people, the bodies. Mrs. Sanchez." She was the only one whose name I remembered. What a crime, that people had died because of something I was involved with, and I didn't even do them the dignity of remembering their names. "Mrs. Sanchez's feet, actually. I don't think this—whatever it is—thing—I don't think it cares about its host body at all. Doesn't feed them, give them water. I mean, it walked the soles of her feet right off. Like not only didn't it care, but it didn't feel the effects itself. So it might not have even thought about it."

"Yeah," he said, and shivered, then unzipped his pack as he walked and handed me a bottle of water.

I felt almost guilty taking it. "That's why we have to get to Jason," I said. "If it cares so little about the body it's *in*, how much less would it care about him?"

Aaron nodded solemnly. "I take your point. But we can only get there as fast as we get there."

"If Hunt's even sending us to him," I said, at last voicing the deepest fear I was holding back. "What if he's sending us on this wild goose chase on purpose, to keep us *away* from Jason? What if he only sent us here because he's targeting Rae, or Suzanne? Or Tamblyn. His brother. Maybe there's some score there to be settled we don't even know about."

Aaron stopped and looked at me sharply. "I know you said they were brothers, but you didn't say much about their relationship."

I took a long breath, longer than I meant to, and Aaron filled the silence. "Let me guess—you'll tell me once we get out of here."

"I know him because he helped get me out the last time," I blurted. "You know I told you I used to be able to... do magic? Well, I used him, cut him, the last time. He let me. But he didn't remember."

I was caught in a whirlwind of thoughts. What was stepping over the line? What part of this story could I tell, and still feel I was protecting Jason, Aaron, and the others? What had I already blithely said, without any consideration, pretending that I was just being as clever as Hunt, to dole out bits of the truth for the sake of controlling the situation instead of helping others understand? Really, I was just leaking like a colander. *My brain is like a sieve...*

"I've said too much, way too much. I wasn't supposed to say anything." My voice was taking on an almost hysterical pitch. This was great—next thing I'd be hyperventilating and fainting. Aaron deserved to know what he wanted to know, but anything more I told him would break that promise I'd made, the promise not to let those who'd shared my time in Char's catacombs even know what they'd suffered.

If I told, what was the point of having kept the secret? And more, what was the point of giving up the one thing that had ever made me feel whole, in the service of being able to keep that secret? Because if Aaron and the others knew, there was no reason for me to have given up my power. No reason to have suffered alone and silent. No reason to have spent the last three years tormenting myself with questions of what might have been.

And in its place would be a big blank slate of possibilities. I might have stayed friends with Jason, become better friends with Aaron sooner. I could have seen Peter. Scott would have understood why I seemed so weird.

My mom would know her house had burned.

But maybe, maybe it wouldn't have been good anyhow. Maybe Aaron and Jason wouldn't have been interested in my friendship once we got back to school. Maybe the trauma of the time below ground would have soured them on me, made them afraid of me even. They would have known the full extent of what I could do. *Once upon a time, I could bring the roof down.* In Char's realm, with my powers raging at their apex, I was afraid of myself. Afraid of what I might be able to do. Had I allowed Hunt to convince me into my final act as much to run away from myself as to benefit my friends?

"Maggie?" Aaron asked. He'd taken the water bottle back, and had his hand on my arm. I hadn't even felt him put it there. Great—now I was zoning out into catatonia.

"Seriously, Aaron," I said. "This isn't the time for all that. I thought we were here for Jason."

And, ignoring the stung expression in his eyes, I shook off his hand and stalked ahead down the tunnel.

It began twisting and turning soon after, and there were several offshoots leading away and into the dark. But the blue lights were only in the main thoroughfare, so we continued on in the way of easiest access. We didn't talk.

I couldn't believe how easy it was for me to turn into a class-A total bitch. And to be a horrible, catty person to just about the only human being in my life who I believed liked me even though he knew something about the real Maggie Stuart.

That was just it, though, wasn't it? I barely knew him, although what I did know I liked. But he knew me from the shadow I'd coaxed into existence to do my dealings in the world for me. Who *was* the real Maggie Stuart? Had she been left behind in Char's throne room, on the bluff above his ruined kingdom? Had she leaked out with my blood when Char's power sheared through my shoulder?

I couldn't help but be the person made by my choices and my

experiences, but who was that? Which of the Maggies I was and had been did Aaron like? And would he run from the others?

I was glad he seemed happy to trail behind me at a bit of a distance. That let me cry without him seeing the tears rolling down my cheeks. So much for the new Stoic Maggie.

Where was Hunt? Would he suddenly appear? We had everything the Thurl-apparition had told us to bring—provided we really were heading toward Jason and his captor. *Your man. Bring your man.* Did the creature mean Aaron after all? Did it know we would grow this close... or at least as close as we'd been a few hours ago?

No, it had to mean Jason. We had the ring, the book. We had to be moving closer to Jason.

And I had to do something to heal the rift I'd torn between me and Aaron. I would show him the ring. I'd let him know that it was an object of power, that we had two magical items with us, two advantages.

And then, with no warning, something sucked all the air out of the tunnel.

It was like a fire backdraft, a huge inhalation that literally tore the air out of my lungs and the strength from my legs. Both Aaron and I went down, he slipping slightly off the walkway into the ever-present ditch to one side.

I couldn't even gasp; there was nothing left in my lungs. All I could do was form his name soundlessly and reach toward him.

The glass of one of his lenses had cracked clear across. Extreme change in pressure. I felt as if every cell in my body was straining outwards into the sudden vacuum. My head ached like a bolt had been driven straight through it.

There was an enormous *POP* sound, and then a chugging noise, like the approach of a gargantuan freight train. Just as suddenly as the air had vanished, it was back. The chugging crested to an unbearable volume, then was gone. I gulped, greedy and raw. My lungs filled like a balloon had exploded inside them. The oxygen rush was painfully intense. Instead of being able to get to my knees even, the pressure of all that air knocked me flat on my back. I had never thought for a moment before in my life of the sheer weight of the atmosphere around me. *Dry drowning,* I thought. I knew it was an interrogation technique, to put a cloth over someone's face and pour water over it until their oxygen-starved body cried out that it was dying.

This was dry-drowning for real, breathing into nothing, like the emptiness of space. But it was over now. I crawled to Aaron and helped him out of the ditch. He was crying too now, so I guessed he'd never know I had started before the air was sucked out of the tunnel.

"Are you okay?" I managed in a whisper. He put his hands on my shoulders and we knelt together for a few long minutes, just breathing and feeling each other's strength return.

Then I was crying again for real, and moved closer into Aaron's embrace. "Don't ever let me get away with being a total bitch again, okay?" I cried. "Please. Make me a better person. Please."

He hugged me close, holding my head below his chin. "You do realize you're asking a teenage boy, right?" he said.

I could tell by his tone he was trying to lighten the mood, and I was almost unbearably grateful. "What, you're just an average teenage boy, Scribner? Since when?"

He laughed, more gently than his you-tickled-me guffaw. "You have a point. But don't expect me to be a saint. And I *never* said 'average.'" He ran a hand across my shoulder blades, and I felt a very un-Maggie-like thrill. But he didn't go any further—not that it was at all the time or place for anything but stupefying fear, of course. . .

We helped each other up, and he shouldered his pack again, wearily. "So. What was that, Maggie?"

"Someone opened the airlock," I suggested. And we both intoned together, "*In space, no one can hear you scream.*"

I laughed. "Sci fi junkie?"

"All-round culture whore," he corrected sternly. "Are we not taking this seriously enough?"

It was my turn to laugh. "Take your pick, Scribner. Go to our certain doom with long faces and shaky legs, or grin like we're the band on the Titanic."

"What happened to the whole heroic *saving Jason* deal?"

"Limited time offer," I said. "I think the *air sucked out of the world* bit was us passing the expiry date."

"You really are a barrel of laughs, aren't you, Stuart?" He grinned broadly, shook his head at the wonder of it all, and gave me a short bow. "Shall we?"

"Certain doom waits for no man," I said, and we went on.

Before we got more than a few steps, a laugh rang out, filling the tunnel. It was nasty and calculating; if it was a color, it would have been some unimaginable combination of chartreuse and puce. *Or, I realized, watery grey green.*

It was the laugh that went with those eyes, the ones that had appeared on my painting while I was off trying to save the world and managing only to screw it up more. It was *it*.

The tunnel went black.

Aaron scrambled for his flashlight, but before he could turn it on, the tunnel was filled with a new kind of light. Not clean and blue this time, now it was reddish and dim, dancing like it came from flames trying to consume the world.

Aaron turned to me. "You think we're in the middle of someone's big budget Broadway production?" he asked. He zipped the pack closed, but kept the flashlight out. I noticed him check its contents carefully before he did it up again.

"Book still there?" I asked, just to make sure. I didn't want it getting away from us again.

"Got it," he confirmed.

"Aaron. . ." I reached into my pocket and held out the ring to him. "Bob gave me this when we were back at the other tunnels, when he gave you Hunt's note."

"I don't understand," he said, taking it and turning it over in his fingers. "Isn't this the ring you showed me before? At Jason's?"

"It was stolen," I said, "in the subway. You remember I said I was caught in a cave-in?" Or maybe I'd only told Rae. Still, he was nodding, so he'd heard either from me or from her. "There was a. . . thing. One of those things, the one that appeared to me looking like my drafting teacher. It told me to come to it, to bring the book, my bauble. . ." I pointed to the ring ". . .and my man."

He smiled faintly. "Recipe for danger? Or salvation?"

"I don't know. But it's all we have. You, me, the ring, and the book."

"I'm your man, then?" he asked, but I didn't reply.

He reached into his pocket, still cupping the ring in his other hand. This time, it was the other paper he handed me, Hunt's map, the one I'd never looked at. "Check the bottom right corner," he said.

I unfolded the page, and traced with my finger a small scribble in the corner in question. "Oh my god," I said. Here, Hunt had indulged in a little rebus mathematics. There was a crude picture of a book and ring linked by a plus sign. After them was an equals sign, followed by a set of prison bars. "Book plus ring equals prison?" I said.

"You got more out of it than I did," he said. "I thought it might just be random, but I didn't really think to put the drawings together with our... resources."

He handed the ring back and I put it back into my pocket. As I did, I felt the remains of the gold chain I'd worn it on before it was stolen, down in the depths of the pocket. I wondered about finding a way to fix the chain to keep the ring handy.

"Aaron, you don't have a paper clip, do you?"

He dug in the front pocket of his backpack, the same one he used for school. I figured the odds were okay that *something* useful might have got stuck in the corners of the bag. His fingers emerged with something even better—a twist tie.

"Yeah, my mom still packs my lunches," he said, faking a tough-guy voice. "You wanna make something of it?"

I stripped the tie down to bare wire, and rigged the ring to the chain. Aaron fastened it around my neck. I felt better with its weight against my breastbone, like it had been for those weeks through the autumn after I'd finally made the trip to the bank. It felt good, felt like a sign that I was actually doing something, taking the lead, instead of just trailing around after Hunt.

The red lights danced like demonic fireflies around us and over Aaron's face. He was gazing at me as if by putting on the ring and chain, I'd turned into someone or something else. "What?" I said.

"You look... stronger," he said. "I think we're ready."

He grabbed my hands between his and squeezed. "This is it," he said.

From the point where the red lights had begun, the tunnel widened and broadened, and twisted more and more. Eventually, we were progressing downwards at about the maximum grade we could comfortably walk, in an almost corkscrew. It made me think of spiral staircases. I hated spiral staircases.

Aaron and I walked side by side, so we arrived together at the point the tunnel ended entirely and opened into a black cavern. The red lights played only a few feet into it, and it was getting chilly. It didn't feel like it was very big, but most of it was hidden in blackness.

"Maggie..." said Aaron quietly. He'd turned the flashlight on again, and the beam had picked out a crumpled shape near the edge of the red light. It smelled bad, like an unimaginably foul kitchen garbage can mixed with a thousand campground outhouses. My nose picked out the distinctive odor of maggoty fly-spawn.

He held his sleeve over his nose and went closer.

"I think we found that TTC worker," he said. The flashlight glinted off the reflective tape of the man's vest. He was shoeless, and the bottoms of his feet were ragged and torn.

"Oh god," I breathed. I knelt, and found a woman's smart purse and briefcase, and a pair of alligator high heels. "I think it has a new body," I said. I prodded the pumps with a finger. "I'm starting to think it just doesn't like shoes. Maybe it's as simple as that. . ."

Aaron shrugged. "As good a guess as any. But I think you're right. It doesn't care about its hosts, at all. Let's find Jason."

Then he straightened suddenly. At the same moment, I became aware, as he had, that we were not alone. Subtly, the red light had spread to include more of the cavern, and a figure was standing not far from us, half-silhouetted by the light.

Even with the dead body right beside us, I expected Hunt, so my surprise was complete. It was a woman, tall and elegant, and well-dressed like a high-stakes commodities broker teleported into the underworld. She had light brown hair with blond highlights, and looked about forty. . . but what stunned me was her face. I realized in that first moment I had found the original of those evil green eyes that had floated their milky way at me out of a painting I had not been responsible for finishing. How had it known? Had it somehow chosen this body months ago, so that it could know to lift the eyes from one of my pictures and plant them in another? Had it chosen its last victim just because of her eyes?

Had it screwed with my memories so much that I only *thought* I'd painted that original picture? After the archive, what could I ever believe I knew for certain?

"Well, you've arrived at last," she said, and paused just an instant before continuing: "Welcome, Aaron."

I stared. Aaron's fists clenched, and he tensed for battle like any good action hero. "Where's my friend Jason?" he demanded. He sounded good. Strong and decisive.

All I could add was, "Yeah!"

*Weak, Mags,* I thought. *Can't you think of anything else to say in defense of your constantly falling status in this adventure?* I also noted his use of the word "my" instead of "our." I felt like the earth had shifted again, like it did so often with anything reeking of Hunt, and I had been relegated to a supporting role.

"Aaron," I cautioned, putting my hand on his arm. "It's definitely one of those things. Look at her eyes."

The red gleam was there, somewhere in the middle of the green, but I wondered if Aaron would see it clearly enough to believe me.

"Yeah," he said. "I know."

I saw an amused flicker go through the sly green eyes of the woman in front of us, and for a moment, as Aaron also turned to me, her gaze met mine. There were volumes in that glance. What was in those green eyes? Amusement, disdain. She was dismissing me to Aaron and communicating something entirely contrary to me.

The woman stepped back further. I was aware again of the coolness of the air around us. She'd been here for some time. The place where she had obviously been waiting for us was littered with cigarette butts and spent matches. Heat, I wondered, as much as addiction?

I saw her bare feet, stockings that had run in a dozen places worn right through at the bottom. Like I'd suggested, it seemed like her ditching of this body's shoes might just be personal preference.

She watched us calmly as Aaron pulled a piece of paper out of his pocket and unfolded it. I took it. It was a color photocopy of the painting I had done.

"Hunt gave this to me," he said. "He said I would know her by her eyes."

Something inside me dropped about twenty storeys. I felt completely betrayed now. How could I ask Aaron why he had said nothing about the picture, when he would only tell me he didn't think it was all that important? More to the point, when had Hunt *been in my house*?

"Mr. Scribner," said the woman, a bit impatient. "You've come all this way. Are you ready to go the final steps?"

He nodded grimly, and peeled my fingers from their grip on his arm. "Maggie. I want you to be safe. You wait here."

"No!" I said. "Don't be dumb, Aaron. *We* came all this way. Not just you. I'm going to see it through just like you."

I wanted to add, *I'm just as important as you,* but I couldn't. Not with her there, a look of amusement spreading on her face.

Then, creeping into my head, I heard her voice. Just like Char used to speak to me, it seemed like proof that she knew more about me than she was letting on. This was what I had seen in her eyes before. The knowledge of what I'd been to Char, once upon a long-ago time.

*What A Little Whiner You Are, Miss Marguerite,* she said. *Is This The Chosen Consort Of The Prince Of Demons? Are You Really As Pathetic As You Seem?*

*No*—she warned as I opened my mouth to answer. *You Keep Quiet, Little Girl. Don't Be More Pitiful Than You Already Are.*

And sad as it seemed, I agreed with her. Aaron followed her as she walked sinuously ahead into the next unknown, and I, feeling like a kicked dog, trailed along miserably.

Soon, the tunnel began to descend again, and shortly thereafter, it turned a sharp corner and dead-ended in a cavern, the depths lost in inky blackness. This time at least, I was spared anything that could have reminded me of Char's palace under the quarry. This. . . cave, I supposed, was as natural as could be. The sound of limestone drips from the ceiling echoed hollowly in the wide space. Stalactites and stalagmites showed that time had passed uninterrupted here for a long age. It was cool, and the air was moist.

The woman shivered. "Do you see?" she said to Aaron.

He nodded. "You stay here, because the others won't look where it isn't hot. That's why you're in that body."

She smiled at Aaron, as if he had won a prize she badly wanted him to have. "Good boy. So smart. And this body is nearly done. Do you want to see my next one?"

She moved with a quick, feral grace behind a lump of curved limestone, and emerged dragging Jason Lawson. He was bound and gagged, looking completely miserable. His hair was matted with dried blood and his expression was tired, defeated. He looked barely conscious.

"Jason," Aaron breathed.

She laughed. "He will make such a nice home, don't you think? Strong, this one. I could live in him for years before I use him up."

Aaron sprang forward, and she raised a hand, indolently, as if his action hardly mattered. Even I who had seen this kind of thing—hell, had *done* this kind of thing once upon a time—flinched at the shock of seeing him batted him to the ground. Aaron was stunned, understandably; me, she gave barely a glance. She hadn't touched him, just waved a hand at him.

But this, actually, gave me hope. She had thrown off his balance, but Char had been capable of so much more. If he'd been here, Aaron would have been pinned to the rock and I would have joined him. So maybe she wasn't all that powerful. And even Char, I remembered, had used technology to keep his palace lit, and little Peter's song to work longer enchantments to freeze people where they stood or render them insensible.

"Oh, Mr. Scribner," she said. "I really don't mean to mock you, but how you amuse me! Do you want him back? Why don't you try to make a deal, instead of fooling yourself that force will make me release him?"

"Aaron," I said. "You know what she wants."

The woman turned in my direction, as if she was only seeing me now for the first time. "Who's your little friend, Aaron?" she said. "Did you bring me an alternative?"

Aaron pulled the straps of his backpack closer to his chest protectively. If she hadn't known where the book was before, she certainly did now. The ring was part of the deal, but let her think he had them both for now.

She smiled again, closing her eyes lazily as if with extreme contentment. "Yes, Aaron. I want the book. That's my price." She didn't mention the ring either, or my *man*. Yes, I was dealing with something at least as devious as Hunt himself. Great.

"But why?" Aaron was fixated now on Jason's lax face. He had shown no signs of recognition or vigor since she had revealed him to us, just kept blinking his eyes and staring blindly into space. Had she given him anything to eat or drink? Had he been lying here in the cold and damp since he'd vanished on Friday?

"*But why*?" she imitated. "Isn't it obvious? I need you to release the rest of us."

The temperature in the cave seemed to drop suddenly. "The rest of you?" said Aaron.

"All of us, imprisoned years ago by a cruel warlord. We thought ourselves doomed to eternal imprisonment. You don't know what it is to languish, without any chance of escape, in a prison of mind and magic. Your little ritual cracked the prison, but only a few of us were strong enough to resist when the charm was dispersed."

By me, but no kudos there from either her or Aaron. Maybe he'd forgotten my actions on the first day of school. It appeared, if she could be trusted, that I had stopped a lot more than a ritual. If they'd continued, would *all* the creatures in that prison have been released? Was Char their jailor? And what, exactly, would have been unleashed if I hadn't been present that day? I figured it would have been a lot more than dogs and squirrels we'd have had to worry about.

Aaron glanced at me. "And what about this warlord?"

"He died," she said, sighing. "But we were not released by his death. Only the book can free us, and only you can read the book."

I put my hand on Aaron's arm again. "She's bullshitting you, Scrib," I said. "No goddamn way. It's just Hebrew."

"Yes, but Aaron has the power to make the magic work," said the woman, frowning at my interruption.

"Bullshit again. Words, diagrams, chalk and blood. That's what it takes. Why didn't you get old greedy-guts Hunt to—"

Something shut me up, and I dove feverishly into my mind to sort it out. Why hadn't Hunt offered to read the spells for her and release her friends? I saw that I'd been half-convinced, even if I hadn't admitted it to myself, that somehow Hunt was actually in league with her and her kind, no matter how he'd implied the contrary.

Not only that, but Hunt might be lurking in the blackness beyond her, but now I rather thought he'd not come at all. Maybe he'd watched us pass from inside one of those black tunnels along the way. Maybe he was feeding us to the lions, and that had been his plan all along.

But then, Hunt hadn't had the book. I saw it now, or at least I thought I did. He'd never had it. Whatever force had put the book into the Scribner's library had not been him. Who had placed it for Aaron to find, and manipulated Jason and the others to find the right page to start the ball rolling? I was missing so many vital parts of the equation. The equation...

*Ring plus book equals prison.* Char's creation of the original prison in which she and the others had been held captive? *Ring plus book plus Aaron equals. . .what? Ring plus book plus Maggie. Ring plus book plus Jason. . .*

"What. . ." I said slowly, ". . .do you get out of the deal? If you want us to believe you're some kind of supernatural altruist, you can just screw off and go bullshit some other gullible kids."

Aaron hissed at me, "Maggie, what are you doing?"

But she seemed amused. "What a brave little girl you brought me, Aaron. Maybe I should take her for my new home, and give you back your Mr. Lawson."

"You're not getting either of them!" shouted Aaron. "Answer Maggie's question, or I dump the book."

That's when I noticed what Aaron had, I supposed, been aware of from the first. In the centre of the chamber, half-hidden from where I stood by pancake-batter piles of limestone, was a hole. It was only about twice the distance across as the one we'd climbed down to reach the first subway tunnel, maybe a meter and a half in total diameter, but it was far more sinister. It was also utterly black. Aaron bent and picked up a pebble from the floor, and pitched it into the hole. There was no sound, no echo of rock hitting bottom. Just that ominous silence.

There had been an extra threat here all along that Aaron had understood, and I had missed. When she had brought Jason out into view, she had also put him within shoving distance of the hole, but on the far side from us where we'd have to circumnavigate it to get to him. No wonder Aaron wanted to make a deal.

But his threat, to throw the book down the pit, seemed to counterbalance the potential she had set up. I blessed him silently. It seemed like a deadlock.

And then, I heard a familiar tuneless whistle. The woman smiled. Aaron tensed. I felt my skin shrink a couple of sizes, felt like I was down to my underwear again. With those reactions as his fanfare, Hunt arrived.

He came striding casually into the chamber like a chief executive entering a boardroom where his word was law, and nothing of importance could be done before he arrived.

"Hello, all," he said. "Not too late for the fun, am I?"

"Hunt. . ." I warned. I didn't want any other factors thrown into the already volatile mix, especially not one as uncertain as Mr. Hunt.

"Don't worry, Aaron," he said, ignoring me completely. "The Calvary is here."

"Don't you mean 'cavalry'?" Aaron said.

"Whatever." Hunt grinned. "Maggie Stuart, I'm a little surprised to see you here."

Aaron shot me a look that said, *what's your deal with this guy?* Damn Hunt, damn the demon. Damn Char for making all this possible.

"You found the book, Scribner?" said Hunt.

Aaron removed his backpack and held it protectively in his arms. "Yeah. You know how to get rid of her?"

Hunt laughed. "Get rid of it? Do you have any idea why it wants to release those thugs it calls its *friends?*"

This was exactly what I'd been trying to discover before, but Aaron seemed to treat it like a new and brilliant question. "No. I was hoping to find out."

"Why don't we ask it?"

The woman seemed annoyed at Hunt's stripping her of a sexual identity, despite the fact she'd been talking happily about possessing Jason a short time before. "Why don't we ask the Hunter why he's here instead? Do you think he does anything without gain?"

"Profit?" I spat. "Is that what it's all about?"

"Why not?" said Hunt. "Money's the great engine, and power is the fuel. How much were you going to charge your fellow felons for their release from bondage?"

She shrugged, grinning. "We'll see what the market bears," she said. "But I think I can ask the world, and get it too."

Hunt moved quickly then, and Aaron didn't see him coming. Before I knew what was happening, Hunt had his signature rusty stiletto at Aaron's throat, and Aaron's arm pinned behind his back. In the hand that pinned my friend, Hunt had also grabbed the straps of the backpack.

"What do you think the boy will bear?" he said. "How about some more cutting remarks? And then we can get down to the real business."

"Hunt, what are you doing?" I cried, but my voice was weak and seemed to get lost in the room. Was it a mistake to have come with Aaron? Maybe I could have let him go alone, and followed with Tamblyn in tow. . . But what more could I have done anywhere else? Coming out of this whole had begun to seem impossible.

I realized now that we'd never talked, not for a single moment, about how we'd free Jason. Not for a moment about anything concrete we could do to beat this thing standing in front of us. All we'd done was put ourselves into the fire without an exit strategy or any kind of plan.

I saw the form of the woman holding Jason shift and become indistinct before she solidified again. *What was that?* I thought that, once inside someone, she would have a solid, real form. Maybe not. Maybe she. . . I don't know, liquified the insides of her host, until she sloughed off what was left of the meat and moved on. *Maybe,* I prayed, *she was losing control of her current body.* Would she evaporate like the apparitions of Aaron and Mr. Thurl had? Or was she a far more complex kind of creature?

Up on the surface, in Westbrook, around town, how many more of them were left? Would what we did here end this, or was there still more to do?

Aaron's grunt of discomfort brought me back to the moment. He had twisted himself in Hunt's arms, but couldn't get away from the older man's strong grip. I'd seen Hunt do one-armed push-ups to embarrass our public school class, so I figured Aaron wasn't going anywhere. "Let me. . . go if you want me to. . ."

". . .Do what, Mr. Scribner?" said Hunt, squeezing him until he groaned. "Say the words that will release a million demons from a bondage placed upon them a thousand years ago? Release, in other words, a million malicious creatures on the world, each one as mad as hell? Do you know the story of the fisherman and the genie? Maggie?"

I did. "The genie was imprisoned for centuries. For the first while, he was going to reward anyone who released him. But when the fisherman finally dredged him up and popped the cork on the bottle, the genie was so pissed all he would offer the fisherman was his choice of how he'd be executed on the spot."

The woman laughed, the sound bouncing around the walls of the cavern.

Hunt laughed too, but shorter and more caustically. "The thing she isn't telling you," he said, "is that the book won't do it."

And with that, he lifted the knife away from Aaron's throat and brought down the hilt of it hard on his skull. Aaron slumped to the ground.

I rushed toward him but Hunt warned me back with the knife. "He's fine, Mags. He's unconscious, that's it."

The woman was standing over the prone form of Jason Lawson. I hadn't see her do anything, but she reassured me, "This one is the same. Unconscious." Then she added, looking straight at me with an expression of hatred and utter contempt, "Princess."

My blood went cold.

"Heir to power, Mags," said Hunt. "Even if you can't use it yourself anymore."

"You hold the key," said the woman, stepping across Jason's body, "and they are the price."

I looked at the still bodies of Jason and Aaron, remembering the feeling of horror the other time I had seen them like this, when I had blasted them both into unconsciousness while trying to escape Char's palace. "You bastards." My whole body felt weak and unsteady. "Why? I have nothing to offer you. I have no power. I can't even read the damn book."

Hunt waved ambiguously toward me. "The book is only part of it."

I finally saw what he was indicating. "The ring," I said. "Aria's ring."

"Remember back in Char's realm," Hunt said. "When you and Jason reached out toward each other to escape? Did you ever figure out why that happened? Or why Jason was the only one who could reach you during the last rite?"

I puzzled it through. "He told me about the glowing ball Char tossed him. It burned Aaron's hands, but when it came to him, it went totally dead."

*Ring plus book plus Jason equals no prison.* Hunt, and the woman, were manipulating me again. They didn't need me. I was just a pawn. They were flattering me now to keep me off balance. What she really wanted was for Jason to hold the ring, and give her the power to release whatever Char had imprisoned a millennia ago. It was all about the games. Misdirection. Keep my ego firmly involved with my own importance, and ignore the real playing field. *Book plus ring...*

"Jason's a *nadir*," said Hunt, "a person who's to a certain extent dead to magic. That's why you were able to do what you did. By holding his hand and using your power, you created a kind of short circuit."

"But I have no power now," I said. "There's nothing for Jason to resist."

And Hunt's eyes fell on me again.

"Give it to me," said the woman. Hunt crossed the short distance between us, and grabbed the chain around my neck, pulling the ring out from its safe haven under my hoodie. He untwisted the tie I'd used to attach it to the chain, and held it up in the flickering red light. Then he grinned, shark-like, and shoved it onto my hand. With horror, I saw Arabella's ring, the talisman which she had used to kill her own brother, sparkling on my finger with more than the light in the room.

"Hunt, don't do this," I pleaded.

"Falling on deaf ears, Mags," he said. "Like you said, what can you offer me?"

Something else penetrated into my whirling mind. "I thought you didn't remember all that stuff in Char's palace. The stuff with Jason and Aaron, I just told you that they were there with me. I didn't tell you anything that specific."

He smiled, and it was the cruelest expression he could muster, I felt sure. "What do you think I was doing with your little love when I had those long talks with him about the situation? Did you ever actually think to ask, or did you just assume it wouldn't be as interesting as anything you already knew?"

I knew an important jab from Hunt, even if it felt more like hooked bait. "What did you talk about?"

Hunt came close. He smelled like smoke from a summer bonfire. "Aaron won't remember. But he may remember letting me... hypnotize him."

I knew about that. Aaron had told me. But how much more could he find out than Aaron would have been willing to tell him in any case?

He leaned closer. "Blood trance, Mags. Did I ever teach you about blood trance, in those famous fond memories of yours? Of course, I could only find out what Scribner remembered, nothing of your experiences..."

"He doesn't remember." I was adamant; I had to be. "I erased everything."

"You buried everything."

Tears formed in the corners of my eyes. "Jan... I mean my mom. She remembers, just a little, something anyhow. I thought it was just a fluke. But if the others can too..."

And Hunt had trespassed on that sacred territory too, into the place I thought I was forever locked out of, into my historic friendship with Aaron.

"And you let him stay ignorant?"

Hunt laughed. "Mr. Scribner's ignorance or intelligence is his own affair," he said, as if it was a particularly witty comment. "I neither decreased it nor returned it to him. It's a darling situation, dear. Such a lonely little girl."

"Such a lonely little girl." The woman glided up to my shoulder. I had almost forgotten she was there. "And you're mine."

I rounded on her, fire in my gut. I had heard much the same line from Char. "I'm nobody's possession," I said. "And nobody uses me."

I broke away from the two of them, the devious duo, and made a great leap over the deadly pit. The floor was slippery wet as I came down, and I lost my footing. I slid a terrifying couple of feet right toward the pit before I could stop myself.

"Maggie. . ." Hunt's tone was teacher-cautionary, but I thought I could detect more of a note of concern than before.

"Little girl—"

"Shut up!" I screamed. "And stop being so goddamn condescending, both of you. I'm not afraid to. . ." And I looked at the slumped forms of the two boys who were again my friends, and I realized there was actually a lot I would do to save them.

"Miss Stuart." The demon woman sounded too smooth now, just as insincere as ever. "I shall reward you as you deserve."

"I think I had a fortune cookie like that once," I said. "You will achieve what you deserve in life. I didn't like it then either. The way I figure, any double-edged sword is going to do at least as much damage to me as you."

She placed a hand on a hip and looked sideways at Hunt, as if to say, *You deal with her.*

Hunt gave her his best *Who me?* and tapped his fingers impatiently on his thigh. "Maggie Stuart. What a surprise you always manage to be."

I inched closer to the hole. "Can we wrap this up, please? The guys will be coming around any time, I'm sure. Maybe I could spare them the trauma of watching me throw myself down this hole."

They both lunged forward but I put up a hand and had the delight of seeing them stopped dead. It seemed I was right about the limitations of her powers, at least so far as they extended to picking me up or throwing me around. *Nada*, just a purely physical response. Maybe knocking Aaron down before had depleted what power she had. One way or another, I seemed to have an edge. "What? Disappointed in my suicidal tendencies?"

"Your terms." She was not disguising the red in her eyes now. The green had been almost completely swallowed in a maelstrom of crimson.

It was my turn to smile. I said nothing.

Hunt picked up Aaron's backpack, and winked at me. He turned away and started to head out of the cavern.

"Where the heck are you going?" I yelled.

"Got what I came for, Mags," he said. "The book was to be my price all the time. If I'd got it before, I wouldn't have needed the elaborate charade of luring Scribner down here at all."

I pulled myself closer to the hole. "Stay where you goddamn are!"

The woman's attention was now split between Hunt and me. "The book is mine!"

"Book or ring," he said, shrugging. "I don't think even you can hold on to them both in the current situation."

He moved to step over Aaron. He was going to leave me here, at her mercy.

"Hunt!"

"Sorry, darlin', " he said, pausing long enough to grin back in my direction.

Aaron rose up, just as Hunt put one foot over his prone body, and slammed into him with all the force he could muster. Hunt went down, the knife skittering across the stone floor toward the pit. Lacking any sort of weapon, Aaron grabbed for the backpack, wrenched it out of Hunt's hands, and threw himself down on the other man with his full weight.

"Scribner!" Hunt roared, and Aaron hit him hard with the backpack.

The demon-woman shrieked in triumph, and jumped toward me. I rolled onto my back instinctively, and kicked out with both my feet. I saw her eyes, watery green again, open wide in shock, and then she overbalanced. Her feet slid out from under her on the bad footing, and she disappeared into the pit.

I lay back breathing hard, then turned myself over onto hands and knees. Keeping my distance from the pit, I crawled as quickly as I could around it and joined Aaron to add my weight to the groaning Hunt.

"Nice move," Aaron said. "Where'd you learn that?"

"Rape awareness class," I said, "which I failed. Huh. What do teachers know, right?"

Hunt attempted to throw us off. He probably would have succeeded if it had just been Aaron or me holding him down. Between us, we wrestled him to the ground again.

"What do we do with him?" said Aaron. I liked the way I was suddenly in charge again.

With the thing down the pit, and Hunt our only problem, I saw an easy resolution. "Let him go," I said.

"You see, Scribner? She knows the score, this girl." Hunt tried again to sit up, but Aaron refused to move.

"Shut up, Hunt," I said, "unless you're ready to tell us what Aaron and his friends actually did that first day, and what she hoped to accomplish here."

Aaron poked him hard with a knee to add emphasis. I was suddenly glad teenage boys had violent impulses. Might come in handy.

"Okay, okay," Hunt grumbled, but he seemed to be complaining mostly for Aaron's benefit. I bet if I could catch his eye, he'd shoot me a wink. "You, Scribner, and your little friends cracked a very ancient— let's call it a genie's bottle—that held an enormous number of truly nasty creatures rounded up over the millennia by an old King of what you might call an underground world."

"Alterna-city," Aaron stated, but Hunt only laughed.

"Not even close. You haven't got *near* that this time, Scribner." And Aaron wouldn't know that at one time, he had been imprisoned himself in one of its palaces.

"That ring of Maggie's is—well, you can call it the electrified fence around the property. When you used the book, you cast a charm that cracked the bars enough for some of those things to escape, but only at a huge cost to them. That's why only the strongest got through, and most were weakened so much they only lasted a short time before getting drawn back. That's the beauty of the original prison: it pulls its inmates back, irresistibly, unless there's some counterforce of enough potency used. I'd bet that no matter what it tried to imply, it's the only one that figured out how to stick around this long."

Hunt was trying to hide it, but I saw him dart a couple of glances toward the pit. I hoped he was just looking at Jason, but I started to feel uneasiness creeping through me again.

"Aaron," I said, "we should let him up."

"Are you kidding? After what he did?"

"He can't help it," I said. "It's his nature. And we probably wouldn't have ever found Jason without his help."

My unease was growing, especially since Hunt *never* gave away information for free, unless he was playing for time.

"That's not true," Aaron protested. "She needed the ring, right?"

I conceded the point. If it hadn't been for Hunt, she must have been preparing somehow to get us down here. The Thurl-apparition hadn't done more than tantalize. "But there's no way we would have been prepared enough to get him back."

Aaron nodded. "I guess you're right." Grudgingly, he copied me as I moved off Hunt and let the other man stand up.

"Good choice, Mags," said Hunt. He reached for the backpack, but Aaron pulled it out of his reach.

A groan came from behind us, and Aaron, the backpack, and I all rushed over to Jason's side. As a bonus, it took us further from Hunt. "What happened?" said Jason, his hand on his head where a big goose-egg was forming nicely in the center of all that dried blood.

"A lot," said Aaron. "You wanna blow this popsicle stand?"

Jason laughed, much like Aaron did when really amused, in that almost snorting manner, but he sounded really, really weak. "You mean *bust a move* don't you?"

Hearing Suzanne's dumb little expression here, so far below the city, brought tears to my eyes. "By all means," I said. "Let's bust one. Or several."

Hunt was between us and the exit, and somehow he'd managed to retrieve his knife.

"Let me get this straight," he said. "You think you're getting out of here."

I put my hands on my hips. "Yeah. You got a problem with that?"

In reply, he let a smile spread as slow as a stain across his face. "Maggie, Maggie, Maggie. You kids made a good start, but I really hate when students don't finish their work."

I looked in the direction he indicated. From the pit, a strange mist was beginning to emerge.

"Oh crap," said Aaron.

We backed away from the hole.

"You didn't think that was enough to stop her, did you, Mags?" Hunt's face was becoming grim. "So, kids... what say you all get behind me a bit?"

Jason and Aaron complied slower than me. I moved aside like someone had lit a fire under my feet. I knew what it was like when Hunt meant business.

"Oh crap," said Aaron again. The smoke was literally pouring out of the hole now, like a special effect in some cheesy skating show. I saw a glint of those green eyes, tinged with their tell-tale redness, and a gleam of white skin. Traveling up the hole had not been kind to the demon, I guessed. She had definitely lost the body she had been using, and was not stable. More to the point, she was pissed.

Her voice echoed through my head, and this time, since Jason and Aaron slammed their own hands over their ears, I knew we all heard it. Her fury was deafening.

*Worms! Die, Stupid Children. Die A Thousand Deaths!*

Hunt was crouched, running in a low-bent circle around the pit. He had a nub of chalk in his hand, using it to inscribe a solid circle around the opening in the ground. Magic preparation. What was he planning?

Jason stepped back. "This bitch is not getting her hands on me again," he said, and I wondered if he had any inkling of the fate she had in mind for him, or, to be fair, for at least one of us.

"Scribner, the book!" Hunt hollered from the other side of the circle.

*Too Late, Too Late,* the demon howled. *My Comrades Will Be Freeeeee...*

Did that mean she—it had given up on the idea of brokering releases for profit, and just meant to break the walls down entirely? I felt a tugging on my hand, and looked down to see a finger of mist latching itself under the band of Aria's ring.

At the same time, an enormous hand formed itself out of the cloud of swirling smoke and enclosed Jason in a full-body grasp. She was definitely more powerful than she had been in her stolen body, although, I guessed, no longer invisible to her fellow creatures. Hardly something important right now, though. The smoke got thicker and blacker so I could hardly see through it to follow Hunt as he put a final touch to the line he had chalked around the pit—and reached out to grab Aaron.

"No time for permission!" I heard Hunt yell, and I stood frozen in horror as his knife rose and came down—in Aaron's back.

I was screaming now, locked in my stupid tug-of-war with the hook of vapor tugging at the ring around my finger, watching Jason swallowed whole by the smoky form, seeing Aaron slump to the ground with Hunt's knife in his back. Hunt paid him no attention, except to plunge his own hand into the blood seeping from Aaron's wound. My former teacher knelt, one hand bright red, using the other to unzip the backpack and free its precious contents.

I was torn now, between hoping Hunt could save us, and wishing he was at the bottom of the world's deepest pit.

Through the mist, darkly, I saw Hunt set Aaron up with the book on his lap. One of Aaron's hands reached for it, and the other made futile swipes at the knife stuck in his back. "Read, Scribner," I heard Hunt say as the mist began to surround me too, and then Aaron's voice rose through the confusion.

It began weakly, that same strange, guttural chanting that had started this whole misadventure. Slowly, his voice began to gain strength. I heard the demon shriek, not even a human sound now, but something that raked its fingernails through my very marrow. "Maggie!" shouted Hunt, breaking through my horror, "under *no circumstances* let Jason touch that ring!"

"You're releasing the rest of them!" I screamed, trying to warn Aaron to stop, but he kept chanting. Wasn't this just a repetition of the first day of school, cracking Char's prison to let murderous creatures escape? The chamber was filling with a stultifying heat, a sauna in mid-summer. I felt like I was dying, melting away, enclosed in the solidifying mist and its smell of sulphur and fire.

## 40

## The Heart's Filthy Lesson

✪

"Jason!" I screamed. I ran to him, grabbed a foot, all I could reach, and put my whole weight into holding him. The ghostly hand was almost, but not quite, strong enough to lift him and me too into the air. I felt the disorienting sensation of my feet leaving the ground only to bump back down. The smoke itself moved into and through me with absolutely no resistance at all. The only sense it registered with was my sight—but although it obviously worked physically on Jason, neither of us was able to touch it. The slickness of the rocks under my feet gave no purchase, and I would have been flat on my ass a dozen times without my grip on Jason's shoe.

Just how was I supposed to save Jason, and also ensure that he didn't accidentally lay a hand on Aria's ring? Did Hunt assume I would be as cold-blooded as him, cold-blooded enough to allow her to either dash him into the pit or steal his body for her own use?

Jason, for his part, was fighting with all his might against what was just about as substantial as a cloud. It held him with an iron grasp, but he could only disrupt its form with his swinging arms while it remade itself and renewed its pulling.

It *wasn't* trying to get him into the pit, I saw, which was a small mercy. It didn't want to pull him away from me, either. All it was doing was shaking him, as if to disorient him was its primary goal.

I was questioning my second assumption about what she/it might want to do to him as well: if he was this *nadir* Hunt had talked about, wouldn't trying to take him over have as an adverse effect on her as it seemed to on other magic things? No, what she wanted was to get the ring and Jason together, and by trying to save him, I might end up accidentally giving her exactly what she wanted.

As the hand shook Jason, trying to disorient me as well I supposed, I felt my gorge rise and was glad that my last meal had been the burgers before Aaron and I had had our long nap. Otherwise, I would be on the verge of puking. Jason had to be going through much worse; at least I was able to feel like I'd reclaimed my bearings whenever I got my toes onto solid ground.

It might not have been the best time to get any deep thinking done, but I thought I saw it now, the whole equation. Make Aaron (or Hunt, or someone) read the spell that weakened the bars of the prison while Jason, the *nadir,* took out the "electric fence." Neither measure on its own was enough to destroy what Char had put in place, as shown by the non-event of Jason putting on the ring at our "lunch meeting," but together. . . How sadly ironic that the first time I encountered Char's world after his death at my hands would be in the process of annihilating something he had created.

Hunt's chalk circle had started to do something odd and creepy— as if the chalk particles had multiplied a million fold, a rough cylinder of matte white powder was rising from it, creating a kind of screen around the hole. Like with the hand, I wasn't sure just how substantial the barrier was, if it would protect me or Jason from an accidental slide into its depths. What was clear was that it was hampering the smoke-form, which couldn't break its rising boundaries. It looked, actually, like Hunt was trying to cut off the "hand" at its "wrist."

Hunt, I saw, was muttering at least as intently as Aaron, painting in the air with the knife covered in Aaron's blood, returning it to Aaron's back now and then to renew the gore on its blade. I was sobbing freely now; Aaron was stabbed and possibly dying, Jason was in the grip of this creature from the black hole, and I was in no way in charge of anything, not even my own emotions.

"Maggie!" Jason reached down toward me with a grimy hand, giving up on his futile fight against his captor. I stretched my hand out —and saw the ring on my finger. I pulled my hand back like I'd burned it. *Ring plus book. . .*

Suddenly, I was second-guessing everything I had just concluded. *Ring plus book equals prison. Ring plus Jason plus book plus Maggie. . .* Either Hunt had told me to keep the ring from Jason for *our mutual benefit,* or primarily for his own. Or he was working his usual double bluff, trusting only in his own estimation of my character. What was I willing to risk? All our lives, more than that even? What would this thing do with the power that might accrue to it when the ring did. . . whatever it would do in Jason's hands?

Whatever Hunt had in mind, I didn't like the way the odds stood at the moment, not at all. Aaron, bleeding and doing whatever Hunt wanted him to with the words in the book. Jason, hovering in a *very* unnerving way too close to the pit, with only Hunt's chalk-dust circle to protect him from death, if indeed it would. And me, clutching a ring, a second-hand power I could no longer even hope to use. . .

None of us, not me, not Aaron with the book he could read but not understand, not Jason who could resist but not attack, none of us had the power to deal with this thing. None of us, alone or together. I let go of Jason's shoe and rolled clear of the pit. Across it, through a curtain of white chalk, I saw Hunt give a brief nod.

The only force I knew of that exceeded what a mere human could do was whatever happened when Jason encountered something magical. Together, at my old strength, we'd nearly blown ourselves into eternity. *Jason plus ring.* It was the only equation Hunt had given us, and Hunt only told anyone what was needed.

With my free hand, I slid off Arabella's ring and, eyes nearly blinded with tears, shouted to Jason as I threw— "Catch!"

The red stone glinted as the ring arced into the air. How much faith in Jason's athletic prowess had gone into my decision, and how much desperation? How much had my memory of Jason and Aaron in our catacombs prison, both blasted unconscious by the mere touch of my hand to Jason's, how much had that memory held me back from the choice I'd just made?

How much was it twisted residual trust, no matter how misguided, of the man who had been my teacher and mentor before he was my captor and tormentor?

Jason's fingers closed easily on the ring, and in that moment, I felt the opposite of the experience Aaron and I had had in the tunnel when the air had been sucked away. Something heavy and invisible blasted me into the dark back wall of the cavern, bruising every part of me. I saw the smoke hand contract, still clutching Jason but beginning to disperse, sparking, disintegrating like paper in a flame.

"Jason!" I screamed, but soundlessly. *I'd just doomed him,* I thought, trapped as I had been inside the... the circle in the barn. That's what Hunt had seen. *I should not have survived inside that circle in the barn.* That pulling I'd felt was the tug returning the creature I'd dismissed back to its prison, and I should have... *gone with it.*

*As Jason would.*

And Hunt must have known it.

I could hear Aaron's pitch change, the way it had when he had neared the end of the ritual in the gymnasium. What should I do now? Stop him before he intoned the final syllables, or would that be more dangerous than letting him complete the text?

And then, he did just that. It was unmistakable, the tone and the finality. Aaron sank down to his side, spent. Hunt, on the other hand, rose to his feet and said something I couldn't hear for the blood rushing in my ears.

With a hollow *boom*, the cylinder Hunt had been constructing flattened and widened, and became just a little more translucent. It flared into a sphere as if to contain the suddenly enormous weight of the air inside it, and I watched in fascinated horror as the grey-green eyes of the woman-thing appeared in the middle of it. But they weren't alone—

I saw, above the pit, a multitude of horrific faces, each with its own expression of evil, or hatred, or insane malice. They seemed to be completely separate from the smoke holding Jason, coalesced together in a kind of fog made entirely of features that were not quite human. Stunned, horrified, I watched the faces multiply, surrounding the struggling Jason with mouths, eyes, teeth... and they looked very, very angry.

The sphere ballooned and contracted, then ballooned again as the faces multiplied, pushing into the smoke like a colony of rogue cells dividing out of control.

I couldn't move, couldn't press myself away from the wall. I couldn't even turn my head or close my eyes as the things swirling around the woman's eyes grew and bloomed with horrible detail. I saw a tiny speck of red in the white of one of the green eyes blossom into a clot and then burst—and another and another pinprick followed, exploding and bloodying the whites, reddening the iris...

I saw Jason, held only by a weakening tendril of smoke, fly clear and away into the wall, no longer above the black hole and finally out of the danger posed by it, at least. I saw Aaron and Hunt pushed skittering along the floor, Aaron nearly out the opening into the tunnel beyond.

Gasping, hardly able to process the heavy, heavy air, I watched as the grey-green eyes were consumed entirely, washed away in blood.

And then, the chalk shell that Hunt had constructed collapsed in on itself, hanging for a moment in the centre of the circle he had drawn around the hole, zipping with barreling acceleration into a white singularity, accompanied by the chugging freight sound we'd heard before. Bob's ghost train? The sound grew in intensity until I had to press my hands to my ears, trying to tuck my head away from the noise, while the air around us seemed to superheat and drive me further into the stone—

—and it was gone. All of it, sound, heat, light, and hideous glimpses of violence.

The red light that had flickered while the creature lived broke into wisps and was gone as well. And darkness—total, heavy darkness—descended on us all.

In the totality of the blackness, the pressure started to flag, like I was trapped in some gigantic blood-pressure cuff slowly sinking back to normal. My ears popped, and I was able to start breathing normally again, but even so, I could hear nothing.

All light had vanished, and I lay on a cold, wet surface, thinking abstractly that I might actually be dead. It felt like there was cotton stuffing my ears, and I realized I had temporarily lost my hearing only when it started to come back. I heard water dripping, and the steady, low warm sound that had accompanied us since we came underground. That was all. And I could see nothing.

A spear of brilliance cut the dark. In it, I saw first Jason, then Aaron, lying prone. Hunt's voice came out of the gloom from somewhere on the other side of the blinding light.

"That was a close one, kids."

Unlike the heroine I wanted to be, I began to cry.

Jason found me, crawling on his hands and knees, and his strong arms encircled me. "Come on, Mags. You did great."

Jason's hands were shaking; I felt it in his hands as he held on tight. In the cast-off from the flashlight's beam, I examined his head, but the wound looked superficial for all it had bled so much. I myself felt bruised, but nothing seemed to be broken or sprained.

Together, leaning on each other for leverage, Jason and I got to our feet and started to make our way toward the light, toward Hunt and an apparently unconscious Aaron.

"Hold," said Hunt, pressing the flashlight into Jason's hands, directing him to focus it on Aaron. I saw the backpack lying open beside him; that's where the flashlight had come from, I guessed.

"He'll be okay," said Hunt to no one in particular, critically examining the knife in Aaron's back before ripping away both Aaron's shirt and undershirt from around the wound and removing them.

"You knew you were going to do this," I said in wonder, seeing him unpack medical supplies from what he'd told Aaron to bring. These were a little more serious than the ointment and band-aids I'd thought to pack. "You knew you were going to stab him, all along, and you got him to bring the supplies to patch himself up."

Hunt grinned at me, and removed the knife in a smooth motion, his eyes never leaving mine. He replaced the knife with a pad of gauze, holding firmly against the wound before taping it in place. He tore strips from Aaron's shirt and used them to bind the dressing in place.

"Didn't *know*, Mags, just to be fair." He rolled Aaron over and set him down, then punched me lightly in the shoulder. "Thought so, but hey. Might have been you, you know."

Was this supposed to make me feel better, I wondered? Hunt's belief system was, as usual, as far beyond me as the stars.

"Is it gone?" said Jason faintly.

I heard the hoarseness in his voice, and remembered that he'd probably been without warmth, food, or water for well over twenty-four hours. I handed him a water bottle from Aaron's pack, and a couple of granola bars I'd packed for myself and hadn't eaten. Between Aaron and Hunt feeding me, I'd actually done pretty well through this adventure, for sustenance at least. I also took out a long-sleeved shirt Aaron had been wearing earlier for him to put on. When he woke up.

"It's gone," said Hunt. I was glad it hadn't been up left up to me to answer that question.

"For good?" Jason said. "How about the other things from September, from the day we let them out?"

Hunt nodded. "Most of them were gone before. But you never know. . . naw, just kidding. Anything that's left will probably stop making your lives difficult. They'll probably leave town, if they can hold onto their forms. And even if they can, well, you showed enough initiative I doubt they'll take any chances with you or yours."

"Are they still killing people?" I said, hearing the coldness in my voice. The image of the poor TTC worker was in my mind's eye. And whoever loved the business woman, her family or friends, would never even have a body to bury.

"That was a particular nasty iteration, your friend with the green eyes," Hunt said, indicating the hole. "None of the others was strong enough to wear a human. It bent a lot of them to its work, but it was the strongest that got out of your little circle."

Aaron groaned, coming to. I was glad he'd been out for Hunt's triage, so I didn't question how he'd come to be unconscious. We'd have to make sure neither he nor Jason was concussed, after of course we got out of here. . . I rushed forward, forgetting for a moment to be cool and collected. I held myself back from actually hugging him—for one thing, he was shirtless and bare flesh was a little too intimate, at least in front of Hunt and Jason. . . and for another, he was obviously in a hell of a lot of pain.

But he was conscious now, and met my eyes with something like his old levelness.

"Are you. . ." I began. "Hunt, uh, stabbed you. . ."

"But I bandaged you up too. All better." Hunt grinned. He punched Aaron playfully, and I winced as he cried out. Hunt plowed on as if he didn't notice. "That was some really nice incanting, Scribner. You could be a pro someday."

Only I knew that he was saying this for my benefit. *Not for you, Maggie May. Magic is a closed book for you now.* I caught his eye as I handed Aaron the shirt, and knew I was right. How Hunt loved the double meanings.

"What now?" I said, at least as much to ignore the jab as to ask seriously. *Get out of here.* That's what we needed to do.

Hunt looked critically at Jason. "You up for a walk?"

Jason nodded grimly. "I want to get out of here. As soon as possible. And then fall down somewhere warm and soft, and stay there for a very long time." A look of panic crossed his face. "Oh, man, my folks must be freaking."

"I *think* we have that covered," I assured him. "Texts and emails, and Scribner's classic Jason Saunders impersonation on your parents' machine."

I looked at Hunt. "Explain this. What happened?"

From what he'd implied, he himself had been the less-than-willing agent of that particular part of the set-up. Or was that a bald-faced lie?

Hunt sighed, put upon. "You, my young friends, have been participants in a fascinating chess game between a creature of rare power and even rarer capitalistic instincts. It was telling you the truth—it was put into a timeless prison a long, long time ago, along with a multitude of other nasties. By that. . .warlord it mentioned." Not even a glance at me, but then, he didn't have to rub this bit in. Char was its jailor, Char and his vanished wife. Was it done out of some desire for supremacy, or was Char protecting the world? I would never know.

Aaron shifted painfully and pulled the map out of his pocket, handing it to Hunt. "In the corner," he said.

Hunt didn't need to look. "It needed the ring, and it needed Jason. The book it planted in Scribner's house, probably the limit of its ability to reach beyond the walls, and probably through some kind of intermediary. The world has always held those who move between the worlds, often for their own profit." *Yeah*, I thought, *takes one to know them, Hunter.* "Sticking it in front of Scribner and Lawson there wouldn't necessarily have proved an irresistible challenge, so I wouldn't be surprised if there was something of a compulsion tied to it." He smoothed his finger over his little bit of word math. "The warlord used the power of the ring in conjunction with some really fancy arcane frippery later transcribed in this book to seal the gates of the prison. Your nasty friend needed both to unravel what had been done, but it didn't want to undo the seal entirely. To coin a phrase, the others would have to pay to play."

Jason turned to me. "You had the ring."

I nodded but didn't want to expand on the *why* of that circumstance. But I *could* use Hunt the same way he'd so often used me. "Hunt made sure of that."

"Bob!" said Hunt, delightedly. "Gotta love that boy."

I was silent, remembering the sight of Scott's jacket on a pile of City-zen belongings. Was it down to Hunt that Scott Saunders had found his way into Bob's world? And what exactly had he paid for? I didn't think I wanted to air those particular concerns in front of Aaron or Jason.

And I noticed that Hunt was avoiding all mention of Jason's

importance in this little drama. The incantation wouldn't have been enough on its own. The creature had needed Jason to kill the power of the ring long enough for it to gain control over the seal. I knew it, as surely as I knew that I wanted Jason to remain ignorant of his own special nature. He didn't deserve to carry the burden I did, the knowledge of being unbearably different from those around us. He could live happily without ever knowing that he was anathema to magic. After all, what was the likelihood he would ever run into the proof of it?

"Hunt," I said, "you still haven't told me the truth about the book. Or at least, your story keeps changing."

"I told you the truth at least once, Maggie May," he said. "I know, I know. Which time, right? That book is a peach, I'll tell you. Contains a lot of lost knowledge. I have no idea where it was before Scribner found it on the shelf. I only knew about it from references, and legend. As to who put it there, again, you got me. All I can tell you for certain is that if I'd got a hold of it before this little match-up here, you'd probably never have seen me again. Bouncing the book around was to stop me from getting it, and quashing its little scheme."

That I could believe. And without Hunt, without the book. . . There would have been a very different ending to our trip underground. He would have walked away from Westbrook, from Toronto, hell, from *Canada* for all I knew, and never looked back. And Jason, Aaron, and I. . . not to mention Rae and Suzanne. . . What would the creature have done if it couldn't get what it wanted? I saw what it was willing to do when it thought it was on a path to success, and figured we'd only seen a hint of its capacity for fury. Worse, what would it have done if it *had* succeeded?

Aaron sat up and looked at me with his eyes narrowed in pain. "What happened? Did I really bring them all back?"

Hunt tsked. "Scribner, if you had, we'd all be dead. No, you just opened the gate between our world and their prison enough for me to let them know what their compatriot there was up to. Oddly, they didn't much like the idea of one creature controlling the keys to the castle. They took care of it themselves."

"They dragged her back into. . .wherever they were," said Jason.

I shivered, wondering what hell our demon's actions would cost her.

"Don't feel sorry for it, Maggie," said Hunt, noticing everything as usual. "It was as bad as a being can get. That's why. . . "

. . . Char locked her up, I knew he meant. But neither of us finished the sentence, and the guys seemed content to let the matter rest.

Jason nodded, but I sensed he was getting impatient. "We've got to get Aaron out of here, and to a doctor."

I became suddenly aware of the weight of Aria's ring on my finger, and stripped it off as if it had begun to burn me. Hunt pretended not to watch out of the corner of his eye as I put it on the chain and twisted the tie back into place. I dropped the chain and its burden back through the neck of my hoodie.

Maybe things could be worse. I had the ring, and I knew now that, even if no one in my current life was aware of my previous connections to Char, other forces were more than cognizant that I had once been powerful, and chosen. With something like that book, I could do what Hunt had done. He'd become a magician without whatever it was that I'd once had. I remembered Tamblyn talking about how he lacked even his brother's capacity for power, but surely I would be able to learn how to do what Hunt did, having once had the ability. Surely I could use the book for example, and. . .

Hunt bent, and picked up the book in question from the tunnel floor where I presumed he'd set it before caring for Aaron. "My payment," he said. I opened my mouth to protest—that book was my ticket, wasn't it? To the life I was supposed to have. But he headed me off neatly. "Don't thank me. I get embarrassed. You have your precious Mr. Lawson back, Maggie May. That's better than you might have come out." And, shades of John Tamblyn, "Don't play with this stuff, Stuart. It'll get you killed." And as he turned away, I thought I heard him add under his breath, "or just suck out your soul." Maybe. Maybe not.

"Shall we, kidlets? Or do you like it underground?"

We followed him, a subdued bunch, out of the cavern where so much had happened and back into the darkened tunnel. He kept the flashlight—another example of Hunt asserting his control, as if I needed another—and led the way. When we reached the place where we'd first met the creature in its woman-disguise, he ignored the dead worker entirely and passed him by without slowing his pace an iota. Aaron, Jason, and I couldn't—I didn't know about them, but I couldn't help worrying about his family and friends. Maybe we could send someone down to bring him back. Anonymously, of course. I thought I still might have Mr. Hapcot's number and extension at the TTC. Maybe Miss Julliard could make a call.

Jason was staring around himself at every change in the tunnel. When we reached the blue glowing walls, I saw his expression take on a happy wonder.

"Cool, huh," I said, the understatement of the century.

Jason smiled at me, as if only then aware of anything but the walls. "Is it natural, magical, what?"

I shrugged. "Got me."

"I have only this vague memory of how I got down... back there," he said. "Maybe I was blindfolded or something. But this is new."

I suspected that his transportation might have been even more dramatic; I had seen Char make people appear and disappear at will, so maybe he'd just been picked up from the middle of the hall at school and just as suddenly found himself in that cave. I wasn't unhappy if he didn't remember all of his ordeal, though. *And this time, I don't have to be the one who makes him forget.* For all the good that had done.

The more I thought about it, the more I wondered if the creature we'd encountered below really had been the only one left, or even the strongest. We only had Hunt's word on that, and I knew what that was worth. If something *had* been able to transport Jason underground, it was more powerful than she'd been when we confronted her—I couldn't stop giving her that female pronoun, even with Hunt's constant insistence of using "it." Either that, or she *had* been depleting herself with every use of her power until that futile swipe at Aaron was all she'd been capable of before she shed the physical body altogether.

I had fallen a little behind, trailing Jason and Aaron who stayed a bit of a distance behind Hunt. "Aaron," I said, and he dropped back from Jason's side to walk in pace with me.

"Yeah, Mags?"

"Just thinking: about Bob. Did you hear the sound Hunt's chalk circle made, just when it was collapsing? And what we heard when the air got sucked out of the tunnel?"

He smiled, giving me a wink with the eye behind the cracked lens. *Chugging, chugging...* "Bob's ghost train, you think?"

"I think maybe."

"In that case, he's right to stay away. Ghost trains can be pretty deadly."

He extended a palm so I could give him a low-five which I connected not too badly, and smiled again before moving back up to lean his weight with Jason's. It looked like they were supporting each other. A part of me was envious. If I hadn't come out so unscathed, maybe I could have made it a trio.

I tried to hold onto the good memories of the past two months, and there had been lots, but it was hard. Even when Aaron shot a look back over my shoulder to make sure I was keeping up, it was hard. I smiled back at him, tentative and unsure, because something either wonderful or truly horrible had just occurred to me. Something deep inside me twisted as we walked. What was it? And then I had it.

Thinking about the creature depleting herself to bring us and the ring and book to her lair made me think of my using up my own powers to erase the memories of a chunk of the population of Toronto. As I walked, aware of the signs of both Aaron's obvious pain and Jason's weakness, I realized I was furious.

And I got angrier and angrier.

I had always hoped, in the back of my mind, that I would be released from my promise someday. I had run every scenario I could think of through my head, but the only one that worked was this: someone else who knew my secret would let the story slip, how Maggie Stuart once gave up her chance at being something special, and used it to make everyone else forget. I didn't even care if I was hailed as a selfless hero, although yeah, that would be nice. What mattered was I would be free to give my side of the story to draw back to me all those I had lost.

But it hadn't been like that. I had been afforded few opportunities to make slips myself, like I had with Rae—with the exception of Hunt and Tamblyn, of course, and with my partial confession to Aaron. I had been willing to believe that I knew a Maggie no one else in the world was aware of, a girl who'd been snatched away because of her spectacular, unique *potential*...

And now, I knew I'd been wrong. This creature of another kind of world, imprisoned by Char for probably a lot longer than I'd been alive, knew all about me. It knew, and it had talked like my role in Char's destruction and the way I'd given up that potential was just common knowledge where it came from. Only in my circle was I a stranger to my own history.

And it had the nerve to stand there grinning its sick grin at me, playing a double game of innuendo and suggestion, one set of meanings for me and another for the person I was beginning to realize I wanted most in the world to be exposed before.

It also confronted me with something I hadn't seen before and I wished I hadn't seen now. Why had I never broken my silence when only a promise to a mercenary had bound me? Why had I never wondered if maybe Rae, or Aaron, would hear me out with an open mind and actually believe me? It hadn't taken Irene too long to accept that the book I wanted so badly had something supernatural going for it. I had wasted three years of my life in self-pity, and there had been no need. None at all. The only explanation? Cowardice. Plain and simple. The fear that I would tell the truth, and it wouldn't make anything better.

My 'secret' was crap.

It probably always had been.

The truth of the matter was that it had been easier to keep my secret than to tell and be forced to go into lengthy explanations and defenses, and to try to prove something that was spectacularly unprovable.

There is no fury like what you direct at yourself.

We were on the raised walkway, already far closer to the surface than we'd been in the cold cavern, but suddenly I felt like I would be better off to be buried alive in the depths of the earth. How had I ever survived Char? What had made me so convinced I could have no identity on my own without magic? Maybe I should just turn, and slip away back into the darkness. Maybe no one would even notice.

Aaron stumbled, and Jason, barely stronger himself, braced him up. They seemed to be leaning on each other just fine. I guessed I was no longer needed. Whatever had passed between Aaron and me, his fingers on my scar. . . would he even want to know now about my secrets, or had I missed the moment for confession? Would everything go back to the way it had been before the first day of this school year, Maggie the outcast, watching from the outside, living in her head and her room, full of regrets and stuck in the past?

Would it have been okay to tell them both the truth earlier? After all, I knew Jason as the kind of person who seemed able to accept anyone for exactly what they were. And if Aaron wasn't quite so accommodating, wouldn't it have been worth the chance? I loved the idea of growing in stature in his eyes; it was—delicious. Infatuating.

There would be no forget-spell after this journey underground. No Hunt whispering his seductive poison in my ear. If I could free myself from the power of my own self-pity, well, nothing said that everything couldn't be different this time. And that thought, at last, made me smile.

I should have been more alert, but I was barely aware of my surroundings by that point. I felt comfortably numb. Amazing, that Hunt had sent us on such a long, complicated journey to which we had committed without a single promise that he'd lead us to Jason, and that I had made him a promise that I'd kept so fanatically, despite the fact that it *meant nothing*.

There was no reason to pay much attention, really. We had enough of the blue glow to walk without any artificial light, and the route was mostly straight at a slight upward incline, and the only exits from the passage were irregularly-appearing openings no more than three feet high and black as night underground which didn't look particularly enticing.

I was so distracted that I nearly jumped out of my skin when Hunt drew a sharp breath, grabbing all three of us and throwing us bodily against the wall of the tunnel.

The ground seemed to tilt under us, that same old sound of the approaching freight coming out of nowhere and cresting to impossible heights in a split second. I fell, Aaron and Jason sandwiched beside me, Hunt on top of us all, and a rain of rock and dust falling over and around us.

I might have actually been unconscious for a few seconds, because Jason had shifted suddenly without my having felt him move. He was shaking me, brushing rocks and debris from my face. We were in total darkness, all the former light from the blue stones extinguished in the same instant as the collapse.

Then, in the flicker of the flashlight he'd turned back on, I saw Hunt dislodging Aaron from what seemed like the worst of the rubble.

"What happened?" Aaron shouted, and I thought we must all be a little deaf. It was maybe the angriest I'd ever hear him, the kind of anger that comes from stark terror.

Hunt looked up, and back at the way we'd come, which was completely buried in broken brickwork and larger rock that had tumbled from the ceiling and beyond the shattered masonry. He looked bemused. "Honestly, Scribner, I have no idea. Maybe I was wrong about that being the last of those things..."

Beside me, Jason drew a sharp, panicked breath.

"...or some kind of farewell it put in place in case it failed."

I stared, letting Jason help me up, still somewhat numb. "Like a parting shot? Or protecting something down there?"

"Yes," said Hunt, and grinned, fully recovered now, and apparently already determined again to be infuriating. "I'd say that's about right." He started off again, down the only route now open to us, and we had no choice but to follow.

## 41

### You've Got A Habit Of Leaving

✪

Hunt seemed to be counting, sweeping the flashlight back and forth whenever one of those dark openings yawned off the main tunnel. Finally, he stopped and indicated one with the light. As if making sure he'd chosen correctly, he bent to his knees and sniffed the air emitting from it.

"Here we are. Fresh air," he said.

I was stunned, watching in disbelief as he slid through into the hole followed by Aaron and then Jason. We were close to an exit, here?

I followed, crawled a few feet, and came to the lip of a hole beyond which there was a maybe five foot drop to the level. Jason caught me by the waist as I landed safely in what seemed to be an absolutely average, brick-lined subway access tunnel. The hole we'd emerged from looked from this side like every other ventilation shaft you saw looking left or right, with just the cover removed. "You've got to be kidding me," I said.

Hunt searched with the flashlight, and found a power box. He threw a switch, and a line of sodium lamps flared to life. He stooped and replaced what I saw was indeed a perfectly ordinary-looking grating over the hole we'd come through.

"Seriously, Hunt?" I said sharply. He'd had us walk for miles, and here was proof he'd had a shortcut planned out all along.

He smirked. "Couldn't have you arriving before everything was ready," he said. "And hey, doesn't it make for a nice surprise?"

He led the way again, but returned the flashlight to Aaron. Jason was still carrying Aaron's overstuffed pack, and I had mine over my shoulder. Hunt just had the book, and hadn't offered to help either of the boys, who were both in much worse shape than I was.

I heard the distinctive rumble of a subway train, somewhere above us, ahead and to the right. This time, it was no ghost train, just the TTC. We were pretty darned closed to the subway line. Unbelievable.

It was only the work of another five minutes or so to reach an escape shaft, just up a ladder and along another tunnel, and through one of those push-doors like the one we'd used near the very beginning of this trek.

Hunt reseated the book firmly under his arm, and led us down a final stretch of corridor to a ladder like the very first Aaron and I had descended. "Ladies first," he said, and I gave him the most disapproving look I could before I started up.

The hatchway at the top gave without much effort, and I opened it up to a dark, cool sky. When I'd pulled myself out and, finally, doffed the backpack, I saw we were not in the same place Hunt had directed us to begin our descent. This was the middle of a park in an obviously more upscale area. Hunt, arriving second aboveground, read the question in my eyes before I could ask it.

"Near St. Clair West Station," he said.

This area I only knew because my optometrist had once been here when Jan worked nearby. We'd managed to traverse half the city underground, all the way past Bathurst north of St. Clair. The train we'd heard below just before the cave-in hadn't even been traveling on the same subway line where Aaron and I'd almost been struck.

I pulled that little travel clock out of my pocket and checked the time. About half past midnight.

"Definitely a different way to see the city," said Hunt, smirking, and extending his hand for the clock. "You think it would excite the tourists?"

"Doubtful," I said, and Aaron and Jason, emerging from the shaft below, collapsed onto the cold grass beside me. Deliberately, I put the clock back in my pocket.

Aaron had his cell out and checked for battery and bars. "Who should I call first?" he asked.

"Let me call my parents," said Jason. "I'll say I just wanted to check in before we went to bed, maybe say we lost track of time or something playing video games." He took his phone, and moved off a short ways to do damage control.

Aaron, looking at me from his spot on the grass, said, "What about you? Need to call home?"

I laughed quietly. "Not a priority." Aaron's eyes were soft on mine. What had I told him about my home-life? Was he actually inferring from what I did and said about my mom that we had a difficult relationship?

I felt Hunt watching us and gave him a nasty look. "What? You need something new to wreck?" He'd spied on me and Aaron sleeping together in that cavern below the city. I felt sure he'd already thought up a million ways to make us uncomfortable or drive us away from each other, probably for no other reason than that it would hurt us. Me, at least.

But he didn't say anything, just gave a short bow, saluted Jason (looking pained as he tried to make excuses for his lack of contact with his parents) and ostentatiously secured the book under his arm.

"You're really taking it and walking away," I said.

"That was always my plan, Mags," he said. "Nice I was able to help you out a little on the way."

As with everything Hunt, I felt like there were levels upon levels of meaning to dissect. And for now, I didn't even have the energy to try.

But he kept looking at me after he'd finished speaking. With a lascivious smirk, he let his gaze wander to the front of my hoodie. Looking at me like a piece of meat, like. . .

And I got it.

The ring. I reached my hand to the chain at my neck, pulling it out of the hoodie's neckline, suddenly aware that its weight didn't feel right. My hands touched two separated ends of chain, but no ring. My improvised fix hadn't held. I cried out, unable to help myself.

"It's gone—I've got to go back. . ." I thought of the pile of rubble blocking the way we had come. Had it gone missing before or after the cave-in? I dropped to my knees. Jason had closed the hatch from the subway egress when we were all safely above ground, and it had locked behind us. One way access only.

Hunt seemed amused. "Oops, darlin'. A little careless with your jewelery?"

Aaron put his hand on my shoulder. Behind him, I saw Jason flip the phone shut and rejoin us. "What?" he asked.

Aaron didn't say anything, and neither did Hunt. "I lost the ring," I said. It was all I could do to keep the emotion out of my voice. I'd lost the ring.

"I'll call Rae," said Aaron quietly. "Do you want me to call your detective too?"

"Yes, do that, please," I said. I pulled my black notebook out of my backpack, and all the while stared at Hunt.

"You couldn't do better," was all he said on the matter. "John'll get you fixed up nice and quiet."

He shifted the book and gave the three of us another little wave. Then, unbelievably, a Beck Taxi pulled up at the side of the park. "Cheers, children," he called back to us as he strode away.

"The ring!" I called after him, with as little hope now as I'd had after the subway cave-in, when I'd realized it was missing from the chain around my neck.

He stopped, turned back. The look in his eyes was mock apologetic; silly girl, Maggie, I could almost hear him say. "Nada. Gone. Wanna go back for it? It's only buried under a thousand tons of rock."

I didn't know if I believed him or not. No, I guess I did. It didn't matter anyhow. He was gone himself a moment later, and the question was moot. Lost to the cave-in or lost to Hunt: what difference did it really make?

Then Aaron was at my elbow. Aaron, who had seen but not judged, who had touched me where I hurt and had not recoiled, to whom I owed some kind of explanation. It would be such a relief to give someone the real one after all this time. I no longer felt bound to any promise I had made to Hunt. But maybe Aaron was going to walk out of my life now too, just like Hunt, just like he had the first time.

He touched my arm, well below the scar hidden under my shirt.

"So—I guess I have a pretty good idea what you were afraid to talk about now."

"Yeah," I said. "Hard to believe I thought it was so scary."

He made that little humph noise I liked so much, when he was genuinely amused. "Yeah, it wasn't so bad. No worse than your average horror flick."

Jason laughed softly. "Little too close for comfort on all accounts," he said.

I picked up the backpack while Jason helped Aaron to his feet, balancing him carefully to not rip off Hunt's patch job.

"I'll call Rae," said Aaron, as if knowing I needed distraction from my thoughts, "as soon as we figure out exactly where *here* is."

The nearest street sign was at the corner of the park. I didn't know if it faced north or south, east or west, but that was really the least of my disorientation. The earth had shifted all right, and it was not just about the final cave-in that had stolen my last souvenir of Char's realm. I started walking, the guys behind me.

We got to the edge of the road, and had just started up the sidewalk when, shades of Friday night, a car passed and U-turned, flashing its beams over us as it pulled into the curb alongside our depleted and battle-weary party. It was a beat-up sedan, an old Taurus like some of the cop cars in town but a hell of a lot more ancient. It was followed by a car I recognized instantly as the one Rae drove belonging to her family.

The first one out was Rae Kennie, followed by Suzanne and, unbelievably, Constable Carla Szaba. Even more of a shock was seeing Detective John Tamblyn at the wheel of the other car.

Rae flew right to me and put her arms around me. "We heard! We got here as fast as we could."

How? We'd only emerged from the underground—where there was no signal and from where I knew for a fact none of us had even tried to contact her or anyone else—minutes before. "Hunt?" I asked, taking what was probably the first safe bet I'd ever attempted concerning him.

"He called me—oh, I don't know, it's probably been more than two hours, but it took a while to get to your house and then into town. I guess it's good it's so late!"

"My house?" I repeated.

"For the cards. That was smart, leaving them for me under the bed." With my portfolio. Tamblyn's and Carla's business cards. Where Hunt knew they'd be. "Your mom was really nice, and she totally believed it was homework you'd forgotten, and that you were in the car. She seemed pretty excited you were having another sleepover so soon, and I guess I'm supposed to go to your place next Saturday." She grinned. "She even gave me a bag of chips for us."

I saw Jason look up, and I remembered how hungry he must be. A quirk of my eyebrows was all that was needed to twig Rae to how much that snack might be needed, and she called over to Suzanne. "Suze! Grab the Doritos!"

Suzanne, who'd been a little too cozily ensconced with Aaron for my taste (as if he wouldn't be more interested in a hospital than a girlfriend at the moment), disengaged and ran back to the car for the chips. Jason unpacked some bottled water and a couple of cans of pop that remained from our supplies and we settled down to some kind of a little post-midnight feast on the lawn.

Tamblyn had a quiet word with Szaba as I sat with the rest of them, conflicted as per usual about my place and too aware of their presence to be totally relaxed. Why was the underground, the world of magic, so much easier to navigate? Although really it wasn't. There was danger, and so much more unknown and possibly unknowable whenever my life and it intersected. To glamorize it was to forget the reality.

Now, the reality was home, and Jan's break-up, and trying not to miss more school. I could live with that. Besides, I kind of had to.

Suzanne now had her arms wrapped around Jason like a kind of human limpet. That tickled me somehow, not to mention easing my mind about Aaron. I owed him a conversation, I guessed, and that was *not* going to be easy. But that could wait, as it really had to.

Tamblyn let me have a few minutes and a few chips before motioning me over. Shades of another evening after another adventure. Carla stood quietly beside him as we younger folk divided our spoils and started telling the story of how we'd all arrived here in mid-town Toronto variously bruised, battered, and bloody. She nodded as I came toward them, apparently in on something more with Tamblyn than she'd been the last time I'd seen her.

"Hey," I said.

"He's gone?" were Tamblyn's first words.

"Yeah," I said. Carla shot us both a sharp look. I guessed he hadn't told her *everything*.

"Good," said Tamblyn. "We better get some medical attention for your friends there."

I nodded. "It would be nice if the emphasis wasn't on the 'attention' part..." I said.

"I know a guy," he said, and stepped aside to use his cell.

Carla put a hand to my chin and lifted my face, examining it critically before releasing me again. "You okay?"

"As well as," I said. "You know."

She cracked the smallest hint of a smile, but I figured that was all I was going to get until I gave her more. "Rough day."

"Yup." I checked over my shoulder to where the other four were almost through the bag of Doritos and into the rest of my granola bars and a baggie of sandwiches Aaron, Bob, and I had apparently missed earlier.

"I'm glad you left my card with Detective Tamblyn's," said Szaba. "Your friend Rae called both of us so he really didn't have a choice about including me. Probably helped I lived closer to her as well."

I chuckled. That wouldn't have pleased Tamblyn much. I figured his entire life had involved one kind of compartmentalization or another.

"Yeah," Szaba confirmed without me having to say it out loud. "Monday at the office is going to be *very* interesting."

"What now?" I said. Tamblyn, returning from his call, answered.

"Doctor, a couple of hotel rooms for the night *which you will owe me for*," he said, "and you can come in Monday for a debrief with me." He glanced at Szaba. "And the constable." I could see how much that cost him, and I thought Carla did too because neither of us remarked on his change of policy.

"Okay," I said.

I wondered if I should say something about Scott, how we'd seen his jacket and knew he'd been underground too in the weeks before leaving town. But that would mean telling someone about Bob's Alterna-City, and that was a secret I felt perfectly comfortable keeping.

I threw another glance over my shoulder. "I think Aaron needs an optometrist too," I said, my mind wandering enough so that I had apparently conflated my reason for knowledge of the neighborhood with Aaron's broken lens. Tamblyn's sharp look demonstrated he had no idea what I was talking about. Instead of explaining, I just grinned. I'd leave explanations for another time.

999

Tonight

✪

Six months had passed since that late October night and the events underground. Six months, in which I had reverted to many old patterns in a way that betrayed everything I had hoped for about optimism and the possibility of people changing in significant ways.

I had coffee every now and then after school with Jason and Aaron, and Rae and I chatted between periods about going riding when the weather was nice or having a sleepover to watch old movies. But the good weather had come, and we were still talking, kind of vaguely, and I realized that I was as limp in my attendance to friendship as I had been in my previously limp friendless state. Suzanne didn't have a lot of use for me, but I gathered that she and Rae had drifted as well. That probably meant that whatever had been blossoming between her and Jason was gone too, and I felt unexpectedly sad for his loss, and hers.

I'd put my head down into my books and managed to pull it together for the principal. Mr. Thurl never really got warmed back up to me, but his course was over in January, and after that I had no reason to be anywhere near the drafting room where I could accidentally bump into him. I only failed one course in my first semester, which I managed to make up in my copious spare time after school in the spring. I guess there were a few benefits to being nearly friendless and without extracurricular activities. It meant I wouldn't have the option of summer school, which might actually be a nice distraction, if I wanted to make sure I stayed away from fun stuff like last summer's McDonald's job.

Irene and I never made up, but it was okay because we only had the one class together, and that had ended in January. I no longer saw her except in passing, and she was studious in ignoring me. She didn't behave as if I was an enemy; she had just apparently replaced where I stood in any given room with a blank spot she could look straight through.

There were lots of looks that moved through rooms between me and Aaron, always when we weren't specifically sitting together. It happened in the cafeteria when I was sitting alone with a book or had been drawn into a game of Euchre after most of the other students had left after eating. He sometimes sat with guys I didn't know, sometimes with Jason, but the looks didn't happen if Jason was there. It was as if he thought Jason had some claim on me that he was loathe to interfere with, despite the fact that my most intimate interactions with Jason had happened in a time long lost to both of us.

No, the looks never happened when he was either with someone I knew from the whole thing with the creature, or when we were having coffee with the gang. It was easy to talk with him when I said very little, and the conversation wasn't loaded with innuendo. It was unloaded, I guess, until we were across the room. And then I was so acutely uncomfortable with the enormous number of things I wanted to say to him that I felt choked by my own tongue and lumpy in my skin. I'd catch him looking my way, with a sensitivity it probably did a teenage boy absolutely no good to possess, and I would timidly gaze back long enough to want to die.

He didn't ask for the explanation I had promised him, and I don't know if he was embarrassed to ask or had changed his mind. I was too nervous to bring it up myself, especially when anyone else was around.

Jan had never spoken about Harrison, or about my disappearance for the better part of twenty-four hours before she could latch onto the idea I was at Rae's, or the fact that we'd passed by my sixteenth birthday without any remark. I wondered if she had actually noticed I was missing, or was so consumed in her own sorrow that she never knew I was gone.

One Saturday, near the end of April, I was sitting in my room with yet another book that I vainly hoped would give me some kind of insight into what Hunt did, without needing to have the innate magical ability I'd squandered. I heard the doorbell ring, but that was like the phone. It was never for me, so why bother answering?

I heard a quiet tap at my door a moment later, and opened it to my mother.

"Someone here to see you, sweetie. . ." Jan trailed off, a vague look in her eye. Either she was trying not to tell me something, or she'd been interrupted in the middle of something.

Perplexed, I said, "Okay," and closed the door again to collect myself and check my hair. Caught a glimpse of myself in the mirror, disgusted with the impulse. It was growing out a little, but I didn't know if it would ever be as long as it had been before my rough initiation into teenage sleepover parties. Whatever. I trailed after her to go downstairs to meet my visitor.

It was Rae Kennie. She laughed at something Jan said, glanced around and nodded, as if appreciating the decor. I saw Jan's hand go self-consciously to her extra-fine blond hair, the strands falling out of their ponytail to her thin neck. Mom looked too skinny. I had hardly noticed her in months. She used to be excessively healthy, tennis and swimming and going to the gym and all, so much so I was constantly embarrassed by my own dislike of and disinterest in sports. I pictured my real father as some kind of super-slug from whom I'd inherited all my sloth genes. But Jan had always been fit and bronzed. Until I wrecked her with the magic. Or until the magic had wrecked me for being able to be a normal daughter.

"Hey, Rae," I said. I was trying not to sound confused about her arrival, but I didn't think I had done a particularly good job.

Especially when Rae's answer was to grab me and give me a big hug. "I'm the worst friend ever," she said, squeezing me.

That made me smile, and Rae gave me another hug after seeing it.

"You wanna play Scrabble?" she said.

". . .Okay," I said. We had a set in the basement, but I figured the dust on it would probably be an inch thick.

"You girls head down," said Jan. "I'll bring you something to drink."

I led the way down the stairs to the finished basement, flipped on the light, and a dozen people yelled, "Surprise!"

Jan, following us down to watch the look on my face, looked almost bashful. "You never got a sweet sixteen," she said. "And I know it's very, very late but. . ."

Since Rae had broken the ice on displays of affection, I gave her a big hug. I don't know which one of us was more surprised.

✪

There was a cake. Actually a cake.

And some Scrabble, and lots of fun finger food, and even a few presents. Was it a surprise? It would have been enough of a shock if anyone from school, or even Jan, had actually said a passing "Happy Belated Birthday," to memorialize my anticlimactic sixteenth. This, this was off the charts.

"Happy birthday, Spook," said Jason, his new and not so pleasing nickname for me. Still, as a tangible measure of affection, I guess I was okay with it. John Tamblyn had mentioned his station nickname was "Witch Boy," probably thanks to Carla Szaba, and almost certainly meant with less affection.

Jason followed up with a quick, very embarrassed peck on my cheek as if I was his wrinkly Aunt Molly and his mom had forced him. Still, it was contact and I was not unaccountably touched. I grinned, and punched him lightly on the nose.

When Jan brought in the cake, the sulfur of the matches drifted in with her from the laundry room, but for once she wasn't making apologies about the scent of something burning. She looked as pleased as the cat with the cream—maybe as happy as I'd seen her since Harrison screwed off.

At the deep end of the evening, Aaron took my hand and pulled me aside. Everyone else was congregated variously through the house, most of them engaged in a ridiculously competitive game of Risk in the downstairs rec room. Aaron and I, arguably the smartest in the group, hadn't survived the first half hour of play.

So we drifted away, and after another visit to the punch bowl in the kitchen, he led me out into the backyard, into the spring evening. Even with the chill in the air, I felt just a little warm. Maybe it was the punch—I could swear someone had spiked it just a tad—but maybe not.

"Rae said no gifts," he began, almost breathlessly, "but I couldn't resist this."

He produced a middling sized package with what was, I thought, an excellent masculine stab at wrapping. At least, it was as good as anything I might have attempted.

I pulled the post office twine off in one piece, not about to dare his Gordion knot. The paper was ducks and ponds, imagery which I quite liked. It might have been left over from Father's Day at the Scribner house.

Inside was something wrapped over and over in tissue paper, something that was unmistakably a book. I rolled it out of its fragile covering, and drew a deep breath.

The book was old, ratty, fragrant with time, its red leather binding showing stained book board beneath. Its pages, when I cracked it open with an audible snap, were yellowed and slightly shiny, like vellum or good parchment.

"Aaron—" I began.

"Yeah," he said, when I didn't go on, giving me a knowing smirk that this time was so far from infuriating me I could have thrown my arms around him right there. He had turned his formidable brain onto tracking down the only thing in the world which could have pleased me.

The pentacle embossed on the marbled endpapers could only be seen when I tilted the book in the light, but it was even without that so obviously a book of... well, something Hunt might have liked to steal from me, perhaps. I leafed gingerly through it. "Is it real?"

"I guess you'll have to find out," he said, and then I couldn't help myself. I threw myself into his arms, and he was there to catch me, his face resting against my neck and mine against his. "I can help with the translation," he said quietly, but with that so-lovely fire in his voice. "It's Latin this time, a hell of a lot easier than that other one."

I laughed, and actually managed to relax into his arms. I felt his fingers lace tightly around the small of my back.

"So," he said at last, as the moon shone down on us, a new world at last, maybe. "I think you still owe me a long and uncomfortable explanation... You wanna go for a coffee sometime?"

Unable to get my mouth to form the word yes, I settled for a smile. He returned it, and started to walk backwards away from me, away from the house, toward the end of the garden, beckoning for me to follow.

This was interesting. Equally intrigued and, well, nervous as all hell, I had already taken a couple of steps after him when a long-lost thought struck me, square between the eyes, and I felt that twinge of joy I sometimes forgot I could feel. Not really knowing why, I took the little black notebook with gold tooling out of my pocket and found with it a stub of pencil I had probably picked up one day at the library.

He watched, pretending not to, as I lay the lead on its side and rubbed the first page, the one I'd always left blank, the one with the faint impressions left by its previous owner.

Words appeared, like a message from beyond. The script was formal, almost Gothic, like someone had left the imprint with a calligraphy pen. The message was short and sweet.

"Don't worry. You're doing fine."

"What's that?" asked Aaron, coming so close to my shoulder I could smell him. Boy scent. Shampoo and something sharper. Did Aaron Scribner wear aftershave?

"I don't know," I told him. "Just a little bit of encouragement, I think."

I smiled, and followed him deeper into the shadows of the far end of the yard, feeling like Mada Premavesi glowing in her pretty party dress. Full of joy.

## About the Author

Jen Frankel is the author of THE LAST RITE and its sequel THE RED RING, the first two books of the Blood & Magic series featuring Maggie Stuart. She writes in many different genres, but speculative fiction of any sort is her favourite.

Her stories, essays, and poetry have appeared in magazines across North America. She also works as a screenwriter/filmmaker, and as a "script doctor" for countless hopeful authors. She lives and works in Toronto.

Coming Soon
## Heaven & Hell
Blood & Magic ✪ Book Three

Now twenty-three and living in Montreal, Maggie is a mess when Hunt wanders back in with an agenda and a challenge: get herself together, and rip off the biggest game in town—a swanky casino called Heaven & Hell owned by her old high school nemesis Scott Saunders.

Back in Toronto, a storm is brewing around Jason Lawson, a tragedy a dozen years in the making. Can Maggie save Jason, extricate herself from Hunt's schemes, and figure out exactly how Scott has inserted himself into the occult world in a way she only dreams of?

Made in the USA
Charleston, SC
17 November 2014